Hagas

Michael Wood

Copyright © 2022 Michael Wood
All rights reserved.
ISBN: 9798363368509

Thank You

Coach Kate, what a ride. Thank you for pushing me, guiding me and laughing with me all along the way.

Chris, my number one fan, thank you for encouraging me, understanding me and putting up with my odd hours to get this done. Love you.

Table of contents

Fuck a duck 1

Puppy love 8

Chan the man 13

On the rocks 19

Take it to go 26

Light up my life 37

Rub-a-dub-dub 43

Going down 54

Head case 58

Stitch 'n' bitch 66

Rise and whine 76

Duck and covers 80

Sun of a 84

Angels and angles 90

Spitting up 99

Nature calls 108

Are we taping? 113

Shaken? Stirred? On the rocks? 121

Promises. Promises. 130

Into the woods 137

A rose by any other name 140

To swim or not to swim? That is the question. 144

The prodigal son 152

What goes up, must 157

Asleep at the wheel 165

Déjà vu all over again 173

Cutting out 177

On the road. Again. 187

One for the road 197

On the radio 205

Farewell and adieu 211

Time keeps slipping 216

Hit the road 223

Pack your bags 232

Dannie with the plannie 238

From the fire to the frying pan 240

The bump from the road 253

Give me a break 262

Just a little prick 269

Wristful thinking 273

Look sharp 280

You can't stop the beat 290

Into the light 295

You go boom 300

Make or break 306

The ties that bind 311

Easy as one, two three 316

One small leap 322

Swing and a 326

Long way from the top 328

Stick the landing 331

Epilogue 336

Chapter 1

Fuck a duck

Raw. The only word Hagas could conjure to describe how he felt. He'd been crouching here for what felt like forever. The cold, wet tongues of the river lapping at the shore muddied the soft ground, its dampness penetrating through his bang-around sneakers and making his feet soggy and puckered.

But here he had stayed with his knees bent far past ninety degrees, his butt perched on a rough, mossy stump. In front of him, a clump of ferns, just unfurling into the season, hid him sufficiently. The constant flow of the dark water, its dull, gurgling roar echoing along the rocks it passed, lulled him into a calm he rarely knew. He let the feeling wash over him.

Hagas looked up to see the sun sinking in the fading blue sky. He lowered his eyes and unfocused them to blur the long, rippling shadows weaving through the pines, birches, oaks, and maples stretching up the banks.

His mind wandered as he thought back to the two kids he'd seen a week before at the campsite across the brook. He'd watched them from this spot, his spot, dying to join them, but fear of Ma's punishment if they told—if she somehow found out he was here—kept him hiding. The boy and girl had exploring rocks and pools by the brook's edge. The girl was younger, giggling all the time. The boy was quieter, but brave, jumping from rock to rock. They reminded him of when he and Angel would just play for hours. But it was their parents that made his heart hurt the most. Their parents were always there, above in their site, watching, smiling. They were good. They loved their kids. He saw it. Somewhere in his very core, he knew it. And he knew Ma had been lying to him all along. *This is the way it's supposed to be. No way everyone is bad out here. Ma's the bad one. And Gigi. And Brian.*

A slight breeze sent a chill reverberating through his body, silencing the warm memory. He fiddled his hands inside his hoodie's pouch. It was all still there. Ready. He had been crouched in this spot for more than four hours. He had been crouching here almost every day—except for Ma's two days off—for the past two weeks. Waiting patiently. Waiting for the right moment.

He had been so focused on his task, that he almost forgot today, May 17th, was his birthday. Thirteen years old by his count. Pulling his left hand out of the pouch, he looked at the digital watch strapped tight around his wrist. *Ten after six. Almost time.* For a moment, he flashed to this day, six years ago, opening the bright wrapping paper covering the watch box. It was a birthday present from Gigi. The last present he'd ever got. And it was the last day he could remember feeling anything close to happy. Today, he was determined to find that feeling again. He shifted his numbed butt and wiggled his legs to get his muscles moving.

Snap! Snap! Somewhere behind him, branches popped on the ground. He jerked his head over his shoulder, looking toward the sound, sucking in his breath. *Chainsaw people! Oh no. No.* Sitting stock still, he strained his eyes to see through the trees. Another snap sounded—this one farther away. *Ah ha!* He caught a glimpse of dark, slender legs moving amongst the trunks and brush. *Deer. Just deer.* He breathed out, feeling his muscles relax. He shivered and jammed his hands farther into the pouch, rubbing them together. Part of him wished he was back on his mattress, curled up under his old blanket. *Colder here than down there. Always cold. Hate it. Hate . . .*

There! There you are. Coming into sight downstream, the mallard bobbed as it worked its way against the fast current toward him. Gobs of sunlight danced off shimmering green and black feathers. *Closer . . . Closer. So pretty. Come on. You're perfect.*

At about ten feet in front of him, the duck reached the still of an eddy and he watched as it put its feet down to connect to the sandy river bottom. Slowly, almost lazily, it waddled toward the edge, toward him. Brush, dense with new buds, overhung the eddy, almost touching the surface at points. The duck's rough nesting spot was perfectly tucked under the natural canopy, almost invisible to any other animals.

Almost.

Closer . . . Closer . . . Now! With a heave of adrenaline, he launched, pushing himself off the stump, landing on his knees as the rest of his body crashed through the brush above the duck. In an instant, he had the duck enveloped in his grip, his hands wrapping around its midsection, pinning it close to his chest. The duck struggled to rise. He felt its muscles writhing, its bones shifting, its wings pushing against his hands. He shifted his weight back, pulling his prize through the protective brush, exposing it to the openness above. For a minute, the duck fought his grip – squirming, squawking, and snapping. Its attempts failed and soon its muscles slacked in his firm hold.

Regarding his prize at arm's length, Hagas soaked in all its details. *So cool up close. All shimmery. Green. Black.* It had more muscle than he had thought too. Its wild fear and fight became waves of full body quivers rippling out from its body. He wasn't sure how long he'd been holding it out like this, and he couldn't see his watch face. *Five—maybe ten minutes? Maybe he's done.* He moved left, bending to lower it down to the flat rock near the river's edge, just past the spot he had been crouching for hours. The duck went still and stopped fighting him. *Too hard?* His mind flashed to Ma yanking him around by his arm. Hoping he hadn't hurt it, he slacked his grip a bit, still keeping it firmly on the base of its neck, just above where its exhausted wings lay dormant. *Okay. Here we go.*

Just like he had pictured in his plan, he released his right hand, keeping his left pressing down as hard as he dared without strangling it. His right hand went methodically to his pouch, and he eased it in to find his treasure. He pulled out the rolled length of connected pieces of duct tape. The sticky side was on the outside of the pieced-together roll, and it was covered with lint, threads, and bits of dirt.

Raising the roll to his mouth, he bit the rough, torn end of the length. Holding it tightly between his teeth and using his free hand, he worked the roll out to its full length, letting the end pile loosely on the damp rock near his feet. He figured it was about four feet long. *Plenty.*

With the tape hanging from his mouth like a giant tongue, he considered the duck held in his hand for a moment or two longer. It made a few feeble squawks on occasion. He felt no remorse, just curiosity. What was the duck thinking? Did it feel afraid? Did it feel helpless? Was it plotting an escape? *She would have loved him.* A tremble from his prize snapped him back to reality and he readied himself for the next step.

Keeping his grasp on the duck with his left hand, he used his right to take the end of the tape from his mouth and positioned it on the middle of the duck's back, sticky side down, pressing just enough to help it get a hold.

Okay. After a few deep breaths to steady himself, he lurched into action. He jerked the duck up and whipped the tape around and under the duck's body, just in front of its dangling feet. The duck writhed but could not force the tape off. Hagas kept going, wrapping the tape down and around again and again, On his last go around, the end of the tape landed on top of the duck. Hagas rubbed back and forth, pressing the tape's end down to secure it to itself. Satisfied, he lowered the duck down to the rock and began easing his grip.

Hagas was momentarily taken off guard when the duck flexed and jerked under his hand, its squawking getting louder and more urgent. It strained its neck to turn backward and bite at him. But its bill couldn't reach him and he held it to the rock until it seemed to calm once again.

"Shhhh. You're a good boy. Good . . . good." He saw its shimmer was gone and realized the sun was much lower and the cool of the forest was creeping in slowly but surely. Looking up at the rushing water, he saw it had gone dark with shadows. A rush of urgency swept through him. He had to go if he was going to get back before she did. He had timed this journey many times now, and he would just make it if he left now.

He released his hand and stood, stepping back at the same time, his eyes locked on the duck. *So cool. Pretty perfect.* The duck sat still for a few seconds, then stood, its little legs working to steady itself on the downward sloping rock.

"You're good. Go on," he urged.

The duck took a step toward the water, then another. It pitched forward onto its belly. He could see it straining to use its wings to right itself, but the tape held true, effectively clipping its ability to get leverage. The duck's feet went into overdrive, propelling its body down the rock to the water's edge. It kept kicking, fighting to get into the water. Its head went under the water briefly, but a final push got its whole body off the rock. Then, it was bobbing, floating, and circling in the eddy.

From the shore, he watched long enough just to be sure the duck would be okay and stay upright. He breathed a sigh of relief as the duck worked its way to its place under the brush. Through the shadows, he watched as it waddled out of the water to the cover of the protective shrubs. *Good boy.*

A quick push to his watch, It lit up with a blue glow. *6:49!* "Shoot! Shoot!" *Got to go.* But he smiled, knowing he would be back here, back to his secret spot, soon enough. The fun had really only just begun.

With a shot of adrenaline coursing through him, he turned to his path to begin the journey home. He moved at a pace close to a jog, his feet sure of the way ahead, navigating the many roots and rocks that existed to inflict pain and injury to the less skilled who invaded his newfound world every summer.

Chapter 2

Puppy Love

May 21, Thursday morning before Memorial Day Weekend

"Hey, Derb—you ready to go to the woods? Are you ready? Yes? Yes?" Suzanne cooed as she ruffled her mutt's ears. He responded by wagging his tail with gusto. "Who's a good boy? You're going to love it. Such a good boy. Do you want to go out before we go? Go out and go piss-piss?"

Suzanne watched Derby's tail wag even faster. She loved how far Derby had come. Fast, too. Housebreaking him had been a snap, especially with Connie being here to keep an eye on him. He was so smart and eager to please. She breathed in deeply, scanning the open-concept kitchen and living room to be sure she'd grabbed everything.

"Okay, one more bathroom run, and we can go."

Suzanne headed to the small foyer to grab Derby's leash with the permanently attached collar. Living in the city meant Derby never left the house off-leash. When she was growing up, she and her family simply opened the back door and—voila—dog goes out and business gets done. Derby danced around her legs once she reached for the leash, making it nearly impossible to snap the collar around his neck, a ritual that always amused Suzanne.

Her iPhone buzzed on the counter, and Suzanne hustled into the kitchen to look at the screen. *11:49a.m. Incoming call – Renee Jordan.*

Sucking in a breath, Suzanne readied herself. Derby sat on his haunches, tail wagging, his head cocked to one side, and his ears semi-perked. Now, leash dangling in her hand, she leaned on the counter, her back and shoulder muscles tensing as the familiar hurt and anger resurged. Forcing a semi-smile to try and make her voice sound happier than her heart, she hit the green button and put her phone on speaker.

"What's up, Doc? I'm just about ready to hit the road. You're not calling to try and talk me out of this again, are you?"

"I just . . . I was . . . I just want to be sure you're ready for this," Renee said.

"Ready as I need to be." Suzanne shot the words out with her practiced confidence, a trick she'd mastered across years of bottling her emotions.

"I know you think you are. And I get it. Really, I do." There was a pause before Renee continued, delivering her words with urgency. "But this—this is going to be heavy. Heavier than you might think. Right now, at this moment, anger is fueling you. But you can't keep running on that. It'll kill you." Dead air hung for a moment. Then her voice came back, calmer. "You need to know I'm here—me, all your friends—we're all here to help lift you out of this. You don't have to go it alone."

Shit. She's a friend. Come on—get real. Suzanne looked down at Derby, who was still looking up at her. She closed her eyes, taking a deep breath before speaking again.

"It's all so frigging messed up already. I need to—I have to—do something. For me. And for Connie."

She waited for Renee's response and kicked Derby's chewed-up toy pig across the kitchen floor. Standing up and fidgeting, Derby tracked it, then looked back up at her. *Wait for it. Wait.* "Okay. Like I said, I get it. Just know, I'm here—all of us are here—just a phone call away."

Suzanne slid her hand to cover the microphone on the bottom of her phone. "Kill, Derby! Kill!" she whisper-commanded.

Derby launched, scrambling across the tiled floor and pouncing on the pig. He came up with it in his mouth, shaking it side to side. *Good boy.* Suzanne smiled with satisfaction and removed her hand from the microphone.

"From what Connie told me, reception gets a little dicey up there, so maybe a smoke signal would be better. Look, I appreciate your concern—and your friendship, but I'll be fine. I'm a big girl." Suzanne's voice dropped. "He needs to know what he did. He needs to pay. And I am going to rip his worthless life apart." She listened into the silence, still watching Derby whip his pig toy side to side.

Finally, Renee spoke. "I know. Just, promise me you'll be careful. It's not Boston. Who knows what kind of people live up in that world? Who knows what this guy is capable of!"

"Connie lived up there!" Suzanne snapped back, lasering her focus back to the phone. "Fuck whatever world it is up there. I don't care. Three years. Three years of everything—good, great, awful—everything. Jesus, she was so fucking broken. By him." She stopped for a second, her eyes stinging from a surge of unexpected, welling tears. "She was my world. That world—that state—did nothing. He will not get away with it. I am going to–literally, physically–do something."

"I know. I know. I'm sorry. You know what I mean though," Renee said.

Shit. Calm it down. Bring it back. Suzanne wiped at her eyes with the back of her hand. "Look, I'm a lawyer, not a fighter." She half chuckled at her one-liner to mask her teary sniffle. "Well, actually, I guess I am a fighter in that respect. But don't forget, I've got sixty pounds of fur tagging along." She glanced at Derby, still going at the pig. "And if he's not enough muscle, well, I've got my mace."

"Just . . . be careful."

"I will. Promise." As much as Suzanne both hated and appreciated Renee's concern, she was done. "Look, I've got to go if I'm going to make it up there in daylight. I'll call you next week. Bye. For now."

"Okay. Bye for now. Call me when you're back," Renee said.

Suzanne watched her screen fade to dark. Derby's demanding whimper/growl lifted her mood a bit. She turned to him.

"Okay. Let's go outside and go piss-piss." She clipped the collar around his blonde neck, grabbed her keys and sunglasses, and headed out the door.

Three flights down, out through the double lobby doors and they were on the sidewalk. Derby quickly found his well-used dogwood tree and let loose.

"Good boy. You done?" Derby's tail whipped side to side. "Okay. Let's do this." Suzanne pressed the fob and the Range Rover chirped out its *I'm open* signal. She popped the back and Derby effortlessly leaped in. "You! You're so excited!"

After shutting the trunk, Suzanne made a quick goofy face at Derby through the glass. *Dammit. never finished my sweep.* "Be back in a minute. Be good. Okay. One more sweep and we're off." She headed back into their building, up the three flights, and into their condo. She looked around and felt confident she hadn't missed a thing. "I am . . . a rock star. East Bumfuck, Maine, here we come. Hope you're ready for us."

Chapter 3

Chan the Man

Piscataquis County Sheriff, Chris Chan was parked at the far side of the Black Bear Market's dirt lot, staring hard into the rearview mirror of his 2010 county-issued Ford Bronco. He glanced at his phone. 6:23 p.m. He'd been sitting here for nearly a half hour, and the simple comfort of his routine Thursday dinner stop was not materializing. Tonight, his slice of pepperoni pizza lay cold and untouched on the passenger seat.

Four years. An anniversary he'd never really envisioned happening. This was the day, four years ago, he had been appointed to the highest law enforcement job in the county, all thanks to former Sheriff John Watkins' implication in a massive bribery scam at the mill, and Governor LePage's need to save some face after his Kennebec County Sheriff appointee debacle.

His official run and win the following November had lifted him like nothing else, not even his marriage and the birth of the twins topped it. But the winning feeling had been short-lived. The towns up here were small, with gossip, prejudice, and backwoods mentality spreading faster than a brush fire in the summer. Now, he found himself wrestling with the idea of running again. June first, the candidate filing deadline, was approaching quickly.

It had been a rough start. Most of the deep locals never imagined—couldn't even fathom—they'd have a Chinese-American running their law enforcement office. Even Chris's parents bought into the underlying racism. They had assumed he would eventually take over Chan Pan, their very popular, modest, small-town Chinese* restaurant. When Chris told them he wanted to go into law enforcement, they had balked, even becoming angry with him. He was destroying their carefully laid-out plan. Growing up, he had tried to tell them it was never his plan. Year by year, he had gotten tired of the bullying, the name calling, and the dirty looks; eventually, he fought back—not just with his fists, but with his mind. Somewhere along the way, he had decided to stand up. And things started to change. Sort of.

Chris looked around. The lot was as empty as his heart felt. *Just me.* He couldn't shake the recent, yet somehow old, scenes of Trish and the boys playing out in his head, cookouts . . . camping . . . movie nights . . . secret signals. *Why? Why leave? You—we—had such a great thing. Didn't we? Knew it though. Should have asked. Tried. Take the girl out of the city, but you can't the city out of the girl. We weren't enough . . . maybe even too much.*

14

Closing his eyes and relaxing his body into the driver's seat, Chris tried to focus his thoughts on whether to run again. The peepers' incessant chirping delivered the white noise he needed to calm his cluttered mind. They were late this year, but a sure sign spring was finally here to stay. *Why put yourself through it? You've served your time. You proved all those haters wrong. Twins are almost ready to start school. You really want them growing up here? Go through all the bullshit? But, but, but—always a friggin' but.*

Headlights splashed across his mist-covered windshield. An SUV pulled in from Route 16, bouncing across the pothole-riddled lot, skidding to a cockeyed stop just to the right of the entry door. "2003 Forerunner. Black. Bondoed driver's side quarter panel," he muttered under his breath, proud of his near-encyclopedic knowledge of vehicle makes, models, and years. He could just see the rear plate, and his cop-trained mind noted it was New Hampshire.

The Forerunner's door flew open and a woman emerged. He thought she looked to be in her late thirties or early forties. Tough to tell with women up here, though. Their incessant smoking always messed with them, graying their skin and aging them prematurely. He watched her lurch to the market entrance, a giant keychain swinging from one hand and a wallet clutched in her other. She fumbled with opening the market's door, fighting against its weight, finally slipping into the glow of the store.

And here they come. Chris was mildly amused. Watching out-of-towners was often close to a spectator sport up here. *Time to go.* He was still the sheriff, and he had work to do before he could call it a night. Chris blocked any lingering, wandering thoughts and wolfed down a few bites of the cold pizza, chasing it with slugs of chocolate milk. He belched.

"You're a healthy one, aren't you," he said to himself, capping the milk.

Grabbing the flimsy pizza box, Chris popped out of his Bronco and strode toward the market entrance. Just as he finished jamming the pizza box and milk bottle into the overflowing bin, the market door bounced open, and the woman emerged, her keychain banging as she struggled through the sliver of an opening the heavy glass door offered her. In addition to the hefty keychain, she now had two jugs of Lord Calvert whiskey and a carton of Old Gold Menthol Light 100s hanging from her skinny arms. In her struggle, she lost her hold of the cigarettes, dropping them on the damp ground.

"Fuckety, fuck, fuck!" she blurted out, then started shuffle-kicking them toward her vehicle.

Chris intercepted her path, picking the carton up and wiping it off with the napkin he still clenched. He held out the mud-smeared box. "Here you go, ma'am." Outwardly, he smiled at the woman. In his head, he was quickly sizing her up. "I guess Jimmy's still being a stickler with handing out bags."

The woman ripped open the Forerunner's rear door and shoved the jugs of whiskey in. Then she spun, snatching the carton from Chris's outstretched hand and flung it into the back seat as well. "Well, thank you, officer." She smiled up at him, revealing her stained, yellowed teeth. "Least someone up here knows how to treat a lady."

The distinct smell of whiskey on her breath was instant. *Shit. Shit.* Chris had zero desire to process an OUI tonight.

16

"Of course, ma'am." He dropped his smile down a notch. "And it's Sheriff, actually. What brings you to town?"

"Oh, you know—coming up for a girl's weekend. Just a little libations and let-our-hairs-down time." She chuckled a little, turning to slam the rear door shut, then yanking her driver's door open.

Glancing in, Chris noted the dirty Dunkin' Donuts Styrofoam cup perched in the cupholder under the console. *That's had some use. Been using it your whole ride up. Dammit.* An old Clash song popped into his head. *Should I stay or should I go now? If I go there will be trouble. If I stay it . . .* "Sounds fun. Where you staying?"

"Oh, not far. Up near the Gulf. Friend's got a place up there." The woman hopped onto her seat, leaving the door open. "Well, I gotta go. Late already. Unless there's anything else—Sheriff?" She fired up the engine.

Almost daring me to do something. Ballsy. No one's out. Only a few miles. Chris went to tip his hat but remembered he'd left it in his truck. *Really time to go.* "No ma'am. You just . . . drive safe. Roads are wet. Oh, I didn't get your name. I'm Chris."

The woman waited a beat before speaking. "I'm Carole. And will do, Officer—I mean, Sheriff! Sheriff! Jeez Louise. My brain sometimes. Thanks!" She shook her head and pulled her door shut.

Chris stepped away, watching her back up and jerk to stop. A flash of flame briefly lit the interior. Then she was gone, with a puff of smoke spilling out her window as the SUV bounced back onto Route 16, heading north.

Back in his Bronco, Chris turned the key and the engine rumbled to life. He secured his seatbelt, flipped his headlights on, and adjusted the windshield wipers to an intermittent setting. *Hate this time of year.* "Just friggin' snow or rain already."

Quick spin, and I'm calling it good. He turned on the radio, permanently set to WTOS, the "classic" rock station broadcasting from the top of Sugarloaf. An old AC/DC song pumped all-too-familiar guitar licks into his head. *Nah. Too much.* He clicked the radio off.

Driving south, he periodically glanced at the dashboard clock, ticking off the minutes, his spirits rising as each one got him closer to his mom and dad's place to collect the twins. The boys were his everything now. *Hope they're awake.* The dispatcher's voice coming over his police radio dragged his mind back to the now.

"Dispatch for Chris. Come in. Over."

Chris sighed and grabbed the microphone. "This is Chris. What do you got, Sheila?"

"We have a 10-42 up at the gulf. Called in from Margaret at the KI check-in gate. Something about a duck. A dead duck. Foul play. No pun intended, Sheriff. Over."

Chris slowed the Bronco, pulling it over to stop on the shoulder of the road. "Dead duck, huh? Well, knowing Margaret, she wouldn't have called if it wasn't something." He paused. *So close to calling it a night. Damn. Twins will definitely be asleep.* "On my way. Over."

After cradling the mic, Chris flipped on his blues and made a U-turn. He accelerated quickly. Even now, years later, he still felt the secret rush of breaking the speed limit and watching cars pull over for him. Tonight, the rush was a little more real; he just wanted to get this call done and get back to his boys. *Dead duck. Come on.*

Chapter 4

On the rocks

The steady mist that had started at the river had become a full-on drizzle when Hagas finally gave up looking for his duck. This was supposed to be his fourth straight day of going out to experiment with it, and he had hoped it would have gotten mellower. He'd been trying to work out how he could make it his friend and, soon enough, coax it to leave with him and Angel. *Rainbow tape's way better than just stupid gray tape. Skinnier now though. Gave it scraps of bread soaked in water. Going to get us all out of here. What's wrong with him? Just needs time, I guess.*

He'd stayed too long looking for it, scouring the bushes up and down the river, looking for signs. Maybe a feather, a hunk of tape. He'd pictured a million different deaths it could have encountered in the woods. Even as he'd searched and searched, in his heart he knew it was gone and he felt the sucking deflation of his plan falling apart. Now, he was on his way back. No duck. No plan. *Was going to be just the three of us. No duck for Angel. Do it again? Find a new one? Take too long.*

"Almost there."

Coming to the end of his private trail, glimpses of the open space, beyond the edge of the trees, filled him with mixed emotions. He felt excitement that he was getting so good at getting back fast, but it paired with overwhelming dread that he was, indeed, back.

A deep shiver shook his body, head to toe. He looked down at the water droplets clinging to the fuzz of his bare shins, soaking into his canvass sneakers. Water was penetrating his thin, too-big flannel, a hand-me-down from Brian. He shivered and bent down, using his hands to wipe some of the wet off his legs. Looking up and ahead through the darkening canopy of pines, beyond the gray cloud of drizzle, he could just make out the dim, darker gray outline of Brian's weathered house. He stood, looked at his watch and let out a deep, satisfied exhale.

"Almost there. Almost there," he whispered. "7:02" *Record time.*

Hagas kicked his soggy feet into gear and wove his way to the edge of the trees. His now-routine, quick glance back up at the dark house had become almost a throwaway with the never-changing scene barely registering in his head. Today though, the kitchen light blazed to life just as he looked up. His stomach yanked into knots and his whole body stiffened with fear. The soft ground seemed to root his feet into place, paralyzing him, just like one of the big trees around him. *But, it's too early.*

It felt like forever that he stood there watching the house for signs of movement. He became aware of his breathing. In his head, he traced the path of the cold, wet air shuttering in and then wisping out of his open mouth. A trickle of water ran down his forehead, pooling in the corner of his eye, bringing his mind back to the now. He looked at his watch again. 7:06 p.m. "Only four minutes." *No. No. No. She's gonna kill me.* "It can't be her. Can't be."

Finally, a shadow moved behind the curtains of the glowing window. His heart skipped a beat. For a long minute, he watched the figure flash in and out of the frame of light. *Looks busy. Doing something. Maybe she hasn't checked. Maybe I can make it back.* He felt a warmth start to spread through him. The locked, semi-comatose state of his body eased out of him, and his blood pumped again, quickening his pulse.

"Gotta try." He forced his wet feet to start moving forward.

Crossing Katahdin Iron Works Road was always the scariest part. He had emerged from the heavy woods and crouched near the edge of the scrappy brush, just starting to pop open its bright green buds. He looked at his finish line, the endless dirt logging road, now a wide, dark brown line from the steady drizzle and fading light. Moving sideways along the brush line, he finally reached the spot where he could see better, past the wall of trees and bushes in front of the house across the road. At the far end of the rutted driveway, parked past the side stairs leading into the kitchen, was an old faded black SUV. He sighed, but not with relief. *Gigi.*

He crouch-ran across the road and stopped just at the end of the driveway, concealing himself from view behind a mangy pine tree just off the driveway. He watched as Gigi moved back and forth across the window frame. Then she paused, fully framed in the window, and tipped a big glass to her face. *She's already into it.* A flash of a memory of her face hovering too close to his made his stomach flip.

The distant sound of tires speeding over the gravelly road caught his ear. He looked down the road and saw headlights and flashing blue lights bouncing toward him, fast. Too fast. Getting too close. "Shit! Shit! Shit!" Looking back at the window, he saw Gigi had moved away. *Gotta hide. Window or car? Window or car? Window or car!?*

He bolted from the tree and raced up the driveway, adrenaline fueling his long, still-growing legs to power him up the incline. He made it to the front of the SUV and slid/collapsed down to the ground just as the cop went hurtling past.

Hagas stayed still on the ground until he could no longer hear the truck as it faded away down the road. After he was satisfied it was gone, he raised up, placing his hand on the front bumper to help leverage himself. *Just gotta get over to the window. Easy. Almost there.* He kept his eyes on the road below, just to be sure no other trucks or cars were coming.

The spray of whiskey hit him first, followed by quick, sharp thuds of ice cubes ricocheting off his forehead. He cringed, dropping onto his haunches, squeezing himself into a protective ball, his arms covering his head.

"What the fuck are you doing out here?" A familiar voice hollered. "C'mon. Answer me, you little shit. Who in fuck are you?"

Hagas peeked through his arms to see Gigi standing no more than six feet from him. Her eyes were wide and wild. She was slightly crouched, her arms stretched out in front of her, ready to fight. Her empty glass was in her left hand and a very large butcher knife in her right. Both were pointed at him.

"It's me, Gigi. It's me. Hagas." He lowered his arms, putting his hands on the ground to steady himself in his crouch, and then raised his head to look up at her. He saw her register. She stood taller. Her eyes lost some of their ferocity as her arms slightly relaxed, dropping just a bit.

"You! You little fucktard. Scared the shit out of me!" She hissed at him. "Friggin' cop flying by. Lucky I didn't start with the knife, boy. C'mon, Get your ass into this house right now."

Hagas pushed himself up slowly and stood in place. The smell of the whiskey soaking into his jacket and hair burned his nose, sparking more flashes of his history with Gigi. His heart sank.

"Right fuckin' now! Move!" she screamed at him, waving the knife and glass in big loopy circles.

He started moving toward the side door. "Yes, Gigi."

"And get right the fuck down into your goddamn room."

"Yes, Gigi."

He made his way up the three side stairs and opened the moss-riddled, wooden screen door that led to the kitchen. Inside, he paused and glanced at the window looking out to the front yard, the same window he had been watching so intently to be sure he did not get caught.

Arriving at the door to the basement, he knew he was stuck. The padlock was still secured, just as it was when he had left that morning. He stood there, not knowing what to do, and stared down at his sneakers and the whiskey-infused water puddling onto the floor around him.

Gigi bounded into the kitchen. Hagas turned his gaze to her. She now had a long cigarette clenched between her lips. She slammed her glass down on the counter and tossed the knife into the shallow aluminum sink. For a couple of minutes, she just stood by the sink, staring out the window, sucking on her cigarette and filling the small kitchen with puffs of smoke. She turned abruptly, looked at him, and breathed out a long stream of smoke as she crushed her cigarette in a plastic ashtray.

"You made me waste my fuckin' drink on you. Shit's not cheap, Hagas. Now I gotta make me a whole 'nother one."

Gigi ripped open the freezer door, pulling ice cubes from the bowl and chucking them into her glass. Once it was half full of ice, she closed the door and retrieved the jug of Lord Calvert from the counter. She filled the pint glass to the brim. Leaning on the counter, she took a long sip and stared at him. Smoke curled around her head.

"What are you doing just standing there? I told you to get down to your room."

He pointed sheepishly at the padlock, watching her work the situation out. Her watery eyes darted back and forth, from his face to the padlock. Then, with a growing, wicked smile, Gigi leveled her gaze at him.

"Oh, oh, oh. I see. Someone's got another way to get out, doesn't he? Well . . ." She took another long, slow pull from her glass, staring at him. " . . . look at you. Aren't you a fuckin' clever—dirty—little—man?"

For a few moments, there was a tense stillness in the kitchen. Hagas looked back at Gigi, trying, hoping, to get in her head and change her plans. *Please help me. Before Ma gets back.* An unmistakable sound ricocheted into the kitchen. *Whip-poor-will . . . whip-poor-will . . . whip-poor-will . . .*

Oh nooo. Hagas shuddered, a cold dread running through his whole body. In his head, pops and chunks of Ma's stories about these evil omens played out. *Not just birds. Where they go, death goes.* He looked at Gigi, praying, she wouldn't touch him.

Gigi's smile dropped as she ran her hand through her hair. "I think you need a bath, little man."

Chapter 5

Take it to go

Chris drove down the dirt road, his mind whirring as fast as the tires of his Bronco. He had the radio cranked—his go-to M.O.—to both energize him for the call and to try and block his churning mind. He was almost to the KI checkpoint gate, where every local and out-of-towner pays their visit fees and registers their vehicle and occupants before driving into the Gulf.

Twins. School. Trish. Why, Trish? Why now?

An overplayed Pink Floyd song faded away and the weeknight host, Jack, started babbling about a classic—*for all those on the lookout for new love this summer.*

He glanced at his speedometer and quickly took his foot off the gas. *Shit. 60! Alright, alright, alright. Coming in a little hot. Pull it together, Chan. Duck. Duck. Duck.*

An all-too-familiar beat kicked in on the radio. "Oh, c'mon! This?" His finger shot to the seek button before the

Silver song really kicked in. But he couldn't bring himself to push it. *Trish . . . Trish . . . Trish . . .*

Starry nights and sunny days
I always thought that love should be that way
But then comes a time when you're ridden with doubt
You've loved all you can and now you're all loved out

Chris couldn't stop the inevitable replay of the dance—that dance—from their reception. Trish pressing against him, holding each other, swaying together. It was the moment he knew they were one. *So perfect . . . so right. Great song. Should've paid more attention to the lyrics.*

Oh Oh Baby we've been a long long way
And who's to say where we'll be tomorrow
Well my heart says no but my mind says it's so
That we got a love that isn't a love to stay
We've got a wham, bam shang-a-lang
And a sha-la-la-la-la –

The road opened up to the large checkpoint area. Chris braked hard, pulling up just after the small brown checkpoint building. He parked and cut the engine—and that song. *Thank Christ! Stupid wedding song.* He took off his seat belt, grabbed his hat, opened the door, and hopped out. *Should've known.*

He took in a few deep breaths through his nose, exhaling slowly to calm himself. After positioning his hat carefully, he strode to the front of the building, pausing to take in the peaceful surroundings. River gurgling. Peepers chirping.

The massive old, stone blast furnace standing tall. Shadows stretched their fingers across the damp ground. A fully loaded logging truck was parked across most of the visitor spots across from the building. *Pretty late for a pit stop. Okay. Let's see what this duck thing is all about.* He stepped onto the porch and swung open the screen door.

"'Bout time, Sheriff." Margaret deadpanned from behind the counter. She peered at him above her reading glasses, perched precariously at the end of her long thin nose. The seasoned gatekeeper had been giving him that same cool look ever since he was a deputy coming up to the Gulf to deal with unruly visitors, illegal hunting, and the occasional logging truck run-ins with visitors' vehicles. Over the years, she had grown to accept him, maybe even respect him, but she always made it clear she was the keeper of the Gulf. This was her dominion.

"Evening, Margaret. Want to tell me what made you call me in about a dead duck? Not exactly six o'clock news material."

Margaret removed her glasses, set them on the counter, and made her way around the counter to join him.

"Well, let's have you take a look for yourself." She motioned for him to go out. "No! Not that door. That's the 'in' door. Use the other one. We've got our rules here, too, Sheriff. You of all people should set an example."

Chris looked at her incredulously, then looked at the two screen doors, no more than six feet apart, shrugged, and took the three extra steps to the far one, holding the door open as Margaret followed him out. They walked to the back of the building and she nodded toward the rushing Pleasant River. Chris followed her gesture and saw a woman scooched down

28

on the grassy bank, looking into a cardboard box, and a hulk of a man stood off to the side smoking a cigarette.

"Jana's got the duck. Found it in an eddy. She radioed it in to me, then caught a ride with that logger and brought it here. Looks to me like some shithead got themself a new take on hunting." "Maybe. Maybe. Let's see what's going on," Chris said.

As they approached the duo, Chris noted the girl, Jana, was young, early twenties, dressed in the khaki-colored uniform of the Gulf's Ridgerunners, those heroes of lost hikers and policers of partiers. The man looked like one of the hundreds of logger clones up here—with an old, beat-up baseball hat, scraggly beard, beer gut, flannel shirt, loose jeans, and heavy work boots.

Jana barely registered them when they stopped a few feet from her. She was just staring into the cardboard, case-sized Shipyard beer box. The trucker looked at them but didn't say anything.

"Evening," Chris said, a little too loud, causing Jana to snap her head toward him.

Margaret wasted no time. "Chris, this is Jana Desrochers, new Ridgerunner this year, and, uh, Scott . . ."

"Cormier. Scottie Cormier. Work for Pine State Timberlands," Scottie interjected, puffing up to his full six-foot-plus.

"Right. Cormier. Cormier," Margaret said.

"Ain't seen nothing like this before. Goddamn duck's all taped up head to toe," Scottie said to no one in particular while scratching at his head under his baseball cap. "Jana here came booking it at me, arms all flailing, just where the river hits Silver Lake. Scared the friggin' bejesus outta me. Didn't think I'd be able to stop in time."

"Well, good thing you did," Chris said.

After a quick, quarter-smile toward Scottie, Chris turned his attention to Jana, waiting for her to add to the account of the story. Scottie started pacing a bit, sucking down his cigarette with quick, aggressive drags. Jana stood up slowly. Puffy eyes and tear streaks on her dusty cheeks clearly showed she'd been crying and just how much this was affecting her.

"Thanks for coming, Sheriff," Jana said, folding her arms across her chest. "I don't understand who would do this. Who would torture a duck like this? Boston maybe, yeah, but here? Where the hell am I, anyway? This looks like some kind of gangland revenge thing or something."

"Before we get too far, let me take a look," Chris said.

Jana took a sidestep away from the box as Chris made his way over. He looked over the top. *Jesus!* Some bright green feathers of the mallard were still visible, but it was mostly covered in what appeared to be duct tape. *Man, oh, man. Shit.* He dropped down to one knee for a closer look.

Definitely duct tape. Mostly gray and—rainbow? Really? Bound tight. This little guy had no chance. He made mental notes of everything he was seeing. *Wings pinned down. Tape wrapped all around it. Feet taped together. Bill wrapped. Nares still exposed . . . so it could keep breathing? Tape looks fresher around the bill. Tape on body looks dirtier, picked at—like it tried to get it off itself . . .*

Chris stopped analyzing and just stared at the gruesome sight, trying to make sense of it. He'd seen—and scraped up—demolished birds, raccoons, skunks, porcupines, deer, and even moose from roads all through the county. But those were accidents, pure and simple. This was different. *Just so cruel.*

"Probably some damn kids or something. Bunch of crazy little peckerheads running around up here," Scottie blurted out as Chris stood back up.

"Appreciate the observation, Scottie," Chris replied coolly, catching a quick memory of the yahoos and bullies from his own school days.

Chris turned to Jana. "What about you? Seen anything, or anyone, unusual on your loops? Anything not quite right?"

Jana looked toward the river for a long thirty seconds, arms still crossed around her athletic body. She turned her gaze back to Chris.

"No, I haven't. Barely anyone up here right now. Hell, I've barely even been up here. Just over three weeks now. Water's still way too cold for most. There are some campers, but they just look like normal people beating the heavy season. RV at Silver Lake 3. A few tenters scattered around—mostly older couples, one young family. Haven't seen anyone finishing the AT yet." She paused. "But, well."

"And?" Chris said.

"This is stupid." She snort-chuckled a little. "There was one day, maybe a week ago, up by High Bridge. I was sitting at the table in High Bridge One, eating my sandwich, when I heard a big branch snap in the woods. Thought maybe a deer, or a moose. Don't know why, but it gave me a jump. Probably too much reading the old stories of the Red Paint People. So, I went back to eating my sandwich, but then it happened again. And again. Like something was moving away from me—fast. I was tweaked out enough. And then adrenaline must have got the better of me. I threw my sandwich in my bag and charged into the woods where I'd heard the snaps. Nothing. And no one. Spooked myself out, I guess. But, until I made it back down, I couldn't shake the feeling of . . . being watched."

"Okay. Well, you're probably right about it being a deer or a moose." Chris turned to Margaret. "Everyone checks in with you, right? You keep visitor logs inside?"

"Yup. No one gets by me or Earl. Well, maybe by Earl, but not by me." She smiled wide, revealing a few gaps where teeth were supposed to be. "You wanna see 'em?"

"Yes, indeed I do," Chris replied.

"But, what about the duck? What happens to him? A burial or autopsy or something? I mean, we have to figure out what happened, who did this," Jana pleaded.

"Fucker got all wrapped up an' then went belly up. Pretty much how I see it all played out," Scottie added with a long exhale of thick smoke.

Chris flashed a stern look at Scottie. *Typical backwoods idiot.* He softened his face and looked back at Jana.

"I'll take the duck with me. Give my buddy a call at the state police. He's Team Commander of their Evidence Technicians." Jana smiled a feeble thank you at him. "I can't promise anything. Dead ducks are probably not exactly high on their priority list. But, this one's a little different than roadkill." He switched gears. "You two can be on your way. I got it from here. Just do me a favor and keep your mouths closed and eyes open around this. We don't want to start the rumor mill."

"Thank you, Sheriff. I will. And, um, please let me know, or let Margaret know, what you find out," Jana said.

Jana thanked Scottie for stopping, then grabbed her gear, walked past the checkpoint cabin and onto Katahdin Iron Works Road, disappearing over the bridge beyond the gate. Scottie dropped his butt on the grass, grinding it out with his boot.

"Gotta get this load to the mill ASAP!" He half-jogged to his truck, coughing along the way.

Idiot. Littering right in front of me. Going to tell your friggin' beer buddies as soon as you get outta here. Chris watched him get in his beast of a truck and tear down the dirt road toward civilization. He grabbed the cardboard box, holding it at arm's length in front of him as he and Margaret walked back to the cabin. He left the duck, in its cardboard coffin, on the porch. Inside, Margaret was already going for the visitor ledger.

"Here you go, Sheriff. Day by day. Week by week. Names. Plate numbers. Addresses. Just like Jana said, pretty light. Only been a handful of people so far."

Chris flipped methodically through the pages. He scanned for names he might have known, any notables that had past brushes with the law. None jumped out at him.

"How about Jana and Scottie? Know 'em well?" he asked, still looking down at the pages.

"Jana's a good girl," Margaret offered up matter-of-factly. "City bred, Boston, but I get a good feeling about her. Been up here a few weeks and she's working those damn loops every day. Rain, snow, or sun.

"Scottie, uh what's-his-name? Cornhole? Dunno. Never talk much to the guys. Used to, back in the day, when I was more around Jana's age. But they don't stop much anymore. They just come in and they go out. Up and down the goddamn road. Logs. Logs. Logs. Never really noticed him before. Beard. Flannel. All of 'em just kinda blend together after a while."

Chris reached the logbook page for today. Five names and addresses were logged. Four locals signed in for day use, three from Brownville and one from Milo. There was one out-of-towner, registered as a camper for a few nights. Suzanne Kelley. Boston address. High Bridge number two. Arrived at 5:30 p.m.

"Who's this? She come in solo?" He looked up at Margaret, simultaneously spinning the log book toward her.

Margaret looked down, sweeping her reading glasses onto her face. "Yeah. She got in a while ago. Her and her dog. Fancy car—SUV. Mass plates. She's at High Bridge number two. Nice enough. Wasn't interested in a whole lot of small talk. Asked her what brought her up this time of year. She said her friend," Margaret used air quotes, "used to live up around here as a kid and told her this was the best time of year. Not many people. Beat the bugs. Who knows? Cute dog. Forget its name though."

"You think she's all set up there? Safe and sound?" Chris asked.

He formed a loose mental image of the solo woman and her dog up at High Bridge. *Probably kids. Teenagers— punks.* He searched Margaret's blank face. *Nothing. She'd have heard. Something. Nothing from any of them on some whack job running around.*

"Who? Jana?" Margaret sounded bewildered.

"Well, yes . . . both. Jana and Suzanne Kelley," Chris clarified. In his head, he worked back to the research he'd

34

done on animal torturers becoming psychopaths and killers. *Classic forming time. Kid or kids maybe. Starting small.*

"Yeahhhh." Margaret rolled out the word slowly. "Jana's fine. She's got a little cabin. And that camper, well, she looked tough enough. And she's got that dog. She'll be fine. Big woods. Getting dark out. Everyone who's supposed to be in, is in, and everyone who's supposed to be out, is out." She pointed her finger at the logbook.

Chris debated driving up to Suzanne to check on her, tell her . . . *tell her what? Just going to scare her. Have to tell all the other campers, too. No facts. No answers. Need time. Still have time. Too soon.*

"Okay. And, with that, I'll say good night, Margaret. I'll be back in a day or so. Try to keep mum on this but keep your eyes and ears open to make sure nothing else weird is going on in these beautiful Maine woods." He tipped his hat and went out the far screen door.

"You let me know what you find out as soon as you find out," Margaret called after him.

Chris bent down and opened the box with the duck. *Jesus. Why?* After snapping a few pics with his phone, he closed the box, opened his liftgate, and placed it in the back as neat and secure as he could. An old sweatshirt was crumpled up against the back seat, and he grabbed it to cover the box. He shut the back and shivered a bit with either the cold catching up to him or the details of the duck's death creeping in.

Starting up the engine, a nameless Journey song immediately assaulted his ears. *Nope! 'Nough of that.* He grabbed his pad and pen, and jotted down his notes, letting the Bronco idle for a minute. *Pieces of rainbow tape. Why? Symbolic? A crafter maybe?* Chris put his truck in gear, turned around in the big gravel expanse, and started back toward the main road. His headlights picked up nature's rush hour of freshly hatched bugs, flitting above the road, many flying directly into their demise, courtesy of his high beams and wall of a windshield.

Yellow light from a window up ahead caught in his peripheral. He checked his speed to be sure he wasn't going too fast. *No need for a report of a speed-freak cop.* The speedometer hovered at about forty-five. Easing his foot off the gas, Chris slowed the Bronco to thirty-ish as he cruised by the driveway. Chris looked up the incline and saw the dark block of the SUV parked near the side porch. The gray Bondo stood out in the porch light. *Busted up quarter panel.* A figure moved across the kitchen window.

"Well, there you are. Least you made it."

Chris glanced into his rearview mirror, just seeing the edge of the box in the way back. After checking the clock, he pressed his foot on the accelerator. *Damn it. Boys will definitely be asleep.*

"We got a wham, bam shang-a-lang, and something is sha-la-la-la-la fucked up out here."

Chapter 6

Light up my life

Gigi let out a short, choking cackle, and gestured at him with her drink. "Look at you shaking in your shoes. What's the matter, little man? You cold?"

Hagas kept his eyes trained on his feet. His whole body was locked in a swirling mess of fears—the whip-poor-will, her, Ma getting home soon. *She doesn't care about the bird. Doesn't know?*

"Answer me," she said.

"Yes, Gigi. Just cold." He whispered the words.

"Well, maybe I can help with that. But first, you're going to show me how you got yourself out of that goddamn basement." She motioned to the side door. "Let's go, genius. I want to see what you've been doing."

Hagas forced himself to look up at her. *Can't just stand here. Gotta do something. The ones who make it to the end of the movie always do something. Don't just stand there.*

Gotta try. He started walking to the side door, focusing on the growing darkness beyond. The extra weight of his soaked clothes made him feel like he was going in slow motion. His sneakers made squishing noises with every step. He couldn't hear the whip-poor-will anymore. *Maybe it's gone.* At the side door, he stood still, waiting, shifting his eyes between the outside and Gigi. *Never make it. Not like this.* He put his focus on Gigi, watching her tilt her head back and drain the whiskey in her pint glass. After a fast swirl of the ice in her glass, she tilted her head back again and slurped down any remaining melty drops. *Maybe she'll be too drunk again.*

Gigi refilled her glass with ice, followed by whiskey, filling it all the way to the top with a shaky pour. She took a big, long swig before slamming the glass down on the counter.

"Wait right there, mister," she said, pointing her bony finger at him.

Hagas watched her wobble across the kitchen, weaving her way down the short hallway to the bathroom. She flicked on the light and bumped into the door frame.

"Fucker!" she barked at the frame.

He heard her turn the squeaky spigot for the tub, and soon, the rushing gurgle sound of the water hit his ears. He pictured the river and his missing duck. Gigi emerged from the bathroom, tossed her hair around, and marched over to the counter for another swig from her glass. She grabbed a flashlight that was perched on the counter before joining him at the side door. With a quick shove, she flung the screen door out and held it open.

"Out. Let's go," she barked. "Tub's filling up. And your ma'll be here pretty soon, too. But I'm betting you probably know that. Let's make this quick." She reached behind him, grabbed hold of his butt with a firm grip, and pushed him forward.

Hagas descended the stairs and positioned himself beside the SUV. *I could drive this. Seen it enough.* He shivered. The drizzle was lighter, finer, but his wet clothes still hung from him, making him colder.

Gigi walked past him, stopping in front of her Forerunner. She lit a cigarette, took in a big drag, then started waving her arms around, circling and pointing them toward the house. In the low light, he followed the zig-zagging, glowing end of her cigarette. His hand went to his butt. In his head, he could see all the scattered scars he carried from Brian's 'teaching' lessons.

Gigi turned on the flashlight, sweeping it back and forth across the dirt driveway as she took a few steps toward him. She put the beam of light directly into his face. "Okay. Show me. Show Gigi where you got—" she hiccup-burped "—got out, Houdini."

Hagas squinted at the sudden, bright light. *What's whodeeny?* His confused face and lack of movement must have come across like he was stalling because Gigi closed the gap between them and got right in his face. She held the flashlight between their heads, pointing it up. The effect was just like that girl with the runny nose in *Blair Witch*, making her look mean and distorted, with dark shadows butting against the lit areas of her face, her eyes black ovals. He fought back a gag at the unavoidable smell of cigarettes and whiskey on her breath.

"Hey. Hey, little man. I'm not gonna tell anyone. Ish me. It's Gigi. You know I love you. Just show me how you got out. Right fuckin' now."

Hagas eyeballed the cigarette dangling beside her and took a step back. *Just show her. Maybe she won't tell. Ma will be here soon. Think. Think. Maybe if I go slow enough . . . just enough . . . she won't have time . . . won't touch me.* "Okay. Promise? Ma will be so mad."

"Jesus," she sighed, moving close to him again. With her cigarette sticking out from her fingers, she touched his face, grazing her hand from the side of his forehead down to his chin. "I promise. It'll be our secret."

Hagas cringed at her touch and the way-too-close cigarette. His heart raced as he pictured the painful punishments Ma, or worse, Brian would do to him if they found out he'd been getting out of his room. *Don't burn me! Please don't burn me. Show her . . . get her on my side. Promised she won't tell.* "Okay. Our secret."

"That's my little man," Gigi cooed, then waved her cigarette toward the house. "Now, where?"

Hagas shuffled around the corner of the house, leading Gigi across the front, past the kitchen window he'd watched her in. Gigi was right behind him, pointing her flashlight just ahead of them, the circle of light bouncing on the ground around him. As soon as he rounded the corner at the far end of the house, he stopped. Gigi swept the beam of light back and forth.

"Where? Your ma's window? Pretty high up."

"No. Not her window, Gigi."

Gigi whipped the beam of light to him. He pointed at the bottom of the house. She traced his arm with the light, bringing the beam to the foundation and spotlighting a tattered screen, hanging slightly ajar in the crumbly cinder blocks.

"Aha! Got you!" she blurted.

Gigi grabbed his arm and pulled him to the small window. It was covered with duct tape strips—a mix of standard gray and pops of rainbow. Gigi crushed her cigarette out on the ground and bent down. She pulled the top of the window outward, shining the light inside.

"Brian's playroom. Hmmph. He does like to keep it dark for them," she said, staring into the gap.

Hagas fidgeted as Gigi pushed herself upright. He felt like he'd given up part of his soul now that his secret was gone. *What now? She going to ruin my plans? Try to keep me here?*

Kicking at the outer edges of the window, Gigi popped it back into place. She turned to Hagas, putting the beam of light on his face again. His hand went up to shield his eyes.

"Your ma will have your ass if she finds out you been getting outta here. How'd you get in his room anyhow? He keeps it locked."

"I know. I know. But she doesn't know. I'm careful. I never go when she's here." Hagas paused, dropping his hand from his eyes so he could look beyond the glare to Gigi's face. "I, uh, figured out the combination for the lock. I kept watching Brian undo it until I got all the numbers. Well, the first two anyway, then I figured out the third just trying different ones." He felt like he'd told her too much.

"Smart little fucker. Smart little man," Gigi said. Then she just stood, cloaked in drizzle and shadow behind the flashlight. After what seemed like an eternity to Hagas, she dropped the beam of light to the ground.

"Still our secret, right?" Hagas asked. He kept his gaze on her face. "You said it would be."

The question hung in the air for a few seconds before Gigi answered.

"Yeah, Hagas. Yeah. Ish our little secret." She let out a low chuckle. "But, but, but, little man – it jush might not need to be a secret much longer. 'Specially if it all works out. We'll see. See how the weekend goes." A quick, full-body shiver shook off some of the wet clinging to her. "Now go. Fuckin' freezin' out here. Go on and get inside. Tub's probably all full up."

Hagas's heart sank. He was hoping she'd forgotten about the tub. But deep down, he knew it was too much to wish for. He turned away from her and began making his way back to the side porch. *What's she mean? This weekend. What's special about this weekend?* Just as he made it to the corner of the house, he took a quick look behind him, watching Gigi stumble and bob back toward the driveway. *How's she even going to see anything this weekend? Drunk bitch. Hate you. Hate you.*

Deep in the woods behind the house, the omen of death called out again. *Whip-poor-will . . . Whip-poor-will . . . Whip-poor-will.* Hagas stood still with anger swelling in him. He raised his head up, listening intently to the bird's call, then slowly climbed the stairs and flung the screen door open. *Hate you.*

42

Chapter 7

Rub-a-dub-dub

Inside, Hagas meandered to the basement door. Waiting. Dreading. Gigi came in and stood by the counter again. She took one more puff from her cigarette and then roughly stubbed it out in the sink. She looked back at him.

"Let's get you warmed up." Her mouth curved into a semi-smile. "Go on in the bathroom and get outta them clothes."

He didn't move. Any hope that she'd just put him downstairs and be done with him was sucked away, sent back into the corner of his mind where his other few hopes lived. *Don't want to do this. Have to keep her happy. Keep her on my side.*

"Now boy. I ain't gonna ask ya twiced," Gigi barked into the air, then took a big swig of her whiskey.

He backed up slowly toward the bathroom. Just as he was ducking in, Gigi hollered down the hall.

"And your underwears, too. Jush leave all your shit in a pile and get in dat tub."

He escaped her gaze when he moved past the door frame and into the dingy bathroom. On the sides of the sink mirror, only the left light was working, and it wasn't very bright, especially with the steam from the tub filling the room. He started peeling off the wet clothes. Bending to untie his shoes, he realized they were caked with pine needles and bits of forest. *Dammit—gotta get that off before Ma sees.* He took them off delicately and placed them under his T-shirt and flannel. Shorts were next. Then his holey socks. He hesitated before removing Brian's old, worn-out, baggy boxer shorts. His last line of defense, protecting himself from her. *Hate you.* He swiped his boxers down and kicked them to the pile of clothes, then made his way to the edge of the water-stained tub, his back to the door. He cupped his dick with his hands, covering himself, even though Gigi was still in the kitchen.

"You in yet, boy? Hurry it up. And turn off that goddamn water!"

He turned off the water. All was quiet. He slid his left foot in. *Yikes! Hot!* His foot recoiled. He tried again, forcing himself to hold his foot in the water. *Not that bad.* The rest of his body shivered. He stared at the water and the suds, and his mind floated back to that day. The water and suds began to still. He heard her little giggle. *Angel. Angel.* His eyes raced back and forth across the sudsy surface. Nothing. The giggle filled his head again. *Angel?*

You promised . . . He heard her words just as he saw the bloody strings of blonde hair on the spigot. *You promised . . .*

44

A pair of webbed feet rose through the suds, then rolled to one side. His shiny, duct tape-wrapped duck broke through the suds. Its head was lolled over to one side. Black, dead eyes stared up at him. Hagas froze, unable to look away. *I'm sorry. I'm sorry. I'm sorry.* The memory of that terrible day came rushing at him, at full speed.

Gigi had come into the bathroom, telling him and Angel to quiet down. Ma had fallen asleep beside the tub, all curled into herself. Gigi had giggled, pointing at them with her glass of whiskey. They ignored her and kept splashing around, covering each other in thick suds, tossing the rubber duckie and frog back and forth. Angel let out little squeals each time Hagas took turns squeezing the duck and frog to make them squeak. It was her favorite game—made both of them laugh every time.

Gigi had shoved Ma with her foot. "Dannie. You 'wake?" she'd asked. She'd poked at her three or four times. Ma never moved. She just kept sleeping. He didn't like her. *Too huggy. Too mean to Angel when Ma wasn't looking.*

The next thing he knew, Gigi put her drink down on the sink, then started undressing. He remembered seeing her naked body. Skinny. Her dirty pillows hanging off her. The big patch of hair between her legs. She'd climbed into the tub with him and Angel. Got right between them with a big splash. her back to Angel. *Too crowded. Too close.*

For a while, she laughed and tossed around their rubber duck and frog with them. Then she got a serious look on her face. Started rubbing suds into his hair. "Such a dirty boy," she'd kept saying, looking past him, like there was something on the wall behind his head.

45

She leaned forward, putting her face really close to his. Her eyes, all wide, were right across from his. He remembered the smell of whiskey and cigarettes on her breath. Her slippery body touching his. *So gross.*

It had all happened fast. Gigi had sucked in a big breath, put her hands beside his feet under the water, then got on her knees in one fast motion and ducked her head into the sudsy water.

At that moment, Angel was toppled over. He remembered the look of surprise and pain as the back of her head slammed into the spigot the first time. At the same time, Gigi's mouth wrapped around his privates. The sensation had been weird. Warmer than the water. Felt like she was using him like a straw. Sucking him in. He watched Angel's eyes close, then she slipped into the water and rolled onto her face in the suds.

After shoving at Gigi for what had seemed like forever, she came up for air. She'd let out a big gasp, laughed, and wiped the suds off her face. She smiled at him.

"You like that? Feels good right?" He'd tried to point behind her.

"Angel."

Gigi took in a mouthful of air and ducked back under the water. On Gigi's fourth time under, he knew something was very wrong with Angel. She was just floating there, face down in the water. When Gigi came up again, he pleaded once more.

"Gigi. Look. Look. Angel."

Gigi was annoyed at him, but she twisted her neck around to look.

"Fucking fuck!" she'd said.

When she spun around, she fumbled, falling onto Angel, pressing her farther underwater. Righting herself, she'd grabbed Angel under her arms and yanked her upward. Angel's head connected with the spigot for the second time. But this time, it was the rough underside. The blood had been almost instant. Over Gigi's sudsy shoulder he could see the chunk taken out of the back of Angel's head.

He remembered staring at the bones popping out of Gigi's back, pushing at her thin skin, when she lowered Angel back into the tub. She'd laid Angel face up and the water had started getting pink around Angel's head. *She's gone . . . dead.* That he remembered knowing. Like one of the birds that smashed into their living room window sometimes—you could just tell they were gone. Gigi had crawled out of the tub and slumped down beside Ma who hadn't even moved. "Fuckety fuck, fuck," Gigi had said.

He'd sat in the tub, numb, staring at the blood seeping into the water, reaching out once to wiggle Angel's toe just to be sure. She didn't move.

And then, Gigi was talking to him, telling him it was his fault.

"Shouldn't have played so hard with her. Roughhousing."

But she said it was going to be their secret. She wouldn't tell. Not the sucky, sucky part either. Their secret. No telling. Just an accident. She'd promised him that now he would get all the love. All her love. Angel was gone to heaven.

"Shit happens," she'd said.

Gigi got dressed, grabbed her drink, and tip-toed out of the bathroom. It had all confused him. He was scared. *Angel's dead. My fault. Gigi said so.* He didn't know what to do. The only thing he could think of was to wake up Ma.

He couldn't remember everything after waking Ma up. She had started hitting him. Yelling. The biggest thing he remembered was that was the day everything changed. After Angel was gone. Ma got meaner. She hit him all the time. Started tying him to chairs when she left him alone in the house. Started . . .

"Go on. Get in the tub," Gigi said in a low, even voice.

Her voice startled him, and he whipped his head to the door. She was squinting at him with that half-smile. He quickly put his other foot in the tub and lowered his body into the hot water. The steamy water stung his cold legs and behind. He sat there motionless, eyes closed, trying to let the heat envelop him. *Just be still. Maybe she'll go back to the kitchen.* Thirty seconds later he popped open his right eye. Gigi was standing beside the tub, drink in hand, looking down at him with one eye squeezed shut.

"I almos' forgot. It was jush your birthday. Look how much you grown."

His hands moved slowly under the suds to cover his dick. He felt the new dark hair, the same kind that had started growing under his arms. He knew he was becoming just like the teenage guys in his movies. They all had patches of hair—legs, pits, chests, dicks. Right now, he didn't feel like one of those older guys. Right now, he knew he was trapped, just like he'd trapped his duck. *Nowhere to go.*

Gigi pivoted and put her drink on the sink. She threw all the clothes, even his shoes, in the dryer. She gave the control dial a quick, clickety crank and pushed the button to start it up, sending all his stuff bumping and tumbling inside its metal walls.

Turning back to him, she smiled and said, "We'll get them clothes all dried. And if you're a real good little man, your ma won't ever need to know you got yourself outside."

She opened the mirror cabinet above the sink and pulled out a plastic bottle of Old Spice body wash. She shook it and smiled as it made thick glug, glug sounds.

"Got this for your ma's man last Chrishmas. Fuckin' Brian. Knew that fucker used it. Uses it all over, I bet." She popped the lid and inhaled deeply, closing her eyes. "Lesh get you smelling all good."

Gigi lowered herself to the side of the tub, one hand on the tiled wall. He closed his eyes, not wanting to look at her. Whiskey and cigarettes filled his nose. *Please don't. Just go. Pleassssse.* It wasn't but a moment before he felt her hand and the cold body wash being rubbed onto his back.

"There we go. Make you smell good." He could smell the body wash now, competing with her breath. He tensed. *Stop. Just leave me alone.*

The next thing he felt was her hands under the water, her bony fingers rubbing at his low, low back. She slowly moved her hands all over him, making him all sudsy. His eyes stayed closed. Her hands moved up his back and onto his shoulders, then reached around him, rubbing the suds into his chest. He heard the wheezing squeeze of more body wash going onto her hands. Then she was rubbing both his nipples at the same time with the cold, thick liquid. He flinched at the weird sensation and the tingles shooting through him. Gigi laughed.

"Look at you all senshitive." She continued circling his nipples with her index fingers.

He didn't like this feeling, all tingles and electricity shooting down to his dick, making it start to swell. He tried to fight it, to stop it. After a couple of minutes, she stopped the circling and let out a sigh.

"Lift your arms up. Come on, little man. Gotta get you clean . . . all . . . over."

Under the water, he clenched his fists into his crotch, squeezing and pushing his dick down. He tried to make it hurt and stop it from growing.

"Lift!"

He obeyed, lifting his arms while squeezing his legs together to trap his dick. He caught a strong whiff of his own smell, sweat from four days of hiking back and forth in the woods. She moved her hands to underneath his pits, rubbing her sudsy hands around.

"Aww, you're startin' to get hair. Look at that."

She bent down to look closer. Her hands rubbed the suds up and down his smooth arms. She squeezed at his forming arm muscles, working her hands up and down their lengths. She finished her exploration by squeezing his hands and then dragging his arms down into the water. Gigi pushed herself up, spinning to the sink. She took her whiskey in long and slow, then almost missed finding the edge of the sink while putting her drink back down.

"Now, lay all the way back, my little man," she said, wiping her mouth with the back of her hand.

Hagas stared dead ahead, focused on the suds and spigot above his feet. The duck was gone. The strings of bloody, blonde hair were gone, too. He was stalling. Waiting for, hoping for, almost expecting, Angel to pop up and give Gigi a heart attack. She didn't. And he couldn't catch a solid

50

thought to help him get out of this moment. He let the gray swirls take over, muting his mind.

"Lay back," she commanded as she lowered herself to sit on the edge of the tub.

Letting himself slip down the back of the tub, he felt the warm water surround his whole upper body. He knew what was coming next and his hands slid back to cover his groin. Gigi looked down at him. She began stroking and swirling the suds above his waist, moving the fading suds out to the edges of the tub.

"Be good and move your hands. We's gotta get you clean all over." Her voice was lower. Hagas didn't move his hands. He lay still, eyes still locked forward on the spigot.

"Move 'em, boy. Show Gigi you love her."

Doesn't matter. Doesn't matter. Keep her on my side. Inch by inch, he moved his hands away, loosening his fingers to create a cover above his groin.

"Move 'em all the way. Put 'em down beside you."

His hands slid past his thighs and he balled them into tight fists beside him. He squeezed his eyes shut and tried to picture his duck, its bill now taped fully shut and its legs bound together. Gigi's hand and the cold body wash touched just below his belly button. She moved her hand up and down his torso slowly, purposefully, methodically.

"Oooooh," she cooed with a gurgly rasp. "You gettin' hair down here, too."

Gigi paused and removed her hand briefly. Then she was back at it, firmly grasping his balls, rubbing the cold body wash around him. He squirmed, a reflex to her sudden, rough touch.

"Be still. Gotta let Gigi clean you up good. Yes. There we go. Yesss . . ."

Forcing himself back to stillness, he felt his dick growing. In his head, he fought against the gray swirls to find the picture of his duck. Gigi kept rubbing, now moving her hand to grab onto his dick. She started her usual slow, tight stroking, and he squeezed his fists harder against the all too familiar feeling.

"That's a good boy. Let Gigi take care of you. You's smellin' sooo good."

Her strokes got faster and her grip tighter as he started getting waves of muscle spasms. His butt and leg muscles flexed on their own. Flashes of scenes from the movies he watched peppered his head. The girls and guys. Tits. Mouths. Hair. Without warning, his dick erupted. Gigi squeezed even harder and his full body twitched again and again for what seemed like forever. Then she removed her hand, wiped it on the bathmat, and pushed herself up.

The dryer buzzed, signaling it was done. *How long had it been? Water feels colder.* He opened his eyes and watched Gigi take a slug from her glass.

"Get up," she said without looking at him. "Grab your clothes outta the dryer and get 'em on."

She walked to the doorway, but stopped and turned, looking at him, her face softening. "Maybe. Maybe. Maybe. 'Cause ish your birthday, you an' me'll go for a real swim. In a big tub. Up to the Gulf."

Hagas's heart leaped. *Go out? For real?*

Gigi's eyes narrowed. "But don't say nothing. 'Specially to your ma. Now, be a fuckin' man and get up. Get dressed.

I'm gettin' the keys. Your ma's gonna be here soon enough." She bumped into the door jamb on her way out. "Fucker!"

His body calmed and his mind began coming back into focus. He stood in the rapidly cooling water and looked down at himself. Milky white goo clung to him just under his belly button. *Gross.* A flash of Brian's hairy, sweaty body standing over him during one of his lessons whipped through his head.

He reached down for the bathmat and wiped himself off with a fury, leaving a red glow on his pale skin. Opening the dryer, he found his clothes were still a little damp, kind of smelling like his room downstairs, but warmer. He put everything back on. Socks. Shorts. T-shirt. Flannel. The good part was that his shoes had shed all their gunk, and he wedged them on as quickly as he could.

Before leaving the bathroom, he took a few seconds to study his reflection in the hazy, fogged mirror. *Hate you.*

He walked out of the bathroom, stopping to wait by the basement door. Gigi was mumbling, swaying on her hands and knees as she rummaged under the kitchen sink. The dirty red cloth that covered the piping and junk stored underneath the sink was draped over her head and shoulders.

"Fucking keys. Where the fuck?" Her head smacked something, sending out a thud. "Fuckety, fuck, fuck!"

Chapter 8

Going down

"Got 'em! Jee-zush . . . Christ . . . Dannie, could ya . . . hang . . . these fuckers any . . . farther . . . back?" Gigi grunted the words as she hauled herself out from under the sink.

The red curtain fell back into place as she emerged, slumping onto her butt, breathing in and out heavily, holding a small ring of keys in her hand. *Ah-ha! That's where they are.* Hagas looked at his watch. *Almost eight. She'll be here soon. Got to get downstairs.* After a long minute, with Gigi showing no signs of getting back to her feet, he mustered up his courage to talk to her.

"Um, Gigi, are you going to put me downstairs soon?" He asked her with a slight hint of pleading.

"S'pose I better," Gigi said.

She pushed herself up, her back sliding against the cupboard doors, her hands grasping the counter. She made it upright and leaned on the counter.

54

"Guessing I'd better get you sumptin' to eat," she said, turning her eyes to the higher cupboard doors.

He watched her open and close the cupboard doors, jostling through boxes, glasses, cans, and packages. He looked at his watch again. *Hurry up. Hurry up. Hurry up.*

"Ah-ha!," she blurted, whipping around with a can of SpaghettiOs held high and almost losing her balance as the tie on her flimsy, shiny robe caught on a drawer handle.

Her robe gaped open as she went to work, twisting and cranking a rusty opener. She got the can open about halfway before giving up. She grabbed a spoon out of the sink and clomped toward him. He could see right down into her robe. The smell of whiskey hit him again when she got in his face.

Dirty pillows! Dirty pillows! Gigi's silky robe barely covering her saggy tits conjured up that scene from *Carrie* when Carrie's mother was trying to get her to burn the dress. *Gross! Gross! Gross!* He wished he could use his mind to send her flying across the kitchen.

"Hold theesh," Gigi said, shoving the can into his hand, then bumping by him to square herself to the door.

Hagas watched as she fumbled through the ten or twelve keys on the ring. She kept one eye closed tight as she examined each key up close, stopping on the sixth or seventh key. It had a purple piece of tape on it. *Gotcha! Could shove you. Lock you down there. Take your car*—"Gotcha, you little fucker." She belted out the words, glanced at him, then turned her eyes onto the padlock.

Gigi managed to open this first lock with relative ease, then took it off the metal latch, and dropped it to the floor. She flung open the door and fumbled inside, reaching around to find the pull string for the light. The stairway light blinked on as she pushed herself back from the door frame.

"Lesssh go. Downstairs." She pointed the keys to the door.

He hated these stairs. Their creaks always alerted him to Ma or Brian coming down. A quick glance at his watch pushed him forward. *Almost there. One more door. C'mon . . . move!*

His left hand pushed on the wall, guiding his steps down the dimly lit stairs. In his right, he gripped the SpaghettiOs and focused hard on not dropping the can. He made it to the bottom and stopped. Another door blocked his progression. Gigi was making her way behind him, cursing at the steep decline and lack of light. She reached the bottom and jerked up the purple-taped key between their faces.

"One more," she sighed as she bent down, getting her face close to another padlock.

Unlocking this one didn't go quite as quickly. He fidgeted, looking at his watch again and again as she mumbled and tried to get the key into the padlock. *Not enough time. Too close. She might get me . . . punish me—*

"Jeezush. Settle the fuck down. You're breakin' my conshentration," she snapped.

He stilled himself and Gigi went back to work. Her wheezy breathing filled the space. Finally, a click signaled she got it. They locked eyes as they both heard the sound of a car rolling on gravel. *Oh no. Oh no. Ma. Hurry up!*

"Fuccckkkk me. Your ma's home," she moaned.

Gigi put her full body weight on the heavy wooden door to push it open.

"Push, you little fucker," she whisper-barked.

Hagas pushed the door with her, using his left arm and shoulder so he could keep his grip on the SpaghettiOs. The door moved enough for him to squeeze through.

Gigi breathed hard. "Go on. Get in there! And push it back from the other side."

He popped sideways through the opening, squeezing his body into the darkness beyond the door.

"Push," she commanded

He set the can of SpaghettiOs down and pushed as Gigi pulled from the other side. Just before it filled the frame and shut out the upstairs, he heard a car door close. He pressed his ear to the door. He could hear the lock clicking back into place. Then he heard Gigi climbing the stairs. The muffled sound of the top door closing. Then, silence.

Next time. Next time you'll be stuck down here.

Chapter 9

Head Case

After a couple of minutes of straining to hear anything from Ma's arrival, Hagas grabbed the SpaghettiOs, walked across the dirt floor to the center of his space, and plopped down on his mattress on the floor. The room was pitch black, but it didn't matter; he knew every inch of it by heart, and right now, he welcomed the uneasy comfort of the dark cocoon hiding him away from Gigi and Ma. *Made it. She'd already be down if she knew. Out of sight. Out of mind.*

He sat in the dark, thinking about how he was busted by Gigi and almost caught by Ma. *Promised she wouldn't tell.* Gigi's twisted face, hovering over him in the tub, invaded his thoughts. *Just better keep her end. Might even get me out for real. Swimming. I did my part. She just better keep her end.*

Hunger pinged his stomach. He hadn't eaten since the day before when Ma had come home and left a Styrofoam container at the bottom of his door. Last night's meal had been her leftover lunch: a cold, half-eaten cheeseburger with a few pieces of limp lettuce hanging off it and some rubbery fries swimming in ketchup.

Reaching behind his mattress, his hand found the old battery-powered lantern. He rarely turned it on because Ma always got mad when the batteries ran out. But he was awake and needed to think, so with a quick twist and click of the lantern's dial, soft, yellow light illuminated the immediate area around his old, flattened mattress.

At the foot of his mattress, an old TV/VCR combo sat on a wooden chair. Around the chair, his stacks of movies were neatly formed into little towers, like a mini city of gore and sex rising from the floor. The cold cement floor was cracked but dry, stretching out to dark, windowless cinder block walls, standing tall on three sides. Layers of paneling, two-by-fours, and beams of wood made up the zig-zag corner and the big door leading upstairs.

Brian's door was in that corner too, and as his eyes got used to the low light, he saw the combination padlock hanging open, dangling from the hinge.

Shoot! In the flurry of getting back down here, he'd forgotten the open lock. *Stupid! Stupid!* Hagas sprang from the mattress, heart pounding, and raced to the door to secure the lock and set the combination numbers back to exactly where they were when he left.

Back on his mattress, his heart slowed, and he began eating the cold SpaghettiOs, stretching out each spoonful to taste the sharp, tangy flavor of the sauce for as long as he could. His gaze found its way to the farthest corner of the basement. The lantern light didn't spread quite far enough to reveal Angel's suitcase, but he knew it was there, sitting in the corner, waiting.

Sorry. Duck got away. I'll figure something out. The darkness forced his thoughts to wander, and replays of his climbs through the lone basement window crept in, the rush of fresh air when he landed in the front yard.

A low scraping sound coming from the corner jolted him. "Just mice. Just mice. Just mice."

He closed his eyes and spooned in more SpaghettiOs. *She won't tell. She won't. Gotta keep her promise.* When he scraped every last bit of pasta out of the can, he got up, walked over to the big door, and set it down. *No mice by me. No siree.*

Pressing his ear to the door again, he listened hard for any signs of life upstairs. *Nothing. Didn't say anything. Kept her promise.* Satisfied the crazy night was finally done, he pivoted around, reaching under the stairs to grab the big coffee can.

He forced himself to pee, concentrating on expelling any liquid left from the day. A nightly ritual started because of that bad run of pissing the bed too often and paying the consequences at the hands of Ma and Brian. He squeezed his dick to be sure every drop was out, then replaced the lid quickly so the smell of piss and shit wouldn't get too far.

Landing on the mattress, he rolled onto his back and pulled the scratchy wool blanket over his fully clothed body. For a minute, he lay still, debating putting on a movie. Exhaustion won out, and he turned off the lantern. Staring into the dark, he found that place where he wasn't thinking about anything. He lowered his eyelids and went deep into the black, feeling the warm nothingness of sleep slowly taking over.

He dreamed of his duck. All taped up. Helpless. He held it in front of him and looked into its eyes to study his own reflection. *I'm so tiny in there.* Swirling clouds and tall trees filled in behind his strange mirror image. *So cool . . .*

Dead leaves rustling around his feet, propelled by a new breeze in his scene, stole his attention from the duck's eyes. The sun was fading, dropping behind the clouds. He looked back at the duck, focusing hard on its black eyes. A scraping sound, soft and sinister, crept into his ears. *What's that? What's that noise?* Tearing his gaze away from the duck, he scanned the darkening woods. *Not leaves.* The scraping was getting closer and closer, louder and louder. *Who's out there?* The duck fought his grip, its eyes darting in a frenzy.

The scraping sound invaded his ears, taking over, wiping away his scene. It was right here. Right on them. Looking into the wriggling duck's eyes again, for a split-second he saw—

"Her . . . Ma . . ."

The duck slipped from his grip and he spun around and around, straining to see into the dark of the woods closing in.

Scrape. Scrape. Scrape. His eyes popped open and he looked dead ahead trying to make sense of the now. His lantern light was on. The scraping sound was coming from him. He felt cold metal on the top of his head. His hair was being pulled and stroked with cold metal. *My knife! Did she find...?* He froze, afraid to move. The stroking and pulling paused.

"I know you're awake," Ma said, barely above a whisper.

Rolling his head, he saw she was kneeling on the edge of his mattress, looming over him. Her face was shadowed by the lantern's light coming from behind her. But he knew her twisted face was there, glaring down at him. She held a pair of scissors, glinting in her right hand.

"Gigi reminded me it was just your birthday. So, I guess being your ma, I gotta do something for you. She gave you a bath, so consider this my gift. Lay still."

The scissors descended and Ma went to work, pulling and chopping off clumps of his hair. Hagas froze in place, afraid to move, afraid of the sharp edges and points, afraid of her. She shoved and twisted his head. The scissors sliced over and over, the sound of metal on metal filling his head.

He knew this was coming, he just didn't expect it in the middle of the night, down here. It was always in the kitchen. Twice a year, once around his birthday and then on Angel's death day, she'd haul him up and go to town on his hair, hacking and slicing. After, down in his room, he'd pick at the scabbing nicks and cuts for days.

Ma paused and released his head. "Turn." She sniffed at her hand. "Fuck! Carole! Goddamn, she knows I hate this smell."

Hagas obeyed her, adjusting and rolling his whole body over to face the opposite way. Clumps of his curly hair prickled at his cheek and forehead and he caught a whiff of the distinct smell of the soap Gigi had used on him.

Please don't cut me. Please don't. Please don't. Ma wiped her hand on the mattress and then got back to work. It wasn't long before he felt the edge of one of the blades zipping through the top of his ear. Still, he remained frozen, even as he felt the warm sensation of his blood trickling

62

down the back of his ear. Ma yanked up his T-shirt and swiped at the blood.

"Christ. You got your daddy's shit mess of hair. Starting to look just like that fucker."

Hagas tried to imagine the "Daddy" he'd never seen. Ma had never told him who he was, never showed him a picture. She said it "didn't matter," and 'the fucker was probably rotting in hell by now."

The pulling and hacking went on, a little rougher, for another few seconds, then Ma lowered the point of the scissors down in front of his face.

"Up. Up. Sit up," she said.

The scissors waved back and forth in front of him, the point swinging in too close, bouncing once off his chin before he could scramble himself up into a cross-legged position. He looked directly at her darkened face, terrified of not knowing what she was thinking or planning.

The cut on his ear stung and pulsed. Ma dug in, working the scissors across his forehead and then back along the top of his head. Finally, the cutting stopped and Ma stood up, dangling the scissors at her side.

"There. Done," she said.

Hagas studied her as she looked down at him. For one short-lived moment, he imagined she was—maybe—smiling. In a flash, she bent, her knees landing on the mattress, her face inches from his, and her left hand, the hand holding the scissors, latching onto his shoulder blade. "Don't you ever forget how good I am to you. Ever. I keep you safe. Feed you. That's what Mas do. All the people in those movies, those are the people, the monsters, out there. Just like your fuck of a Daddy. I keep you safe down here. You're so lucky. So . . . fucking . . . lucky."

Those last words, she whispered menacingly, then shoved him down and clicked off the lantern light. With a quick push off the mattress, she was up and walking away into the darkness.

Hagas watched her shadowy shape open the big door. The stairway threw a shard of light across the floor. Ma turned toward him before going into the stairwell.

"I hope you liked your bath time with Carole—Gigi. I have to go make some fucking money, so she's going to be here with you all day tomorrow. And you better be good to her. Do what she says. You don't want me or Brian coming home and hearing that you'd been a bad boy."

With those parting words, she slipped through the opening and pulled the big door shut. The padlock clanked and banged on the other side. In the dark, Hagas lay motionless until he heard the stairs creak, signaling she was on her way up.

She's gone. She's gone. She's gone. He flicked his lantern on, sank deeper into the mattress, and stared at the dust- and web-covered beams above. Thick tears welled and spilled from his eyes as he felt around his choppy, short hairs. *Not good to me. Never ever, ever, ever. Hurt me. Hate me.*

He licked his right pointer and middle fingers and dabbed at the cut on his ear. Pulling his hand down to the light, he focused on the watery, red blood coating the tips of his fingers. Anger, pain, and hate filled him. *Hate you, hate you all. Going to get out of here.* He reached down, feeling for the hard bump of the old jackknife he'd found on one of his outings. *There you are.* It was still hidden, jammed into the side of the mattress.

Afraid of making a mess on the mattress, Hagas licked the blood from his fingers. The metal taste was something he'd gotten used to over the years, and it barely fazed him anymore. He clicked off the lantern and let his body start to release. His mind began swimming again. Flashes and pops of Gigi, Ma, and Brian swapped and mixed. Then he found her. Angel floated in, her blonde hair filling the black.

His last semi-conscious thought came easily. *Going to kill you.* He slipped into sleep.

Chapter 10

Stitch 'n' Bitch

Carole was slumped over the kitchen table. Messy curls of hair hid most of her face which was planted on her bent left arm. Under her outstretched right arm were smears of drying blood. Her pint glass of whisky was sweating, leaving a puddle on the table, just shy of fingertips. A cigarette with an ash a solid two inches long, hung in the well-used plastic ashtray, sending up a thin stream of smoke.

"Wakey. Wakey," Dannie said.

Carole coughed into her arm. For a moment, she looked like she was coming to, but then she went limp and settled back into her passed-out position.

Such a fucking mess. "Jesus, Carole. Wake up." Dannie's thin veil of patience caved. "For fuck's sake, Carole, open your goddamn eyes!"

Shaking Carole by the shoulder, Dannie grabbed the cigarette, took a long drag, and then smashed it out in the ashtray. She slammed the scissors onto the table, bent down, and blew a forceful billow of smoke into Carole's face. Her eyes blinked open.

"Da fuck you do to me, Dannie? Fucking bleeding out over here," Carole whined.

"Oh, shut it, Carole. If you weren't so fucking drunk, you wouldn't have tried grabbing the fucking scissors from me. Just a haircut, Carole. A haircut. Hell, seemed like the right thing to do, especially since you'd given him that nice bath. But you fucking act like I'm going to cut off his goddamn balls."

"Whatever," Carole said, raising her head and pushing herself upright.

"Ha. Whatever? Think you can just sit there on your high horse and tell me to give that little shit a break. Telling me he's a good boy. Well, fuuuck you, bitch. You only give a shit because you don't want your fucking toy to get broken. Good boy? You know better. You fucking know what he did. He needs to be reminded—to pay—for as long as he's living."

"You do whatchoo gonna do no matter what the fuck I say anyways."

Dannie leveled a cold glare on Carole, locking eyes with her. *Don't you even think for a minute you're in charge of this shit.* She grabbed Carole's right arm and jerked it up for a closer look. Carole yelped. *Ha. Got you good, bitch.*

"Goddamn it, Dannie—fuckin' go easy, for Chrissake!"

"Oh, fuck off, Carole. Just take another swig, you pussy. Got to get this shit cleaned up before you bleed all over my house. And don't you fucking pass out again. You and me, we have some business to discuss."

67

Dropping Carole's arm, Dannie stomped away from the table and yanked open a drawer by the sink. She pulled out a variety of pens and pads of paper before finding what she was looking for. She turned toward Carole and held up a plastic sewing kit.

"Voil-fucking-la. Going to get you all fixed up."

Dannie grabbed the bottle of whiskey and some paper towels from the counter. She sat at the table, scooting her chair closer to Carole. Unscrewing the whiskey cap, she smiled, filling up Carole's pint glass with a steady pour. *You just keep drinking, bitch.* Carole reached for the glass and took a long pull. When she set the glass down, watery blood was smeared all around it. "Now, I'm not gonna lie, this is gonna hurt you way more than it'll hurt me," Dannie said, still smiling at Carole.

"Whadda you talkin' about?" Carole asked.

"This."

Dannie grabbed Carole's forearm and yanked it toward her. Before Carole could react, Dannie poured whiskey directly onto Carole's sliced palm. Carole howled, bouncing in her chair, trying to yank her arm back. Dannie held firm and doused her palm a second time.

"Bitch! Bitch! Bitch! Fuck you! Owww. Stop it. Fuuuck," Carole said through gritted teeth while pounding her free fist on the table.

Dannie released Carole's arm and set the bottle down. Grabbing the paper towels, she mopped up the puddle of whiskey—getting some of the blood, too. After shoving the soggy pile of paper towels aside, she selected a needle from the sewing kit and held it pointy end up between her and Carole.

"Now, you're gonna sit real still right there. Me, I'm gonna take this needle and thread and stitch that nasty shit up. And maybe while I'm stitching you back together, you can tell me why I'm fucking short a grand this time 'round. Sound good to you?" Dannie asked.

Carole averted her eyes, grabbed a cigarette and, with a shaky hand, lit it, pulling in smoke with quick puffs. Dannie selected a tiny spool of black thread, unrolled almost three feet of it, and snipped it off. Carole watched through slitted eyes as Dannie pushed one end through the eye of the needle, matched it up to the other end, and tied a messy knot.

Dannie reached for Carole's right arm again. Carole tensed, sucking hard on her cigarette.

Holding firm, Dannie twisted Carole's hand palm-side up and examined the cut. The scissors had made a clean, straight slice, running from just below Carole's index finger down through the meaty part where her thumb connected. *Got you good. Serves you right. Stealing my money.* She released Carole's hand and sparked the lighter. For a few seconds, she held the needle tip in the blue-orange flame.

Dannie started pressing the hot needle into Carole's flesh, about a quarter inch outside the cut. She didn't break the skin—yet. Carole flinched and squeezed her eyes shut, scrunching up her face.

"It's been, what, five months since you been up here?" Dannie asked.

"Yeah, 'bout that I guess," Carole said.

"Exactly that. Christmas to now—end of May. Five months. January, February, March, April, May. Five checks. Same amount each time. Not real fuckin' rocket science to figure it out. Nine thousand . . . four hundred . . . and fifteen . . . dollars."

Dannie pulled an envelope from her back pocket and slapped it on the table. The number '9,415' was crossed out in jagged, angry scribbles. Underneath it, '8,415' was followed by three pronounced exclamation points. Carole looked down at the envelope, then looked away, staring toward the kitchen sink.

"Look at me! You think I don't count the money every fucking time you show up to get your fix with my kid?"

Dannie pressed the needle a little harder. Carole winced and snapped her eyes back to Dannie's.

"I was gonna talk to you. Little bitch at the bank—ow!—recognized me. I had to give her some money to keep her fat fuckin' mouth shut."

"Recognized you? What the fuck does that mean?"

"It means I was taking the money outta your account, using your ID. Fuckin' drive-through. Who the fuck woulda known that little bitch would grow up and get herself a job at the bank?"

"Oh, wait. You didn't go to the branch in Hampton, did you? Oh, you fucking did, didn't you? Jesus, Carole! You stupid fuck. Who is she?"

Not getting busted. Not when I'm this close. No fucking way. Dannie eased off the pressure of the needle. Carole sighed and opened her eyes.

"Cathy Dodge. Her and her ma lived down the road from me years ago when I was livin' in Canaan. Little fucker used to come to my door every other fucking week tryin' to sell me some shit. Cookies. Wrapping paper. Popcorn. Magazines. Always fuckin' savin' the world or somethin',

70

who knows. She recognized me all the way from the drive-through window. Said so, too. Long story short, she gave me the money. Knew I was upta somethin' though. Told me we should catch up. Soon. Like, that day. Said to meet her at the Baptist church down the road. Lunchtime."

Carole went for a drag on her cigarette, but Dannie latched onto her wrist and pushed her hand down, guiding the cigarette into a slot in the ashtray. *No, no, no. Don't you . . . snap your fucking wrist if I want to . . . don't fuck with me.*

"Uh-uh. Finish your goddamn story."

Releasing her grip, Dannie sat back and crossed her arms, knowing she'd made her unvoiced physical threat crystal clear. Carole let go of the cigarette, shook her hand, and let out a sigh.

"All right. All right. Jesus. Well, I go to the church. Wait almost forty-five minutes. And just when I think she's not gonna show, bitch does, all smiles and shit. Tells me she looked at the account. Saw the deposits all coming from the state. Then she fuckin' says she won't say nothin' if I cut her a piece. Two hundred bucks a month. Says she figures that'll make up for all the shit I never bought from her. So, what the fuck was I supposed to do? Gave her the money right there."

"You know that's my money you're fuckin' with."

"Fuck you, Dannie. Our money. I'm the fuckin' one running this little shitshow for you. My ass is on the line, too. State ever finds out, you're fucked. I'm fucked. Woulda given that bitch two thousand. I ain't goin' to jail. Not that fuckin' hard up for Hagas. I got plenty of other young bucks on my watch—"

Like a tiger grabbing hold of its prey, Dannie seized Carole's fingers and stabbed the needle into her palm. Carole screamed as the point drove in. Dannie pushed, sending it through the wall of flesh under the cut. The point popped out on the other side. The long tail of black thread hung behind, but Dannie remedied that, pulling it through the fresh tunnel as slowly as she could, sneering at Carole's red, contorted face.

Finally, the rough knot of black thread anchored on Carole's pale white skin. *Yeah, we're going to get this shit all fixed, bitch.* Carole wavered, her eyes rolled back and she slumped forward, landing her face on her left arm, almost in the exact same position Dannie had found her when she had come upstairs from Hagas's haircut.

"Yeahhh, there you go. Pass out again you fucking moron. Just some blood, lightweight. Well, maybe a whole lot of hurt, too."

Chuckling, Dannie released her grip, put down the needle, and took the cigarette out of the ashtray. For a minute, she took slow puffs and stared down at the crown of Carole's messy hair. She crushed the cigarette and went back to stitching.

"I give you friendship. Let you do whatever the fuck you want to my kid, you twisted bitch. I get the cash. That's the deal. My deal. No way you're gonna fuck this up for me."

Stitching fast but steady, Dannie made wide looping arcs with the thread, doubling back in places to be sure it looked ragged and rough. *Yeah, good luck grabbing hold of his dick with that clusterfuck.* Carole never moved from her passed-out stupor.

Dannie looped the needle through the end stitches of thread and pulled tight to knot it off. She snipped the hanging tail of thread off and put it in the ashtray.

After a quick wipe around Carole's hand, Dannie grabbed the envelope of cash, threw away the soggy whiskey- and blood-soaked paper towels, and walked out of the kitchen.

She paused at the basement door, pulled on the padlock, and looked back at Carole, who hadn't moved an inch. With a flick of the switch, the kitchen light above the table went off and Carole became no more than a dark lump in the mix of moonlight and shadows.

Dannie walked in the darkness down the short hallway and into the bedroom she shared with Brian—on occasion.

Without turning on any lights, Dannie got down on her hands and knees near her side of the bed and folded back the frayed, braided rug. She dug her fingers under her special floorboard, but paused, listening for any stirrings from the kitchen. Silence answered her, so she proceeded, reaching her fingers in farther, lifting the board up and out.

Pulling the envelope of cash from her back pocket, a jolt of anger hit her as she shoved the thick row of identical envelopes, neatly lined up in her hidden cubby, to one side, making room for the new one.

Each envelope had a number on it, all almost the exact same number, except for the ones where she'd dipped in to pull a little for some drug-fueled fun. She knew exactly how many were in there, the running tally etched in her mind, getting her closer to what she'd figured out for a year's worth of rent and lay-low time. This new one though—no good excuse for the lower amount she'd written on it. *Fucking bitch. Everyone wants a piece. Brian. Carole. Now this bitch at the bank.*

"Fuck you all to hell."

Dannie jammed the board into place, pushing hard all around it to be sure it was snug. She folded the rug back down, pushed herself up, and crawled onto her bed. Her phone showed 1:12 a.m. when she checked it for the last time to be sure the alarm was set for 8:00 a.m.

Still fully clothed, Dannie stared up at the ceiling and the shadows twisting and turning in the moonlight. *Almost a perfect hundred. So . . . fucking . . . close. Fuck perfection. I'm close enough.* Kicking her legs out, she splayed her body as wide as she could across the bed, feeling the permanent dent on Brian's side. *Fuckhead's home tomorrow.*

Right now, she could almost smell him, his sweat mixing with ocean and dead fish. The phantom scent nauseated her. And she'd grown to hate sharing her bed with him, even as rare as it was. He'd served his purpose at first, giving her—and Hagas—a place to lay low and let the plan play out, but now, he was just another hairy, smelly, twisted fuck she had to deal with. *Carole's bright fucking idea.*

Snapshots of stinging memories popped around her. Angel's limp, dripping, blood-streaked body. Hagas, staring, giggling. Herself, helpless, horrified, scared, shattered. *Should've killed him. Could have. But couldn't. Goddamn it!*

Joyless visions of Hagas's birth resurfaced. She had been alone, angry, trapped. *Fucking weak! Should've gotten rid of him before he was ever born. Fuck!* She hated herself for not having the balls to do it. Today, at this moment, she hated him for even existing; touching him and that Daddy question he'd asked all making her remember so much bullshit she wanted to forget.

But deep down, snaking into those thoughts she refused to let fully unwind, threads of doubt about her planning, constantly drew her away from the surety she could do it now. *Kid's getting too fucking old. Figuring shit out. Fuck! Fuck! Fuck!*

Whipping her legs in tight, she folded her arms across her chest and focused on the shadows above. *Almost a perfect hundred. Maybe close enough. She's going to fuck me.* It was another couple of hours before she finally saw Angel's blonde wisps of hair flowing in the streaks of light between the shadows. *Time to fly.* Calm washed through her, and she allowed sleep to creep into bed with her.

Chapter 11

Rise and whine

"Mmmmmm. C'mon . . ." Suzanne groaned. A dream, *Connie . . . me,* flitted behind her eyes for a second, but she couldn't hold onto it.

Rolling her head side to side from her near horizontal position in the driver's seat of the Rover, Suzanne willed herself out of sleep, shoving at the too-hot sleeping bag covering her and squeezing her eyes shut to avoid the dapples of sunlight hitting her face. In the back, Derby whimpered, signaling his building staccato of urgency.

"Okay. I know. I know, Derby. Calm down."

After rubbing her eyes open, Suzanne powered her seat up. She grabbed the hunting knife she'd tucked between her thighs, plunked it on the dashboard, and scanned the surroundings.

The rising sun was starting its daily battle against the dark of the towering, dense trees, sending swords of light through them. Just below the site, the White Brook's spring pace fueled a constant white noise, penetrating the Rover's windows. Unseen birds and critters chattered. Derby's whimpering mixed into the growing sounds of the forest.

"I know, buddy. Give Momma a minute to pull herself together," Suzanne said, looking at Derby in the rearview mirror.

With a quick turn of the ignition, the Rover roared to life. Its dashboard array washed the interior in a soft blue glow. Suzanne's phone buzzed with the new jolt of energy coming into it. The screen lit up: 5:37 a.m., Friday, May 24.

Her printout of Portland's fishing boat arrivals report was rumpled and puckered from the nearly empty bottle of Sauvignon Blanc laying on top of it. She'd opened the wine soon after making the decision she was too tired and too keyed up to deal with pitching a tent in the drizzle of last night. *Now, that's camping. Polishing a bottle of wine in your car in the middle of the woods.*

Picking up the phone, Suzanne looked for bars. She waved it around briefly, but the status remained as it had since her arrival, even when she went wandering around the site and down the dirt road. No bars flickered in.

"Shit. Of course not."

Tossing the phone, she glanced at the passenger side mirror and stared at the road beyond the entry to the site. *Am I doing this? Could just turn around and head back to the city.]*

"Fuck."

She popped open the glove box, checking for the umpteenth time to be sure the taser was still in there. It hadn't moved. She slammed the glove box shut, and then gripped the steering wheel with both hands, stretching her arms.

After a minute, Suzanne turned off the ignition, removed the keys, and with a quick press of the fob, unlocked the Rover's doors. She pulled her sleeping bag into a ball and tossed it into the back seat. After one big stretch, she got out of the Rover and walked around to the back, pushing the fob again to unlatch and raise the liftgate.

Under the interior light, Derby sprang to attention, still whimpering but wagging his tail as he scooched to the bumper's edge, waiting for his leash to be put on. He jumped out as soon as it clicked into place, circled once, then dropped himself down a bit, jettisoning a solid stream of overnight water.

"Sorry, buddy. Should've walked you one more time last night." *Should've walked me, too. Damn. I gotta go.*

Derby finished up, rising from his half-squat, his tail wagging with relief. Holding the leash loosely, Suzanne strolled Derby around the open space of dirt and pine needles. At the tent spot she had scouted out last night, an overgrown path led to a dark green outhouse, visible through the swath of trees. She had yet to nerve herself up to use it, opting to drop and squat at the side of the path's entry instead.

A shudder rolled through her, making her body vibrate in quick waves. With a quick swipe, her sweats were down and she assumed the position. Relief came instantly. Sometime midstream, she let go of the leash and Derby sat on some soft moss, looking up at her as she did her business.

God, that felt good. Suzanne stood, hiked her sweats back into place then raised both elbows up to shoulder height.

After a half minute of upper body twists, she began to feel a little less antsy and a lot more . . . her.

The sun was gaining ground on the darkness and the site was starting to feel warmer, at least in appearance. Derby's low whimpering brought her back to the moment. His tail was doing a slow sweep, moving back and forth across the moss and pine needles.

"Okay, Derb. Let's get you fed and get me some caffeine. We're going to get this place set up. Legit camping. No revenge mission, right? Just a girl and her dog enjoying a little break from the city . . . and putting a fucking scumbag out of commission. Right? Right? And don't you tell anyone we slept in the truck last night."

She bent and ruffled Derby's ears, grabbed his leash, zipped her fleece all the way up and the two hustled back to the Rover.

Chapter 12

Duck and covers

Chris's eyes were already open—had been for ten minutes already. His internal alarm clock was trained and set at this time for nearly four years. But his ritual never allowed him to pull the sheets back until 7.00 a.m. on the dot. The fifteen extra minutes he spent in bed were usually reserved for reflecting on the day ahead. Today, his thoughts were focused on the night before . . . and Trish, always Trish as of late. *Hated my punctuality. Never spontaneous.*

Staring up at the white expanse of the ceiling, Chris let everything he'd registered wash through his mind. The duck. The duct tape. Jana. Margaret. Scottie sucking down his cigarette. It all tumbled together as Chris searched through the fragments for meaning and connections.

At 6:56 a.m. Chris looked back at his clock. He adjusted his position, roughed up his pillow, and closed his eyes, trying—but failing—to find that zen place in his mind where he could start outlining his next steps with clarity. *Jana. Just no way. Scottie . . . Cormier. Got to look him up. Rainbow tape. Check the list Margaret gave me.*

Chris opened his eyes and looked at the clock again. 6:58 a.m. "I'll show you spontaneous."

Throwing the sheets back, Chris leapt out of bed. He grabbed his thick, chunky robe from the back of his bedroom door, tied it around his waist and crept down the hall to the twins' bedroom. He was primed to do his daily knockety, knock, knock, but stopped himself just before his knuckles connected with their door. *The duck. Shit. Can't let these guys see that thing.*

Tiptoeing down the hall, Chris made his way to the side door, connected to the garage. He jammed his bare feet into his flip-flops and did a quick twist and pull to open the door and pivot himself through. Standing on the steps in the garage, he eased the door shut behind him, trying to be as silent as he could so he didn't wake the boys. A push of the wall button sent the garage door groaning open, its pullies rattling overhead.

It all sounded exceptionally loud in the still of the morning and Chris rolled his eyes, realizing his attempt at staying quiet was failing hard. For a moment, he pictured his Bronco as a sleeping bear and him the hunter, stalking up on it in the early morning sun.

Opening the liftgate, Chris gagged a little at the forming smell of decay. He covered his mouth and nose with his forearm as he pondered the blanketed body in the box. *Dammit. Dammit. Not good.*

"Sorry, bud. Have to get you out of here."

Chris removed his arm from his face, held his breath, and grabbed the box with both hands. Holding it as far away from his body as he could, he walked around to the side of the garage. *This'll have to do for now.*

Chris placed the box down on the crushed stone perimeter and flipped open his old barbecue storage bin. Inside were a couple of old crumpled bags of charcoal, some lighter fluid, a rusty grill grate, and a charcoal chimney starter.

After some quick reorganizing, he had cleared a space for the box. Taking a couple of deep inhales, Chris held his breath again and placed the box inside. The lid almost closed. Almost. *Good enough – least the smell will dissipate out here.*

Determined to get the morning back on track to normal, Chris walked to the end of the driveway and retrieved the *Bangor Daily News* from its cubby attached to the mailbox post. Newspaper in hand, he scurried back through the garage and into the house, leaving his liftgate and the garage door open to ventilate both. He kicked off his flip-flops and shut the side door. A look at the clock showed it was 7:05. *Not too behind.* Back on tiptoes, he crept down the hall to the twins' door. He gently tapped with his knuckles.

"Knockety, knock, knock. Seven o'clock. Time to rock."

He heard the boys groan from the other side of the door. Chris peeked in, directing an exaggerated, screwed up smile at them. They both giggled.

"Morning, guys. Let's get going. Sun's up and I think the paper's got a fun word jumble today. You can help me solve it before I go to work."

The boys peeled off their covers. Satisfied and smiling, Chris gave up the tiptoeing and full-on flip-flopped his way to the kitchen to start their breakfast. Opening the fridge, he quickly scanned the inventory. *Milk. Juice. Leftover Chinese. Half and half. Grapes. Lettuce. Eggs . . . eggs.* His stomach gurgled slightly. *Nope. No eggs today, guys. Cereal and juice it is.*

After the boys were fed and the word jumble solved, Chris sent them to grab their gear for the day. With a sigh, he looked once again at the pictures of the duck on his phone. *Man. Okay. Let's see what we can do.*

He scrolled through his contacts until he reached Paul at the State Evidence Team. Five rings later, the line connected, and Chris listened to the recorded message informing him Paul was out on vacation.

Just as Paul's voice was telling him who to contact instead, the twins came bursting into the kitchen with their overloaded backpacks. *Dammit. Call back after I drop them off.* He lowered the phone, watching his boys, squealing and all energy, fully engaged in playing their human bumper cars game, slamming their backpacks into each other and, literally, bouncing off the walls. Chris smiled and pocketed his phone. *Maybe try the warden department too. They deal with dead animals all the time.*

"Okay, fellas, time to go. Let's load up." He switched his voice into sing-song mode. "Over the river and through the woods . . ."

The boys jumped in with their part, shouting in unison, "to grandmother's house we go!"

For a brief, shining moment, Chris felt the warm glow of happiness tickling at his soul.

83

Chapter 12

Sun of a . . .

Sunlight began peeking through the kitchen window. Carole hadn't moved from the table. Her head still lay in the crook of her left arm, while her right arm remained outstretched. Dried blood and whiskey peppered the table. The ashtray was filled with crushed butts. A blood-fingerprinted pint glass held an inch of light brown watery whiskey.

Brilliant, new light cut through years of dust to illuminate the shoddy surroundings—peeling cabinets, cracked floors, dirty refrigerator, greasy stove. Slowly, steadily, the white light washed across her face.

Dannie sighed when Carole shifted her face away from the sunlight, disappointed her 'friend'—this moron of a human—hadn't died overnight. *Should've just let you bleed out.*

"Mmmmm. Jesusss Christ. Am I dead?" Carole's eyes fluttered, squinting against the fierce sunlight. Turning her head away, she began the slow process of pushing her hungover body up from the table.

"Morning, sunshine. How's that hand?" Dannie said from near the basement door.

Carole jumped, her eyes opening instantly. "Fuck! Jesus, Dannie. You trying to scare me to death now? You already hacked up my hand."

"*You* hacked up your hand, Carole. I was simply trying to give my son a little birthday trim. But you didn't think that was a good thing to do. Made your opinion pretty clear. So, really, who was right and who was wrong here?"

Holding her right hand up in the sunlight, Carole's mouth gaped open as she looked at the ragged crisscross of black thread holding the vicious cut together. Grumbling under her breath, she made her way to the sink and turned on the cold water.

Dannie snickered when the water hit the fresh cut and Carole stomped her feet. *Serves you right.* After the quick rinse, Carole ripped off a couple of paper towels and wrapped her hand.

Back at the kitchen table, Carole sat with a heavy sigh. She propped her right elbow on the edge of the table, positioning her wrapped hand upright like she was about to take an oath. It didn't take long for blood spots to dot the makeshift bandage.

She lit a cigarette, swearing and coughing as she tried to manage the process with her left hand. Finally, she bowed her head. Smoke curled around her. Dannie moved to the coffeemaker and began prepping a pot.

"Look, let's just move on. I'm fuckin' spent over here," Carole said, still looking down at the table.

"Love to, but . . . ." Dannie let a pause hang between them. "Here's the thing, Carole. You, uh, owe me some money, based on what you told me last night. You remember? *You fucked up.*"

Carole rubbed her forehead with the back of her left hand, cigarette locked in position. Dannie leaned back against the counter, crossing her arms, waiting to hear whatever feeble excuse Carole was churning around in her head to get out of paying up. The coffee began its slow, gurgling drip, hissing and spitting boiling hot water. Finally, Carole looked up.

"Goddamn it, Dannie. If I told you the deal, then you know the deal. That little bitch will turn me and you, and Brian, and even that kid in. I gotta give her a cut. No way around it."

Dannie looked hard at Carole, uncrossing her arms and gripping the counter behind her. Carole looked back at her with a 'that's that' look on her face, eyes wide, mouth tight.

"That's not my deal, Carole. That's your deal. You still owe me a thousand dollars. It's that simple. Now, if this bitch—Cathy, was it?—is a problem, then she is one hundred percent your problem. Not mine. And you need to take care of that problem. Got it?"

Carole looked down at the table again and sucked on her cigarette. Dannie continued staring at her. *You won't fucking win.* The tense silence between them was broken only by the coffee sputtering. Minutes ticked by.

Carole broke. "Fuck. Fine. I'll get you your money back. I promise. Just . . . just don't cut me off from him. I . . . I need him. You don't understand."

"I don't give a . . ." Dannie paused and cleared her throat. "As you and me discussed a long time ago, you can do

86

whatever the fuck you want to with that bastard. I don't give a shit. You just need to give me what's due. It's. My. Money."

The coffee finished brewing with loud, strong blasts of steam coming out the top of the machine. Dannie opened a cabinet and took out two mugs. Grabbing the coffee pot, she walked to the kitchen table and set down one mug. She hovered the second mug in front of Carole's face. Carole stubbed her cigarette out and reached up for the mug.

"No, no, sunshine. Let's see how my handiwork is holding up. C'mon, hold out your other hand."

Carole pulled her right arm against herself. Dannie continued holding the mug out in one hand, and the glass coffee pot in the other. Steam trailed up, mixing with the lingering smoke.

"Hold out your hand, Carole," Dannie said in a slow, measured command.

Carole slowly offered up her trembling right hand. The bloody dots on the paper towels had now merged together. With great delicacy, Dannie placed the mug into Carole's palm. Carole closed her fingers around it, hooking her thumb through the handle. Her face twitched, but she managed to grip the mug and look up at Dannie.

"See. Look at that. It works just fine," Dannie said, releasing the mug.

Carole said, "I'll get you your money."

"I know you will." Dannie offered a menacing smile.

Raising the pot of coffee to a foot above Carole's quivering hand, Dannie kept smiling as she poured a thin stream of steaming coffee directly into the mug. Carole's hand shook more. The mug filled to the brim, just to the point of spilling over. Dannie stopped pouring and lowered the pot to the table, pulled out a chair, and sat down.

"Been doing this too long to fuck things up now," Dannie said after taking a slurp from her mug.

They remained silent for the next ten minutes, drinking coffee and smoking cigarettes. Dannie looked at the clock, shoved her chair back, and popped up.

"Shit. Well, this has been nice, but I gotta get going, sunshine. Busy fuckin' day at the shop. Tons of fuckin' outta-staters coming up this weekend to open their camps and put their docks in. Docks in. Cocks in. Ha! I made a little funny there."

Carole didn't laugh. Dannie ignored her silence and continued.

"Hate those rich fucks. I almost shaved, but fuck it. I figure I'll make three or four hundred bucks just opening my mouth one by one. Well, unless Billy tries to fuck me over again. Fucker took twenty percent last week. That's why every penny counts here, Carole. Every fuckin' penny."

Dannie shoved her mug into the sink, adding to the collection of dirty dishes. She looked back at Carole. *Bitch looks beat the fuck up. Fuck her. I win.* Dannie hustled around the kitchen, searching for her car keys and sunglasses, and swiping a pack of Carole's cigarettes. She grabbed the scissors from the kitchen table and jammed them back in a drawer.

"So, anyway, you're going to stay here and keep my little bastard company, yeah? I'll be back about eight o'clock. We'll drink. Get back to being friendly. Shit, Brian should even be back tonight. I know you want to see him, and you know he'll want to see you. He's been out almost three weeks on that fuckin' boat. Probably all horned up."

"Yeah, I'll stick around. Be good to start over tonight. I'll go down and make sure Hagas is being good."

"Fuck him. You fed him last night, right? I saw the SpaghettiOs can. He can just sit down there. He's got his movies. Unless you . . ." Dannie paused. "Whatever. Do what you do. Just watch yourself. He's getting smarter. Something's rattling around in that pinhead of his. I can tell."

Slinging her beat-up, oversized bag over her shoulder, Dannie strode to the side door. She stopped midway across the threshold, one foot in the kitchen, one on the porch, fishing around in her bag. Her hand emerged with the sunglasses she'd stuck in there moments before, and with a one-handed flick, opened them and jammed them onto her face, blocking out the fast-rising sun. Turning back to look at Carole, her mouth curled up. *Next time I leave this shithole, it's for good.*

"Gonna be a hot one today," Dannie said.

And then she was gone. The screen door banged shut, leaving Carole sitting in a halo of smoke surrounding her at the table.

Chapter 13

Angels and angles

Dannie raced along Route 11 out of Brownville, crossing into Milo. The drive to Billy's Antiques and Pawn shop in Corinna was about an hour if she pushed it hard. She was already on edge, with a million thoughts ricocheting around her head, stemming from her coffee chat with Carole.

She came up fast behind a loaded logging truck. Riding its ass made it impossible for her to see around the pile of freshly hacked-down trees, so she veered out every few seconds to see if she could get around him--a dicey prospect with morning traffic, even up here. She banged her fists on the steering wheel. *Fuccck. C'mon. C'mon. Fucking trucks!*

Now on Route 6, almost to the edge of Milo, just before the Dover-Foxcroft line, Dannie got her break on a long stretch of wide-open road. She floored the accelerator and swerved beside the truck, her car straining to pick up speed. Down the road, she saw a yellow blob coming at them.

Plenty of time. Come on. The trucker beside her was picking up speed as well.

"Fuck! Cut the shit, fuckhead!"

The yellow blob was getting closer, revealing itself as a school bus. Dannie continued stamping on the gas, now making headway in a slow-motion creep past the truck at about 65 m.p.h.

Finally, she poked past the truck's rumbling front tires. Looking in her side mirror, she could see she was almost clear enough to get in front of it. *There we go.* She kept pressing the accelerator and glanced to the rearview mirror, seeing the full truck, now well behind her, like it had slowed down. A surge of victory displaced some of her angst. *That's right, asshole—back the fuck off.* Dannie swung into the right lane, still looking behind her. Satisfied she'd ditched him, she turned her eyes back on the road.

The red, flashing stop sign of the bus was maybe two hundred yards ahead on the opposite side of the road. Dannie squeezed the steering wheel and slammed both feet on the brakes. Her car screeched and swerved. Dannie hung on and mashed her eyes shut. After what seemed like an eternity, the car stopped, jerking Dannie forward. *Fuck me. Fuck!*

Pounding the steering wheel with her fists, Dannie opened her eyes. The bus's yellow and black nose was right there, in the opposite lane, parallel with her front bumper. Inside the bus's cab, just beside the blinking swing-out stop sign, a meaty woman, hands in the air, glared down at her. Dannie stared up at her, dumbstruck, waffling between pissed-off and pure relief.

A hand slapping on her passenger window grabbed her attention. Dannie turned, seeing a woman with a face almost as red as the stop sign screaming at her, sending a flurry of muffled words into the interior. *"What is wrong with you? . . . should be arrested . . . calling the cops."* The woman kept going on.

Dannie explored the woman's face, avoiding eye contact, focusing on her mouth, growing mildly amused as the woman's flapping lips fired off threats. She let her eyes wander past the woman's red face.

Her amusement snuffed out when she saw the young girl, crying and heaving, wrapped in the woman's arms. She looked to be about four or five years old. Dannie fixated on the little girl, all blonde hair, blue eyes, and sporting a light gray sweatshirt with bright pink flowers on the front. A brutal wave of memories crashed around her head. *Angel.*

Behind her, the logger blared his horn. Dannie snapped out of her daze, glaring into the rearview mirror. He was right behind her. From his window, the driver flailed his arm. Dannie cranked her window down and gave the driver the finger.

Bringing her gaze around, she looked back up at the bus driver. The driver's arms were still up in a what-the-fuck pose, shaking her head. *Fuck you.* Dannie pivoted her hand, raised it higher, and saluted the bus driver with her middle finger as well. Pulling her arm in, she whipped her head to the side, locking eyes with the mother, who was still spewing venom. Dannie raised her right hand and uncurled her middle finger. The mother's face sucked in, shocked. And, with that, Dannie punched the accelerator and began tearing back down Route 6. *Fucking fuck! Late as fuck. Stupid kids.*

Dannie drove fast, but not as fast as she had been going. She scanned the road for more buses or cops. The little girl kept creeping into her thoughts. *Same look. Same look. Mama better take care of her. Got to watch her—all—the—fucking—time. Little bitch will get run over next time.*

Angel was barely four when it happened. The whole thing was still fucking blurry and drove her crazy every time she tried to put the story together; a piece of her never quite believing she knew—or was told—the whole truth.

Blame, rage, and guilt swirled just under her hardened surface, bubbling over often. Her Angel. The one she wanted. The one she thought he wanted, too. From the moment Angel was born, Dannie knew in her heart her little girl was destined for more. She'd tried, putting all her focus on raising her out of the cycle of shit she'd managed to get stuck in her whole life.

For a while, everything was going in the right direction. He worked at the Shipyard. She thought, or at least convinced herself, he was different, even promising marriage. Her golden ticket to game changers like insurance and money.

When they first met, he had reluctantly accepted Johnnie was in her world. And she had tried her damndest to make her firstborn mistake seem like a background fixture, like some old piece of furniture that was simply there, too heavy to get rid of but still in need of the occasional dusting.

He was excited, or said he was, when she got pregnant. He painted a room and fixed the crib. In her heart though, as the days ticked by and her belly got bigger, a tiny spark of doubt grew into a steady, annoying flame as his enthusiasm faded away. It had all been too damn good to stay true. She knew it. Always had. She could have written the script.

After Angel came, he changed. Stayed out late, eventually not even bothering to come home some nights. Fighting replaced fucking and any talk of marriage dried up along with his contributions to the household.

Then one Monday, just after Angel turned two, he was gone for good. It hadn't taken long to find out he'd quit the Shipyard and moved south—Georgia, she'd heard—with some little bitch bartender from the pub. She hadn't bothered to find out more. *Fuck him.* But that little annoying flame in her mind became a full-on fire, fueling her will and actions to get her and Angel out of the shit.

The master plan had taken shape out of necessity, born straight from her worst nightmare. Carole had come over for Dannie to sign some more papers. They started drinking like they always did. Whiskey and gingers. One after another. Laughing about the 'System' and how they had it by the balls. Easy money. Homeschooling bullshit. Fuck work. Blind people jokes followed, with Dannie putting on her prop oversized sunglasses and using an inverted broom to smack her way around the kitchen—"Just in case any nosy fuck's looking through the windows."

It had been a shitty afternoon, rainy and cold—the perfect kind for drinking the day away. Johnnie and Angel were outside jumping around in mud puddles that peppered the small dirt yard behind the house. She always hated Johnnie roughhousing with Angel, getting her pretty, blonde hair all messy and dirty. But Angel seemed to like it—seemed to like him, maybe even more than her.

After a couple of rounds of drinks, Carole broke out some pills. "Jush take a half. Shit'll fuck you up." Dannie took a whole.

The next thing she remembered was Johnnie throwing lukewarm water on her face, rousing her back into semi-consciousness. She remembered her whole body feeling warm and tight, all curled up on the floor, beside the tub. But her head felt like it was wrapped with every towel in the bathroom, almost detached from her.

Johnnie's panicked yelling had sounded distant and faint. Gradually, his voice grew stronger and louder, and she opened her eyes. He was standing over her, his pale, skinny body naked and dripping, pleading with her to get up.

He kept darting his eyes between her and the tub, yelling "Ma! Ma! Ma . . ." and pulling on her arm. She cursed at him and told him to "Settle the fuck down."

She hadn't wanted to get up and was more than annoyed at Johnnie's pleading. But a twinge in her head—*what, motherhood?*—pushed her to move.

As she struggled up to a sitting position, her hand gripped the icy porcelain of the tub. That sensation was her most vivid memory. The one that made the twinge in her head scream. Even today she could feel a tingly wave of cold come over her whenever she got in the shower.

Rubbing her eyes, she looked back at Johnnie. He just kept pointing into the tub, stamping his feet, his face all screwed up. She remembered turning her head to see what he was freaking out about. The water was milky pink, studded with patches of white bubbles, and for a split second, she wondered what the fuck they dumped in there.

Then she saw Angel. She was on her back, her face just under the water's surface, bright blue eyes open, her head surrounded by a ring of white, foamy bubbles that seemed to have clung to her. At the top of her head, the bubbles morphed into a much darker pinkish red. Too red.

Dannie remembered screaming and shoving at Johnnie, pushing him to the floor to get him out of the way. She remembered grabbing at Angel to pull her up. Angel's body flopped into her own on the edge of the tub. Blood was seeping out of the back of her head. The tub spigot had blood and strands of blonde hair stuck to it. She remembered reaching for the gash in Angel's head, trying to stop the blood, then squeezing her tight, feeling her cold, limp limbs, and then the awful, sinking realization that she was gone.

There was wailing. Maybe sobbing. Maybe both. Time seemed to have stopped—or fast-forwarded—and she couldn't recall how long she sat there with Angel in her arms. But ultimately, she laid her perfect little girl back down in the water.

The image that continued to burn in her mind to this very day was Johnnie cowering in the corner by the door, his knees pulled up to his chest, his whole body shaking. He looked like he was trying to hide—and something worse.

He looked like he was laughing, laughing like a stupid—fucking—boy. Laughing at her because her Angel was gone. Rage overtook her quickly. She remembered leaping across the floor and pummeling Johnnie with her bloody fists until he stopped screaming and simply lay still—a lumpy ball of pale flesh.

Her next memory was when she screamed at Carole, who was dead to the world, her skinny body pressed into the living room couch. A half-empty pint glass of watery brown whiskey was perched on the edge of the coffee table. She doused Carole's head with the liquid before throwing it to the floor. Everything blacked out after that.

The next day, she found herself on the living room floor and Carole hovering over her with a look of wild fright in her eyes. There had been a feeling of numbness overwhelming her. Not like the drugs she'd been on. It was different. Like her mind and body decided on their own to disconnect.

Somehow, Carole had risen to the occasion and convinced her to hide Angel's body and carry on with the plan, telling her, "No one ever needs to know Angel is gone." The only catch was she'd have to get out of New Hampshire. Too many people knew her and her Angel. Too risky to stay. Too many questions to deal with. Oh, and fucking Johnnie. Eventually. Literally. Every time she looked at her bastard boy after that night, he looked like he was laughing at her, hiding giggles just under the surface. No matter how much she tried to smash them out of him, he just kept laughing, mocking her.

For a while his very existence consumed her. She couldn't stand to say or hear his name. *Fuck you, bastard. Killer. Should be dead. Should have gotten rid of you eons ago, before you ever saw the light of day.* But as much as she wanted to crush the fucking life out of him, to make him suffer and pay, part of Carole's plan meant keeping this little, soulless fuck alive.

Carole had convinced her that one dead kid was manageable, but two—two would be much harder to pull off. *Should have known better. It was always about Carole and what her twisted twat wanted. One hundred K. My magic number to get me the fuck...*

A horn blared. Dannie flinched, jerking the wheel to get her car back onto the right side of the road. *Fuckers!* She passed the *Welcome to Corinna* sign. Her car clock read 9:13 a.m. Banged her fists on the steering wheel. "Shit!"

Billy's was just ahead. Pulling into the large dirt lot, she saw two muddy, jacked-up pickups were already there. As usual, Billy's shiny, precious jeep was parked cockeyed in the far corner. *Fucking douche. Don't matter. Fuck him. Chill. Gonna be a good fucking day.* She snorted. *Ha! I made a funny. Payday, bitches. Almost time to adios this shithole.*

Chapter 14

Spitting up

In the basement, a soft glow cut through the dank and dark of the basement as Hagas watched the tiny old TV intently. A young woman was being screwed by four guys in a field. Hagas couldn't look away. Even as the woman screamed and begged, all he could focus on were her little dirty pillows bouncing all around. The scene got him tugging fast on his hardening dick. *Look at 'em—what'd he call 'em—titties. Yeah, them titties.*

I Spit on Your Grave was one of the thirty-seven VHS tapes he had been given by Ma. This one had become one of his favorites. He hadn't understood the sex stuff as much when he was younger, but his growing curiosity of the world, and certainly his uncontrollable dick, helped him make sense of it now. He watched it a few times a week and knew exactly when to push the Fast Forward button on the VCR to get to the good parts.

Until recently, movies were Hagas's only connection to life outside. Ma would tell him to watch them so he'd understand why she had to keep him safe in the basement. "People are all fuckin' crazy out there, just waiting to kill you, or eat you, carve you up, or even send you straight into hell," she'd say.

Titles like *The Omen, Friday the 13th, Carrie, Maniac, The Fog, The Exorcist, Cujo, Last House on the Left, Basket Case, Sleepaway Camp,* and the many others that featured gore, demons, torture, and all kinds of gruesome deaths, painted for Hagas a very clear picture of what people were like outside of his home, and according to Ma, not so far away.

"This is the only place you're safe. New state. New house. Even a new fuckin' name. None of them whackos will ever know you're here. Can't get at what they don't know exists," she'd tell him, scowling and laughing at him simultaneously, each time she'd brought him a new movie. "Watch and learn," she'd say. "Watch and learn."

"Shoot!"

The movie was at a dull spot. Hagas pushed the Stop button, then hit Rewind. Ticking off a count in his head, waiting to hit Stop at the right moment, he let his hand drop to the floor. His hand landed on soft clumps of his hair—just when he'd managed to push Ma's visit out of his head. Now it came flooding back as he reached up to feel the choppy remnants on his skull. Her dark face, hovering over him, came into focus. The scissors, so close—

"Shoot! Shoot!"

The count in his head was gone. He jabbed the Stop button, anxious to get back to the good parts. *Aaargh.*

Where'd I land? With a push of the Play button, his movie glowed back to life. The guy, Johnnie, was in full frame, smoking a cigarette, staring down at the naked woman.

Hagas froze, lost in the moment, unable to stop his mind from rewinding to his own similar scene. On the screen, Johnnie morphed into Brian, raising his head, his eyes looking out of the screen. Looking right at him. Brian took a drag from his cigarette, then blew smoke directly toward him, and Hagas' mind pushed play on that awful night.

After cramping up from scarfing down old, greasy Chinese food Ma brought him, he put in *Cujo*, hoping if he lay there, focusing on the movie, his body would calm down. It didn't. He quickly filled up his coffee can with sour puke and diarrhea.

Sweating and exhausted, he curled onto his mattress, his stomach cramping and spasming even more. He didn't even remember falling asleep, but the creak on the stairs jolted him awake. The TV screen was blue. Then he felt the cold and wet around his butt. It took a second to realize he'd shit himself in his sleep. And in that same moment, he knew he couldn't do anything about it. The door was already opening.

Brian stomped directly over to the door to his special room. Hagas balled himself up, trying to look like he was dead asleep, yet watching Brian through squinted eyes, hoping he'd ignore him and go into his room. But that didn't happen. Brian paused, one hand on the door handle, lifting his head up like a bear sniffing the air before spinning around.

"You little fuckhead!"

"Sorry. Sorry . . ." Hagas said, over and over. While his mind clung to some tiny, shriveled kernel of hope, his tensed-up body knew something was coming. It was a useless attempt to apologize. It always was with Brian. A new lesson, from the hands of the master, was coming.

The next thing Hagas knew, Brian dragged him up the stairs. Bumping his shins on every step, squeezing his ribcage so hard he couldn't breathe. Brian hollered for Ma and the two of them took him out behind the house. He could tell it was late afternoon because the sun was sinking fast and it was really cold. Winter was creeping in.

Brian made him strip down naked and commanded him to put his shit-covered clothes in a pile on the frosty dirt. Shivering and hugging himself, he watched Ma pour lighter fluid on his clothes, then flick her cigarette onto them. The pile went up quickly, sending up smelly black belches of smoke. "Shitfucker!" she called him. "Wasting money and ruining things."

Brian lit a cigarette before dousing Hagas with icy water from the hose, the nozzle on high pressure. Hagas looked at Ma, silently begging her to make him stop. But she just stood there, her arms wrapped around her chest, watching the fire with a dazed look on her face.

Things got worse when Brian made him bend over, then jammed the hose up his butt to "douche that shit out." He remembered how much it had hurt, the metal end scraping his tender poophole and the water gushing in, filling him up. Brian yanked it out when they all heard the distinct grind of a chainsaw cutting through a tree in the distance.

"Hear that?" Ma asked. "That's the chainsaw people. They're probably coming to get us 'cause they smelled your shit floating through the air."

Brian turned off the faucet and threw the hose down, back onto its heap of twisted rubber. "Guess we better get us all back in before those fuckers hack us all up into mincemeat," he said. Pondering his half-smoked cigarette, he stepped back over to Hagas.

"Squat, boy."

Hagas bent his knees slowly, shivering and hurting with his bowels filled up with the icy water.

"Now, you gotta get that shit water out of you before we put you back inside. Ain't gonna go stinking up my fuckin' house again leaking that shit outta you all over the goddam place. My castle ain't your shithole," he said.

"What do you mean? What do you want me to do?" Hagas asked through chattering teeth.

"Ha! What do I mean? What the fuck do you think I mean? Shit it out, boy. Push like your life depends on it. 'Cause it does," Brian said as he bent down beside Hagas.

"Okay. I'll push," Hagas said.

"Let's sweeten the deal. Let's see if you can shit that out before my butt connects with your butt," Brian said, looking at Ma and snickering.

Brian took one long drag from his cigarette, then began inching it under Hagas's behind.

"Let's go, boy. See if you can douse this fucker before I put it out in your ass," Brian said.

Hagas pushed as hard as he could, but his mind and muscles weren't connecting. Fear took over as the cigarette got closer and closer. Looking to Ma for any help was no good. She just kept staring at the fire, swaying, mumbling under her breath. He couldn't do it. He couldn't make himself let it go.

"Almost there. You better hurry the fuck up and push," Brian said.

The white-hot pain was instant when the cigarette made contact with his poophole. Brian crammed it right against him, and it felt like a knife had stabbed through his whole body. He pitched forward, his reflexes kicking in to try and get himself away from the pain, but Brian held him in place with one meaty hand locked on his shoulder.

When nature finally took over, he let loose a vicious, stinging stream of icy water. Then, the lesson was over. Brian scooped him up again with one arm, yelling at Ma to get the door, then brought him inside, banged him down the stairs, and dumped him back onto his mattress. He got no food or new clothes for three days, just a new coffee can.

The woman in the movie screamed out, jolting Hagas's mind back to the now, back to focusing on his task at hand. He pumped and pumped, watching the scene play out, and was starting to feel that warm rush starting at his face and neck when he heard the creak of the stairs. *Shoot! Shoot! Shoot!*

The jerky nature of the creaks made him think it was probably Gigi. He jabbed the Stop button and turned the TV off. He looked at his watch and saw it was almost 10:30 a.m. *Too late for Ma.* The dull clanking and thumping of the padlock made his heart race. *Shoot. Fake it.* He pulled the thin sheets up, almost covering his head, and forced himself to lay still, curled up on his side, his back to the door. *Dammit. Underwear. Underwear.* Hagas quickly felt around by his feet. Nothing was there. *Must've kicked 'em off. Shoot. Dammit! Dammit!* The door groaned open and the light from the stairway slid over him. He froze in position.

"Mornin', Hagas. Ish Gigi. You 'wake down here?"

Hagas did not reply. He closed his eyes as she began a slow, tip-toe shuffle toward him. He could smell the whiskey when she stopped at the edge of his mattress, bumping it with her foot. "Aww, looks like you been watchin' your movies," she said.

The VCR! I forgot to turn off the VCR! Hagas clenched his teeth and kept his stillness.

"Oh, and what's this? Whadda we got?"

Gigi's face was a couple of feet above the mattress and her breath was wafting over the sheets to Hagas. The smell of whiskey and cigarettes made its way further into his nose, making him cringe.

"Oooh hoo. It's your underwear, idn't it," she said, giggling.

Leave me alone. Go back upstairs. Hagas tried willing her away with all his might. *Go away. Go away.*

Behind him, Gigi's shoes skidded across the floor. He heard her zipper going down and then fabric hitting the floor. Gigi grunted as other pieces of clothing followed, making barely a sound as they landed softly. Hagas squeezed his eyes harder, trying to block the picture of her naked body from forming in his mind.

"Brrr. Cold down here. Getting hot upstairs. Gigi's gonna show you some lovin' and make you all warm," she said.

The sheet pulled away as she crawled and adjusted herself onto the mattress. She yanked the sheet back into place, and then he felt the awful, warm connection of her naked skin pushing against his backside. She rubbed his chest.

"I know you're feeling this. Show Gigi you love her. Jush like we talked 'bout," she whispered.

Her hand moved down, circling his belly. Waves of her smoky whiskey breath hit the back of his head, faster and faster.

"C'mon, little man, turn around. Show me you love me. Then I'll take you outta here for real today. No sneakin'. Jush you an' me," she said.

Her hand made its way farther down. He hadn't had time to fully calm his body down from the movie and he knew, could even feel he was still semi-stiff. She squeezed him, hard, just like she had in the tub. *Please stop. Please stop. Stop. Stop. Nooo. Don't.* Hagas kept his eyes squeezed shut and his muscles tensed, making him rigid from head to toe.

"Maybe we'll even go do that swimmin' thing if you're real good to me. Huh? You wanna do that? Gonna be hot out. Get you all cooled off," she said.

Swimming. Out of here. For real. Hagas shifted his body and twisted so he was facing Gigi. Their faces were just a few inches apart. He tried looking directly into her eyes, straining to see if he could believe her, but the light coming from behind her head made her face dark and he couldn't see them clearly. *It's a start. Maybe I won't have to . . . can get her to . . .*

Gigi rubbed her hand up and down his side now, lightly grazing his ribcage down to his hip bone. Her breath was raspy.

"You really going to take me swimming?" Hagas asked.

"Yeah, I'll take you swimmin'. Jush gotta be back before your Ma. And 'member, it's our little secret, right?"

"Right, Gigi. Our secret."

Hagas pushed his waist into Gigi, connecting their lower halves, and brought his hands up to feel for her dirty pillows.

Titties. Titties. Titties. That's what they are. He closed his eyes, racing to the secret corner of his mind, his special place filled with pictures, scenarios, and thoughts. *Her titties. Yeah. Yeah. Nice.*

Somewhere, in the dark, far away from his mind's secret corner, he heard Gigi's violent coughing, followed by a muffled spit into her hand. Rushes of warmth, tightness, and pressure began fueling the movie playing in his head.

Chapter 15

Nature calls

At High Bridge #2, the sun climbed higher, bursting through the trees and steaming off the dew and drizzle from Thursday night. Suzanne set up the tent in record time, even breaking a sweat to get it all done by 10:00 a.m., her self-imposed deadline, driven by a mild annoyance at choosing the lazy route of crashing in the car and not doing it last night. *Way to go, city girl.*

"There. No one will ever know we slept in the truck," she said to Derby.

Derby didn't react. He lay on the ground by the picnic table, eyes shut, napping in a bright patch of sunlight. Suzanne grabbed the air mattress, sheets, and pillows from the backseat. She eased the door shut, trying not to wake Derby.

Back at the tent, she threw everything inside, wrestled with the mattress, and hooked up the air pump. Glancing at

Derby, she paused before turning the pump on. *Eh. Gotta do it. Here we go.* The pump surged to life, its loud whirring breaking the morning calm. Derby jerked his head up.

"It's okay, buddy. It's okay. Almost done. Shhhhhh," Suzanne said.

Trading glances between the mattress and Derby, she smiled as he came alive from his post-breakfast daze, lifting his haunches, stretching his front legs far out in front of him, yawning, then finally standing tall with tail wagging. He woofed a couple of times in Suzanne's direction. *I know. I know. Play time.* She looked back at the mattress which was maybe a quarter of the way filled. She fiddled with the nozzle, pushing it into the mattress to keep a tight fit. *Come on. Hurry it up, piece of shit.*

Derby began to whimper. He tugged and paced against the leash tethering him to the picnic table. Suzanne looked back at him. He stumbled over a root and went down. The leash wrapped under his belly and around his left leg as he got himself back up. He looked genuinely confused by his predicament. Suzanne let go of the nozzle. *Dammit.* Walking over to Derby, Suzanne scanned around the site. *Okay. Okay. Pretty open. Where's he going to go?*

"You want to explore? Do you, buddy?" she asked.

Derby stopped whimpering and his ears pricked up at the tone of her voice. Suzanne unfastened the leash from the picnic table and ruffled Derby's head. He responded with excited wags. *Shit. Thinks we're going for a walk.*

With leash in hand, Suzanne guided Derby toward the tent, allowing him to ramble a little as they went, hoping he'd just pee already. She looked inside the tent and saw the air mattress was almost half full. Taking one more look around their site, she dropped the leash. Derby stood where he was, looking up at her, waiting for their walk. Suzanne motioned to the site.

"Go ahead Derb. Go piss-piss," she said.

Derby hesitated only for a moment, then put his nose to the ground. He sniffed and circled near the tent entrance.

"Derby. No, no, buddy. Look. Look. Go over there," she said, gesturing again around their site.

He seemed to get it and Suzanne watched him move farther from the tent, letting his nose guide him around the site. He wasn't moving fast, but his tail was wagging with the excitement of freedom. His leash trailed behind him, until it snagged on a root, holding him fast. He tugged to no avail. The whimpering began and Suzanne sighed. Abandoning her grip on the pump, she walked over and freed him. This scenario happened two more times over two minutes. On the fourth, Suzanne's patience was threadbare. *Dammit, Derby. Give me a break.* Placing her hand on the leash's clasp fastened to his collar. Suzanne pulled Derby's face toward hers to get his attention.

"If I do this, you better promise you won't go far. Promise," she said.

With a quick click, Derby was free. Suzanne watched him explore. He had a bit more zeal now without the leash dragging him down, and his nose went to work sweeping the ground. He sniffed and meandered his way right back to the picnic table, then proceeded to lift his leg and let out a mighty stream right on the bench he had been tied to. *Of course.* Suzanne chuckled to herself. Her jovial mood evaporated when the air pump switched from its white noise whirring to a dull roar. *Shit. Shit. Shit! Knew it! Popped out.*

Derby looked over at the tent briefly, but his nose had him glued to a path only he could see. For a moment, Suzanne watched him walking in tight little circles. *You're fine.* She hustled back to the tent and reconnected the pump to the mattress. The mattress resumed its steady inflation. Suzanne held the pump's nozzle in place, scooching down to be sure the mattress filled to capacity. *Guess I have to babysit you, piece of shit.*

Finally, the pump hit its high-pitched sound indicating all the air it could squeeze into the mattress was in. Suzanne flicked the switch off, and the whine stopped immediately. With fast, fluid skill, she yanked out the nozzle and capped off the port. *Success!*

Suzanne made quick work of putting on the bedding. She tossed her pillows to the far end of the mattress. *Voila.* After backing out of the tent, Suzanne zipped it up, leaving just a bit of the flap open to let in some air.

She turned to see what Derby was up to. He was nowhere to be seen. She quickly scanned the site, listening for his movements. It struck her how very still the woods were. The first pangs of nervousness hit her.

"Derb. Come here, buddy. Derby!"

Derby did not answer. No woof. He did not come running to her. Suzanne waited and listened. She began walking the site perimeter, calling out his name into the woods, pausing, listening for sounds.

Birds and squirrels chirped and chattered a bit, but Derby didn't respond and no clumps of bushes rustled. Her walking became more urgent. She walked, stopped, called, and listened for nearly fifteen minutes. Derby was nowhere to be seen.

"Derb. Come on, buddy. Derby!" she shouted again and again.

Looking past the Rover and up the little turn-off that led into their site, she could see the dirt road above. Turning left led to the Appalachian trail entries. Turning right went back the way they had come in from. Her heart sank with the growing realization Derby had wandered far past earshot.

She raced up to the road, darting her head left and right, looking for any glimpse of Derby. *So many friggin' trees. Jesus.* The brook's rushing water sounded louder. *Shut up, stupid river.* "The water. Shit!"

In a full-on panic, she sprinted to the open-sided wooden bridge connecting the main road twenty feet above the fast-running brook and its steep, jagged rock walls. Standing at the edge, looking down, the water swirled and broke over unseen rocks and logs under its surface. It was as black as the sheer wet walls it had carved over time. Its racing flow echoed and reverberated up the walls, making it sound like a roaring animal. *Oh no, no, no.*

Chapter 16

Are we taping?

Once again, for the fifteenth day in a row (although, to him, it felt like it had been months) since Trish had left, Chris made it through a frantic morning of getting the twins up, dressed, and fed. Breakfast came and went with no issues. No burning questions about Mom. The Chan clan, minus one, was out the door and over to his mother's by 9:00 a.m.

He put up a good front at the door, even managed to smile, assuring his mother he was managing his new single parent status just fine, even with a small measure of success. *Just up and leaves. Who does that? Her kids. Me. Not the woman I thought I knew.*

Sitting in his Bronco, its back end tucked into a conspicuous spot at the Bear Market, Chris watched the slow trickle of cars and trucks pick up in frequency, ferrying their passengers to their work-a-day drudgeries.

His very presence kept the pace slow and steady, and he not-so-secretly loved his command of that, like a conductor silently controlling his musicians. No need to break out the radar gun for the early locals; they all knew the song and played by his rules. Usually. *Until one of them tortures a friggin' duck. Or, just leaves her family high and dry.*

"Hmph," he grunted.

Chris shimmied around to a more comfortable position. He closed his eyes. Began taking in deep breaths through his nose and exhaling slowly through his mouth, willing his mind to quiet, focus, and slide into deeper thought. His morning mission: get back to the challenge at hand. *Duck. Duck. Duck. Dead, dead duck.*

Holding the steaming cup of coffee just under his chin, taking in slurps, he eased into his mind. *Damn duck. Told her I'd contact the staties. Margaret knows more. Doesn't know it, but she does.*

Chris grabbed his phone, looking for any missed calls from his forensics contact. *Nothing.* He pulled up pictures he'd snapped when wrapping up the duck. He scanned each, zooming and pinching in, looking for anything that might help him. *Duct tape. Friggin' every corner store sold that. No good prints. But, rainbow tape? Wait . . .*

He tapped the map app and typed in 'craft store.' *Shit.* There were four stores within a twenty-mile radius of where he sat. One here in Brownville, two in Dover-Foxcroft, and one in Medford. *Frig me.* The closest one was five miles away on Route 6. They opened at 11:00 a.m. The time was 10:34 a.m. *Figures.*

114

According to his phone, the farthest store was seventeen miles away. Hobby House. Dover-Foxcroft. Open now. Twenty-five-minute drive.

Chris drummed his fingers on the steering wheel, debating whether to hold out for 11:00 a.m. opening time. Impatience got the better of him. *Close enough. Hobby House, here I come.* After a long swig of coffee, Chris pulled out of the lot and quickly exceeded the posted speed limit of 35 m.p.h. *Show's over, ladies and gentlemen. Elvis has left the building.*

The twenty-five-minute drive to Dover-Foxcroft took just under twenty with Chris putting a little urgency onto the gas pedal. He slowed in the town center and did an illegal U-turn to park directly in front of the shop.

Exiting the Bronco, he grabbed his state-issued campaign hat. He hated its old school look, but he always put it on when he wanted to impart an air of authority. One quick adjustment, a final check in the side mirror and he was satisfied he looked the part. *Chris is ready to kick ass and take names.* And, with that, he strode to the Hobby House's entry door.

Bells clanged, chimed, and jingled as soon as he swung the door open. They brushed the top of his hat and sent it askew on his head. *Dammit.* He swiped it off and held it under his arm.

Two women, one behind the register counter, and one in front looked at him. They didn't seem disturbed, merely inquisitive as to why a sheriff would be in the shop. Chris stood in the entry area and scanned the store. *Jesus. Packed with crap. Smells funky. How's anyone find anything in here?*

"Help you, Sheriff?" The older woman behind the register called out to him.

Chris smiled and approached the two women. They both had that small-town busy-body look, their expressions clamoring to know why he was in the store. *Don't need them to know about a dead duck.* He nodded at the slightly younger customer as she gave him space at the small counter without breaking her gaze on him.

"Yes. I hope you can," Chris said.

After addressing the clerk at first, he soon found himself talking to both women as he was unable to escape the customer's eyes.

"My twins are starting to get into all kinds of crafts. Picked up the bug at school. Fun stuff, for sure. They just did some kind of duct tape project. But it wasn't gray duct tape. They had all kinds of colors in these crazy flowers they made. At least, I think they were flowers. Ha."

The women were not amused. *Take this craft stuff seriously.*

Chris carried on. "Anyway, they asked me to get some more tape for them. But they wanted me to see if there were different kinds, beyond solid colors. Maybe like rainbows or something? Is there a special duct tape section?"

"Do we have a duct tape section? Lord, have you come to the right place, Sheriff," the clerk said with a laugh. "Come on. I'll show you."

She made her way around the counter. "Hang tight, Mary. Be right back," she said to her customer.

"Paula, by the way," the clerk said, guiding Chris through a maze of displays filled with supplies including fabrics, brushes, paint bottles and tubes, markers, stickers, and bare wooden kits.

"Good to meet you, Paula. Thank you for taking the time to help me. You could have finished with your customer."

"Who? Mary? She's no customer. She's my sister. Well, sister-in-law if you want to get technical. Just here to bug me," she said. "Here we go."

The display shelf in front of Chris had more duct tape than he could have ever known existed. There were all kinds of different colors, sizes, and patterns. And, at least three rainbow variations he could see at first glance. Wavy. Striped. Blended.

"Wow. That's a lot of tape," he said with genuine shock.

Paula looked at him, smirking with a 'duh' expression aimed right at him. Chris grabbed one of each rainbow variety he could find.

"Better get one of each. Tell me, do all the craft stores carry the same brands? Same variety?"

"Hmmm. Not sure. There are only so many suppliers, and our customers all tend to like the same stuff, especially around here."

"Okay. Would you have records of when inventory was sold – maybe receipts of transactions from the past year?"

Paula let out a grunting laugh. "Oh, sheriff, my records are probably the biggest crime in here. Besides, most of my customers are paying with cash still."

Chris handed Paula his state-issued credit card, paid for his six rolls of duct tape and exited the store with his flimsy plastic bag, opening the door a little more gently to avoid the chaos of the bells. He had a pop of hope that maybe finding a match wouldn't be too hard.

Back in the truck, he pulled out his phone and looked at the pictures of the duck again, zooming in to see the tape. Holding up each roll of duct tape, one by one, he compared the picture to his purchases. *Nothing. Nothing. Nothing. Dammit. Come on.*

After shoving the tape back into the bag, he tossed it onto the passenger-side floor. At 11:06 a.m., he was on the road, heading back to Brownville. *Alright Keera's Krafts, you're open now. Let's see what you've got.*

Keera's place turned out to prove Paula right. The same mish-mash of junk rambled around her shop, and pretty much the same selection of duct tape held its special spot. There was one different style, but that was only because it was so old and had been slightly hidden, jammed into the back of the display and layered with a few good years of dust.

Chris purchased the one roll and went back to his Bronco. The same results followed, no match. *Knew that was coming.* Chris studied the photo to cement the rainbow pattern into his brain. *Wavy. Stripes for sure. A little bleed, almost blending. Vertical orientation on the roll.*

Starting up the Bronco, Chris sat for a minute, looking at his phone map and the little dots of craft stores peppered around it. He hit the home button and caught sight of the Amazon app's logo smiling up at him. *Jesus. Of course! Why drive around town when they can just order on-line. Waste of time.*

With a flurry of dust, Chris headed back toward Gulf Hagas and began working out how in the hell he would go about acquiring duct tape purchase records from a behemoth like Amazon. His annoyance faded a bit with the drive and he mellowed his thinking. He had to talk to Margaret again.

Turning onto Katahdin Iron Works Road, Chris was almost fully back to his centered, logical self. He took note of the dusty road and the plumes of tan clouds billowing behind him.

At just over three miles down the road, Chris glanced up at the lonely house he'd passed a million times in his career. He'd never given it a second thought. Hell, there were hundreds of isolated cabins and hunting camps around his territory. Too many to care about unless they gave him cause to care. *Ugly thing.*

Maybe it was the sun, or maybe he was being "hyper-aware Chris," but the busted fender of the Forerunner and its New Hampshire plate caught his eye. *New Hampshire plate!* He pushed the brakes on the Bronco after he'd gone a hundred yards past the house. The truck skidded to an abrupt stop.

Was that . . . ? Aaaah, dammit. Chris threw his arm over the passenger seat and reversed, crawling back down the road, careful to keep the dust at a minimum. He eased to a stop at the end of the long driveway and looked up. The Forerunner was still there. *At least you're staying put, lushie.* Chris put the Bronco into drive and slowly crept away, only picking up speed when he was back to his skid marks about hundred yards away.

He couldn't shake the feeling something was more off with that woman than being a drunk. Chris turned on the radio. Journey blasted above the grumbling tires tearing up the dirt.

Don't stop believin' . . .
Hold on to that feel-a-yin.

Chapter 17

Shaken? Stirred? On the rocks?

On the front porch of the check-in cabin, Chris was getting frustrated with Margaret straining to recall details. Nothing seemed out of the norm to her. She knew a lot of the locals who had come in for day trips, just for a hike or some fishing. Some repeat visitors, but that was normal. Away people were usually day trippers at this point in the season, apparently a lot with fancy cars and silly footwear according to her. A few bold couples and families had started camping out for a night or two. But no one stood out to her as off. *Come on Margaret. Rack your brain. Think.* A radio crackled to life inside the cabin.

"Ridge Runner, Jana, for Margaret. Over."

Margaret scurried into the cabin, the screen door smacking off her butt as she crossed the threshold. Chris looked in, watching Margaret fumble with the radio. Jana's voice came over the radio again.

"Hello. Jana for Margaret . . . or Earl. Or whoever's manning the gate. Over."

"Yup. Yup. I hear you. Go ahead, Jana. What's up?" Margaret answered.

"If that woman at High Bridge Two comes looking for her dog, tell her I found him. Over."

Chris shook his head as a look of utter confusion took over Margaret's face. She stared into space.

"Whose dog? Over."

"The woman you checked into High Bridge two yesterday. Her and her dog. Tell her I found her dog. Bringing it back to her site. Over."

"Oh, yes. That woman. Roger. I'll tell her if she comes down looking. Over."

"Thanks, Margaret. Over and out."

Chris opened the door and Margaret, leaning on the counter, looked up. To him, she still looked confused. *Jesus, it was just yesterday.* He went in, and they continued reviewing her spotty memory for anything out of the norm.

Jana's second call came in maybe ten or fifteen minutes later. Her tone coming over the radio was much different. Anyone could have picked up on her fear.

"Margaret. Jana again. Over."

Margaret's response was quicker this time. "Got you, Jana. No sign of that woman down here yet." She paused. "You okay? Over."

"No. I'm not really. Found a bunch of frogs. I counted six. All of them taped up, like that duck. All of them are dead. Near High Bridge one."

Chris and Margaret exchanged eyes before he dropped his head, trying to process this new development. *Duck... frogs ... and more tape. Jesus. Jesus.* Margaret cleared her throat.

"What am I telling her?" she asked Chris.

"Tell her... tell her to stay put. I'm going to her."

Margaret held the radio to her mouth. "Stay put, Jana. Chris is here. Sending him up to you. Over."

"Understood. Over."

"Jana. You got your mace and your knife? Over."

"Affirmative. I'm with the dog at number two. We'll be waiting. Margaret, tell him to hurry."

Margaret's face dropped a little. Chris could tell she was disturbed, too. She sucked in a deep breath before speaking into the radio again.

"I will. Sheriff will be right there. He's on his way now. Stay calm. Over and out."

"Copy that. Over and out."

Chris spun on his heel and pushed the "in" screen door open. He paused halfway through.

"Margaret, need you to see who's camped out at High Bridge one this season. Actually, I need you to write down everyone who has stayed at any of the High Bridge sites. Names. Hometowns. Dates. And please write down anything, anything at all, you remember about them."

"Just this season?" Margaret asked, pulling the logbook closer to her.

"Yes. These animals would have never made it intact over the winter."

Just as he was reaching his Bronco, Chris had another thought. *Shit.* He turned and walked back to the porch,

123

raising his voice to carry through the screen door to Margaret.

"And, if that woman, Suzanne, shows up before me and Jana get back, don't say anything. We don't want to upset her. Just have her hang out until we get back."

"Well, what am I supposed to tell her? I don't want to scare the bejesus out of her," Margaret yelled back with a hint of annoyance.

"I don't know. Use your imagination. Tell her I need to file a missing dog report or something. I need time to figure out exactly what to say to her, what to ask her. Remember, not a word to her or anyone."

Chris tore up gravel speeding away from the check-in lot. He'd registered the urgency and fear in Jana's voice. The nearly six-mile ride to High Bridge took Chris almost fifteen minutes, swerving around dips and tree debris, but also glancing down the many unmarked offshoot roads and clearings to see if there was anything, or anyone, unusual.

Slowing way down to cross the narrow High Bridge just before number Two, Chris forced a smile and waved down to Jana. He kept an eye on her as she got up from the picnic table, walked over to the dog, and crossed her arms, hugging herself.

He grabbed his hat, thought better of it, and tossed it back on the seat, and got out. He walked down the short entry into the site, approaching her as calmly as he could. The dog watched Chris descending into the site and gave out a low woof.

"Hey, Jana. Sorry it took me a little bit to get here. You good? Want to show me what you found?"

"Hey, Sheriff. I'm, um, okay. Took some pictures. Found them at the end of a little trail off High Bridge one."

"Okay, great. Let's see what you've got. And thank you. Should have you on the force." He fake-chuckled. "Hey pooch," he said, looking down at the blonde mass of fur and muscle.

Jana pocketed her mace and pulled out her phone, handing it to Chris. He scrolled, zoomed, and scrutinized each photo. A wave of nausea hit him, but he forced himself to focus. *Damn. No rainbow.* Jana fidgeted beside him. He handed the phone back to her.

"Same M.O. right, Sheriff? I mean, come on, it's got to be the same person. Twisted."

"Yeah, I imagine it is. These look like, what I'd say, starter projects."

"Jesus. What does that mean? Where exactly does the duck sit in that spectrum? Midway? What's the final project? The dog? Me? Maybe Margaret?" Her voice wavered at the end.

Chris was pissed at himself for saying that, but it was out there. And it struck a nerve. Jana bent down, scratching the dog's ears, hiding her welling eyes from him.

"I don't know, Jana. I could be way off. Maybe it's done. Maybe it was just some punks with a warped sense of fun."

Jana continued scratching the dog's ears, but she looked up at Chris. Tears flowed down her dusty cheeks.

"I can't do this. Just not what I signed up for. Picking up people's trash and cleaning out the toilets I can handle. But I just can't be the girl on the news who got tortured or raped or killed out here in the middle of the woods."

Chris put his hand on her shoulder, trying to comfort her. She trembled under his touch. "You're not going to be, Jana. I promise you that."

"You can't promise that at all. Jesus, look at me. I carry around mace and a knife for the bears, or so I thought. Not the whacko backwoods people. Oh, who knows. Weird shit happens up here. That I'm sure of. You should hear Margaret's stories on some of the crazy things people leave behind. Sex toys . . . lingerie."

Chris said nothing, just his hand on her shoulder to let her know he was there. Wiping her eyes and nose with her sleeve, Jana stood up, looked across the bridge to High Bridge number one, and pointed.

"They're over there. Take the little path off the back of the site. Probably fifty yards or so, you'll hit the edge of the river. Keep going a little farther along the shore and you'll find them." After another sniffle, she bent down to ruffle the dog's head. Chris saw a hint of a smile on her when the dog's tail wagged in response.

"I'll be right back. Stay here with the dog. Keep your radio handy. Channel seventeen, right?"

"Yeah. Seventeen. I'll wait here. Please make it quick."

On his way out of the site, Chris swung by his truck to get his gloves and see if he had a container. Rummaging in the back, he found an old plastic Hannaford bag. *Have to do.*

Glancing back at Jana and the dog as he crossed the bridge, Chris felt unsettled. He hadn't dealt with any cases like this, hadn't even heard of anything like this. Kids shooting cats with BB guns, sure, but this was next level.

He put his mind on high alert as he followed Jana's directions to the barely-there path. Stepping onto the semi-flattened grasses at the path's beginning, he noted the overgrowth was narrow for him.

Brushing shrubs and trees with his body, he looked down and around every step he took as he made his way to the edge of the stream. No tape was stuck to anything, and the path itself stayed faint, like someone had whispered through it instead of walking on it. No broken branches or torn-up grass, just pine needles, moss, and brush.

Finally, the edge of the river appeared. He looked closely at the shore where the river lapped at the rocks, mud, and moss. Nothing seemed out of place. Jana's footprints were there, but only hers. He followed them upstream, walking the edge. And then, there they were. Six taped-up, fly-riddled frogs.

The carcasses were neatly lined up in the order of their different stages of decomposition. The worst ones were tucked farthest away. What looked like the most recent one, seemed slightly fresher, but still beginning to rot. *Why in hell do this?*

Chris took photos and reassessed the area. No other footprints but his and Jana's. Squatting down, he used his gloved hands to delicately retrieve each frog and place them in the plastic bag, registering each variety as best he could.

He hated the squishy feeling of them as he tried to be delicate. Some were squishier than others, and he caught himself a couple of times holding his breath as he worked. When he was done, he had two leopards, three bulls, and one tree frog in his bag.

Turning to head back to Jana, a large gray rock caught his eye. It wasn't remarkable by any means—one of the thousands deposited on the river's edge. This particular one, tucked just under a scrubby bush, had tall, thin grass around it.

At first, it looked like other micro-scenes all over this spot. But at this rock, the grass was bent down, flattened to the ground. He realized this was probably the perp's spot. *Hiding and waiting, weren't you? Just sittin' on the dock of the bay.*

A few looks around revealed no more evidence than the flattened grass and no visible footprints. He took a few pictures of the area before lowering himself onto his hands and knees. He twisted his body down and peered under the bush, straining to see in its dark shadow.

A small scrap of something was on a smattering of smaller rocks. He stretched his arm around the back of the rock and grabbed it. Pushing himself up, Chris looked at the wadded-up piece of tape in his hand. *Rainbow. Course it is. Aren't quite as tidy as you think. Always clues. Always. Always.*

The bag of frogs and the piece of tape went into the back of the Bronco before Chris returned to Jana. She sat at the table, facing the brook. The dog lay right at her feet. She looked deflated and Chris felt for her but he had to keep moving on this development.

"Look, let's get you out of here. I packed up the frogs. Got everything I could find, including a piece of that rainbow tape. Need to get back and see what Margaret's got for me."

"You going to have your friend examine it?"

"I'll get it looked at, I promise, but I don't have a lot of hope. Looks like the frogs and the tape have been out here a while."

"God. I've been up here so many times. He could've been here while I was doing my rounds. Probably was. Watching me. Jesus."

"Let's go, Jana. Get you back down to the check-in cabin. You've had a rough day already." Chris motioned to his Bronco.

"What about him?" she said, pointing to the dog napping on the ground. "I'm not leaving him here tied up to a picnic table like a piece of bait."

"Right. Okay. Let's bring him along. Leave a note for his owner. She's bound to be back soon. I'm sure she's driving around looking for him. Just write that we took him down to the check-in cabin."

Jana reached in her pack, emerged with an index card, and scribbled a note. *Hi. Your dog is fine. Found him walking around on the road up to High Bridge. Didn't want to leave him alone. Took him down to the KI check-in cabin. He'll be waiting for you. – Jana, KI Ridge Runner.* She placed it on the picnic table and put a glass-jarred candle on top of it.

Driving away from the site, Chris and Jana said nothing. The dog, however, woofed often, pacing the back seat.

Chapter 18

Promises. Promises.

In the dark of the basement, Hagas and Carole lay still on his old mattress. The only sound was snoring as she heaved in and out with raspy breaths. Her naked back side was up against him and he could feel her bony spine pressing into him. *Her bones.* He didn't need to see them to remember the look of them. They were a permanent part of his nightmares since the tub all those years ago.

Things had taken a new turn with Gigi a few weeks after the tub day. He sensed something was coming when Ma marched downstairs to tell him she was going out with some guy. She laughed when she told him Gigi had come over to watch him. So, instead of tying him to his chair, she hustled him upstairs.

For an hour or so, Gigi was doing her normal whiskey drinking and cigarette smoking while they sat on the couch watching some game show. She kept scooching closer to him. Then, she made him take his pants off. He remembered the weird sensations in his dick as her hands got busy rubbing him, only pausing when she smoked or took a swig of her drink.

Eventually, she put her mouth on him, sucking him like a straw again, like she'd done in the tub. But this time, she fell asleep while she was down there. His dick was still in her mouth and he sat, frozen, afraid to wake her up.

Ma came home that night and caught Gigi with her face buried in his crotch. She was so mad, swearing and screaming. She ripped Gigi's head up and slapped her awake, ripping into her about "doing shit out in the open" and calling her "stupid" and "twisted bitch." She finally screamed "get down to your room," and kicked at him as he ran away to get downstairs.

The room. The smell. The dark. He hated it down there. He slept on a cot down there ever since Angel came along and Ma had given her the small bedroom next to hers.

Since the tub day though, Angel was down there too, closed up in two old suitcases, one inside the other, and tucked into a far corner on the concrete floor.

He had nightmares about the tub every night. And worse, he was too afraid to open his eyes because he kept seeing Angel floating around the room. In his dreams, she was always floating right above him, staring down at him with her dead blue eyes. *Sorry, Angel. My fault. All my fault. Sorry. Please don't be mad.*

Now, from his mattress, he could barely see the outline of Angel's suitcase, lying on its side in the dark corner. It didn't smell anymore, or at least he couldn't smell it, and he didn't see her floating around as much in this new house.

Gigi shuffled beside him, stirring awake. She turned to him, her face inches from his. She smiled at him. Hagas forced a smile back. The smell of her breath on his face was making his stomach flip.

"Gigi, you promised we'd go swimming. Think we can still go?" he asked.

"Oh, my little man, I don't know. It's getting late id'nt it?"

"But you promised. And it's not that late. Look. One thirty."

He showed her his watch to prove it. She sighed and closed her eyes, draping an arm over him.

"Aww, Hagas. Wouldn't you rather lay here with me? It's all warm in here."

"I. I. I love it here with you, but you said we could go. We can be quick and come back down here after. Promise I'll be good." *Good and gone maybe. Please.*

Gigi sighed and flipped onto her back.

"Jesus. This is stupid. Dammit. Shit."

"Please. No one will know. Our secret. Remember?"

Looking back at Hagas, her smile morphed into a serious expression. She pounded the mattress with her fists.

"Nobody can see you. Got it?"

"Got it! Promise. Let's go!"

Hagas bolted off the mattress. He threw on his underwear and found some shorts and an old T-shirt of Brian's. Carole peeled herself up, sitting on the edge of the mattress, rubbing her head and draining the remnants of her watery whiskey. She fastened her bra and put on her sweatshirt. She stood, her bare bottom facing Hagas, and yanked up her underwear, followed by loose sweatpants that she cinched up tight. She pointed to Brian's special room.

"Open her up. Let's get some gear. Gotta be sure no one sees you. You're s'posed to be homeschooling in New Hampshire. I don't need any damn questions."

He obeyed, and Gigi turned on the light.

"Aaaaah, Brian. That's my boy," Gigi said, looking in from the entry. She was smiling again.

The room was Brian's playground. A variety of leather straps hung on the walls. In the center of the room sat a big chair with arm and leg restraints. Rubbery tools, metal chains, shackles, and bottles of oils and lubes cluttered a workbench. On one wall, a bunch of masks hung in tidy order, all mostly leather, all black.

Gigi put her hand on a mask, caressing it, and almost took it off the wall before switching gears and selecting a full headcover one. "Here we go. Try this on for size." She handed the mask to Hagas. He examined it, pretty sure Brian hadn't used this one on him yet.

Hagas sniffed it. The smell reminded him of Brian and the tangy sweat that dripped all over him during his lessons in the chair. But he ignored the smell, pushing past it and slipping the mask over his head.

He was plunged into darkness, and he bolted into that corner of his head where he could detach from the physical world around him. Gigi grabbed hold of the mask and spun it around. Tilting his head back to look through the two eyeholes that sat too low on his face, Hagas could see her droopy eyes looking him up and down.

"Well, look at you, my little man. You look all growed up."

She wrapped her arms around him and pressed his face to her chest. *Dirty pillows. Gross.* After a minute of them standing there, body to body, Hagas coughed to break her out of the moment. *Come on.*

"Can we go now?"

"Yes, you little shit. We can go now."

They left Brian's room, being careful to lock everything up, and went upstairs to the main floor.

"Stay put, little man. I just gotta grab a couple things." She went down the hall to Ma's room and he heard her opening drawers. Hagas stood where he was, not daring to move yet, but looked hard into the kitchen. *Stupid mask. Can't see.* He stiffened when less than a minute later, Carole emerged, wearing a black bathing suit that had replaced her sweatshirt. Her sweatpants stayed on. She shoved a canvas tote bag at him.

"Hold this."

Next, she went into the bathroom. Again, rummaging around. He heard her mumbling, cursing Ma about no clean towels. The fire of freedom sparked, and Hagas lifted the front of his mask to look down into the bag. Sweatshirt. Bra. Underwear. Some old boxer shorts. He looked back at the bathroom, and then quietly walked into the kitchen, his heart pumping hard. *Got to be something I can use. Think little. Some kind of tool or knife.*

Three lighters were on the counter. He swiped one and jammed it into the inner pocket sewn into the waistband of his shorts. A full roll of duct tape sitting on the bottom shelf of a cabinet caught his eye. *Tape her up! She's going to fall asleep.* He heard the toilet flush.

"Hagas!"

He lunged and grabbed the roll of tape, shoving it into the bottom of the bag, and then stood still in front of the refrigerator. He pulled the mask back down just as Carole emerged from the hall. She narrowed her eyes. He held his breath.

"What're you doing in here?" she asked, appearing at the edge of the kitchen.

"Nothing. Waiting." *Keep her happy. Keep her moving.*

"We need anything else?"

"Here. Put these in the bag."

She handed him two bluish, threadbare towels and a huge bottle of suntan oil. Next, she found a big water bottle and filled it with ice and whiskey, taking a healthy swig direct from the whiskey jug before putting it back on the counter. She shoved things around the counter near the two remaining lighters.

"Where's my fuckin' Patriots lighter? Fuckin' Dannie. Bitches about her money, but all good with swiping my shit. Every fuckin' time. Swear to God, I show up and half my shit disappears. Love that fuckin' lighter."

Gigi hung the padlock key back under the sink.

"Can't forget about this, can we?"

Hagas nodded. She laughed at him, then grabbed her car keys, wallet, and sunglasses.

"Let's go 'fore I change my mind."

They exited the side door and Gigi pulled it shut. Opening the back door to her old Forerunner, she motioned for Hagas to get in. He threw the bag on the floor and hopped in.

"Lie down and get comfortable," she said, slamming the door behind him.

Hagas lay on his back, straining to get the right angle to see through both the mask and the Forerunner's blacked-out rear windows. He was already beading with sweat from the trapped heat of both the mask and the interior of the truck. *Guess no one will see me in here. Could sleep in here and no one would see me.*

Gigi popped into the driver's seat and fired up the truck. He watched her, studying what she did to start the truck. After taking a big swig from her water bottle, she turned on a fan, then yanked on the stick in the middle of the seats. She twisted her neck around, one-armed the passenger seat, and sent them speeding down the driveway backward.

He couldn't gauge where they were on the driveway, but they must have made it to the bottom, because she cranked the wheel, stopped, then began flying forward at an even faster speed.

From his position, all Hagas could see was the sun flicking between the treetops. It was plenty. *Away we go. On the way to my world.*

Chapter 19

Into the woods

Oh, God. It'll be over soon. It'll end. Don't let her turn around. Hagas lay in the back seat, eyes closed, gripping the door handle, sweat pooling under his mask, and focusing intently on not getting sick as they bumped and swerved down the road. Just when he thought he wasn't going to make it, they slowed, turned and stopped.

He eased himself up. The sheer relief of not moving was almost instant. He saw Gigi had pulled into the small parking area. Her head swiveled side to side a few times before finally craning around to look at him.

"Wait right here. And don't sit up. I'll be right back," she said, shutting down the truck and grabbing the keys.

"I won't move. Promise," Hagas squeaked.

Once her door closed, he sat up fully and watched her walk to the little cabin. When Gigi finally came out the door, holding a piece of paper, a truck with a rack of lights on top pulled in and parked just a few feet away from Gigi's truck. Hagas ducked down. *No. No. Don't wreck this for me. Just get in, Gigi, and we'll go.*

Hagas heard two doors open and close. He could barely see out the window, but he caught a glimpse of a woman. Then he heard whining and a woof. A man kept saying, "Come on. Down, boy."

Then a girl's voice chimed in. "I got him, Sheriff. Come on, buddy."

Gigi's voice came next. "That's a handsome boy right there."

Her words were followed by more woofing and whining. The girl's head jerked around, close to Hagas's window. "Don't worry. He's just a little anxious," the girl said.

"Well, good thing he's tied up," Gigi said. "Maybe you can yank him back and keep his goddamn nose out of my crotch."

The Forerunner started blasting its horn and flashing its lights. The dog began barking. Hagas almost popped up in the back seat.

The man's voice came back. "Geez. Hey, hey. Calm down. Calm down. You all right ma'am?"

"Fine. Fine, Officer. Just hit the wrong damn button. Friggin' thing."

The truck finally silenced and Gigi let out a weird laugh. The dog's barking was getting farther away. Her door opened and the heat and light flooded in. She hopped in. But before she could shut the door, the man spoke again.

"It's Sheriff. Met you last night at the Bear Market. Remember? You okay? You seem a little, uh, agitated."

"Oh, right, right, right. Sheriff. Me? I'm all good. Just forgot how friggin' pricey it is for walkin' 'round the woods. I remember when nature used to be free."

"Okay. Well, I think it's worth it. Take it easy up there." He paused before resuming in a louder voice. "Let's go, Jana. Let's get him tied up out back and calmed down. I need to check in with Margaret. I'll get some water for him and she's probably got a treat or something kicking around."

Gigi slammed her door shut and then whipped her head around.

"Lie back down!"

He hadn't realized he was still perched halfway up from the jolt of the truck's blasting horn. He obeyed, dropping down flat again. Gigi didn't do anything for a few seconds. Then the truck fired up and she wrestled with the stick again, yanking it back and forth.

"Jesus Christ. Can't get away from that fucker. Fucking pig," Gigi said.

They tore away from the lot, spitting up dust and dirt as they lurched ahead, rumbling over the bridge leading into the woods.

Chapter 20

A rose by any other name

"Hey, Margaret, we've got the dog. Jana's tying him up out back. Do you have a water bowl, maybe a treat or something we can give him?" Chris asked.

"Oh good. Course I do. I'll dig up something from out back. What's the name? So I can write it down," Margaret answered.

"Not sure. Find anything interesting in the logbooks?"

"Sheriff, I swear, I have looked and looked. Nothing. Two overnighters up at High Bridge so far. But that was almost two weeks ago, and they've been coming here for years. I even called Jill up at Hedgehog. Tried Cheryl at Jo-Mary, too, but she didn't answer. I told Jill what was up. Had to. She was pretty shocked, but she hasn't seen anyone strange either. We pretty much concluded all's been good in the woods. Well, current situation not included."

"Okay. I figured as much. I'll still take the names and info of those overnighters though. You never know."

"Yup. That's for sure. You never know." Margaret sighed. "I'll get that water and see if I've got some treats or food or something for Derby. Poor thing."

"Thank you, Margaret. Wait. What did you call him? Derby?"

"Yes. That's what the young woman called him when she checked in yesterday."

Chris shook his head as Margaret wandered away. Jana came into the cabin, the screen door banging behind her.

"The dog's all good. He's wiped. Basically flopped onto the grass as soon as we got into the shade. Any news in here?"

"Nothing," Chris answered. "Oh, except the dog's name is Derby."

"Aaah. Good ol' Margaret. Coming through in the clutch. Figured there wouldn't be any earth-shattering news. It's been pretty much locals and some seasonal regulars. Kind of doubted anyone would drive all the way up here just to torture a duck and some frogs. You think it's someone local then?"

"I believe so. Can't rule anything or anyone out just yet though. People can be, well, people can be a little strange sometimes. Everyone's got something no one else knows."

"I hear you. But I, for one, feel exponentially better just being down here. And, sorry, I was pretty freaked out up at High Bridge. And, honestly, Sheriff, not sure I can go back."

Jana hugged herself. Experience told Chris this whole situation was probably going to stick with her for a good, long while. He felt for her. Hell, she reminded him of Trish when she was younger. All fire. Pretty. *Enough!*

"I understand, Jana. Pretty messed up situation. And it's absolutely your call. No one would fault you for leaving."

"Thanks. I just need to think things through."

"That sounds like a good plan. Take all the time you need and do what's right for you."

Margaret emerged from the back carrying two old plastic bowls, one with water slopping out and the other with a few broken pieces of what were once bone-shaped dog biscuits. Jana met her at the counter and took the bowls.

"Um, I'll just go outside and give these to *Derby*," she said, looking at Chris.

"Who? Did you say Derby?"

"Yeah, Derby. Remember? He's the dog I found up near High Bridge. He got loose. Just keeping him here until his mom, Suzanne, comes to get him."

Chris's eyes rolled back all on their own. He was already fried, and it was barely midday.

"I need to call it a day up here. Got to see what else is going on in the world. You got that woman's name who came in before we got here?" Chris asked Margaret.

"Indeed I do. Carole . . . or Coral . . . nope. Hold on. Carole something."

Margaret flipped pages of her binder, looking for the copy of the check-in form.

"There we go. Rose. Carole Rose. New Hampshire."

"Hmph. Well, she's anything but sweet, I'll say that much. I'm going to borrow that sheet if you don't mind. Just do a little checking to cover our bases."

Margaret handed over the sheet without a word.

142

"Ladies, I'll take my leave. I'll be back tomorrow."

Chris left the cabin and got in his Bronco. He paused before starting it up, scouring Carole Rose's check-in form. Something's off with that woman. Why was Derby going bonkers on her? Did she have a dog? Maybe in the back seat. Nothing recorded on her check-in. Just her. Skittish. Nervous. Again.

"Tomorrow's a brand-new day. Guess I better finish this one first," he said to the faded picture of the twins taped to the dash.

Once on the road, he fiddled with the radio to find some music to drown out the crunch of dirt under his tires. Led Zeppelin's overplayed epic filled him with melancholy.

When she gets there she knows,
if the stores are all closed,
with a word she can get what she came for.
Ooh, ooh, and she's buying a stairway to heaven . . . '

Chapter 21

To swim or not to swim?
That is the question.

The narrow view through the mask's eye holes provided Hagas with a kaleidoscope of muted light and color as the canopy of trees and sky flew by. His stomach was churning again, but his mind was churning faster. *Maybe I can take her car. Think I can figure it out. Keep feeding her whiskey. Leave her stranded. Where do I go? Must be a town somewhere where the people all come from. Find someone nice, like that family. What if I can't?*

Hagas' thoughts were interrupted as he shot off the seat and landed on the floor. The truck had swerved hard to the right, now heading uphill. Gigi turned her head and laughed at him.

"Friggin' turnoff snuck right up on me," she cackled.

Pulling himself back onto the seat, Hagas decided to sit upright. He caught a glimpse of Gigi's eyes in the mirror. One was partially squinted closed. Looking out the side window, he opened his dry lips, feeling them stretch apart, stuck together by gummy spit. He could taste the smell from the mask. It was overwhelming him.

"Gigi, okay if I sit up for a minute? My stomach feels all funny."

"Shit. I guess so. No one's around. You just be ready to get back down if we see another car. Got it?"

"Got it. Can you put the windows down?"

"Christ. Anything else, your highness?"

Gigi put the rear windows down about halfway. Behind the mask, Hagas closed his eyes, letting the wind from the window wash over him as he breathed in the smells of pine, earth, and freshly cut wood. *My world. I am king here.*

Gigi lit a cigarette and puffs of smoke started wafting through the Forerunner, squashing the purity of the air coming in. Sweating and still nauseous from the bumpy ride, Hagas scowled under his mask. *She ruins everything.* Concentrating on the landscape whizzing by them, he began seeing signs of familiarity. The huge dried-out area, studded with old stumps and leftover scraps of wood, the field going downhill toward the trees. *This is it.*

Gigi slowed as they approached the turnoff to the High Bridge sites. Hagas slid across the back seat, pressing against the door to see the brook sparkling through the trees below.

"Well, looks like we made it," Gigi said, flicking her cigarette out the window.

Hagas slid to the other side of the seat and looked into High Bridge number one as they passed by its roadside parking spot. *My spot. Can get in there fast. Lose her.*

Gigi crept the Forerunner across the high wooden bridge spanning the river. Hagas poked his head out the window, marveling at the rushing water and how high up they were. *Maybe she'll fall off. Or push her . . . or . . .*

The window surprised him, connecting with his neck and pushing his head up. It started dropping down and he yanked his head back in.

"Get your ass back in the car!" Gigi yelled from up front.

"Sorry, Gigi. Sorry," Hagas stammered. "I'm just excited to go swimming."

Both back windows shut tight, cutting off the fresh air.

"Rules, little man. Rules. Don't start gettin' all cocky with me. Friggin' hauling your ass up here. Respect. Respect. Respect. Better do as I say. Got it?"

"I got it. I'm sorry."

Just after the bridge, barely past the number two site's entrance, Gigi pulled over and parked. From behind the darkened windows of the Forerunner, they both looked down at the site. Within it, sat a bright blue tent, a folding camp chair by the fire pit, and a picnic table peppered with gear.

"Well, shit. Guess we got some company," Gigi said.

"But, there's no car. Maybe they're gone." *Don't say no.*

"Gone? Jesus, Hagas. Open your eyes. Look at all that shit. They're here. Just hikin' or fishin' or somethin.' Fuckers." She paused. "What time is it? Check that beautiful watch I gave you. My clock's broken."

146

Hagas raised his arm, squinting at his watch through the mask. "Almost one o'clock. No! Almost two o'clock." *Don't say no. Don't say no.*

"Shit. Shit. Shit. Goddamn stickin' to this seat. Gimme my flask. I need a friggin' drink."

Hagas rummaged through her bag and found the flask. Gigi reached back and grabbed it from him. She unscrewed the cap and tilted her head back to take a long swig. A little more went into her water bottle. She screwed the cap back on and shoved the flask back to Hagas, wrenching around to look at him.

"Well, frig it. I'm hot as hell. We're going to Haybrook. I gotta take a piss. Wait here. Gonna be quick."

Hagas crinkled his nose as he caught the smell of the whiskey, drifting from her as she spoke. *Yes! We're going. Hurry up.*

Gigi lit a fresh cigarette and got out of the truck. It chirped and the locks all clicked at once as she moved away. Hagas watched her walk into the site, creeping toward the tent. She got to within a few feet of the entry and bent down. A thin line of smoke rose straight into the dead air. Gigi made her way up the site's incline, walking past the truck toward the bridge. Hagas swiveled in the back seat. *Where you going?*

Gigi paused halfway on the bridge, shuffling toward its edge. She swayed a bit before stepping back. Then she ripped down her sweats, yanked around her bathing suit, and squatted in the middle of the bridge. She took a few puffs from her cigarette as she hovered. When she was done with her business, she flicked her cigarette over the side of the bridge and walked back toward the truck. *C'mon. Hurry it up already.*

A slow rumbling sound made its way into Hagas's ears. *Car!* Gigi froze halfway back. He spun around, straining to see between the front seats and through the dusty windshield. An SUV rounded the corner a bit farther down the road, heading right toward them. Spinning again, he saw Gigi hustling forward. *Hit her. Hit her!*

Gigi made it to the back of the Forerunner just as the SUV pulled up. She was heaving a little. The SUV stopped and the passenger window rolled down. Hagas, crouching down, peeked around the back seat. *Good or bad? Good or bad?*

"Hi there," a woman said from the driver's seat.

"Um, hi," Gigi responded. "Help you?"

"That's my site down there. Been out looking for my dog. He got away from me this morning. And I can't get a damn cell signal to call the check-in cabin. You haven't seen a blondish guy, sixty pounds or so, running around here, have you?"

"Oh. Well, that's just awful. No, we—I mean I—ain't seen a dog. Jush got here. Was thinkin' of goin' swimmin' but I don't know. You know? Looks kinda rough here. Hot though. So I don't know. Dogs go wandering up here all the time. Probably fine. Usually just show back up."

Gigi was talking fast. Hagas strained to see out the back window, rising higher in the back seat, looking past Gigi, but the woman sitting in the driver's seat was just a shadow. He put his hand on the door handle. *What if I just jump out? Move, Gigi. Good or bad?*

"Um, yeah. I'm sure he's fine. I'm going to check the site again before I keep looking," the woman said. "Are you . . . you okay?"

148

"Me? Oh, I'm fine. Jush hot, I think. Sun or my friggin' hormones. Thinking I might go down to Haybrook instead. Quieter. The water's quieter. You been down there? Anyone there? You alone?"

"Yeah. I was just down there looking for him, but no sign. All's quiet. No one's there."

"Good. Good. Well, you got yourself a good weekend. Jush you be careful. Pretty young girl alone up here. Horny buggers all over these woods."

"Yeah, I'll be fine. Just need my bodyguard back here. His name's Derby, by the way. Big boy, but super friendly. He might come to you if you call him. You know where I'm at."

Derby. Derby. Derby. Blondish. Sixty pounds. She's nice. She's good. Maybe now. She'll help. Hagas slowly pulled on the door handle. It didn't open. He pulled again. Nothing. It wouldn't budge. The SUV began sliding forward, then stopped.

"Oh, wait, who's that in the back seat? Maybe they saw Derby?" the woman called out.

Hagas winced when Gigi turned, looking into the back of the Forerunner. She smacked the window with her hand. Hagas flattened himself to the seat. *Oh no. She's gonna kill me.*

"That's uh . . . that's jush *my* dog. Been back there the whole ride up. Don't think he's seen yours. And if he did, he's not talking." Gigi let out a raspy, coughing laugh.

"Yeah. Okay. Well, like I said, I'll be here if you see any sign of him." The woman's SUV began inching away, turning down into the site.

"You bet. Bye now," Gigi yelled.

Hagas put his hands between his knees, as Gigi jammed herself back into her seat. He put his energy into hoping she'd keep driving, keep going to Haybrook.

"Well, we're getting the hell outta here. Stupid bitch and her dog. Don't need any part of that shit. Going to Haybrook instead. Quieter." Gigi said while maneuvering out of their parking spot. They began bumping along the High Bridge road, heading deeper into the wood. Hagas turned to look behind them. The woman was standing at the entry of the site, seeming to watch them drive away. *Bet she's a good one.*

"Friggin' dyke should know better. Just lettin' her dog run around. I wouldn't let you go runnin' rampant up here. Gotta keep you safe. Right, little man?"

"Right, Gigi. I know you . . . you love me." *The woman was good. Know it. She saw me. Help me.*

"Friggin' right I do. Now, lay your ass back down. No more sitting up, or we're turning right the fuck around. 'Sides, we got a bumpy road a coming."

Hagas slumped his body onto the seat, once again squinting through the mask's eyeholes to see the world go by him. *Gotta get back up there. She'll help me. Maybe. Two versus one. We can take Gigi. I think.*

Branches screeched relentlessly on the sides of the truck as they made their way down the road. Gigi cussed with every fresh scrape. After what seemed an eternity of deep dips and big bumps, Gigi slowed, and the sky opened up ahead of them. She turned sharply and stopped, shutting off the engine.

"Je-zuss Ch-rist. Road was never that friggin' bad," she said.

Gigi's head and body twisted in her seat, scanning all around. She lit a cigarette and then looked at Hagas.

"Well, looks good, little man. Jush you an' me. Let's go. Out. Hot as shit down here. We're goin' swimmin'."

Hagas reached for the handle and pulled on it. The door didn't open. He pulled again. Nothing.

"It's not working, Gigi."

"Dammit. Right. Right. Right." She opened his door from the outside. "Child locks. Like I said, gotta keep you safe. Wouldn't want you fallin' out unexshpectedly."

Hagas got out and breathed in the fresh air, relieved again to be sucking in better smells than the ones inside the mask.

"Grab my bag. Need a drink before we go up."

Hagas retrieved the bag and handed Gigi her flask. She took a long swig. Her whole body shuddered, and she let out a loud "aaaah" followed immediately by a rough coughing fit.

"Alrighty, little man. Let's go. That way." She pointed toward a large open area dotted with tall pine trees. "It ain't High Bridge, but it'll do. Let's go get our swim on."

Gigi led them on a meandering path through the large swath of land, covered in soft, dead pine needles, passing three designated camping sites and two outhouses. They made it to the far edge of the sites, and she continued guiding them up a short trail.

At the end was the coolest, clearest pool of water Hagas had ever seen. It was carved out of the rock, some fifteen feet above the stream below, with a steady trickle of water coming into it from up the hill behind. *Wow.*

"Whoooeee! This is it. Go on and get outta them clothes, little man. Let's you and me get wet."

Chapter 22

The Prodigal son

Suzanne stood at the top of the entry to her site, her hands on her hips, watching the Forerunner drive away. She couldn't shake the feeling that the woman was off somehow—so jittery, like she was caught doing something wrong. And she was ninety-nine percent sure that was not a dog in the backseat. If it was, it was super mellow.

Adding to the swirl in her mind was the gnawing feeling she'd seen that woman before. But up here, all the older women seemed to look alike, their weathered faces blending into one archetypal image. Her heart sank, feeling the sheer weight and vastness of the woods surrounding her as she watched the woman drive away.

After the Forerunner's dust trail settled, and she was very much alone again, Suzanne decided to walk the road between the three High Bridge sites one more time to look for Derby. She went in the direction the Forerunner had gone to check out number three first. Walking and calling out every thirty seconds or so, her dismay grew deeper with every step.

Myriad visions of Derby's fate ricocheted through her head. Crumpled in a riverbed. Bloody and fileted from a run-in with a bear. Flattened by a logging truck on one of these endless dirt roads.

Arriving at site number three, Suzanne forced herself back into the moment. *Come on. Stop it. He's out here somewhere.* She walked the site, finding no signs of Derby. No little tufts of hair stuck to the picnic table. No paw prints in the wet and muddy spots. She had little hope she would find anything. At this point, she knew Derby had to find her.

Suzanne left the site and started back toward her own. She gave up calling out, choosing to just listen to the woods, holding out a sliver of hope she might hear a bark. As she got closer, she heard something. A faint rumbling. An engine. *Car coming. Maybe? Someone from the check-in cabin?* Hope sparkled in her heart, giving her a quick rush of energy. She jogged the remaining hundred feet or so to reach the top of her site entry.

The green pickup came into view just past the bridge. *The truck from the check-in cabin. Got to be that woman.*

An arm stuck out the window and gave a thumbs up as the truck slowed for the bridge. Whoever was driving crept across the wooden planks painfully slow. Suzanne's impatience rose. *Jesus, come on, it's a bridge, not a tightrope.*

Finally, the truck pulled up to the entry. A young woman, dwarfed by the size of the truck's double-cabbed body, smiled from the driver's seat.

"Um, hi. Are you missing someone?"

"Oh, I am. I am. My dog. He's blonde, about sixty pounds . . ."

The rear window behind the young woman slid down. Her heart filled and a wave of euphoria and relief flooded through her.

"Derby! Oh my God! You're okay. Hey, buddy."

Derby jerked his head up from the back seat. His tail kicked into fast-wagging as he pulled himself upright to greet Suzanne through the window. Slobbery face licking was next. Suzanne was just fine with that.

"Took a chance you might be back here," the woman said.

Suzanne opened the back door and Derby hopped out, trailing a long piece of rope. *Not again.* She snatched up the rope and bent down in one fluid motion, hugging Derby's head.

"Oh, thank you. Thank you. Mama missed you so much!"

"I left a note earlier but figured I'd give it one more try. Besides, he wasn't liking being tied up at the check-in cabin. And he was vocal about it. Margaret was going to keep you there if I didn't catch you here."

Suzanne released Derby's head and stood to properly address the woman.

"I didn't know what to do. No cell service, so I thought maybe I'd find him if I just drove around here a little. You said you left a note? Dammit. Where? I just got back a little bit ago. I didn't see anything. I'm Suzanne, by the way. Suzanne Kelley."

"Jana. Ridge Runner up here. Yeah, I left it on your picnic table." Jana pointed. Suzanne saw the small white piece of paper jutting out from under her candle. *Ugh. That would have been helpful.*

"Oh, man. I was so focused on looking for him. I didn't even see it. Wait. How long has he been down there?"

"Maybe an hour, a little more maybe. Why?"

"Well, a woman was up here when I got back. I asked her if she'd seen him, but she said no. But, she must have been at the check-in gate. Must have heard him."

"Hmm. There are other checkpoints to get in here. But there was indeed a woman who checked in solo just as me and the sheriff got down there. She was in an old Forerunner."

"Yeah. Got to be her. But, she wasn't solo. There was a kid or maybe a dog in the back seat. I couldn't tell—tinted windows. She was all nervous. Hell, for a split second I thought it might have been Derby and this woman had kidnapped him."

"That is odd. I remember she said she was alone."

Derby began pacing, pulling at the rope. Suzanne was pretty much done thinking about the past few hours. She just wanted to get back into the site and regroup. *Bigger things to get back to.* She smiled up at Jana. *Cute.* Any other time she would have asked her down for a drink. *Not today. Back to the plan. Time to get ready.*

"Hey. Thanks again, Jana. I'm going to get this guy some water. Maybe a treat if he promises to chill. Why was the sheriff with you, though?"

"Oh, um, no reason. Just, um, routine. He's up here sometimes. Just checking stuff."

Suzanne registered Jana's fumbles. *Jesus. How many tweaked-out people can there be in one chunk of woods?*

"Okay. Well, we're off. See you around, Jana." Suzanne watched her as she made a six-point turn to get the truck pointing back toward the bridge. Jana rumbled across it, just as slow as before. *Sheriff. Up here? Hmm.*

Suzanne tied Derby's rope to the picnic table and retrieved the rumpled printout from the Rover. She sat down at the table and read the fishing boat arrivals and departures information for what was probably the hundredth time. Now that Derby was back, she could feel her vigor and focus returning at full speed. Timing calculations ran through her head.

See you soon, Brian.

Chapter 23

What goes up, must . . .

When Gigi ordered Hagas out of his clothes, he was mildly excited that he finally got to take the mask off. Removing the leather hood, he sucked in the humid air surrounding them, reveling in the fresh smells of rock, dirt, leaves, and water.

He removed and rolled his shorts carefully, keeping the stolen lighter hidden. His T-shirt followed. He placed everything on a flat section of the rocky ledge, and then stood tall, letting the sun's heat seep into his skin. Brian's oversized boxers were damp with sweat and sticking to his legs and butt. *Please let me keep them on. Please. Please.*

"Off," Gigi said, pointing at the boxers. She was sitting on a rock, smoking a cigarette and sipping from her flask. Hagas looked at her skinny frame and the shimmery sweat forming just above the top of her black bathing suit.

"What if someone comes? I feel funny being naked out here. I'm okay with getting them wet," Hagas said.

"Take 'em off. Ain't no one coming up here. Look, I'll take my top down and prove it."

Gigi placed the flask down and stuck her cigarette between her lips. She grabbed each of her suit's shoulder straps, yanking them down and wriggling her arms through them, finally freeing herself of the stretchy fabric. Her dirty pillows sagged in front of her. She took the cigarette out of her mouth and exhaled a huge cloud of smoke. "Whew. That's better. Your turn, little man. Off with 'em. Lesh go."

Hagas turned away and slid the boxers down around his ankles. *Hate you. Ugly. Gross dirty pillows.* He stepped out of them, then added them to the rock with his other clothes, laying them flat to dry them in the sun.

"Come over here. Lemme look at you," Gigi said, waving her arm at him.

Hagas walked over to her, hanging his head down, feeling more naked than he had ever felt before. He stood a few feet away from her. Even in this open space, the smell of whiskey and smoke wafted up to him. *Hate you. You smell. You're gross. Don't touch me. Don't. Please.*

Gigi stuck the cigarette back in her mouth and leaned out from her perch. She placed her hands on his hips and started rubbing up and down his waist and legs. "Mm, mm. You are turning into a fine young man."

Hagas tensed as her hands explored his front side. *Too close. Don't burn me. Gross. Stop it. Stop it. Please. Stop.* Gigi pushed herself off the rock, staggering upright to stand just in front of Hagas. She threw her cigarette into the pool of water, then pressed her body into his, wrapping her arms

158

around his back. "Mmmmmm. You're so warm. All shlippery." She started moving her crotch up and down against him.

Let go. Stop it. Stop it. Get your dirty pillows off me. The friction from her bathing suit rubbing against his dick started the tingling sensation and he felt himself hardening. *No. No. No. Stop it.*

"Um, Gigi, maybe we can go swimming for a minute first." The rubbing kept going. "Gigi?"

Gigi stopped moving and pushed herself upright. "Aww. S'pose you're right. I promised. Jush get me goin', little man." She chuckled. "Well, maybe not so little," she said, flicking her fingers at his semi-hard dick. She started laugh-hacking and backed away, launching a big gob of phlegm into the pool.

"Jeeeeezus! Fuck."

"You . . . you okay, Gigi?"

"Shit, yes," she said, shaking her body. "All right, go on then, antsy pants. Get in. You first."

Hagas felt the burning shame of not being able to control his dick. *Hate you. Touching me. Making me . . .* He walked to the edge of the slowly churning pool. Dipping his foot in, he felt the cool water swirl around his toes. *Wow. Cold. Awesome.* It calmed him. He sat down, putting both feet in up to his knees. Leaning over the water, squinting against the sun, he strained to see how deep it was. *Just a few feet . . . maybe. Hope so. Can I still swim?*

"Wait! Wait!" Gigi barked. "Gotta put some lotion on us. Get that lotion and the spray outta my bag."

Hagas stood and crossed over the rocks to the bag with their extra clothes and towels, leaving wet splats along his path. Both the big container of lotion and the skinny spray bottle were at the bottom, just beside the big roll of duct tape.

He pulled them out and studied the spray bottle. Some of his movies had words on the bottom of the screen when they played, and he picked up a game of matching the words with what characters were saying. He'd gotten good, not that anyone cared. But now, he cared a lot and he put his skills to the test.

S-P-F 6. Warnings. Do not use on dam-aged or bro-ken skin. Keep away from face. Do not spray on or near eyes. Fla-mm-able. Contents under press-ure, pressure. Do not use near fire, heat, or while smoking. Flam-mable. Flame able. He held it up high. "This it, Gigi?" *Flammable. Lighter's in my shorts.*

"Hurry up. Bring 'em over. Don't need you getting a burn, or your Ma will know you were out."

With sure feet, he hopped over the rocks to Gigi. She stood when he reached her.

"Now, be a good little man and spray me all over. Don't miss anywhere."

Hagas popped the lid and started spraying. Gigi closed her eyes and held her arms up and out.

"Mmhmm. Cold! Feels good. Get it all over."

Hagas sprayed and sprayed. Face. Chest. Legs. Back. Gigi turned as he went, even lifting her dirty pillows so he could get under them.

"Atta boy. Get me good. Says I'll get a solid tropical tan."

"More?"

Hagas stopped spraying, surveying her shiny body for any spots he might have missed. Gigi looked herself over, twisting and bending to check herself.

"Nah, looks like I'm covered. Your turn."

She took the big container of lotion and squeezed out cold mountains of sunblock onto Hagas's chest, shoulders, back, and legs. Making quick work, she rubbed the mounds into his skin, paying careful attention to get a lot into his face, neck, and head. Some got in his eyes, stinging him, but he squeezed them shut and held back the reflexive tears. Finally, Gigi finished by wiping the excess from her hands all around his dick.

"Go on. Now you can get in."

He sat on the edge and dangled his legs in the water again for a few seconds. *Mmmmmm.* Sucking in a deep breath of air, he launched with a quick shove, flinging his whole body. He let himself sink under as bubbles escaped from his nose. *Cold. Cold. Cold.* Opening his eyes, he felt the cool water washing away the sting of the lotion; he fluttered his hands to swish water around. He felt so . . . free. No sounds. No smells. No one messing with him. When his breath was gone and he started feeling the urge to suck in, he popped up with a triumphant splash. He felt re-energized. His body had cooled quickly in the chilly mountain water and any leftover pukey feelings were gone.

"Yes! So nice, Gigi. You, um, coming in?"

"In a minute. Soaking up this sun. Shit says iss waterproof, but I don't trust it."

Sliding to the far edge, looking down at the shallow brook below, he got back to trying to form a loose plan. *Would hurt her for sure. Maybe, maybe kill her. Or tape her up and leave her up here. Lighter. Flammable.*

Gigi was leaning back on her rock, eyes closed, propped on her elbows, her dirty pillows flopped over to her sides.

Sucking in as much air as he could, Hagas plunged under the water again and again, his mind racing through scenarios as he sat on the bottom of the smooth rock bowl. *Says no one will be here. Gotta keep her happy. Maybe she'll fall in. Drown. Take her car. Think. Think. Think.*

Flashes of Angel, floating in the bathtub, floating beside him in here, kept interrupting his thinking. With each plunge he stayed under, trying to zero in on a plan until his lungs burned for air. On his fifth or sixth resurfacing, just as he slipped above the water, he saw Gigi squatting at the edge of the pool, watching him. She had one flip-flop on and was holding the other, rubbing its bottom against her butt.

"Get out, little man. Time to give your Gigi some attention."

Hagas pushed off the bottom, moving backward to the far wall. *No! Not now. Not again.* His heart was beating fast. He didn't know what he was going to do next, but there was a new feeling rising in him—scared but strong at the same time.

Squatting neck deep, he pressed his back against the hard, smooth wall. He could hear the water flowing over the rocks below.

"No. I don't . . . I don't want to. I just want to stay in here."

"What? What the fuck you doin', little man?" Gigi yelled.

"I'm—I'm staying in here."

"Hagas, what are you doing? You know I love you, sweetie. And I know you love me right back. So . . . okay, we can have it your way."

Gigi let out a raspy sigh, then lowered her body into the water and began shuffling toward him. She was smiling.

162

Hagas's gut tightened. He pushed harder against the wall, trying to back up, trying to get away. Gigi crept closer.

"You don't love me. You . . . you killed Angel. I remember. I saw what you did. You killed her! And I hate what you do to me. I . . . I . . . I hate you."

She was on him. He could feel her body heat as her legs connected to his under the water. Her breath cut through the air. He had nowhere to go. His heart beat faster and his jaw clenched.

"Aw, Hagas, I was jush protectin' you. You know that. Your ma wanted to kill you. I stopped her. You're my little man. She doesn't love you. I love you."

Gigi's hands touched his waist. His reaction was instant, unthought. He shoved her hard and made her wobble a little. Her smile dropped and she came at him again, grabbing his wrists. He grabbed hers, too. They wrestled each other, making the water churn and splash.

With a heave, he spun her against the wall, reversing their positions. She stopped fighting, releasing his arms.

"What are you doing? Hagas, you better get in line right now!"

As she yelled the words, he watched her struggle to stand as tall as she could against the wall. Her dirty pillows sagged, almost touching the water, rising up and down with each wheezing breath. Something was different though. She looked smaller, standing there, shaking. There was still anger, but . . . her voice—he heard it. *She's afraid. Gotta do it. Her or me. Her or me.*

With as much control as he could muster, he yelled, "I'm leaving, Gigi."

"You stop it right now. You aren't leaving me. Where you gonna go? Huh? Huh? Where you gonna go, Hagas?"

"Away from you. Away from Ma. And Brian. That house. And . . . and everything. I—I don't belong here. It's not right. All you all do is hurt me."

Rage bubbled in Hagas's belly. He couldn't contain it, and he liked it.

"But, I love you, Hagas. I told you. Look. Look. I took you swimmin', didn't I? I do love you. You love me, don't you? You're my little man."

Gigi reached out to him, but he recoiled before she could touch him. She opened her arms, spreading them wide, inviting him into her. A crooked smile took shape as her lips jerked up. But only making it halfway. Angel's voice whispered in his ear. *You promised, Johnnie. You promised to protect me. Get her. Get her. Get her . . .*

"No. I'm not! Not anymore!"

He lunged, his hands hitting her chest with every ounce of strength and fire in him. Gigi screamed as her upper body shot backward and her waist lifted, upending her over the rock wall. After he pushed, everything seemed to happen in slow motion. Her face vanished as her bony legs rose out of the water, going almost vertical before dropping out of sight. He heard the thud from below. *No more!*

It took him a minute to calm a little. Still heaving with adrenaline, he stepped to the wall and looked down over the edge. Gigi lay twisted on the rocks below. Water bubbled and flowed around her. He watched, not quite believing what had just happened. But there she was, down there. And she wasn't moving. *She's . . . dead. Dead. Dead! Got her, Angel. Got her.*

Chapter 24

Asleep at the wheel

Dragging Gigi's crumpled body from the stream was hard. Gripping her by the ankles, Hagas yanked her over rocks and roots. He kept looking back at her as he made his way, partly to be sure she wasn't going to wake up, partly because she looked so . . . broken.

Her left arm flopped and bounced while her right arm with the big bone sticking out, stayed bent, stuck in a weird, almost backward direction. His stomach churned. As much as he tried to stop himself from looking at her face, covered in streaks of blood, he kept fixating on the huge section of skin hanging off her forehead. *Just like Angel.* He tried to focus on his destination, the outhouse. Sweat poured from his head. *C'mon. Pull. Pull. Pull. Almost there.*

With a final burst of energy, he made the last twenty feet or so, stumbling and almost falling over a couple of times.

165

He released his grip and dropped her legs to the ground. *Finally.*

Breathing heavily, he slid his butt down the door of the outhouse, landing on the soft pine needle-covered ground. His mind was spinning as he looked at her. She was covered with smudges of dark earth, and pine needles stuck to her skin. Her dirty pillows hung to her left. He kicked her foot. *Hate you.*

Hagas gave himself a couple of minutes to get his wind back. Looking away from Gigi, his eyes darted around the site, peering past trees, squinting in the blasts of sunlight. He listened to the brook gurgling along and the occasional chatter of squirrels. There were no signs or sounds of any other people. No hikers. No cars coming down the road. No chainsaw people. They were alone. His mind slowed, calming his whole body as he processed his next steps to freedom.

Pushing himself up, Hagas felt ready. *Okay. Gotta do this.* He swung the door open and grabbed hold of Gigi's ankles again. Backing into the outhouse, he got her in almost to her waist. The rest of her was hanging out of the opening. Jumping over her, he landed back outside. Then, grabbing under her shoulders, with a mighty heave, he folded her into the outhouse.

She was in, bent at the waist with her head toward her feet. *Good. Good. Okay. Just gotta go get the bag.* Gigi's upper half started tilting backwards toward the opening. *Shit! No. No. No.* Hagas slammed the door shut and put his weight against it, all in one jerky motion.

Just after swinging the blocker down, he felt Gigi bump onto the door. He jumped, adrenaline flooding back into him as he spun, backing away from the door, picturing Gigi just behind it.

"Got to hurry. Move. Bag. Keys."

He jogged across the site, making his way back up the trail to the pool. Working quickly, he scooped up their towels, her flask, his mask, and suntan spray. He grabbed the one flip-flop by the edge of the pool and looked around for the other one. *Shoot. It's down there.*

In his head, he flashed to seeing it on her foot as she fell over the edge and remembered taking it off before he began pulling her to the outhouse. *Stupid. Stupid.* He peered down, using his hand to shade his eyes against the sun. *Nothing! Must've floated away.* He finished his sweep of the rocks. *That's it. Got it all.*

After stuffing everything back into the bag, Hagas pulled on his shorts and squirmed into his T-shirt. *Least they're dry now.* Weaving his way back down, his mind raced again, mixing excitement with panic. *What if someone finds her? Will Ma know? Me? She will. They will. Brian's coming home. Gotta get far away. Somewhere. Somewhere. Anywhere but here. Can't just hide her. Need to get rid of her...* He slipped a little and felt the lighter jam into his hip. The idea hit him and his mind screeched to a halt. *Gotta do it. Get rid of her. Who cares? She's already dead.* He looked across the site to the outhouse.

After piling little mounds of sticks and pine needles all around the walls, Hagas doused them with splashes of whiskey. Stepping back to look at his work, he was satisfied it was enough. He took the lighter out of his pocket and bent down by the door. It took him six tries of spinning the little ridged sparker before a flame finally jumped up.

With a shaking hand, he lowered it to one of his piles. It immediately lit, and the flames carried across the top and down into its center. *Working!* Shuffling around the perimeter of the outhouse, he carefully lowered the lighter again and again, lighting each of his piles. *Ow! Ow! Hot.* Before he could get to the last two piles, he threw the lighter to the ground. Standing upright and stepping back, he sucked on his burnt thumb. *Stupid lighter.*

The flames grew, licking and crawling up the sides of the outhouse. Curling smoke, black and white, mixed, rising into the umbrella of pines high above. *Shoot! So much smoke. Can anyone see it?* Panicking, Hagas kicked dirt at the outhouse, racing around to put out the fire. The flames kept climbing, putting off more heat with layers of paint blistering and the dry wood popping.

Hagas backed away from the burning outhouse, picking up the lighter from the ground and bringing his arm up to cover his nose and mouth. The flames continued rising and the smoke grew thicker, wrapping around every side of the outhouse. *Too late now. I'm sorry, Gigi. I had to. Had to.*

He picked up the bag and walked away. He thought of Angel's suitcase, sitting in the dark basement, waiting—waiting for him. He paused to look back at the fire. Tears stung his eyes. *I'm not sorry. You killed her.*

"I hate you! I hate you! I hate you!" He yelled, wiping tears from his eyes.

Then he was off, rage racing through him again, powering him away from the fire, away from her, heading toward the Forerunner parked in the little dirt lot.

Hagas dug into the bag, finding the jumble of keys at the bottom, tucked near Gigi's wallet. When they left the house earlier, he'd seen Gigi press the chunky, black plastic thing hanging off the key ring to unlock the doors. Sucking in a breath, he pressed. The Forerunner's response was instant, and its horn began screaming, its lights flashing on and off. *Shit! Shit! Shit!* His heart went into overdrive as he stabbed at the thing again.

The horn and light show stopped. His heart still racing, he whipped his head all around. The lot remained still and silent. Breathing again, he looked intently at the black mechanism, now seeing the two buttons with padlock drawings on them, one showing open, the other showing closed. After a slow, cautious push, he was rewarded with the sound of the driver's side door unlocking. *Ha!*

He hopped in and threw the bag on the floor in front of the passenger seat. He found the key with black rubber coating on its end. *That's the one she used.* Bending down and looking under the steering wheel, he found the metal slot for the key and pushed it in.

Holding it for a few seconds, he waited for the sound of the engine. Nothing happened. *Dammit. Okay. Okay. Think.* He searched back in his mind. *What did she do? What did she do?*

He turned the key toward him. The dashboard came to life, lighting up, and a steady beep started chirping, but the engine did not. He pounded the steering wheel. *What am I doing wrong? Why won't you start?* He turned it away from him. The sensation in his fingers as the key moved through hidden mechanical clicks lifted his hope. The engine roared to life. "Yes!"

Hagas closed his eyes, trying to picture Gigi in the driver's seat. *What did she do? The middle thing. She moved*

169

it. Then she used the pedals on the floor. One to move. One to stop.

He opened his eyes and studied the handle Gigi had used. It was all the way forward, slightly illuminating a "P." *Okay. Okay. She moved it back. But to what? R ... N ... 4D ... 3 ... 2L?*

R. R. R. Rewind? Makes sense. Gotta just try one.

Looking under the steering wheel, he found the pedals and positioned his feet on each one. *Perfect.* His mouth went dry and his muscles tensed up. But he was ready. Gritting his teeth, he tried moving the handle down. It didn't budge. Pulling harder didn't work.

Frustrated, Hagas pounded the steering wheel and pushed his feet down on the pedals, making the engine roar. *Whoa.* He yanked his feet back and the engine calmed back down. *Okay. Okay.* He pressed the left pedal. Nothing. He pressed the right and the engine roared again.

That's the one. That will make it go. He pressed his weight onto the left one, using both feet. *Got to be the stop one. Okay.* He tried the handle again, this time pushing in on its side button. It moved right past the "R" and clicked in at the "N."

He let some of the pressure off the stop pedal, slid his right foot to the top of the go pedal and pushed. The engine roared again. But the truck sat still.

"Shit! Come on!"

He let go of the steering wheel, retracted his foot from the pedal and grabbed the handle again, yanking at it. It slipped to "4D" and the Forerunner started creeping forward, toward trees just past the edge of a grassy spot. In a flash, his hands went back to the steering wheel. *Shit! Shit! Wrong way!*

In a flurry of panic, he pressed down on both pedals. The Forerunner's engine roared again but kept its slow pace toward the trees. Sweat poured from him as he spun the steering wheel back and forth, making the truck zig and zag, but still moving, still getting closer to the trees. *No. No. No. No...*

It finally stopped when it hit a big pine tree. Hagas bounced on impact. The engine kept running, holding the truck in place against the tree. Green pine branches covered the front of the truck. He took his feet off the pedals and pounded the steering wheel again.

"Shoot!"

I can do this. Got to get out of here. Pressing both his feet down on the stop pedal, he grabbed the handle again. *R. R. R. Rewind.* He moved the handle forward, clicking through "N" and landing on "R."

"Got it!"

Hagas lifted his feet off the stop pedal and the Forerunner began moving backwards.

Here we go!"

With the force of stomping a spider in the basement, he jammed both his feet on the go pedal. Hagas screamed as the Forerunner shot away from the trees, zooming across the parking lot. But his feet stayed put, locked, pressing down on the go pedal. The Forerunner's back end launched up and Hagas jolted forward, smacking his chest off the steering wheel.

Snapping his head around, he saw a new bunch of trees coming at him fast. Before he could even form a reaction, the truck slammed to a stop and his forehead ricocheted off the steering wheel. The engine shut down with a gasp and a hiss.

Dazed and disoriented, Hagas looked around, touching the window, wondering if he was seeing dust or maybe smoke swirling around outside. It seemed like it was getting much darker out. A blurry glimpse of orange glow from the fire at the outhouse was the last thing he saw before he closed his eyes and slipped into the blackness.

Chapter 25

Déjà vu all over again

The time spent at the gulf today had taken Chris longer than he wanted or expected. His mind drifted in and out of full observation as he maneuvered along the lonely stretches of road connecting myriad small towns. Small, run-down houses, old trailers, and occasional sprawling farms peppered his path. *So many assholes.*

After almost four hours of canvassing his county roads, making his presence known to both the locals and out-of-towners trickling in, Chris pulled into Bear Market and shut the Bronco down at the gas pumps. He got out to fill up the tank.

A loud, jacked-up pickup truck flew by, heavy metal blasting from its open windows. Chris sighed, turning his attention to the pump, watching the numbers tick up, up, up. *Nightly fill up, courtesy of all you assholes.*

Easing back to the road, finally heading to his mom's place to get the twins, he couldn't shake the feeling something bigger was happening in the gulf. *What's next?* Visions of his school days popped like flashbulbs, sparking through his head. Name calling . . . shoving . . . taunting.

Pulling into his mom's, Chris flicked the blues on, his ritual when picking up the twins. For now, it still thrilled them to see the whirling blue lights coming up the drive. Today was no different. His mom opened the side door and the twins ran out, bounding down the stairs, waving colorful pieces of paper. *Mom. Always keeps 'em busy. Need to make more room on the fridge. Does she even miss them, even think of them at all?* He got out and opened the back door, scooping each boy up with a hug and play-tossing them into the back seat.

"Belts on, guys."

The boys wrangled the seatbelts over their bodies. He shut the door, muffling their giggles. He got back into the Bronco, waving goodbye to his mom as she leaned against her side doorway. He didn't have the energy for chit-chat today. And, he didn't want to be asked again about her. *Same story, different day, Mom. No, there's no new news. No Trish.* Turning off the blues, Chris backed down the driveway, thoroughly ready to end his day. The radio crackled to life. *"All officers available. We have a ten forty-eight, possible ten forty-nine. Gulf Hagas. Haybrook camp sites. Fire dispatched to scene. Request any officers in vicinity for assist. Ten ninety-three. Over."*

Chris jammed the brakes, skidding to a quick stop. The twins giggled behind him. *Shit!* He threw the Bronco into drive and crawled back up the driveway. His mom raised her

174

hands in the air, questioning his return. He parked and jumped out.

"You forget something?" she called out to him.

"Need you to watch the boys, Mom. Probably for the night. You have their emergency overnight gear, right?"

"Yes. Okay. Why? What's happening? Patricia call?"

"It's not Trish. Just need your help. Police business. Can you watch them?"

"Okay. Okay. Yes, of course."

Chris opened the back door and scrambled the boys out. They were no longer giggling, instead looking up at him with somber faces.

"Come on, guys. Sleepover at Nai Nai's."

"I want my bed . . ."

"Been here all day . . ."

"Wanna come home with you . . ."

He ushered them toward the house. His mom bent down, smiling wide and opening her arms to welcome the boys back. "Let's go, little dumplings. We'll have fun!"

She squeezed the boys to her, and then shooed them into the house. Chris hustled back to the Bronco, pausing at the door and looking back at her.

"Do me a favor. Be sure you and Dad lock the doors tonight. Got my babies in there."

"Be careful, son. You're still my baby."

His mom stood tall and then backed inside her house, pulling the screen door closed. Back in the Bronco, he took a moment to collect himself before grabbing the radio. He took a deep breath, and then clicked the talk button.

"Ten-four. Chris here. On my way to the gulf. Additional responders, go ten twenty-one immediately. Meet me at the

KI check-in. Do not proceed until I'm on site. Once we're in the gulf, it's code four. No lights. No sirens. Dispatch, get a K-9 team moving. Over and out."

Chris reached over to the passenger seat and adjusted his hat, positioning it for a quick grab when he got back to the gulf. He clicked on the radio and turned up the volume. AC/DC's "Hell's Bells" blasted, midway through the song. He waited until he was a half-mile away from his mom's house before turning on his lights and sirens, and then pressed down the accelerator.

His trusty old Bronco roared, picking up speed. One by one, cars and trucks pulled off to the side of the road, letting him race ahead unimpeded. *Too fast. Too soon. Too friggin' soon. Come on! Has to be something else. Just an accident. Happens. Has to be.* In front of him, brake lights continued illuminating and pulling to the side. *Just like Moses, except I've got no people. Heading right back into this mess.*

Chapter 26

Cutting Out

Dannie leaned on the back wall of Billy's, smoking a cigarette while counting the cash she'd been jamming into her pockets all day. *Three hundred. Three twenty. Three forty. Three fifty. Three sixty.* She fished out more crumpled bills from her pocket and smoothed them out.

"All fives. Who the fuck pays with fives? Jesus." She whipped through them. "Sixty-five. Seventy. Seventy-five. Eighty. Three eighty."

Her eyes narrowed. She clenched her cigarette between her lips, digging back into her pockets, pulling their linty linings up, and turning them inside out.

"Mother fucker!" *One of those fucktards shafted me twenty bucks.*

Beside her, the back door banged open and Billy leaned out. "Hey, Dannie, what the fuck you doing? Got a customer in here."

177

"Fuck you, Billy. One of those fuckers stiffed me twenty bucks."

"Well, shit. That sucks." He paused. "But that's on you, Dannie. It's not coming out of my take. I counted ten guys so far. That's a hundred bucks."

"Oh, fuck off. You'll get your cut. Just wanted to get the fuck out of here. I had a goal for today."

"Well, hey now, day's not done. You got a fresh one inside. You coming or what?"

Dannie looked down at the rumpled wad of cash clenched in her hand. *Jesus. What in the holy fuck am I doing? Fuck do I care if I'm not at an even one fifty? Close e-fucking-nough. Plenty enough to get me way the fuck out of this place, away from all these fuckers. Fuck! Where's doc? Fucking promised . . . Asshole.*

Billy swung the door open wider. Dannie glared at him. *Little fucker. Definitely going to key your jeep when I leave.* She stuffed the cash back into her pocket and flicked her cigarette across the dirt lot. Forced out a last puff of smoke. Watched it fill the air against the setting sun.

Dannie tussled her hair as she walked back into the dingy shop. She hated the musty smell of all the old junky crap Billy had stacked and jammed into every corner. *Who even buys this shit? Whatever. Almost done. This whore's got two more scores!* She giggled under her breath, happy with her rhyming skills. *Ha. Made a funny.*

"He back there already?" Dannie asked as Billy turned to go to the cash register at the front of the shop.

"Yup. Waiting on you. Better hustle." Billy laughed at his little play on words.

"Very funny, asshole."

Dannie walked to the dark velvet curtain separating her small back room from the rest of the shop. *Two more.* Lifting the heavy fabric slightly to one side, she slipped her body past it, stepping into the dark cubby. She took in a shadowy figure seated on the metal folding chair. *Short, round, kind of tensed up. There he is. 'Bout fucking time. What's up, doc?* A smile crept across her face.

"Hey, baby. Been waiting on you. Didn't think you were coming. Thought maybe you forgot all about me."

The man spun around. His face was still dark, but Dannie could see beads of sweat poking through strands of dyed, black hair pasted to his forehead.

"Oh, hi, Dannie. I'm so sorry. My wife was at me all morning. I'm so sick of her. Wanted to come up with me. Must have taken a hundred "nos" before she finally gave up. I'd never forget about you. I just couldn't get away sooner." He paused, sucking in his breath, staring up at her for a minute before blurting out, "You look so beautiful."

Dannie forced her smile wider. *You stupid, pussy-whipped asshole. Going to get trounced the rest of your stupid life.* Stepping into the room, the curtain fell shut behind her. The little room got darker, blurring the doc's face in the darkness. Behind him, her hands found his meek shoulders, and she circled them down to his soft, damp, squishy chest, pulling him against her pelvis. *Jesus, your tits got bigger than mine.*

"Oh, baby, it's okay. I understand. She doesn't get you like I do. I'm going to make you feel real good."

"You already are," the doc groaned.

Dannie rubbed his chest, unbuttoning his polo shirt and sliding her hand inside to get him revved up. She was repulsed by his slick skin. *Fucking hairless wonder. You better have come through for me.*

"First things first, though. Did you bring me the goods like we talked about?"

"Mmmm, you know I did. Well, only three. I couldn't get four like you asked. Would have been too risky."

Dannie stopped rubbing as the doc reached around for his jacket that was hanging off the chair. *Carole and Hagas were one each. But Brian. Fuck! Douchebag.* The doc's hand found hers, pressing three cool, smooth, plastic cylinders into her palm.

Dannie closed her fingers around them, her mind fast-forwarding to the bright, beautiful vision of her flying down the open road, sun shining, windows open, and warm wind blowing all around her. *But three. Only three.* An image of Brian, bumbling around the kitchen, flailing his arms, refusing to go down, popped into her head. She slid the syringes into her bag, wiggling them down to the bottom, then went back to rubbing the doc and processing the wrinkle in her plan.

"Aw damn, baby. Last I checked, you were the owner of your little critter hospital. I told you I really needed four. My man's a big guy. Don't you have one more? Maybe in your car?"

"I don't, Dannie. I tried. Took me a few weeks to get three. People will notice if too much of this stuff goes missing. It's all over the streets now in Portland. People are dropping like flies. I just . . . I just ran out of time. But it's potent. Trust me, three will work. I believe that. We'll—I mean you'll—be rid of them. You can get out. By the time the cops find them, they won't be able to figure out where it came from. Then, I'll come. Leave that nagging bitch of mine for good. We'll both be out of here, together. Start fresh, just like you said."

"Just like I said," Dannie echoed the words, staring into the dark. Anger bubbled in Dannie's gut, as she slinked around to the front of the chair, raking her nails down the doc's arms, just hard enough to make him squirm, but not enough to break his skin. *Fucking four. Simple ask, you idiot fuck.*

As she unzipped his shorts, she squatted down between his knees, staring at his doughy face. His eyes were closed and his brow crinkled as he waited for her to go to work. The thought of chomping his tiny dick clean off made her smile for a second. *Eh, too messy. No need to cause a scene. Better to just leave him hanging. Ha! I made a funny.* She giggled out loud. The doc looked down at her with questioning eyes. *Moron.* Dannie dropped her smile and yanked open his shorts. Just as she started lowering her head, the cubby's velvet curtain ripped open, and light flooded in.

"Hey! Hey! Hey! What are you doing?" the doc blurted out.

Dannie whipped her head up to see who dared invade her space. *Fuck! Cop?* The silhouetted figure, holding the curtain open with one arm, said nothing and just stood at the entry. *Tall. Wide shoulders. Not a cop. No uniform. Built. Eh, better than most of the old fat fucks.*

The doc was scrambling, shifting in the chair, pulling at his shorts in a fury. Backing away from his thrashing, Dannie stood, her hands going to her hips in a pose of both defiance and annoyance at the intrusion. The smell of Old Spice mixed with a slight undertone of old fish caught her nose, overtaking the normal, dank mustiness of her 'office.' *I know that smell. Jesus Christ . . .*

"Hey, baby. Been on the road all day." Brian's growl whispered into the cubby.

Thinking as fast as she could, Dannie glanced at her bag, picturing the needles tucked away at the bottom. *Fuck. Fuck. Fuck. Dick can't just leave me the fuck alone.* The doc was on his feet now. *Don't be an idiot. Don't say a –* The doc's gut sucked in as he puffed his chest and opened his mouth. In a flash, Dannie put her index finger on his lips and leveled a 'keep your fucking mouth shut' glare on him before turning to face Brian's silhouette.

"Smells like you've been in the water all day, baby," Dannie retorted through a forced smile.

"Been working my ass off for three weeks to get back up here. You 'bout done with this fucker or what?" Brian asked.

The doc stood still as Dannie let her finger slide down his lips, tapping her nail twice on his chin. Her eyes widened, meeting his, then dragging his gaze toward the door. *Don't say a word. Just go.* The doc seemed to understand, and he began deflating, slipping back into his normal blob of a man. He turned and took two steps to the door. Brian stood exactly where he was but lifted the curtain higher in a 'get the fuck out of here' motion. After a quick, pained glance back at her, the doc squeezed past Brian and stomped away. *Adios, doc.*

With Brian's question answered, Dannie concentrated on making things all good with her man. *Fucking dumbass.* She launched at him, dropping to her knees, wrapping her arms around his waist. Her face pressed against his stomach.

"Shit. I didn't think you'd stop here. You know I hate it when you see me at work."

"Aww, fuck, baby. Whatever. Come on. Let's get the fuck outta here."

"But I haven't met my goal. Doing my part. For us. Some prick stiffed me twenty bucks. Gotta make it up."

Brian stepped into the cubby, letting the curtain fall shut behind him. He pulled Dannie up and pressed against her.

"Fuck that. I'm horny as shit. 'Sides, I made coin this trip. Consider it a gift."

As Brian's strong arms pulled her in tighter, Dannie felt his cock hardening against her. His scent filled her with disgust, yet she still felt some wave of raw, animal attraction to his physicality that made it easier to pull off her acting.

"Mmmmm. You have been away, too long, baby," she purred.

Pushing up between Brian's arms and standing on her tiptoes, Dannie pressed her mouth onto his—hard, forcing her tongue inside. *Fucking stubble. Fuck. Ow.*

"Mmmmmm . . . fuck. Get off me. Fuck! Tastes like a goddamn cum dumpster. How many guys you blow today?" Brian pushed Dannie off, bumping her against a side wall.

"Jesus, Brian. What the fuck? You don't bitch when it's yours you're tasting." She glared up at him, wiping the wet from her lips with the back of her hand. "Fuck, you ask for it."

"Yeah, yeah. Just hate you doing this shit, and giving that little prick, Billy, a cut. Fuck though if it doesn't turn me on. I just wanna get at you. But not here. I need more than a hummer. Get your shit. Let's go."

"Shit. Fine. You're cool. I'm cool. Fuck this place," Dannie said, snatching her bag. *Got to set the scene. Get him all primed.* "Ooh, shit. Forgot. Carole's up. You cool with that?"

"Cool with that? Shit, yeah. Always. We'll get her in the fun. Bitch might even have some new tricks to teach her old favorite student. She all good and sauced?"

"Oh, yeah. Drinking whiskey like water. Had to cut her up a bit last night. Little fight. All good."

"Ha! Atta girl. And the kid? He behaving, or does he, uh, need to take a turn in my chair for a little discipline?"

"Depends. He's been okay. But I'm sure he's been up to something, at least in his head, anyway. You want him in your chair for a while? Get you all primed up."

"Yeah. Yeah, I do. Gotta keep him in line. Be sure he knows who's boss."

"Well, let's hit it."

Brushing past Brian, Dannie swept the curtain aside and headed toward the front, with Brian trailing right behind her. *Fuck! That smell.* Billy looked up, put his phone down, and threw her a lopsided smirk.

"Shit, that was quick," Billy said.

Dannie fished out her wad of bills and counted off one hundred dollars in twenties. Slapping them on the counter, she peeled back a wicked smile at Billy.

"Here's your cut. Why don't you get yourself something nice and big so you can go fuck yourself."

She marched toward the front door, pausing to look back at Brian. At the counter, Brian stood tall, staring down at Billy. Brian placed his meaty paws on the counter. Billy stared up but seemed to shrivel down at the same time. *This should be good.* After a brief, wordless stare down, Brian landed his index finger on a single twenty-dollar bill, from

184

the five splayed out on the counter, and dragged it toward him. When it reached the edge of the counter, he pinched it in half and pocketed it. Dannie smiled, remembering a flicker of time when she liked this dumb hunk of menacing meat. *Ha. Good for something anyway.*

"Dannie got stiffed twenty bucks. Now, really, go fuck yourself," Brian growled.

Billy was stone-faced and silent as Brian cracked his neck to one side and walked to Dannie. As the pair went out the door, Dannie gave an over-the-shoulder one-finger salute to Billy, cackling as the door swung closed behind her. *Oh, that was rich. Fucking moron. Made my quota after all, and a bonus in my bag, too. Adi-fucking-os you*—Brian's too-hard smack to her ass slammed her back into the now.

Caught off guard, she yelped, instantly pissed at herself for letting out a sign of weakness. *Fucking fuck!* Brian said nothing, spinning off to go to his truck. He didn't look back at her as he peeled out of the dirt lot. His pumping fist raised out the window, soaring high above the trail of dust left in his wake as he barreled down the road. *Idiot.*

Dannie, still seething, whipped open her car door and dropped onto the seat. A punch of the gas pedal jerked the car backward. *Shit! Almost forgot.* She jammed the brake down, threw the shifter into park, and shut the car down. Grabbing her keys, she popped out of her car and half-skipped over to Billy's shiny, black jeep parked in the far corner of the lot.

Working quickly, Dannie balled her keys, selecting the rugged car key for her task at hand. She started at the back fender on the driver's side, digging the key in as hard as she could, working her way across the door, looping under the handle, all the way to the front fender. Gouging through the paint to make a rough, wavy, silver-white line from tail to tip. *Oooh, this feels good.* Stepping back, she put her hands on her hips and admired her homemade pinstriping capabilities. *Damn. Almost looks good. This backwoods crafting bullshit has made me all fucking artistic.*

"Gonna take more than eighty bucks to fix this shit, Billy," she said to her hazy reflection looking back at her from the side of the Jeep.

Dannie jogged back to her car. Her spirits rose again as she double-checked her bag. The three syringes sat at the bottom, under a crumpled, red bandana. *Let's get this party started. Thanks again, doc. Nothing like a good, regular customer. Ha. Maybe I will out the fucker to his wife on my way out.*

It was nearly 6:00 p.m. when Dannie tore out of the lot and onto Route 6, holding up a long, twirling one-finger salute out her window.

"Fuck you, Billy. Fuck you, Corinna, stupid-ass town. Fuck you, Brian. I am fuckin' outta here."

Chapter 27

On the road. Again.

Thwump. Thwump. Thwump. The noise echoed in Hagas's swimming mind. Behind his closed eyes, he zoomed past Gigi's bony back, fixating on the out-of-place, shiny, wet spigot at the far edge of the rocky pool. Sunlight sparkled on its metal skin. Thwump. Thwump. Thwump.

Angel burst up from the water at the far edge of the pool, her forehead connecting with the metal edge of the spigot. *Noooooooo! Angel!* Her eyes locked on his for a moment, just before blood gushed down her face. Then, she slipped under the water.

He pushed off the rock beneath his feet, trying to get to her. To save her. *Almost there.* Under the water, Gigi grabbed his ankles, holding him in place. She was too strong. He couldn't move. He kicked, wiggled, and stretched out toward Angel. Gigi laughed at him.

A foot below the water, Angel's blue eyes pleaded with him through clouds of blood and blonde hair, swirling around her tiny face. The torn skin from the gash in her forehead flapped open and closed. Her hands were floating, suspended just above her in the cool water. Stretching. Stretching. Gigi's grip tightened. *Almost . . . there.* His hands were just a few inches from Angel's. His lungs were burning. Air bubbles gushed out of him. *Angel! Angel. I'm sorry. I love you.*

Thwump. Thwump. "Kid! Hey, kid!"

Thump. The noise was closer. Louder. *Angel. Gigi.* Hagas peeled his eyes open. Everything around him was soft and fuzzy. His head throbbed as he tried to make sense of the now. *The car. Gigi. Am I dreaming?* Thump. Shifting his eyes to the left, Hagas saw big hands pressed on the Forerunner's window. A shadowy figure gazed down at him. *Big beard. Who are you?*

The man spoke. "Kid. Thank God. You alright? You hurt?" The man's hand pointed down. "The doors are locked. Can you hit the button? Hit the unlock."

Eyes squinting, searching for the button that he saw Gigi use to unlock the doors, Hagas obeyed the stranger's order. Reaching forward, he watched his arm move out in front of him. It didn't feel connected to him. *The car. The outhouse. Gigi.* His finger hovered, just grazing the hard, plastic button.

"Stay with me, kid. Go ahead. Press the button," the man said, his voice calmer and clearer.

Hagas looked up at him and let his arm drift back to his side.

188

"Come on, kid. Gotta get you out of there," the man urged.

Wait. No. No. Gigi. Dead. Gotta get away. Did he see?

"Okay. Okay. It's okay. Um . . . I'm gonna get a rock. Break the window behind you," the man said.

Hagas's focus sharpened as he watched the man spin away.

"Matt! Jesus! Matt! Matt! Holy shit!" From far away, a woman screamed. The man jerked upright.

"Matt! Matt! Oh, God. Come here! Hurry!" The woman's voice was high, almost screechy. The man glanced in the window, putting both hands up for a brief second, before bounding away from the Forerunner.

"What? What? Hang on. I'm coming," the man called out.

Oh no! She saw her. Gigi. Dead. Dead. Killed her. Gotta get away. Hagas rubbed his forehead, feeling a lumpy line under his skin. *Angel.* Looking up into the mirror, he saw a diagonal reddish swath above his eyes. Details began popping back. Bouncing in the seat. Racing across the dirt road. Pushing in his mind, he tried to find the rest of what happened, but all he could see were dark gaps and just a few little pieces of pictures.

Forcing himself to move, Hagas felt a swell of panic rushing in. His stomach tensed and his blood pumped faster. *Gotta run. Gotta get away.* Clicking the seatbelt open and sliding it away, he turned to look out the window. He couldn't see the man or the woman, but he could hear their voices rising and falling. *They know. They know. Get my gear and go.*

Working fast, adrenaline and panic fueling him, Hagas reached down to the passenger floor and hauled the bag up to the seat. He looked around with panicked eyes, stuffing everything he could see back into the bag. *Okay. Okay. That's good.* He looked out the window again, straining to see beyond the bushes, and held his breath. He couldn't see the man or the woman that had called out, but he heard muffled voices that seemed far away. *Still down there. In the site. Now. Got to go now.*

Pressing the unlock button, he cringed when the doors all made the popping sound. In slow, measured moves, he pulled the door handle and pushed the door open. The fresh, hot air washed over him, giving him a boost of energy. He swung his legs over the edge of the seat and paused, sucking in short breaths.

The voices were clearer now without the door and glass muffling them. *Still far away.* The woman was crying. The man was talking. "Getting help . . . find a radio . . . doubling back . . . stay with the kid . . ."

Hagas looked down at his watch. 4:42. *Whoa. How long? How many hours?* Looking up, he could see the sun shimmering just above the tree line. *Dark soon. Gotta hurry. Angel. Get her. Get out. Fast.* Clutching the bag to his chest, he slid off the seat, landing with a soft thud on grass and weeds. *Too loud.* His breath caught. He listened. *Still in the site.* Digging into the bag he found the leather mask and slipped it out. *Maybe he didn't see my face good.* He set the bag down and dropped the mask over his head. The familiar, pungent smell hit him hard, and he gagged a little but pushed through the feeling.

Yanking the mask into place around his head, he got it to the spot where the eye holes allowed him to see dead ahead

190

but cut off any wider side views. Pulling on the leather straps, he tightened it into place. *Won't see me now.*

The man's voice called out. "Wait here. Sit. Breathe. I'm just going to see if the kid is okay." *Closer. Louder.* Hagas's heart pumped faster. *Got to go.* He snatched the bag and started up the road. Moving fast, he tried to be quiet, sticking to the weedy-covered edges.

Just as he got to the entry to the Haybrook sites, a woman emerged from the shadows of the trees, stepping onto the road. Hagas braked, skidding his sneakers on the gravelly dirt road. The woman jerked her head up, eyes wide. Clear trails streaked her dust-covered face. *Younger than Ma. Pretty.* The woman's mouth dropped open and she stumbled backward, making strange choking noises. Hagas cocked his head, regarding her. *No. No. Oh, please, don't. Don't say anything.*

He raised his index finger to his mouth, hidden behind the leather. "Shhhhh. Shhh. Please. Shhhhhhh."

The woman, grabbing at a small tree trunk, screamed. It was raw and loud, piercing through the leather covering Hagas's ears.

She followed up with quick bursts of "Matt! Matt! Matt!"

A burst of panic took over Hagas, propelling his legs to move as fast as they could. *Run! Run! Run!*

Behind him, much too close, the man yelled out. "Kid! Kid! Come on! Wait! Wait! Where you going?"

Run! Run! Run! Hagas did not look back. Running at full speed, heaving in wet gasps through the mask, he sprinted up the rutted road, bobbing and weaving around rocks and giant divots.

Branches scraped his arms and bugs ricocheted off him as he invaded their flight plans. He made it around three sweeping curves before his legs could pump no more. He stumbled, losing his balance, crashing down onto the dirt. He had swung the bag out in front of him, sparing himself from a full messy wipeout. He lay still, frozen for a long few seconds. *Shit. Shit. You're okay. Come on. Gotta get back up.*

Hagas swiped at his shorts and shirt, sending dust out in small bursts. Moving his head down and around, looking through the eye holes as best he could, he scanned his body for any serious injuries. His left palm had a few dirty scrapes, barely seeping blood.

Touching his right knee, Hagas yelped as he grazed the open flesh. Torn up with gravel sticking in it. Dark red blood snaked down his shin. *Ow. Ow. Ow.* He tested the pain, squatting to bend his knee, grimacing behind the leather mask in full anticipation of pain. *All good. Okay. Just a cut. Just a cut.*

He popped upright, swiveling to look behind him. The road was silent. No movement. Just bugs flitting around in the low rays of the sun. *Phew. Nobody coming. Gotta wrap it up. Gotta keep moving.* He pulled at the mask's ties, yanking the leather hood off his head, sucking in great breaths of the hot air.

Fishing around the bag for something to wrap his knee with, Hagas pulled out one of the towels. The old towel had more than a few holes in it. Using both hands, he pulled at one of the bigger holes, tearing off a long strip of cloth. *Perfect.* He winced as he dragged bits of gravel out of the wound, and then he wrapped the strip of the towel around his knee, tying it tight in double knots to keep it in place.

Standing tall and wiggling his knee to check his handiwork, Hagas was ready to move on. After stuffing the remains of the towel and the empty flask back in the bag, he picked it up, noticing its weight for the first time. He set it down. Assessing each item for any use, he launched unneeded things as far as he could into the surrounding brush. *Flask. Yep, for water. Ripped towel, nope, keep the good one. Shorts, nope. Boxers, no. Lighter, yep. Tape, yep. Suntan lotion, nope. Wallet . . . hmm.* He flipped through its chambers and slots, removing a few bills and two credit cards, then Frisbeed the wallet away.

Digging into the bag farther, he was surprised to discover a skinny, white zipper running along one side, almost hidden. *Hmm. What's in here?* Zipping it open, and peering in, his eyes widened. Gently, slowly, he pulled out a small gun. The metal exterior glinted in the sun. *Whoa. Heavy. Real. Why? For animals?* After laying the gun on the dirt road, he dug back into the secret compartment.

Hagas pulled out the three envelopes. Two looked older, kind of dirty and tattered. He flipped them around in his hands, then set his mind to working out the words on the outside. The address on the front of each was to Carole Jenkins in Hampton, New Hampshire. *Ma had called Gigi that a few times. Carole. Drinking usually.* "Jenkins. Jenkins." *Last name. Gigi Jenkins. Carole Jenkins. Let's see.*

He chose one of the older ones and pulled out the card inside. A single red heart was printed on the front with a blue ink doodle of a dick sticking out of the heart and raindrop shapes coming out of the end. *Gross.* He opened the card, furrowing his brow to try and work through the messy blue words.

Miss you . . . need you . . . pussy . . . taste . . . fuck . . . weekend . . . Dannie . . . bitch . . .

At the end of the note, there was no name, just a dash followed by a single, swoopy *B*.

Hagas selected the next tattered envelope. Same address. Inside this one was a folded-up piece of paper. Flattening it out revealed more blue ink doodles. Dicks, raindrops, and stick figures, all stuck together in different positions, peppered the edges of the sheet. Tan splotchy stains had smudged some of them. The note was mostly the same stuff.

Come up . . . taste . . . too long . . . want me . . . taste you . . . cock . . . fuck . . . found the money . . . floorboard . . . bedroom . . . hiding it . . . need you . . . let's go . . . At the end, again, a dash was followed by a single, big, swoopy *B*. But this one had two blue dots in the open areas of the *B* and open lips with a tongue sticking out right beside it. *Brian and Gigi. Gross. Gross. Gross.*

The third envelope was cleaner—newer. Inside, was another piece of paper. No doodles, though. Just Brian's same messy writing, but in black ink. *Last run . . . tired of waiting . . . need you . . . fucking not fair . . . Memorial Day Weekend . . . got to do this . . . get it at Sig Sauer . . . call my buddy . . . use Dannie's ID . . . got a plan . . . take the money . . . you and me . . . start over. B.*

Hagas looked down at the gun. In his head, he heard Brian's growly voice. *I got a plan. Take the money. You and me. You and me. Just you and me . . .*

Realization hit him. *Gigi was gonna kill Ma. Or maybe Brian was. What about me? Just you and me. You and me.*

They were gonna shoot me, too? Rage swelled in his gut. Flashes of Brian's chair ricocheted around his head. His hands and feet strapped down. The cigarettes burning into his stomach and balls. The hard things Brian stuck into his butt. Brian in his leather stuff, standing over him. Ma watching. Laughing. Crying. *Serves you right. Devil boy. Devil boy. Serves you right. Killed my Angel.*

A guttural scream erupted from Hagas. "Noooooooo. I hate you all, you fucker shits! She killed Angel. I didn't do anything! Anything!"

Ripping the envelopes and notes, grunting, tears streaming freely down his face, Hagas ground the pieces of paper into the dirt, kicking them and shredding them. Dust billowed all around him.

Finally, his rage slowing, he stopped kicking. He used his foot to sweep the scraps together into a small pile. Squatting down, he got the lighter out of the bag. Wiping his face and sniffing up dusty snot, he sparked the lighter to the little pile. Even with dust all over it, the paper ignited quickly. Flames spread through with blobs of white-gray smoke rising.

Hagas sniffled, staring down at the small fire, watching it flare, sending orange-edged bits of paper floating up. After a minute or so, it was just a black, flaky pile. He stomped on it, grinding it into the dirt again, squelching it out all the way.

"Wish you'd all burn. Just like Gigi."

Picking up the gun, he pondered it, feeling its weight. He held it up, squeezing his left eye shut and pointing it at trees around him. He thought back to the movies he watched. *All of them just point it at someone—something—and pull the trigger. Sometimes a few times.* After a couple of minutes of reenacting scenes he remembered, he felt sure he could use the gun. He put it back in the secret compartment and zipped it closed. *You can do this. They were going to shoot me.*

Hagas stood tall, using his hands to rub his eyes and wipe his face clear of streaks of tears and snot. The sun was sinking, the sky changing color, and he knew light was going away fast. *This is it. Got to move. Can still beat Ma home. She'll never know. The money. Get the money. Get Angel and get gone.* Brian's face popped into his mind. *If you're there, I'll shoot you. I will.*

The hood felt different going on this time. Hagas adjusted the eyeholes into position and tightened the strings, securing it in place. The smell didn't bother him as much. He felt a turn inside, a sort of power welling in his gut. *No one can see me. Can't get what they can't see. Can't see me.* Grabbing the bag, he continued his journey up the road. Heading home for one last time.

Chapter 28

One for the road

God, she was beautiful. Drank like a fish. Never put on a fucking ounce! Suzanne, squatting beside the fire ring, gazed into the low flames, a red Solo cup in her hand. The rising, curling licks of orange and yellow flames reminded her of Connie's hair waving in the late-day breeze on the beach in P-town, just the two of them. Holding hands. No booze, no cackling, tipsy friends circling them.

Derby, laying in the dirt and tethered once again to the picnic table, whimpered. Suzanne eased out of her trance, turning her head to look at him, then stood and swirled the melting ice around the bottom of her cup. *Time for a refill.*

"Who's a good boy? Who's a good boy? Little shit. Running away from Mommy." Suzanne smiled as Derby stood.

Walking over to give Derby a little love, she smiled as his tail wagged with more fervor as she got closer. She stopped just short as he strained his body against the end of his tether. She put her cup on the bench of the picnic table, ruffled his ears, pushing him back at the same time to ease the tension on his tether. Lulled by the affection, his tail slowed and he stopped pulling on his tether, then finally, sat on his haunches.

Suzanne stood and pointed at Derby in a silent command to tell him to stay put. She opened the cooler and pulled out limes, tequila, agave syrup, and a bag of ice, setting it all on a massive cutting board on the picnic table. *One margarita coming up. Fuck. How many times did I say that to her?* After a couple of deep breaths, she reached back in the cooler and pulled out a bag of marinated chicken, a container of refried beans, tortillas, a bag of shredded cheese, and a tub of fresh salsa—the kind Connie loved. She admired her pre-camping prep work. *Voi-fucking-la. Your basic tacos and tequila night.*

Smiling at Derby, Suzanne reached down to ruffle his head again. *Don't worry. Dinner's coming for you, too.* She cut two limes in half, both a little off center. Just as she started pouring tequila into her cup, Derby's ears pricked up as the sound of a low rumble made its way into the site.

The rumble grew and Suzanne stood tall, looking down the road, past the bridge. Derby growled as headlights breached the hilltop just past the bridge. Suzanne looked in disbelief as a bright red fire truck crept across the wooden planks. *What the . . . what?* The three guys in the front all had their heads turned to the site.

Suzanne put the tequila down and began walking up to the site entrance, folding her arms across her chest as the truck slowed, coming to a stop. On the side, in gold, read

'Brownville Fire Department.' Derby woofed from below. From the cab, the three men kept their eyes on her.

The driver rolled his window down. "Afternoon, miss," he said.

Trying to process without panic, Suzanne responded with an inquisitive but upbeat tone. "Hello, fellas. What's going on? Are the woods on fire? Do we need to get the hell outta here?"

"No. No. Well, we don't think so. Small fire down at Haybrook sites. Dispatch said it's pretty much out. So, nothing to get worked up about," the driver said in a quick clip.

His forced half-smile told Suzanne that something was off. She looked past him at the other two men in the cab, bearded replicas of the driver, sitting silent, staring down at her. Derby barked and whined from his tether at the picnic table.

"I mean, well, good. That's good that it's out," Suzanne addressed the driver.

The driver continued looking down at her for a moment too long. *You're not telling me something.*

"Is there something else?" Suzanne asked. "Is someone hurt? I know a woman was going swimming down there. She stopped here when she was driving down. I talked to her."

Suzanne watched, furrowing her brow as the driver looked over at his two guys. She studied their darting eyes. After a few seconds, the driver turned his head back to Suzanne.

"Ummm . . . we, uh . . ."

"What about the woman?"

The two silent guys turned their heads to look straight ahead. The driver fidgeted. "We need to go check everything out. Can't confirm anything yet – not until we're eyes on," the driver said with a hint of authority in his voice.

Derby barked again. Suzanne looked down at him. He was tangled around the legs of the picnic table. Her mind raced, processing. *Jesus. Seriously. This is fucked up.*

"Shit." She addressed the driver. "Okay, so now what? Should I have a fire, or are you putting a kibosh on that?"

"No. No. You should be fine. Just keep it in the ring. We'll check things out and clean up down there. Dispatch said some hikers had mostly put out any remnants."

"You never answered me. What about the woman?" Suzanne asked again.

"Like I said. We'll check it out. The sheriff has been dispatched, too. He should be up here soon. He can let you know what's what. If he can."

"Got it. Well, appreciate the heads up. I'll let you get moving." Suzanne's hands locked onto her hips in an involuntary, practiced power pose.

The driver rolled up his window with some uninspiring parting words. "Be safe."

The truck resumed rumbling up the road, its taillights fading in the dusty cloud hovering above the road in its wake. After watching the truck drive away and round the corner leading to the Haybrook sites, Suzanne relaxed her posture, taking in a few calming breaths, before turning and walking back into the site. Derby remained tangled, pulling on his tether and looking up at her. Suzanne looped Derby around and out of his maze, freeing him to roam his area again.

Shit. Really? Really, Suzanne? Her mind wandered as she finished cutting limes. *Bunch of fucking whackos up here. We've got Larry, Daryl, and his other brother Daryl from some crack fire department on the case, though. Could've been some twisted religious thing gone wrong for all they know.* She went back to work with the knife, hacking at the limes, then squeezed them into her cup. She finished the tequila and lime with a splash of orange juice, and then went back to the fire ring.

Tossing sticks on top of the now-smoldering orange coals from earlier, her mind drifted. *Am I really doing this? They weren't tweaking out. Just another thing. This is the woods. Shit happens.* Closing her eyes, she took in a few deep inhales and exhales, enjoying the smell of the fresh, dry wood catching. *Calm. Calm. Get it together.* The sticks crackled and popped. Suzanne opened her eyes and stood, crossing her arms, looking at the growing fire as it sent smokey tendrils into the shadowy trees above.

Knew she was off. Probably killed herself. Accident maybe. Whatever. It's done. It's done. He said the fire's out. She grabbed two large pieces of firewood and placed them on top of the raging pile of sticks. *Derby. Fire. Dead lady. I've seen her before. Have I? Shit. What else could possibly go wrong? Just a full-on confrontation with a backwoods fuck . . .*

A half-hour later, Suzanne caved to Derby's whining and released his tether from the picnic table, but she kept it attached to his collar just in case he started wandering too far again. The fun of tossing his ball around the site, watching him scramble to grab it as it ricocheted around roots, lost its magic in minutes. Every throw followed with the inevitable untangling of his tether from the myriad exposed tree roots. *Dammit. This sucks.* Suzanne scooped up the dusty tether, leading Derby to the fire. Ball in mouth, he didn't resist, collapsing down beside her and releasing the dirty, slimy ball to rest between his front paws.

Suzanne dumped her barely touched drink onto the ground. *Not working for me. Shit. What the fuck am I—*

Derby growled, jerking his head up, looking up at the entry to their site. He started barking.

Suzanne spun. *What the . . . ?* A figure stood still in the road, shoulders squared to the site entry, looking down at them. Between the growing shadows and her panicking mind, the figure was tough to process. *A man—a boy?— holding a bag. Is that a mask? Come on. What the hell is this? Fuck. Fuck. Fuck.* Her heart raced, and her mouth went dry.

"Hey, buddy. You lost?" Suzanne called up to him, summoning her best attempt at steadying her voice and normalizing the situation.

The boy did not move. Derby continued barking, low and slow, hackles raised. He slinked past the picnic table, heading up the site entry toward the figure.

"Derby! No! Stay here!" Suzanne yelled, realizing the distances between her and Derby and the figure were shifting.

Instinct kicked in, and she raced to catch the end of the tether trailing behind him. One big lunge brought her foot down on the end.

"Gotcha." Derby strained, barking and barking.

Suzanne snapped her head up just after her foot crushed the tether. *Shit! Shit! Wide open. Too close.* The boy bent down in the same instant, his hand jamming into his bag. In a flash, he was upright again, with what was clearly a gun. Suzanne raised her right hand automatically, squatting down and holding the tether firm in her left.

"Shit. Shit. No. No, kid. Easy. We're good. He's good. Don't do anything rash. Derby stop! Come here!" Suzanne pleaded.

Suzanne reeled Derby in while he fought the pull, barking and scratching at the ground. She tried to even out her voice. Her eyes went to the gun.

"Hey. Hey. It's all good. He's not going to hurt you. Are you okay? Are you lost? What do you want? Derby—shush!" *Oh my God. Oh my God. Please don't do anything. Why are you in a mask? Jesus. Jesus.*

The boy stood his ground without responding, the gun dangling by his side, bag at his feet. His head lilted to his right shoulder. Suzanne continued wrapping the tether around her hand, slowly dragging Derby toward her, her eyes locked on the gun. *Come on, Derb! Fuck. Fuck. Fuck! Stop fighting.*

"Do you want food? We've got food. Yeah?" Suzanne asked, her voice rising.

The boy's head rose. He took two small steps forward. Derby lunged, barking louder than before. The boy's arm jolted up, pointing the gun into the site.

"No! No! Derby! Stop! It's okay. *Jesus.* It's okay! Please don't shoot!" Panic seized Suzanne and her arm waved back and forth on its own. *Fuck. No. No. No.*

The boy shuffled backwards, grabbing his bag at the same time. He sidestepped toward the bridge, gun pointing down into the site. As he passed the scrub brush beside the site entry, he ran.

Suzanne watched him race across the bridge, arms pumping with flashes of the gun's metal going up and down. He made a hard, skidding stop on the other side of the bridge and spun around to look back toward the site. He jammed the gun into the bag before taking off again, flying by the entry to High Bridge #1, then veering left, going up the road that forked off just after the site's parking area.

Derby was calming. He stopped pulling and let out a few final woofs. Suzanne crumpled, landing in a squat position, a tremble rolling through her. *Jesus. Did that just happen?* She reached out to Derby, pulling him to her and scratching under his ears.

"Oh, my good boy. Good boy. Good boy." She said, burying into his forehead.

Her body still spasming with the aftershocks of primal fear, Suzanne looked past the picnic table at the low, crackling fire and the darkening shadows creeping into the site. Visions of the masked boy lurking in the shadows raced through her head.

Her fear, her humanity, annoyed her, making her feel like a scared little girl instead of the confident woman she thought she was. *I'm fucking alone out here. Get out. We're going.* She shot a glance down to Derby. *Too much. Not worth it. I'm sorry, Connie.* Anger trickled through her. *Move . . . your . . . ass, Suzanne!*

Chapter 29

On the radio

At 6:05 p.m., Chris turned onto the KI Road for the second time that day. His gut tightened as he progressed past the mile markers, getting closer to the check-in cabin. Even his radio blasting out Steppenwolf's "Magic Carpet Ride" did nothing to alleviate his angst. He glanced at his phone in its holder, hit the 'Home' button, and smiled back at his two boys looking out from the screen. *Least you're safe and sound.*

The phone buzzed, surprising Chris, its picture switching to the brick exterior of the Piscataquis County Jail, snapping him back to the moment at hand. "Dispatch" accompanied the image on the screen.

Chris pushed the radio off. "Chris here."

"Sheriff, it's Marie. We have a new devel—" Marie's voice cut off mid-sentence.

"Marie. Marie. You there?"

"I'm here, Sheriff. You said no radio, so I'm calling to let—know—left scene."

"Marie, you have to repeat that. Reception is in and out. Say that again." Chris gripped his steering wheel tighter, his frustration growing.

Come on. Come on. He slowed to a crawl just as he neared the lonely house at mile marker five. *How in hell do people live out here with no reception?* Looking at his phone, he scowled at the reception bars waffling between one and none. He parked.

"Marie. If you can hear me, repeat what you said." Silence followed, but the call was not dropped. "Or just text me, like I'd asked you to. Try that."

Finally, Marie's voice again. "... opment—jew—nile—maybe—ickel—unknown—foot." The phone chirped out three beeps, and the picture of the jail vanished.

"Shit!" Chris rapped the steering wheel and pressed the accelerator, Marie's half words jangling around his head. *Jew. Jew. Jew. Nile. Nile. Foot . . . Foot. Come on Chris. Think. Jew. Jew. Juvenile! Ha. Juvenile.* Chris turned up the radio, pressing harder on the accelerator and spewing a huge cloud of dust in his wake.

Well, you don't know what we can find.
Why don't you come with me little girl
on a magic carpet . . ."

The song dropped away as Chris dialed the volume down and rolled into a spot across from the check-in cabin. Two of his deputies were leaning on the rear of one of their cruisers. Margaret and Jana, both with arms crossed, standing close to them. All of them watching him pull in. Chris shut down the Bronco and grabbed his hat. *Show time. Game face on.*

Positioning his hat on his head and pacing his walk to exude confidence to the group, he addressed each person by name as he approached, locking eyes on each callout. "Deputy Clark. Donnie. Thanks for coming. Margaret. Jana. Appreciate you two waiting for me."

"Got a burned-up outhouse and a dead woman in my woods. Where else would I go, Sheriff?" Margaret asked.

"I hear you. So, let's start with you giving me your account of what happened," Chris said, opening his pocket notepad, then glancing at his deputies, telling them to do the same without saying a word.

"Well, I was just wrapping up the logbook for the day when—" Margaret started saying.

"Actually, I got the call first," Jana interrupted.

Margaret pursed her mouth shut, shooting Jana a side-look.

"Okay. Tell me about the call, Jana. Who called?"

"On my radio. A guy named Matt. A-T hiker, all the way from Georgia. Him and his girlfriend found the fire . . . and the woman . . . and the kid."

"The kid. Okay. Go on," Chris said.

"He told me about the fire. The outhouse burned to the ground. And the truck. With the kid inside. And he told me a woman was dead, stuck under the rubble of the outhouse. I don't even know how that could . . . unless she was . . ."

Stop detectiving! "Jana, let's just stick with what you know for sure."

"There was this one pretty weird thing too, if it can get any weirder."

"What?" Chris pressed her. *Come on. Spill it already.* He noticed his deputies fidgeting, both crossing their arms and adjusting their perches on the cruiser. *Okay. This should be good.*

"Well, he told me the kid had gotten out of the Forerunner when he went to check on his girlfriend. Next thing he knew, the kid was booking it up the road, carrying a big bag. And, here's the weird part. He said the kid had a leather mask on. Said it covered his whole head. His girlfriend ran right into him. But the kid just took off running again."

Jesus. "Has this masked kid been seen since?" Chris looked at his deputies. *Come on, guys.* The two deputies shifted their stances. "Donnie, what's the word?"

"Uh, we were waiting for you to arrive before taking any action, as instructed, Sheriff," Donnie responded.

Numbskulls. He sighed. "Okay. Okay. You're right."

Chris shifted his eyes to Margaret, who was still pursing her lips, eyes locked on the ground. *Pissed? Confused? Just worried?* "Do I even need to ask, Margaret? The Forerunner?"

Margaret snapped to attention. "Yes. Matt gave Jana the plate number." She motioned to the check-in cabin. "Wrote it down inside. It was that woman who came in this morning. The one gone swimming. Alone. Remember?*"*

Dammit all. I knew it. He flashed back to that run-in with the woman at the Bear Market. *Something was off. Shit.* "Yeah, I remember." He breathed in, steadying himself before speaking again. "Jana. Margaret. You can go now. I'll swing back before I leave the area."

He waited until the two women had made it back into the check-in cabin before addressing his deputies. "You guys it? Anyone else coming?"

"Just us. Didn't hear from or see anyone else on our way," Donnie said.

Clark nodded. "Yup. But Brownville fire and rescue already showed. Probably down there already."

"Okay. We're losing daylight, quickly. We've got a dead woman in a torched outhouse. We also have a kid running around the gulf in a leather mask. *The kid. In her car? Did he..?* Here's the plan. You two will scour the area in your cars as best you can. Get maps from Margaret and make yourselves a coverage plan ASAP. Split up and check out the roads. See if there's any sign of that kid. No blues. No sirens. Try to be low-key. Campers are scattered all over here. *Three cop cars. Like we're having a blue light special in the gulf. Yeah, that's low-key.* I'm heading to the Haybrook sites. Meet right back here in two hours. Let's roll. Two hours."

Jana blasted out the door of the check-in cabin, thrusting her radio in front of her as she jogged over to the three men.

"Sheriff. Sheriff. Take this!" She pushed the radio into his hand. "It's the fire guys, down at Haybrook." She stepped back, eyes wide, watching Chris.

He put the radio up to his mouth and pushed the talk button. "Chris here. Over."

The radio crackled. "Sheriff. It's Jon, Brownville fire. We got a situation down here at Haybrook. What's your twenty? Over."

What now? His deputies and Jana were staring at him. Waiting. Margaret had appeared on the porch of the check-in cabin. *Shit.* Chris pushed the talk button. "I'm at the KI check-in cabin. Just about to head down to you guys. What you got? Over."

"Sheriff. Still alive. Woman in the outhouse. Burned up to hell, but she's breathing. Barely. Keeps trying to say something. Need you down here. Trying to stabilize her. Can't get her up that road. Air lift, maybe. Not sure she'll hang on that long. Over."

Chapter 30

Farewell and adieu

Chris watched his deputies, Jana, and Margaret all tense up. He processed the message in seconds. *Jesus. Gotta move.*

"On my way now. Try to keep her stable. Over."

"Ten-Four."

"Deputies! Get those maps and get moving. Two hours. Back here." Chris's orders kickstarted his guys, popping them off the back of the cruiser.

He handed the radio back to Jana. "Need you to stay with Margaret tonight."

Jana shook her head side to side in a casual no-no-I'm-fine way. *Stupid. Cut the shit, Jana.*

"No? I mean it, dammit. I think our boy in the mask might be a very troubled young man. I think you believe this, too. We don't know anything about him. So, you're staying put with Margaret."

A tear rolled down her cheek as she crossed her arms and walked slowly back to the check-in cabin. She turned halfway there, looked back at him, wiping her eyes with the cuff of her jacket.

"Be careful, Sheriff."

He didn't respond, too unsure of what would even come out of his mouth. His mind raced as he hustled to his Bronco and tore out of the lot. He pounded the steering wheel as he raced through the gate, crossing over the bridge.

"Shit! Shit! Shit!" *My town. Fucking kid. Who is he? Shit!* Tearing down the KI road, he lost track of his speed. The Bronco ate the road up, like it devoured the gravel. A blaze of fire to the left caught his eye and he slowed, realizing he had just told his deputies to be mindful of campers. *Urgency, not lunacy.* He braked, cruising by Pleasant River # 5 at a modified clip, looking at the young man and woman huddling by their campfire. They glanced up, but he didn't see them register any alarm. *Just a routine sweep, folks.* He kept going. *If they'd seen that kid, they would have flagged me.*

"Damn it!"

Jamming on the brakes a little too hard, he skidded to a stop a hundred yards past the site. *Easy. Easy.* He shoved the shifter into reverse and rolled the Bronco backwards to the site entry, slowing to a stop, simultaneously rolling down his window.

"Hey there," he called out.

"Evening, Sheriff," the man called out. "Everything okay?"

"Got a kid wandering around. Not sure if he's lost or . . . ? Seen a young boy by himself? Probably a little skittish."

The couple shook their heads "Nope. No lost kids down here."

After telling them to contact the check-in cabin with any information, Chris pulled away and scanned the upcoming sites for any signs of life.

Chris whipped the Bronco onto the road leading uphill. Bouncing across some potholes, he glanced down at the speedometer, its needle just past the forty. He didn't even register the headlights coming at him until the last second. A horn blared, and the lights whipped to the right. "Shit!"

Chris cranked his wheel to the right, his foot slamming his brake pedal. The two vehicles missed by mere inches and skidded to stops, sending clouds of dust swirling around them.

Jesus! He blew out a tremendous breath, his body shaking. He looked out his rearview mirror. Like him, the Range Rover was sideways a bit down the road, its ass-end half on the KI Road.

A young woman jumped out of the car and looked herself and her car over. She jumped up and down, her hands balled into fists at her sides. Chris got out of his Bronco and hustled to her, relief washing over him that she was in one piece.

He recognized her as one of the campers he'd spoken to earlier. "Oh, hey, hey. I'm so . . ."

The woman cut him off in a nanosecond. "Jesus Christ, Sheriff! Are you insane? What are you doing?" She marched toward him, fists still clenched.

Chris raised his hands. "Whoa. Hey, calm down." *Jesus. She gonna hit me?* "Like I said, I'm sorry. You okay? Suzanne, right?"

213

"Fuck!" Suzanne said under her breath, looking down at the ground.

Past her, through the open door, Chris saw Derby's blonde head poke around the front seat. Suzanne spun at his whimper-growl. She turned back to him with a sigh, raising her hands to her head, raking her fingers through her hair. Chris caught a hint of alcohol in the air between them.

"Yes. I'm fine. I am just trying to get the hell out of here. There is a goddamn kid, in a fucking leather mask, running around with a fucking gun out here. Did you know that? I mean, Jesus! What is this place?"

"A gun?" he asked, his voice ratcheting up an octave. *No one else mentioned a gun. Kid with a gun. Burned up lady. Come on!*

Suzanne released her grip on her head. She kicked small rocks around. "I can't deal with this shit. I'm going back to Boston." She looked up at Chris, sucking in a deep breath. "Somewhere past my site, some weird woman is dead. I know it. And a kid in a friggin' S&M mask is running around out here with a gun. There is something really, really off out here."

"You're right. Something is off." He paused. "But you're here too." He let the words hang for a second before continuing. "And I might say you are out of the norm up here too." He scanned her for anything that would tell him she was more than a scared young woman. She narrowed her eyes at him, seeming to steel herself back into composure. Any other time, he would have called her out for being a bit beyond buzzed and driving around. But not now.

"I'm going. The woman at the gate has my info. You can get a hold of me if you need to."

Derby whined and Suzanne glanced over at him. Chris's head was spinning. *Too much right now. She's not part of this. Nope. Figuring her out will have to wait.*

"I understand," he said.

Suzanne slapped her hands to her thighs and threw her head back, then returned to her vehicle and started the engine. She paused by him on her way out. Chris's training pushed him to tell her to stay put, or at least stay at the check-in cabin.

"I left a bunch of my stuff in the site. And I'm sorry for that. You or the lady at the front can fine me whatever you need to, but I have to go now."

As Suzanne rolled away, Chris caught sight of his reflection in the dark glass of her window. He noted a very similar, pained expression on his face. Same one he saw on Suzanne.

Crazy? Maybe. Hell. I wouldn't stay here now. Chris got back in his Bronco, and proceeded back up the hill, keeping his speed in check and his eyes open for any signs of the kid.

The uphill drive leveled off and he slowed to a stop at the mouth of the High Bridge #1 site. He shined his flashlight out the window. *Nothing. Should get out. Damn it. Got to get down to Haybrook to that woman. Later.*

Chapter 31

Time keeps slipping

The road to Haybrook was worse than he remembered. Potholes, ruts, and branches abused his Bronco, forcing him to adopt a slow and steady speed. *Jesus. All I need is to wind up in the trees.*

Nearly ten minutes after rounding the corner, he arrived at the parking area for the Haybrook sites. He pulled in next to the fire truck. *Bet their ride down here was fun.* Getting out of the Bronco, he threw on his hat and grabbed his notepad, ready to scribble whatever he could get from the half-dead woman at the outhouse. He noted the familiar black Forerunner squashed into the brush. *Shit. Could have guessed. Here's where you landed. Let it start gelling, Chris. Let it gel.*

He called out to the crew on site. "Sheriff Chan here. Heading over."

An urgent voice yelled back from beyond the trees, somewhere in the interior of the clearing of campsites.

"Hurry up, Sheriff! We're losing her."

Chris ran. He came to the site opening, his flashlight helping him see ahead of him. A man and a woman were standing, holding each other, while three men—two standing, one squatting—gathered near pieces and piles of still-smoldering black wood, presumably the outhouse.

As Chris got closer, he saw that the squatting man held a small oxygen tank over the victim's face. *Oh God. Jesus. Jesus. Is that her?* The woman's hair was gone. Her facial skin, what was left of it, was black, and her lips were gone, exposing her teeth like a gruesome, living skeleton. Her left eye was missing, seemingly melted into her. Deep red crevices exposed wet muscle and tissue underneath her charred skin. The rest of her body had been covered with a light blue sheet, peppered with splotches of her blood. Chris's hand went to his mouth. His stomach flipped. His mouth went dry as he forced himself to hold back from retching.

"Jesus Christ."

The woman's remaining eye seemed to squint ever so slightly. Chris took a deep breath and dropped down to one knee, readying his notebook and pen in his shaking hands.

The woman let out a long, wet, raspy breath. "Herriff . . . Herriff."

"Ma'am. I'm so sorry." Chris reached toward her, stopping short of touching her. *Jesus! Jesus.* A futile attempt to comfort her. He pulled his hand to his chest.

"Who did this to you? Just give me a name. Did you do this to yourself? Was it the boy?"

The woman's breathing was heaving, gurgling. Her head moved, ever so slightly, side to side. *No. No. She's saying no.* Rough sounds, not quite words came out in whispered fits. Chris strained to make sense. He scribbled the noises down as she wheezed them out.

"ohhh... ih... huzzz... kilt... eh – knee... ehny ... annie."

"Annie. Annie. Is that who did this? Are you sure? A woman named Annie."

The woman delivered one more garbled statement. "Duhhhh." Wet bubbles spewed out her last word. "Annnnie."

Her eye rolled, locking on the dark canopy of branches high above the group. Chris studied her face for a few more moments, horrified and mesmerized at the same time.

The fireman pulled the sheet over her face. All three men looked at Chris waiting. He rose, steadying himself before addressing them.

"Thank you, guys. I know this is hard and you did all you could." He glanced at the couple, still holding each other. "Wait here for a minute. I'm going to go talk to them."

Chris approached the couple, and they stared blankly at him. The woman's face was tear-streaked. He felt for them, but time was wasting and he needed information. *Got to plow through. Come on, Chan.* He blocked his emotions as best he could and asked them to recount their timeline of events.

As they told their story, he jotted down notes. The part about the kid yielded no new useful information. Satisfied he had everything he could get at this moment, he thanked them, getting their contact information and asking for their discretion. He looked over at the three Brownville firemen.

"These guys are going to give you a ride into town. We'll get you a room for the night. Go ahead and wait by their truck. We'll get you going shortly."

He watched as they made their way out of the site toward the fire truck. The man never let his arm leave his girl's shoulders. Trish's face flashed in his mind for a split second.

Back at the body, the firemen were now deep into discussing possible scenarios, pointing around the site as they spoke in hushed but animated voices. Chris's approach silenced them. He had one of the men remove the sheet covering the remains.

Almost retching again at the sight of her fully charred and twisted shape, Chris bent down, partly to stop the woozy feeling in his belly and partly to get a closer look. Scraps of skin and cloth were fused around various parts of her. *Jesus. Nothing about this mess is going to help me figure this out.*

"Guys, I need your help. I'm losing daylight, and I need this area searched for any evidence. Anything that might help connect the dots. We have a crime scene and we don't have time to call in the CSI team, so I need you to put on your rubber gloves, split up, and scour the site. Carefully. Look for scraps of paper. Clothes. Lighter. Matches. Grab anything that looks recent." The men jumped into action, digging into their gear for their gloves. "Whatever you find, again, grab it carefully. Keep things as intact as you can."

The men snapped on their gloves and moved out in three directions, heads down as they canvassed the site. Chris tiptoed around the remains and debris, staying just outside the burn perimeter.

Using his phone, he snapped pictures as best he could, trying to get as many angles and shots of the scene as he could. All the while he kept picturing the woman's dead eye following him with every click and flash. *Nothing. Nothing. Nothing. Friggin' fried to hell. Unreal. Why? Why do this to someone? Payback? Jilted lover? Money? Jealousy? What? What?* His search revealed nothing to help him, just blackened ash and wood. He looked down at the woman's body once more. *Shit. Got to get the coroners moving.*

Chris looked up when one of the men called out near the brook's edge on the far side of the site.

"Hey, Sheriff! Got something."

The fireman came running across the site with something dangling from his outstretched hand. A shiny flip-flop. Under the canopy of trees, darkness was creeping in fast. Chris shone his flashlight onto the flip-flop, looking it over. On the sole, a torn and worn piece of tape stretched across a crack. It was old and scuffed up, but it was rainbow. *Shit! Looks like someone graduated from wrapping up ducks.*

"Duct tape. Of course," Chris said under his breath.

The fireman looked at him. "What do you mean, of course?"

"No need to get into it now. Let's get this bagged."

Chris walked away, signaling the fireman to follow him. They went to the Bronco where Chris opened a fresh evidence bag, and the fireman dropped the flip-flop in.

Chris was about to shut the tailgate but caught himself and decided to leave the Bronco open, anticipating more items would soon be joining the lonely flip-flop.

"See if you can find anything else. I'm going to check out the Forerunner."

The fireman gave a gloved thumbs up before jogging back into the site. Chris made his way to the Forerunner, searching the surrounding ground every step of the way, his flashlight's beam bouncing across gravel and sporadic weeds. *Nothing. Nothing. No scraps.*

At the vehicle, he noted the series of smallish shuffling footprints. He did his best not to disturb them as he leaned inside. *Gotta get prints ASAP.* The waning light from the sinking sun made it tough to see in the shadows. Interior details receded in the darkening corners as he scanned the seat and floor surfaces. *Dirty. Reeks of butts. Nothing on the seats. No real signs of the kid. Dammit.* Careful to not mess up the footprints, he hopped over them and slide-landed onto the driver's seat. *Friggin' graceful.*

Chris opened the glove compartment, pulling out a stack of rough, worn papers. A classic Stones song began creeping in, just under his racing thoughts. *Time. Time. Time. Not on my side . . .* He flipped through the papers as fast as he could, scanning each for something, anything.

The registration triggered his memory of his encounter with the woman at the Bear Market. *There you are. Carole Rose, forty-one, Alexander Drive, Hampton, New Hampshire.* He flashed back to earlier in his long day. *That's her. All skittish, checking in solo this morning.*

The rest of the paper stack revealed nothing more. Old gas receipts. An old, tattered Boston parking ticket. Fast food napkins, some of them obviously used and stuck together. Disgust and annoyance mixed in his head as his reworked Stones lyrics grew louder. *Time. Time. Time. Not on my side . . . no it's not . . .*

221

He opened the center armrest next. Empty, crumpled cigarette packages filled it. After digging them out, one by one, and placing them in a pile on the passenger seat, he looked hard into the dark void of the cubby. He fished around. Bumps of old chewing gum (he hoped) peppered the bottom. *Gross! Jesus. Come on. Come on. Give me something.* His hand landed on a flat, rigid something, wedged against the side of the cubby. He lifted out a plastic card, swinging his body to the open door so he could get his flashlight on it.

Staring back at him from the driver's license was the shiny fake-smiling face of Carole Rose. The only problem, this license declared her name as Danielle Bernier, fifty-three, Garland Road, North Hampton, New Hampshire. He took in this new info. *Shit. Who are you lady? Wait. You were at the store. The house. The check-in cabin.* Chris tried to focus in on what the deceased woman had been trying to say. *Duh-Annie. Duh- Annie. Dannie? Dannie. Shit. Danielle. Who in hell are you? One of you is fake . . . And one of you is dead. Or . . . you're both very real. And that kid is wrapped up in this. Somehow.* That tune roared back into his head. *Time. Time. Time . . . Is not on my side.*

Chapter 32

Hit the road

Keep going. Keep going. Muscles in Hagas's legs screamed at him as his breaths heaved in and out under the mask. Between his wipeout leaving Haybrook, running full speed up the road after his encounter with that lady in the site, the mask jostling around his head, and the clunky bag swinging every which way, he was losing physical energy.

But he did not give in, focusing on the peak of the third rising hill of trees, the final one before he would be on the all-downhill section of his trail. He kept his eyes trained on the dark, pine needle-covered trail, feeling the rhythm of his feet, willing them to keep up a steady pace. *Almost there. Get to the log. Get to the log. Little further. Keep going feet. One. Two. One. Two. One. Two. One . . .*

Finally, the ground leveled out and he looked up to see a familiar shape materializing ahead. His 'thinking' log waited for him, just as it had over the weeks and months he'd been forging his private trail into the gulf. *Made it.* Slumping onto the log, Hagas wiggled the damp leather off his head, sucking in the crisp air.

Twisting and turning his body, he looked all around to be sure no one was following him. Then sitting still for a moment, he listened to the darkening woods. *Nothing. No one but me.* The bag slid off the log, thudding onto the ground. "Shoot!" *Just how it went off before. Careful.*

He reached in the bag and found the cold steel of the gun. He lifted it out and squinted as he examined its shape. *How many bullets you got left?* He positioned it in his hand the way he'd seen guns held in his movies, squeezing the handle to get a feel for its weight. *You gotta have one more in there. One more for Brian. At least. One for him. Had to be one for Ma, too. Letter said. Maybe . . . one for me?*

Standing tall, Hagas raised the gun to chest height, pointing it at the thick, black trunk of a pine a few feet away. His hand quivered and he brought his other one up to steady his grip. *I can get you. Just gotta get close.*

With the sun almost gone, and his muscles calming, the heat that had been pumping through him faded away and cold seeped in. His sweat-soaked hair wasn't helping either. A shiver ran through him. He looked at his watch. *7:24. Late. Late. They'll be home soon.*

Scanning the sky through the trees, he saw the first glimmers of stars. Down his trail, the glowing edge of sunlight was barely hanging on to the treetops below. *Okay. Okay. I can do this. I can do this. Get inside. Hide. Wait. Their bedroom? Bathroom maybe? Behind the shower. Figure it out when I get there.*

224

He placed the gun on the log and tapped inside the bag again. *Keys. Keys. Keys.* His tapping became more urgent, turning into frantic shuffling all around the bottom. *Come on. Where are you?* He upended the bag, spilling its contents onto the ground, then rifling through everything. There was no metal jingle. "Oh, shoot." His mind flashed to High Bridge #2, remembering the feeling of the bag slipping out of his hand when the dog barked. The gun dropping. The huge bang it made. His panic. Running away as fast as he could. *Gone. Must've fallen out. Now what? How'm I gonna get in?*

He shoved everything back into the bag. *The window! Slip back in. Shoot! Gigi! Put the lock back. Be stuck in there. Think. Think. Outside? Maybe hide by a tree. Wait. What if he's there right now? What if Ma's there? No. Too early. No one's there. Can't be. Sneak in after he gets home. Screen door.* The gun was the last item he put in the bag, and he laid it on top, nestling it into a towel. Looking and listening to the silent woods around him, he was almost sure no one was around. Almost. Behind him, a whip-poor-will broke the silence, calling out from the trees again and again. Whip-poor-will . . . whip-poor-will . . . whip-poor-will. *Death is near.*

Grimacing, he snatched the mask from the log and sucked in one more mighty breath of air before pulling it over his head and tightening the ties. *No chances. Death won't find me.* Focusing his mind on the next phase of his mission, Hagas paused, turning in the direction of the bird.

"Shut up! Shut up! Stupid bird!"

The whip-poor-will obeyed. The woods fell still again. *Hmphhh. Stupid bird. Shoot you next time.*

225

Bag in hand, Hagas started back on his quest in earnest. His legs were feeling closer to normal from the short rest. Blood pumped through him, again fighting the chill off. Hastening his pace to a jog, letting gravity pull him downward, he whipped through scenarios in his head. *Brian comes home. Goes inside. I run from the big oak tree. Blast in. Surprise him! Pop him in the head. No . . . He'd see me coming. Bathroom! Always hits the bathroom. First thing. Ma might get home first. See me. Get mad. Might not believe me . . . Has to believe . . . She's gotta remember. She's gotta see what Gigi did – what – what her and Brian – what they were going to do. Angel. Angel. She's gotta believe me.*

Scenarios and outcomes continued as Hagas flew down his trail, getting closer and closer to home, the prison he'd finally escaped just hours before. The ground began to level out as he neared the edge of the trees. He stopped just shy of breaking out into the big open area between the trees and the road.

Crouching and peering from the edge of the trees, he watched the last blurry line of sunlight fade into the blackness above. Drifting his gaze lower, down past the silhouettes of trees, he landed on the house. His house. Harsh yellow light spilled out the kitchen window. To the right, the spotlight above the side steps was attracting bugs, dancing in and out of its beam. Farther right, hulking in the driveway, was Brian's big silver truck.

"Shoot. Damn. Damn."

Weren't supposed to be here, yet. Ma's car's not there, though. Now what? Think. Think. No hiding under the porch. Hagas scanned the front of the house, locking on the darkened far left corner. *Maybe. Yeah. Yeah. Sneak around.*

226

Maybe he's in the bathroom already. Check the window in back. Sneak in the screen door if he is. Then . . . boom! Surprise him while . . .

Hagas's head snapped to the right as a shadow appeared in the frame of the kitchen window. A large figure, in profile, raised his arm, tilting a glass to his face, then spinning, placing both hands down on the ledge of the window, his full form blacking out the kitchen's yellow light. *Brian. Definitely.*

Hagas tensed, crouching deeper, shrinking into himself. *What's he doing? Is he looking for me? Did he go downstairs? Too soon. Always comes down late. He can't know. Maybe Gigi? Gotta be. Cheaters! Wondering where his gun went off.* Brian stood and moved out of the window frame. Hagas stood and felt for the gun through the bag. *It's coming, Brian. It's coming.*

He crept across the open span of grass, shrubs, and weeds, leaving the safety of the trees behind him. He kept his eyes locked on the kitchen window and moved faster, feeling more exposed with every step. *Halfway there. Don't look out. Don't look out.* Walking became jogging. *Just gotta get to the trees on the other side.* Brian appeared in the window. Hagas halted, dropping to the ground, pressing his body into the hard earth, not daring to move, his breathing short and fast. *Did he see me? No. Please. No. No. No.*

A full two minutes passed before Hagas gathered his nerves enough to raise his head, inch by inch. *Be here by now if he saw me.* The kitchen window was empty again. Rising a little more, Hagas scanned the driveway and road. Brian was not coming for him. *Didn't see me. Phew.*

227

Pushing himself to his knees, he pulled the bag to him, feeling inside to make sure the gun was still there. The hard lump was right on top, just where it should be, resting in the towel. Adrenaline coursed through him. *Gotta run for it. Now or never. Get to the trees! Go!*

Looking through the mask's eyeholes, he locked on his target and ran at full speed, his feet sure beneath him as the distance to the trees shortened. Soft earth turned to the gravel of the road. *Go! Got this.*

There was no pain at first. Just surprise as he briefly flew up. Then crashing down on metal and glass, his head bouncing, and finally landing on the gravel road with a flurry of lights washing over him, cutting through the fresh cloud of dust.

Hagas lay still, focusing on the gun a few feet away, its metal skin glowing red.

"Kid! Kid!"

That's not Brian.

"Jesus! Oh Shit! Shit! Kid!"

Ma? Feet appeared in front of him.

"Kid! Oh my God. Fuck! Kid!" The voice echoed in Hagas's head. He followed it, gliding with it into the darkness of his mind.

Hagas opened his eyes as he came to from the feeling of his body scraping across the gravel. Searing pain shot through his middle, like knives stabbing his ribs. He felt detached though, like it was all a weird dream.

"Help me get him to the house. Ribs are broken." A man's voice rose above the crunching and dragging.

Brian. Brian. Brian! Hagas lifted his throbbing head to see the people pulling him. Brian's gnarled face, almost smiling, looked down at him. Hagas realized Brian's hands were under his arms, gripping tightly. Beside him, the woman from High Bridge #2 was rocking and circling. *Oh, I guess I didn't shoot you. That's good.*

"Fuck! Shit! This is insane. We need to call the police. You shouldn't move him. We don't know how bad he's hurt! Who is he? Is he yours? Fuck! Fuck! Fuck!" The woman's panicked, high-pitched voice rapidly fired out the words.

The dragging stopped, and Hagas felt his body slump into softer sand and grass. He couldn't make his muscles work.

"What we needed to do was to get him the fuck off this road. You want a fuckin' logger to run him over?" Brian, smiling, looked down at Hagas again and whispered, "Shouldn'ta been out here, boy."

"Shit. Okay. Okay," the woman said while spinning around in the road, her arms raised high, stabbing at the phone in her hand. "Fuck!" She jammed the phone into her pocket.

"We got a radio inside. Just help me get him the fuck up there. Can't leave him here."

"Oh, fuck it," the woman said, stomping over to Brian and Hagas. "How are we going to do this?"

"Get in between his legs and grab onto his thighs. Legs might be all jacked up, so watch where you hold on to him."

Hagas tensed as Brian's hands latched onto him again, digging into his pits.

"Know that I'm against this," the woman said, bending in front of him, her hands searching his legs. "Fuck. Here we go."

Her grip was sudden and hard. White-hot pain shot up his left leg. He screamed. Images of hot cigarettes coming at him, leather cutting into his skin, and Angel's head hitting the spigot flashed and popped in his mind. He slid away again, giving in to the sensation of floating as they lifted him.

"Just a little more. Get him in!" Brian shouted, jolting Hagas back into reality.

He opened his eyes and the bright kitchen light flooded his vision. Brian was a blurry shadow above him. The woman was on the porch, maneuvering his legs through the door. *What are you doing? Don't bring me in here. Please. Please.* Sharp waves of pain spiked through his leg and ribs. His head, lolling on his chest, felt wet and heavy in the still air. He smelled stale cigarettes. *My mask. Gone. She sees me.*

"I'm trying! Jesus. Fuck. You're the one who said be careful. Just . . . about . . . there."

Hagas lay on the cold kitchen floor, pain throbbing through his whole body. He stared up at the overhead light, trying to think, trying to make sense. *The gun. Brian. My plan. My plan. Ma. Money. Where's the gun?*

"Okay. He's in. Where's the radio? We have to call," the woman said.

"Wait here. Keep an eye on him. I gotta go get it. And what's your name, little lady?" Brian asked, walking away.

"What? Oh. My name is Suzanne. I'm Suzanne. Please, just hurry."

Hagas listened to Brian's footsteps going down the hall toward the bedroom. He looked up at the woman—*Suzanne*—staring down at him, her arms crossed tight and her face all crinkled. *You gotta get out of here.* He opened his mouth, straining to make it move.

Suzanne bent closer to him. *You gotta get out of here.* His mind raced, searching for the right word. *Get help.* Suzanne lowered, her eyes searching his face.

"What? What is it? Tell me. Can you talk?"

Pushing his throat muscles with all his might, his voice bubbled up, hoarse and garbled. "Ruh-uh-uhnnn . . ."

Thwang! The dull metallic sound hung in the air as Suzanne lurched forward, her eyes bulging momentarily before crumpling to the floor. She landed just beside him. Her open, unseeing eyes looked into his as a trickle of thick red blood made its way down the side of her face. He looked away in slow motion, confused, turning his gaze to see what happened. Standing in the doorway, Ma was holding a shovel, raising it above her head. She glared down at Hagas.

"Well. Well. Well. What the fuck do we have here?" Ma asked.

The last image Hagas saw, the one he feared most, was Ma's lips curling up at the sides, ever so slightly. The sound of Brian plodding back into the kitchen dulled as he slipped into unconsciousness again.

Chapter 33

Pack your bags

In the darkest corner of the basement, the suitcase shifted slightly. Hagas's breath caught in his throat. *Did it? . . . Just move?* He stared at it, focusing hard to make out its shape against the dark walls. The suitcase remained still. *Couldn't've. She's gone.*

A corner of the suitcase lurched forward, scraping across the rough, concrete floor. Hagas's breath came short and fast. *It moved! It moved! No. No. No.* The suitcase swung its other side forward, scraping against the floor. Hagas's eyes widened. *Run!* But he couldn't move; he was frozen, muscles locked.

The suitcase lurched forward again. He could see some of its details now—the zippers, the broken handle, the leather straps. It lurched again. *Oh, God.* And again. *No. No. No. No.* Getting closer.

232

He could see the dark, wet trail it was leaving behind. Scraping wildly, the suitcase wriggled to within three feet of his mattress and stopped. *No. No. No. Can't be.* The zippers moved in opposite directions from the top of the suitcase, inch by inch, rounding the top corners, going down the sides. Finally, the zippers stopped at the suitcase's stained, wet bottom corners, and his staccato breathing was the only sound.

A tiny, wet hand burst from between the zipper's open teeth and grabbed the leather strap wrapped across the top, just to the right of the handle. With jerking tugs, the hand moved the strap around the top right corner. The suitcase yawned open. Hagas sucked in his breath, waiting.

"Hagasssss." Blonde hair, matted and streaked with dark splotches, rose from the open corner.

Angel! Angel. Can't be. You're gone. "Angel?" he whispered through his trembling lips.

Angel's head, severely angled down, kept rising, giving way to uneven, twisted shoulders. Her little body kept rising, her pale, arms wrapped around her dirty torso, clutching something to her chest. *What is that? What do you have?*

"Angel." Hagas gulped. "Angel. It's me."

The little girl raised her head, revealing rotting, black holes where her bright, blue eyes used to be.

"You got her, Hagas. You got Gigi." Angel smiled at Hagas.

"Yes. I got her. She's gone. Angel, I'm so sorr-"

"You said you would protect me. And, she got me," Angel gurgled.

She twitched, and then popped her right shoulder into place. Squeezed her arms tighter around her middle. His stomach churned.

"I'm sorry. I'm sorry." Hagas began sobbing. "I couldn't – I couldn't get to you fast enough. She was blocking me. I'm sorry."

"I know, silly." Angel fidgeted, twisting her little body side to side. "We were having so much fun. Remember? Splashing and laughing. Playing."

Blood flowed down the sides of her head, snaking around her neck and chest, pooling at the top of her folded arms. She began twisting faster.

"Remember, Hagas? Splashing! Laughing! Splashing! Laughing! Splashing! Laughing! Splashing! Laughing! Splashing! Laughing! Splashing!"

In a flash, Angel heaved the dead, duct-taped duck at Hagas. *No. No. No. No.* It hit him square in his belly and sent waves of pain through every part of him.

Hagas popped his eyes open and saw Ma peering down at him. She was tearing a piece of rainbow duct tape with her teeth.

"Aww, what's the matter, sweetie? Too tight?" She looked into his eyes. "Too fucking bad!"

Laying on his side, Hagas sensed the rows of tape wrapping around his middle, pressing on his tender ribs and securing him to the mattress. His hands were behind him, bound together by tape. *Please. Please, don't.* Ma shifted her position, scooching herself down by his legs. She grabbed his feet and yanked his legs up.

"Owww! Ow. Ow." He winced in pain. "Ma. Please. Pleeeease."

234

She didn't respond, and he felt her wind the tape around his ankles before dropping his feet back down to the mattress. Hagas grit his teeth, stopping himself from crying out. Ma stood, backing a few feet away from the mattress and looking past Hagas.

"There you go, babe. He's all yours," she said.

Hagas couldn't see him, but felt Brian behind him, sinking onto the mattress just behind his head. The smell of cigarette smoke wafted to his nose. Brian's hot breath hit just above his ear, sending a stream of smoke curling across his face. *Oh no. No. No. What are you gonna do to me?*

"Where'd she go, boy?" Brian growled.

"Who? I . . . I . . . I don't know. Who do you mean?" Hagas answered, his voice shaking.

"You know who. Gigi." Brian blew another cloud of smoke over Hagas's head, then sat behind Hagas's back. "Where'd she go? She take you outta here?"

"I. I . . . I don't remember. She . . . She . . ."

Burning pain flared as Brian's cigarette connected with the tip of Hagas's left pinky finger.

"Aaagghhhh–ahhh! Stop! Stop! Please!"

Brian held the cigarette in place for a few seconds before taking it away. Then his hot, smoky breath was back in Hagas's ear.

"You know that game twenty questions? Well, you got ten fingers, ten toes. How many questions you think it'll take for you to tell me what I wanna know? Now, I'll repeat that last question. Better listen good, boy. Where—did—she—take—you?"

Hagas's watering eyes searched the room and landed on Ma. She looked down at him with a slight smile on her face as she dragged on her cigarette. *Hate you. They were going to . . .* He fast-forwarded through every move he could have made differently. *Should have run.* Panic began creeping in. Everything felt different, just like the end of one of his movies. *Everything ends sometime. Gigi's dead . . . No one's gonna help.*

Brian's room spilled light from its open door. Hagas let the scene swim into focus. In Brian's special chair, a woman slumped forward, held in place with the chair's various leather binds and straps. *Woman from the road. Su – Suzanne. She dead?* The panic rose higher, but it was shifting him, funneling his mind down to the now.

"Time's up, boy."

Answer. Answer. Answer.

"She took me swimming. Down to a waterfall. I. I. I didn't wanna go. She made me." Searing pain shot from the tip of the finger next to his smarting pinky.

"Stop! Please! I answered! I answered!"

After a few more agonizing seconds, Brian removed the cigarette. Instant tears welled in Hagas's eyes again.

"A waterfall, huh? Did this waterfall have a name? Or, maybe it's just some fuckin' magical la la land place? Better think quick, boy."

Hagas fixed his eyes on Suzanne who was slumped in the chair. *What was it called? Think. Think! Gotta come up with something.* Suzanne began raising her head in halting lifts, her hair falling back from her face as it reached its final upright spot. *Not dead!* She flexed her hands against the leather binds holding her arms down.

"She's . . . She's awake," Hagas whispered.

"Who's awake? Fuck does that mean? Where's fuckin' Gigi, you shit?" Brian barked into his ear. "Looks like you need a little more motivating."

"She's awake! The lady! The lady in the chair." Hagas blurted, desperate to deflect Brian's attention. *Sorry, lady. Sorry.*

Brian's weight shifted. "Well, lookie lookie, Dannie. Seems our girl has finally decided to join the party."

Chapter 34

Dannie with the plannie

Dannie turned her attention to the room, pausing before looking back toward Brian, trying to make a quick plan of attack. She darted her eyes down to Hagas. *And what the fuck did Carole tell you? Bitch took off didn't she? You're up to something too.* She looked back to Brian who was now pushing himself up from the mattress. *Now you're all worked up aren't you, you big dumb fuck?* The bright orange cherry on her cigarette sizzled as she took one last drag, dropped it onto the concrete floor, and used her foot to grind it out.

The woman strapped down in the chair had thrown her for a loop. Unexpected. Unwanted. Now, unavoidable. But with Carole out of tonight's picture, the situation was not necessarily bad, just different. Dannie liked being quick on her feet and now that she'd mulled things over, she had the first sparkles of immediate next steps. *Let's get you good and distracted. Shit's going down tonight. Getting out of here, come hell or high water.* Exhaling a slow, steady stream of smoke, she forced her lips and eyes into *that* smile before turning *it* full on for him.

"Why don't you get on up, babe? He's not going anywhere. And sure as shit, Carole's gone. She and me got into it a little last night. I say fuck her! Taking that little fuck outta here to piss me off. Her bony ass better be back in New Hampshire already."

Dannie took a step toward the mattress and glanced into Brian's room, gesturing her head toward Suzanne. "Besides, we have a new friend to play with. And she's been a bad, bad girl. Running over Hagas. She needs to be disciplined." Her lips curled higher. "Hell, she looks tastier than Carole and her nasty, old dried-up twat. Come on. Let's you and me have some real fun."

"Amen to that!" In a flash, Brian shoved himself upright and clapped his hands together. "Let's see what this little bitch is made of."

Dumb fuck. That was easy. Dannie walked into the room with Brian following right behind her. He started pulling the door closed behind him, but Dannie stuck her arm out to keep it fully open. "Gonna be a good show. Don't want the boy to miss anything," she said.

Brian stretched his arms out, locked his hands together, and cracked his knuckles one by one, sending wet popping sounds into the basement.

"Back with you soon enough, boy. Don't go anywhere," Brian said through a laughing sneer.

Chapter 35

From the fire to the frying pan

Standing at the edge of the Haybrook site parking area, just beside the Forerunner, Chris urged his mind to disengage from emotion and think objectively. *Staying at her friend's – that house. The house on K1 road. Was she plotting to take the kid? Which one is she? Dannie or Carole?*

A fireman approached, disrupting his thoughts. "Sheriff, we've got her bagged. Going to head out and get her to the morgue at Northern Light. Assuming you'll be requesting an autopsy?"

"Thank you. Yes, an autopsy is definitely in order." He paused. "How are you and your guys doing? Tough thing to see. You okay?"

"We're okay. A little tweaked out. Tired, too, I guess. Not your everyday gulf situation, that's for sure." The fireman shifted his stance, folding his arms across his chest before continuing. "Do you . . . do you, uh, well, we were talking and, uh, do you think there's some sort of friggin' – I don't know – psycho running around out here? I mean, we all got families. Kind of want to know if we should be locking our doors."

Chris stayed silent for a moment, looking past the parking area into the shroud of darkening trees as he considered the question and its potentially much bigger ramifications, depending on which direction he chose to go.

"I don't think you have anything to worry about. But I'd go ahead and lock things up. It's like I always tell my kids, better safe than sorry." He cleared his throat, stood taller, and looked into the fireman's eyes. "And, no need to say anything. To anyone. That's both a favor . . . and an order. All Northern Light needs to know is they have a deceased female and the cause of death is under investigation. Until I get more information and can figure out what is going on, I don't want any old ladies freaking out and I certainly don't need the whole damn county going all vigilante."

He moved to his Bronco, waiting to get in, watching their taillights rocking and bouncing up the road, and picturing the woman in the body bag jostling around like a lifeless rag doll. *Why? Why kill her? What did she do to you?* Images of his twins, their faces hidden behind leather masks, flashed into his mind. *What sick shit happened to you? Come on kid. Need to find you – help you.* The taillights rounded a corner and disappeared. Shortly after, the rough groaning sounds from their trek back up the road trailed off, and Sheriff Chan breathed in the quiet of the night, closing his eyes, listening to the brook babbling away in the distance. *Kid was at the house. With her. Need to end this – whatever this is.*

After wrapping the Forerunner with yellow crime scene tape, he fired up the Bronco and made a long, slow U-turn, following his high beams as they swept across the Haybrook site, illuminating the Forerunner and cutting through the trees and brush. Bugs flitted in the beams of light. *So peaceful. So perfect. So false.* He drove away from the parking area, pausing where the site's entry area met the road. He got out, hustling behind his truck to wrap yellow tape around nearby tree trunks. After a few rounds and crisscrosses, he was satisfied the message would be crystal clear to anyone who may venture down before the crime scene unit could get there the next day. *Course, they won't obey it.* He got back in the Bronco and began the bouncy ride back up to High Bridge. *Shit. Maybe someone will find something we didn't.*

Nearly ten minutes later, Chris was rounding the final corner, thankful to be off the rough uphill road. His headlights pierced into the opening of High Bridge #3, and he stopped for a moment to investigate the empty site, half hoping, half dreading the kid would pop out of the shadows. *Nothing. All clear.*

He steered the Bronco into a hard right, heading down the road, scanning ahead and to the right. He turned into High Bridge #2, pointing his headlights down into Suzanne's abandoned site. A thin stream of smoke still rose from the firepit, twirling lazily in the wash of light from his headlights. He pounded the steering wheel, frustrated at how much all of this situation felt out of his grip. *Time. Time. Time ... is not on my ...*

As he crossed the bridge, Chris slowed to a crawl, rolling by High Bridge #1 and shining his flashlight into the site.

The beam of light revealed nothing new of interest. *Jesus, Chris, what'd you expect – kid would just be sitting here wrapping up a squirrel or something?* He stopped at the fork. *She said he went left. Why?* He debated taking a quick spin up the road. A push of his phone brought the screen to life, showing it was almost 8:15. Breathing a sigh of frustration, Chris sped up, heading to the check-in cabin to meet his deputies, all the while trying to piece what he knew together.

Kid banked left. Why? Nothing up there . . . that we know of. No marked trails. No marked. What about unmarked? He pictured all the hunters with their secret spots—that only they knew how to get to. *What about your own trail?* He jammed the brakes.

"Dammit!" He turned on the overhead light and reached into the glove compartment, pulling out his old map of the gulf. Using a red pen, he marked each incident.

"Duck . . . I'll mark you as originating near the frogs at High Bridge #1 . . . Dead woman at Haybrook . . . Kid sighting at High Bridge #2 . . . Dog ran off . . . found on road past High Bridge #2 – right about where I am now. *Caught scent of something . . . someone?* Kid goes – left."

The red Xs clustered quite near each other, considering the vastness of the gulf. Chris hovered the pen at the fork in the road near High Bridge, then traced it up the road where the kid ran. The road meandered, sometimes splitting off into other veins, finally ending near Spruce Mountain Pond. *Too far.*

"Shit. If I lived up here, I'd know every inch of these roads and woods. Get from point A to point B lickety-split."

243

Chris stared at the map. If the kid lived around here . . . in a house . . . His eyes swept over the woodlands to the right of the road and landed on the next major line, the KI Road. *Point A to point B.* He rested his pen on the spot where the house would be, then dragged a straight red line to the fork by High Bridge. He was surprised at how short the line was compared to the twisting roads and trails of the gulf. *Point A to point B. Duck in. Duck out. Whenever you want.* Looking into the darkness surrounding his Bronco, for the first time in a long time, he felt small and vulnerable in these woods.

A million scenarios, none of them good, peppered his mind as he raced down the road from High Bridge. Skidding left onto the KI Road, he picked up speed. The string of Pleasant River sites came into view, ticking by. He noted the flickering campfire at #6 and eased off the gas pedal for a couple of seconds. The young couple's tent was dark and still. *Kid was never down here. Too far from home.* Ten yards past the site, he pushed back down on the gas pedal.

The check-in cabin came into view, its porchlight throwing out a soft yellow glow and drawing in countless moths to dance in its warmth. His deputies' cars were lined up, one in front of the other, just past the porch. The two men were leaning on the far car's trunk, clearly engaged in an animated discussion.

Chris parked and exited the Bronco, habit spinning him back to reach for his hat on the passenger seat. *Screw it.* He left the hat where it was, slammed his door shut, and walked toward the two deputies, now standing at attention.

Margaret appeared in the screen door. "Any new news Sheriff? We've all been waiting on you. Fire guys said you'd be coming right behind them. What took you so long?"

Chris paused just past the porch, shooting an all-business look up to Margaret. Jana shadowed her in the doorframe.

"Been doing cleanup and evidence gathering. The woman... She didn't make it. Passed away just after I got down there. I'll be right back to talk to you Margaret – you too Jana."

Sheriff Chan approached his deputies. "Gentlemen, I can see by your enthused expressions, you have no great revelations to share with me."

Donnie spoke first. "Unfortunately, Sheriff, we got nothing. Split up and canvassed as much as we could. Both of us spoke with a few campers. No one had seen anything off. Definitely no kid in a mask."

Clark chimed in. "Sheriff, aside from a dead woman, everything seems pretty normal. A whole lot of still woods. A few deer. Two raccoons. Even heard some whip-poor-wills. Just a few campers peppered about. One couple I spoke with did seem concerned that I was cruising around looking for a wayward kid. Probably because they had two of their own toasting marshmallows at their fire while I was talking with them. Did my best to assure them it was probably nothing." He hesitated. "I'm not so sure I told them the truth."

"I'm not sure you did, either." Chris looked back and forth at the two younger men. "There's more."

He proceeded to tell them about the duck and the frogs, the duct tape, connecting the small, individual instances to the much darker picture taking shape. He brought it back to the dead woman, recounting her arriving to the area a couple of nights prior at the Bear Market, then seeing her SUV at the house, running into her here at the check-in cabin earlier today, and finally her demise. He showed them his map of duct tape incident occurrences and the kid's presumed path. Finally, he shared his feeling that the dead woman and the kid—and probably someone or someones else– were all somehow connected at the house just a few miles up the road.

The deputies listened in silence. When he was finished, Chris gave them a moment to process, watching their faces as they churned through the information. Donnie looked simply lost, staring into the night sky. Clark's furrowed brow and direct eye contact gave Chris hope that he was truly trying to connect the dots.

"Well," Donnie said, breaking the silence. "I got nothing." He crossed his arms, sinking back onto the cruiser's trunk.

Chris wasn't all that surprised by Donnie's response. *About as bright as that porch light, aren't you?* "Anything firing for you, Clark?"

"Well, the duck and frogs could've been any punk kid— or kids—from around here. Hell, when I was a kid at Foxcroft, me and my friends used to stick firecrackers up frogs' asses and blow 'em up." He looked back and forth between Donnie and Chris. "Stupid, I know, but kids are assholes. Just not sure why that woman would be involved in that. And, she wasn't here long enough, that we know of." Clark looked hard at Chris for a moment before launching back in.

"Maybe the kid. I mean, he obviously seems off kilter. But, was he kidnapped? And, from where? No missing male juvenile kid in any of the sites here. And nothing reported recently, statewide anyway. I checked. And I've got Marie looking into the national registry. But if he was kidnapped, why not just run for help when he got free today? Anywhere. Anyone. The hikers that found him and the woman. Why not tell them? I mean, if it were me, when I was a kid, I'd have grabbed anyone who would listen."

Clark paused, regrouping from his onslaught of questions and string of thoughts. It was a full three seconds before he started in again, now with his arms animating his flood of words.

"If he did kill that woman – why? Because she kidnapped him? You said the woman was in a bathing suit, right? I mean, who kidnaps a kid and takes him swimming? Doesn't add up." Deputy Clark stopped talking and his eyes bored through the darkness, locking on Chris.

Logic crammed Chris's head, battling his gut, telling him it was too soon to tell if he was right in his suspicions. He drew in a breath of the cool night air, exhaling slowly before speaking.

"Deputies, I do not have the answers. Not yet anyway. What I can guess is this kid is probably very scared and very confused. That said, we will get to the bottom of all this as quick as we can—with evidence and facts. Gate's closing. No one's going in or out of there tonight. So, Donnie, I need you to head to Haybrook and babysit the Forerunner and the site. Clark and I are – "

Donnie jumped from the trunk. "Jesus, Sheriff. You want me sitting solo down there with all this going on?"

"Donnie!" Chris cut him off. And as fast as he'd barked out the deputy's name, he reined his voice in to his usual cool delivery. "Go. To. Haybrook. That's an order."

Donnie kicked at the gravel as he spun and went to his car. Chris addressed his remaining deputy. "Clark, you're coming with me, but hang tight for a minute while I wrap up with Margaret."

Chris strode across the porch and entered the check-in cabin. Margaret hunched over the log book, scrolling through the pages, while Jana stood nearby, her arms crossed in a self-soothing hug. The door smacked shut and they both looked to him.

Chris took a deep breath as he went up to the counter and addressed Margaret. "Woman up at High Bridge #2, her name was Suzanne, did she stop here on her way out?"

"Yeah. Said she decided it was too much, too much going on here to stay. Got her contact info right here. Mentioned you'd probably want to talk to her." Margaret stabbed the logbook in front of her. "Promised to pay for the trouble of leaving half her stuff behind. Said she couldn't even get her dog to calm down. Funny."

"What's funny, Margaret?"

"Oh, nothing, really." Margaret looked at Chris hard. "Just funny how they know something's going on. Dogs. Always got that extra sense of stuff."

"Well, anything?" Jana asked, her shoulders and palms both up and her impatience shining through.

"No, Jana." He snapped his head, looking Jana square in the eye. "Nothing. Nothing I can share." *Dammit. Too harsh.* He softened his tone. "You're all set to stay with Margaret tonight?"

Jana didn't reply. A twinge of something, maybe worry, shuddered through her.

"Yes, we'll be fine," Margaret answered, shooting a reassuring look at Jana. "It'll be good to have company. Get you out of these woods for a night. Girls' night. And hell, I'll feel better having someone else around, too."

"Thank you, ladies. Margaret, you mind getting here about seven tomorrow—earlier the better—to unlock the gate for us?"

"No problem, Sheriff." She cleared her throat. "Please, um, please figure out what's going on. My woods are too beautiful to be marred by all this bullshit."

Chris eased the door closed behind him, being sure not to let it bang. Driving away, he kept thinking about that word. *Beauty. All around.* Before he got into the Bronco, he lit up his phone and looked down at his boys smiling up at him. *We'll find that kid. Figure this out.*

As they drove to the house, Chris relied on the light from the high beams to scan for any signs of the kid, while Clark shone his flashlight out his window. Just as they neared the house, a glint caught Chris's eye on the edge of the woods.

"What's that, Clark?"

"Car – no. SUV."

Chris slowed the Bronco to a stop and backed up, swinging the nose slightly to point into the woods. The black Rover revealed itself. Its front end was partially covered by brush. A familiar dog popped up in the rear passenger window, front paws on the inside edge of the door and his tongue hanging out.

"Shit."

Chris grabbed his flashlight, told Clark to stay put and keep an eye on the house and watch for any signs of life. He exited and began walking toward the Rover, sweeping his light in front of him as he made his way. As he got closer, he called out.

"Suzanne! You here?"

No one answered him. He looked down, training his light on the ground. No footprints yet. The beam from his headlights dissipated as he got closer to the Rover. Dread sank into his stomach. *Be okay. Be okay.* Behind the windows, Derby let out a dampened couple of woofs as he got close.

He finally saw footprints beside the driver's door. Some shuffling was obvious. *Sporadic.* They appeared to go away from the vehicle. *You walked away? Why? Where?* He put his flashlight on the driver's window. The keys were in the ignition. Derby woofed again.

"Shh. Shh, Derby. Good boy."

What are you up to, lady? He lifted the handle and was going to open the door but thought better of it as Derby vaulted into the driver's seat. *Dammit. Don't need you running around.*

Training his flashlight back to the ground, Chris followed the sporadic prints in the dirt and brush. The prints morphed from full tread to just the toe end, leading him past the back end of the Rover toward the road. *Running. She running?* Thirty yards away, getting closer to the road, he spun around, looking back at the Rover, then spinning again to look across the road. He saw a single square light shining out from a house, a black silhouette in the darkness. That house. *She hurt?* He jogged back to the Rover. Derby was woofing harder, almost barking.

"Shh. Shh. Shh, boy."

250

Chris pointed his flashlight into the interior again. *Gear's in back – a mess. In a hurry.* A crunch sounded behind him and he whirled around. The spray connected directly with his face, and pain instantly seared his eyes, nose, and mouth. He yelled out and threw his arms up, flailing at his unseen attacker while trying to block the burning stream coating his face. *Pepper spray! Jesus! Bear spray!*

"Stop! Police! . . ." His lungs screamed, and he began hacking, stumbling backward into the Rover, dropping his flashlight as his hands went to his face. "Stop! Jesus! Clark! Clark!"

Derby was barking nonstop. The spray stopped, just as a foot connected with his knees, swiping him off his feet. The back of his head banked off the side of the Rover and he landed on the ground, with a painful thud. Chris gagged and coughed, *Can't open my eyes. My eyes. Jesus! Fuck!*

"Sheriff! I'm coming! Police! Stop! Down on the ground!" Clark called from what seemed like a mile away.

"Who's there? Answer me!" Dazed, he felt, rather than saw, his face bathed in light. He struggled to force his eyes open. At barely a sliver, all he could see was blinding white light. *No. No. No. Fight back, Chan. Fight!* He tried to push up, but his arms felt like hundred pound weights he couldn't move.

"Ooooh hoo hoo. That's gotta sting, Sheriff." The voice was deep, growling. "I was bringin' it for the dog, but, hey, here you were." The man's voice dropped to a whisper. "And . . . here comes your pal."

Dammit. Fight! Again, Chris pushed at the ground trying to right himself. He sensed the unknown man moving away as the air around his face opened up. He couldn't get a bead

251

on where the guy went. But he heard Clark's footsteps getting closer, pounding on the dirt.

"Clark! Clark!" Chris gasped. "Careful! He's out here. Got friggin' bear spray!"

"Where!? Where'd he go?" Clark paused and then yelled out. "Sheriff's department! Show yourself right now!"

Chris felt Clark's heaving breath in his ear. "Sheriff, what happen—"

A wicked cracking noise cut through the air. Clark screamed out, and his full weight landed on Chris.

Clark fought to push himself off Chris. Another crack rang out. "Fuck! My arm!" Clark yelled. "You broke my fuckin' arm!"

Beams of light darted all around in front of Chris's dime-slot eyelids. Another hiss of a spray. "Motherfucker! Fuck! Fuck! Cut the–" Clark pleaded, his voice faltering. *Crack!* Wet hit Chris in the face. Clark's shout was gurgling, incoherent.

Jesus. Come on. Get up. Clark! Get up! Clark continued pushing against him, and Chris could feel Clark's hands loosening. *Oh, God. He's struggling. He's losing. Shit–* Another crack followed by a sickening thud against metal. Clark slid beside Chris. Another crack. Another spray. Silence. Then Clark's shallow, wet wheezing just beside his ear.

"Clark. Clark," Chris whispered. Then louder. "Stop it. Jesus! What do you want?"

Crack! Spray. *Oh, God! Oh, God! Oh, God! Oh, Go–* Crack!

Chapter 36

The bump from the road

Somewhere in the recesses of her unconscious mind, Suzanne became aware of smoke surrounding her. *Nasty. Stupid Nightclub. No smoking, my ass.* Connie was pressing tight against the back of her body, making them one unit in midst of the loud, thumping crowd, her hands gripping her own. *Jesus. Lighten up. I'm right here. Hate coming here. Should just go home.* Squinting through the haze, Suzanne found their friends dancing in a sea of sweaty women and men. Lights, sweeping the club, flashed into her eyes and bounced all over gyrating bodies. The music, the never-ending, unrecognizable mashup of beats, throbbed in her head. *Oh my God. I fucking hate it here.*

From the middle of the dance floor, a shadowy figure caught her eye as it walked directly toward them. Connie's hands gripped tighter. *Who's this? Not Lorea. Jess? Did Noelle show up finally?* Suzanne looked past the figure at their friends, grouped together, bobbing up and down in a tight circle.

The figure drew closer, backlit by the lights, its face remained cloaked in shadow as it slipped through the tight crowd. Behind Suzanne, Connie pressed into her harder, pinning her arms by her sides.

"It's him," Connie whispered into Suzanne's ear, her voice shaking. "He's coming to take me back . . ."

The figure kept coming, slicing through the crowd, getting larger, blocking Suzanne's view of people beyond. She felt the music slow and dull, becoming a deep bassline pulsing through her, making her hyperaware of her heart flexing, pushing blood in and out. The figure stopped a few feet away, face lowered, still hidden in darkness. *Who is this guy?* Suzanne steeled herself, rising taller, filling her space in an instinctive reaction to an imminent threat, focused on protecting Connie, who was quaking behind her.

"Who are you?" Suzanne forced her words out in a slow, measured delivery. "What do you want?"

Connie's grip tightened on her hands, twisting her wrists. The figure said nothing. *Fuck this.* Her adrenaline kicked into high gear.

"Hey, man! What the fuck do you want?" Suzanne yelled.

The figure raised a cigarette and lifted his head. The man spewed a mighty stream of smoke. Suzanne squeezed her eyes against the sting. *Fuck. Move. Move! Why can't I move!?* After what seemed like an eternity, the smoke stopped.

Suzanne forced her eyes open. The extreme close-up view of the man, now just inches away, wheezing putrid breath into her face, sent an instant shock through her. She groaned, trying to push away, to back up, but Connie was rooting them to the floor, clutching at Suzanne, shuddering. The man's mouth opened.

"Time to go home, sweet . . . sweet . . . Connie," he wheezed. "Daddy's waiting."

"Noooooooooooooo! You fucker! Noooooo!" Suzanne screamed, thrashing with all her might, trying to break free of Connie's hands.

The music seemed to be getting louder, faster. *Fuck! Let go of me. Jesus! Got to get you away! Get us out of here! Let go . . .* Smoke streamed from the man's mouth again as he reached around Suzanne's shoulder, toward Connie. The smoke thickened in front of her, obscuring the man's face. *It's him! Fuck! Fuck!* The smoke began morphing, forming into something. A face she'd seen . . . on a dirt road . . . at the top of her campsite. *You! You! You're the fucking—the fucking caseworker! You bitch! You got him off!* The woman's smoky face, now forming a twisted smile, rushed at her.

Suzanne's eyes flipped open and bright light flooded in, blinding her. *Shit. Where am I?* Her head pounded with sharp pain. Cigarette smoke singed her nostrils. She quickly realized her mouth was stuffed with some foul-tasting cloth. Tight tape stretched across her lips, chin, and cheeks, preventing any mouth movement.

She tried moving her head but discovered it was secured to the back of a chair with a strap, pressed tight against her forehead. *Shit. What happened?* She wanted to fan the smoke away, but her wrists were tied tight to the arms of a hard, wooden chair. *Fuck.*

Her lower body was cold. A dull, rhythmic ache in her legs. *Jesus. My pants. The gun.* Straining her eyes, she saw her smooth, naked legs splayed out across the seat of the chair, and though her feet were out of sight, she felt the tight restraints locking her ankles in place. *Oh, God. Oh, God. No. What are they doing to me?*

"Well, fuck. Guess you're not dead." A woman's voice came into Suzanne's ears as a smoky, exasperated sigh. "Took you long enough to wake up."

Suzanne struggled to look ahead. The light blinded her, shining directly into her eyes. Fear bubbled up from her gut. "Who are you? Why am I tied up? What do you want?"

The tape across her mouth muffled her words. A billow of cigarette smoke poured across her face. She flexed her whole body, pushing against all the restraints. *Fuuuuuuck!* She narrowed her watering eyes, forcing a glare into the direction of the light.

"Aww, you're a feisty little bitch, aren't you?"

The woman circled the chair to stand in front of Suzanne. With the light behind her, the woman's face was a dark, featureless shadow, surrounded by a mass of glowing hair. Smoke curled up from a cigarette dangling at the woman's waist. Suzanne squinted harder, trying to force-focus the woman into view. Finally, the woman took a drag from her cigarette, bent down, squeezing her hands over Suzanne's wrists, and positioned herself inches away from Suzanne's face. Dread seized her and she held her breath—waiting for the unknown. The woman exhaled a long stream of smoke into Suzanne's face.

"Now, I've got a couple of questions before my man gets back to have his fun. He won't be long. Just went to check on your fucking yappety dog and pull your car in the driveway."

Suzanne's eyes widened. *Derby! Jesus. Don't you fuckers hurt him!* She thrashed against the restraints, grunting out blasts of obscenities.

"Christ, lady—Suzanne is it?—You're not going anywhere." The woman squeezed Suzanne's wrists harder. "Suggest you settle the fuck down."

Suzanne stopped thrashing, heaving breaths in and out of her flaring nostrils.

"That's better. Like I said, I got a couple questions. I'm going to go ahead and take my man's old jock out of your mouth so you can answer them." The woman rose, placing her cigarette near Suzanne's face. "And, don't you even think about yelling, 'cause nobody's going to hear you out here. Plus, I can't stand yelling and begging and all that bullshit. So don't. Got it?"

Suzanne closed her eyes and nodded. In a flash, a searing wave of pain hit her as the woman ripped the duct tape away from her face, taking bits of skin with it. Her eyes squeezed tight as she wailed through the muffle of cloth inside her mouth.

"No yelling. And quit your crying. Jesus." The woman mocked her before shoving her hand between Suzanne's lips to yank out the damp wad of cloth.

Suzanne gasped, sucking stale, smoky air into her dry mouth, filling her lungs. Her face was on fire. In her head, words were not forming fast enough. *Is this it? Am I going to die?*

The woman shoved a handful of rumpled papers to Suzanne's face. "Found these in your jacket. How about you tell me why my man's goings-on are all over these? Looks like you've been a busy little bitch."

The woman ground the papers into Suzanne's cheeks. Suzanne screamed in agony. Bloody smears appeared on the bright white pages when the woman pulled them away. Suzanne grit her teeth, her breath coming in short bursts.

"Fuck you!" Suzanne yelled.

She looked around the room with wild eyes. *Where the fuck am I? Basement? The house.* Her eyes caught the open door. She saw a rumpled human shape in the darkness beyond, mounded on the floor. Her stomach sank. *Is that the kid?*

The woman laughed. "Ha! Fuck me?"

Suzanne saw a blur of orange just before the woman jammed the cherry of her cigarette into Suzanne's midsection, connecting just under her belly button.

"Fuck you who, who!"

"Stop it! Stop it!" Suzanne screamed, bucking and writhing against the agonizing pain.

The woman pulled the cigarette away, standing upright.

"Let's try that again. Why the fuck do you have all these notes on Brian? Who the fuck are you? Cop?"

The woman took a slow drag from the bent cigarette, rekindling the orange glow at its end. Suzanne squeezed her eyes, fighting back the tears forming from the fresh burn. *Fuck. Fuck. Fuck. Tell her. Something. Make her understand.*

"He, he, he killed Connie! My girlfriend! She's dead! Because of him! He did it."

The woman crossed her arms and looked down at her with zero readable expression.

"Huh. Well, fuck, that seems about right. He does get a little excited sometimes . . . you know, when he's playing." She uncrossed her arms, pointing at Suzanne with her cigarette. "So, what? You came here to kill him?" The woman seemed to get introspective for a moment, almost side-barring to herself. "Shit. That would have been handy," she muttered before turning her attention back to Suzanne. "Where? Where did he kill her? I don't remember some fucking Connie coming here."

The woman bent down again, grasping Suzanne's wrists. "And, what the fuck does Carole have to do with this. She do it, too? That bitch fucking around with my man again?"

She doesn't know about Connie? Carole getting Brian off? Fuck. Fuck. Doesn't matter. Suzanne's mind raced, trying to connect the dots. The cigarette connected to Suzanne's skin a second time, just at the top of her pubic hairs. Suzanne screamed, her muscles tensing in shock. The smell of burning hair assaulted her nose.

"Brian's her father. Fuck! Please! Please. Please stop!"

Suzanne flexed and bucked against the inescapable pain. *She's going to kill me. Oh, Jesus. Please.* The woman yanked the cigarette away. *Oh, God. Oh, God . . .*

"What? Shut up! Brian. A real daddy?" She laughed, throwing her head back. "Sweet Jesus. Who the fuck knew? Fucking moron."

Taking a drag from her cigarette, the woman stared past Suzanne for a moment before looking back at her, dead on.

"So, you're telling me Brian is your little girlfriend's— Oh, I'm sorry, your dead girlfriend's—fucking daddy. Ain't that a trip." She laughed the last words out, low and mean.

259

The woman looked Suzanne dead in the eyes. Suzanne searched the woman's eyes boring into her. She couldn't speak, couldn't think of anything *fuck, fuck* that would pacify this woman. *Tell her. Something. Tell her. Fast. Jesus. She's going to burn me again. Tell her.* Suzanne's eyes darted to the door, stealing a glance at the lump on the mattress. *Tell her what you think. The kid.*

"What the fuck you looking at him for? He can't help you." The woman leaned in, her smoky breath hissing at Suzanne.

Suzanne broke. "I think . . . I think . . . I mean – I heard . . . you were asking him—the boy—about your friend. Your friend—your friend's dead." Suzanne watched the woman's eyes go wide. "I, I don't know for sure. An accident. Something. In the gulf."

Suzanne chanced another quick look out the door. *The kid. Did he . . .* A slam of a door somewhere in the house cut off her thoughts.

"Hey, baby! I'm back. Brought some new friends, too." Heavy, muffled footsteps plodded, getting louder.

Suzanne flexed against the restraints. *Jesus. No. No. No. Fuck. Fucking help me. How many people are here? Think. Think. Shit.* The woman pushed back from Suzanne and marched to the door. "What the fuck? Are you fucking crazy? Who are . . ."

Suzanne heard loud crashing on stairs outside the room, a massive series of thudding and cracking. *He fell. He's dead. Be dead!* A body landed just outside the door with a wicked, final slap onto the concrete floor. *Tan pants, dark green jacket. Not what he was wearing.*

260

"Are you fuckin' kiddin' me, Brian! You killed a cop?" The woman walked through the doorway, into the other room in the basement, yelling up the stairs.

"Re-fuckin-lax, Dannie!"

Before Suzanne could process the situation, a second round of cracking and thudding commenced. The woman backed away from the stairs as the thudding intensified. Another body rolled onto the floor.

Suzanne gasped out loud, letting a breath of her hope escape into the stale air. *No. No. No. Not the sheriff.*

"Fuck! What the fuck?! Brian! Two! Jesus Christ! You are so—" the woman screamed.

"Oh, relax. Say hello to our new friends. I call them alibi one and alibi two."

Chapter 37

Give me a break

Giggling faces . . . tiny hands scribbling crayon drawings . . . a skinned knee . . . blankets piled high on twin beds . . . moonlight spilling in from a cracked window . . . crying . . . running . . . muddy grass . . . inconsolable . . . Trish . . . squeezing . . . darkness . . . pain . . . slipping . . .

Chris stirred, fighting his mind from rushing him out of his private home movies, moving him into the now, his senses awakening as the soft pillow of unconsciousness gave way to the hard, cold concrete his head rested on. *The road. The Rover. Clark. The dog. Him.* He felt something wet surrounding the left side of his face. He struggled awake, blinking his eyes open. *So dark.*

Automatically, his hands moved to reach out and touch the liquid. Except there was no movement. *What the . . . ?* His hands were immobile, clasped behind him, wrists pinched in cold metal. *Cuffs.* He shifted his body, sending a flash flood of pain up his left arm and crashing into his shoulder. *Shit! Broken. Broken.* He crunched his teeth together, instinctively stifling the scream trying to force its way out. *That guy. Bear spray. Hit me. Where am I? Shit. Shit. Where's Clark?*

Focusing on the pain washing over him, he stilled his mind to follow the blood pumping through him, mentally checking for other damage. *Ribs. Maybe a crack or two.* The searing pain in his arm and shoulder began subsiding into dull, throbbing heat. His head radiated waves of staccato, painful bursts.

Something about his right knee was feeling horribly wrong. Nausea swirled into his gut. He tried bending. An instant blaze of blue flame surrounded his knee. *Oh God! . . . Jesus!* His right knee was inverted, resting on top of his left leg, bending the wrong way.

"Keep that little bitch warm! Be right back baby." The man blurted out from close by.

Narrowing his eyelids into slivers, Chris tried to find a focus point in the scant hint of light cutting across the floor. Everything in front of him looked soft, fuzzy, and dark. *What's that?* A lumpy form took shape. *Is that a mattress? Shit. Who is that? Alive?*

Barely six feet away, the top of the lump stirred and turned, exposing one wide eye that picked up a hint of the light as it peered towards him. *The kid. The kid!* The kid's eye shifted slightly up. *Shit. What?* He felt the presence of someone just behind him.

A woman screamed out somewhere behind him. *The woman – Rover – Suzanne. She's down here –* In the next instant, a heavy knee slammed onto him, delivering crushing pain as his ribs cracked under the weight. Chris howled in pain as his duty belt began yanking and twisting at his waist.

"Get – off – me-e-e-e!"

"Come on fucker – un – fucking – hook," the man grunted.

The man twisted and yanked at the belt. Chris's body sent fresh, hot flashes of pain rifling through him as his breaks and cracks were all shaken around.

"Get – off . . ." Chris tried getting the words out again, forcing out air between his clenched teeth.

"Fuck you. Shut up."

The man gave a final jarring tug and Chris's keys detached, jangling and skidding across the concrete floor behind him. The man gave a mighty shove-off, driving deep into Chris's ribs one more time. Taking in breath, wincing as the air filled his lungs, Chris grit his teeth against the radiating pain and turned his head toward the man behind him.

"What – are you – what do – you want?"

The man stood tall above Chris. "Me. I'm gonna do exactly what you said. I'm gonna get off." The man spoke the words in a dead calm, letting them hang in the air.

His foot connected with Chris's lower back. Chris yelled out in agony as his body convulsed in white hot pain.

"Whooo-eeee! We got us a party down here to-fuckin-night!" He was almost laughing, jumping up and down.

"Jesus! Fuck! Quit dickin' around. Hurry the fuck up and go get their goddamn truck off the road." A woman's voice barked out from behind Chris.

Their. Clark! Clark's in here. The man was now hovering above his ear, blowing into it. Slowly. Intentionally. The

264

sensation of hot, smoky breath wafting over him was chilling, sending shudders down his spine. Chris froze. Helpless. *Jesus. What are you doing? Oh Jesus. This can't be happening.* After two long, slow blows, the man whispered into his ear.

"Like that? Just cooling you off. You're all worked up." The man blew into his ear again, before continuing. "You know, we've never been able to get Chinese delivered out here. But look at this shit. You just showed on up. A big fuckin' pig, all dripping with sweet sauce. Too bad your buddy couldn't stick around to enjoy this."

"Where's – Clark?!" Chris blurted.

"Aw, well, that poor fucker's dead. Just over there actually." The man's tongue lapped from Chris's chin to his temple. "Fucker's head cracked open like a fuckin' fortune cookie when he hit the floor. Must've tossed him a little rough. S'alright though. We still got us plenty a party right here."

The man's tongue circled the edge of Chris's ear. *Clark. Clark. Noooo.* Booze and smoke drifted into Chris's nose. *Get off me. Fuck – you sick fuck.* Rage and hate were working for him now, distracting him from the pain.

His mind raced, searching for a plan, a possible way out of this. Something. Anything. The man pulled away, rising in one motion. The next thing Chris heard was the man bounding up the stairs. His boots thudded on the wooden treads, then across the floor above. A door banged shut and the thudding stopped.

Chris heard the woman speaking softly behind him. He heard "be back" and "have us some fun" but couldn't make out much of anything else. He strained his hands. Bolts of agony shot through his left arm with every shift, but he fought it, focusing through it. His right hand, uninjured, took on the work and connected with his duty belt.

The only piece of luck he could have hoped for was in his grasp. He pulled at the compartment tab, grimacing as his wrists pressed against the handcuffs and the strain on his broken left arm threatened defeat.

Sweat beaded on his forehead. *Come on! Do this!* After a few tries, pulling with shaky fingers, the tab released with a dull pop. *Shit!* He stiffened, sure the noise had echoed throughout wherever he was. He waited for Dannie. She did not come. Her whispery voice drifted out to him. He continued digging his fingers into the compartment. *There you are. Gently. Gently. Come on. Easy.*

His small, spare cufflinks key dangled precariously between his index and middle finger as he lowered his hands to the floor. His wrists were on fire. His left arm screamed. *Almost. Almost. There.* Sucking in a deep breath, sure of the pain he was about to bring on, he tensed his muscles and shifted his body, twisting his backside over the key. His eyes bulged as the pain shot forth from his knee, ribs, and left arm. *Did it. Breathe. Focus.* He closed his eyes, exhaling and riding out the pain until it had subsided into tolerable. He willed his hands to stop shaking. *Okay. He'll be back. Move your ass, Chan.*

He inched forward, bursts of pain shooting through him with each shuffle, but feeling the key under him, picturing it getting into position. After a few micro-shuffles, he lowered his cuffed hands, stretching his right hand down as far as he could. *Got it!* Pain grew along his left arm. *Time to go to work, Chan.*

He opened his eyes. Reflecting in the dim light, the boy's wide eye stared back at him. Chris stared back. *Friend or foe?* He could think of only one thing to do.

Chris whispered, barely above a breath, "Shhhhh."

He never broke eye contact with the boy. A long couple of seconds passed. The boy blinked, ever so slightly nodding his head. Chris conjured up a slight smile toward the boy, the best he could offer. Working in silence, he maneuvered the key between his fingers, positioning it to expose as much of the bit as possible while still keeping a secure grip on its bow.

From the mattress, the boy stared toward him, probably trying to make sense of his contorting facial expressions. *Hang in there, kid.* He closed his eyes, picturing the key, focusing his finger movement on bringing the bit closer to the tiny keyhole in the cuff. Pain increased, radiating down from his shoulder, clouding his focus. Fresh beads of sweat formed near his hairline. *Come on.* The key made contact with his skin.

He guided it across his wrist until it hit the edge of the cuff, then eased it up over the edge of the metal and dragged it across the surface. *It's right there. Easy now. Let it find its mark.* The key's bit gave way slightly. *Bingo! Got it!* Squeezing the bow a little tighter, he pushed. The key moved deeper into the keyhole. Popping his eyes open and exhaling, he felt a truer smile pulling up the corners of his mouth. *Phase one. Done.* The boy's eye had an inquisitive look to it, his brow tightened into a shallow furrow. Reaching for the right word, something to reassure the boy, Chris mouthed out "O—kay," being sure to make his mouth form each syllable clearly. The boy's expression softened. Then, for the second time, the boy's gaze shifted up a bit. Chris tensed.

"Hey there, Officer?" Behind him, just above his head, a woman's low, gravelly voice doused the brief glimmer of hope Chris had. "You think getting those cuffs off is going to change anything?"

A stream of cigarette smoke swirled around his face.

Chapter 38

Just a little prick

After Hagas figured out what the policeman was doing, he was rooting for him. *You're picking the cuffs? Yes. Yes, you are.* The man's eyes had been closed the whole time once he got going, like he was sleeping but moving at the same time. Hagas watched the sweat bead then drip into the tightened slits of the man's eyes. *Keep going. Hurry. I can help you. Show you my knife. Right under my feet.*

Just as the man had opened his eyes wide and a smile sparked from his mouth, is when he saw Ma tiptoe across the floor, stopping behind the policeman. Her cigarette glowed, dangling from her right hand.

But in her left hand, she clenched something else. His eyes went back to the policeman's face as Ma bent down, hovering over the policeman's ear. The policeman's smile dropped away. Hagas's body froze. Even if the tape holding him down was gone, he wouldn't be able to move. He was locked on the helpless policeman's face, watching the streams of sweat running. The policeman looked back at him, and Hagas could read the fear. He thought of all those movies he'd watched down here. Watching the people try to run or hide or fight back. He knew. He knew now, just like he knew when those people in the movies were not going to win. *I'm sorry. I can't help you. Sorry. Sorry. Sorry.*

Ma jammed the cigarette into her mouth. The cherry glowed as she sucked in and Hagas could see her dark eyes looking down. *No. No. Please don't hurt him more. Please don't.* She unclenched her fist to reveal a whitish tube. A long, thin spike of a needle jutted from it, glinting in the cigarette's glow. *Seen that before. In that movie. The plunger thing. Brought dead people back. But he's not dead.*

Ma transferred the tube to her right hand, steadying it with her left and pointing the needle end upward. A spurt of liquid arced from the needle, landing on the policeman's cheek. Her lips twitched, curling up at the edges into a sinister smile.

Hagas glanced back at the man. The fresh drops of liquid were mixing into the sweat. The man's eyes searched Hagas's own. *Sorry. Sorry.* Hagas looked back at Ma as she bent down, her cigarette still stuck in her mouth.

The man grunted, coughing words out between breaths. "Ma'am—Dannie, right? Not too late. I—I can help."

Ma yanked the policeman toward her. He let out a high-pitched squeal. The sound hit Hagas's ears loud and raw, instantly flashing back to the memory of Brian killing that kitten, bashing its head with a sledgehammer. Hagas squeezed his eyes to shut out the image. When he opened them a mere second later, he saw the man's eyes were wild, darting left and right.

"Ma! Ma. What are you—"

She jammed the needle into the man's leg and flashed a menacing 'shut up' glance at him. Hagas flinched, watching her thumb pushing the needle down, down, down—sending something bad—into the policeman. After a few seconds, Ma pulled the needle away.

"Time for officer asshole to go bye-bye."

She took the cigarette from her mouth and leaned down to the man's ear. "Oh, Sheriff. You tried. Oh, you fuckin' tried. I'll give you that." She chuckled. "But, like my dumbass Brian said, you're our new best friend, Alibi. Yep. The story is you came in and found that crazy bitch fucking with us. She damn near killed all of us—but you—you showed up. Tried to save us all. I think that sums it up nicely. You? Good? Good. And, if I'm being totally honest, jail isn't really going to fit in my plans."

Hagas focused on the officer's sweaty face, watching his features slide, transforming and softening his skin. The officer's frantic, tensed eyes relaxed, becoming glazed-over orbs behind drooping eyelids. His lips parted, moving for a moment, but no sound came out. *Can you see me? Are you still here? Are you . . . dead?*

The officer's empty stare became too much for Hagas. He turned his head, looking up at the dark ceiling as a tear ran down his cheek. *Sorry. Sorry.*

"Well, one down. Now, who's next?" Ma said matter-of-factly.

She walked away, back toward Brian's room. *She's gonna kill me. Or he is. I know it.* Anger and hate churned in his gut. *Get unstuck. Have to.* He wriggled his hands under the bands of tape. They were strapped tight, but he could move them. *Got to try like he did. Got to.* He kept wriggling, and the tightness began feeling different. Some parts of the tape detached from him, tearing at his skin a little. *Keep going. Come on.* His wriggling grew faster; his wrists warming from the friction. *Come on.*

"Ow!" The sound just popped out, stopping his hands instantly.

Did she hear me? He froze in place. Waiting. On his left wrist, the buckle clasp from his watch dug into the tender underside of his wrist. It stung. *Ow. Ow. Ow.* He couldn't wait anymore and shifted his hand up. The watch came undone, hanging—barely—on his tender wrist.

A lightbulb fired on in his head. *Sharp. Use it.* Contorting his wrist down, his fingers found the strap of the watch. Maneuvering it inch by inch, he grabbed the buckle, pinching the sharp clasp between his thumb and index finger. Twisting his wrist around, he poked at the tape binding him. It took effort, but the clasp was punching through. *Okay. Okay. Keep going.* Hope and determination took over; his poking became more rhythmic and energized. He could feel the pressure and pop with each stab. *Keep going. Keep going. Angel, if you can hear me, help me.*

Above, the unmistakable slam of the screen door halted Hagas's mission. Thudding footsteps clomped across the kitchen floor. Hagas's stomach flip-flopped; he held his breath in, listening, mapping the steps, waiting. *Brian. No! No! Need more time.*

272

Chapter 39

Wristful thinking

"What did you give him? What did you do to him?" Suzanne asked, her voice shaking in an unavoidable moment of panic. *Damn it! Get a grip if you're going to get out of this. You are strapped down and half-naked in – a – fucking – torture – chair!* Fear pulsed through her, fighting her ability to do any methodical thinking.

With her head strapped down, she couldn't turn much, so she darted her eyes around, trying to make sense of the room. *Stairs just outside the door, past the sheriff. Shelves beside the door. Loaded with tools. Jesus. Gear. So much gear. Window! Yes. Covered. But—*

"Oh Jeezuss, chill out. Was just a little something a friend gave me. Something to help him relax. Fuck. Dunno though, that shit may just put him right into la la land for good. You see that leg of his? Shit's nasty."

Dannie breezed by, flicking hot ash from her cigarette down onto Suzanne's lap as she went. Suzanne flinched. "Got one for you, too. Maybe—and I do mean maybe—if you're a good girl, and you 'fess up to all your shit, I'll even give it to you before he starts really going at you."

Suzanne flashed to Connie. *The stories. The nightmares. The joke of a fucking trial. Brian. Daddy.* The shift began. Behind her fear, creeping in, her anger grew.

She continued grinding her feet and wrists against the thick leather straps, hoping the constant movement would start loosening them. Stealing a glance out the door, she saw the lump of the kid moving a little.

He was looking in, his eye catching and reflecting a hint of light. *What are you doing? Don't stare!* She fixed her gaze back to Dannie who was blowing out smoke, looking toward the ceiling and shaking her head as footsteps stomped above.

"Fucker's going to take a dump. Yup. I goddamn knew it." She turned back to Suzanne. "Like a goddamn kid. Gets too excited and can't even keep his shit together. Literally."

"Maybe he's nervous. I can help. You can stop this before—before it goes any further. You don't have to—" Suzanne cut herself off.

Dannie's face hardened, and she let out a chuckle, buried within a heavy sigh. Looking back up at the raw wood beams supporting the floor above, Dannie spoke into the air.

"Fuckin' two cops in here and he's takin' a goddamn timeout to take a shit. Moron. Fuckin' idiot. Fuck, I'm gonna miss his sorry ass." She fell silent, staring up at the beams, her cigarette sending thin, twisting slivers of smoke up, up, up.

Suzanne thought, maybe, just maybe Dannie was working out a different scenario. *Come on! Make a new ending to this fucked up story you bitch. Jesus.* She continued flexing and twisting her hands and feet against the straps. In an instant Dannie was on her, one hand latching onto her throat and the other jamming the cherry of her cigarette into the back of her left hand.

Suzanne's fist clenched, her muscles seizing as she screamed out at the fresh pain. Her scream was pitiful—a gurgling, stifled yelp—due to Dannie's hand squeezing her neck. Dannie kneed her exposed, naked crotch with a wicked force. Black stars popped and danced in front of Suzanne's eyes.

"What the fuck you keep wiggling around for? Think you're going somewhere? You think you're the first little bitch that's been in this seat? No. No. He plays *allll* the time. And Hagas over there is his little practice bitch."

Suzanne's body spasmed, trying to get away from the pain, trying to get air. *Jesus! You psycho!* Then Dannie was twisting her head, forcing it to turn under the restraining strap. Her hair pulled under the leather. Dannie kept twisting until Suzanne was facing out the door and looking toward the lump on the floor. *Hagas. Hagas. Jesus –*

"And he always wins, doesn't he, boy?"

Dannie was looking out the door too. Suzanne saw Hagas was still now, his one illuminated eye looking back at them.

"Say hi, Hagas. Say hi, my little fucktard."

Hagas remained silent. For a fleeting moment, Suzanne's heart and head filled with sorrow. *Just a little boy. How can they do this? Connie. Connie. Connie . . . He did this to you. He broke you.* Her sorrow began heating, igniting a primal rage in her gut. *I'm going to fucking fight or go down swinging!*

Dannie lifted the crumpled cigarette, now fully extinguished, and examined it briefly before flinging it to the floor. She rubbed vigorously at the charred back of Suzanne's hand, smudging the remaining ash in and around as Suzanne moaned in pain.

"Shit, that smells," Dannie said with a grimace on her face. "Fuckin' messy."

Dannie released her death grip on Suzanne's neck, pulled her knee back, and strolled away from the chair. Suzanne felt immediate physical relief, gasping in air, coughing and hacking as she filled her lungs.

"Fuck!" She sucked in air. "What is wrong with you? Listen to me." Suzanne forced her words out through staggered whispers. "I don't have anything to 'fess up to. I don't know you. I don't care about you. Fuck! I mean, you, you, you, yooou have nothing—nothing to do with me or with Connie. I just—just wanted him to pay. To hurt." Suzanne stopped. *Please. Please.*

Dannie sparked a new cigarette. She leaned casually against the big, blocky shelving, its surfaces filled with a variety of masks, whips, and mean-looking sex toys. Restraints, chains, and other varied, torturous-looking things Suzanne had never seen, or even imagined, hung from hooks along the face of the shelves.

A boom box, half-covered in old pieces of cloth and towels, looked out of place sitting on a shelf among all the other devious devices. Gazing across at Dannie and this wall of insanity, all Suzanne could think about was which things they were planning to put to work on her body. Her heart pounded. Rage continued rising in her. *Fuck you. Sick fucks. I won't be your victim! I won't.*

Through a billow of smoke, Dannie responded. "You know, you did run down my boy with your fancy, schmancy truck. Banged him all the fuck up. I think you understand fair is fair and that there is something that needs reckoning with before I go." Oh wait." She snickered. "I made a rhyme—*fair is fair* and *that there*. That's fuckin' funny."

Dannie pushed away from the shelf, pacing, inching closer and closer to Suzanne. Suzanne trained her eyes on the glowing cigarette, its cherry elongating with each of Dannie's inhales. Her hand throbbed.

"I am kind of curious what he's thinking of doing to – I mean 'with' you. Well, not that you've got much say in anything." Dannie's pacing quickened. "On the other hand. I just want to get the fuck out of here. Maybe I'll just take your fancy truck and go." The cigarette was making wide jerky arcs. "You know what I mean, right? Fresh starts. Out with old. Be done with it. Move the fuck on."

The toilet flushing from above snapped both women to attention, and their eyes jerked up. For a couple of seconds, Suzanne followed the sound of water and foulness coursing through the pipes hanging along the wood beams. *Shit.* Remembering the moment at hand, Suzanne quickly looked back down at the menacing cigarette, just a few feet away from her face.

"Guess he's done." Dannie shook her head, like she was trying to get something out of her hair. "Aww, fuck it. One more show. Fuck."

Dannie spun and walked back to the shelf, positioning herself into the same relaxed pose she'd struck just a minute before. Softly, she began whistling in time with the footsteps.

"Swooo swoo swee. Swooo swoo swee. Swooo swoo swee."

Over and over, she whistled the same staccato chirps as Brian's footsteps thudded across the floor above. Then the steps were on the stairs. Thudding. Creaking. Closing. Getting louder with each bounding clop on the stair treads.

"Swooo swoo swee. Swooo swoo swee. Swooo swoo swee." Dannie matched the sound level, picking up the pace of her whistling.

The clodding on the stairs stopped. Dannie stopped whistling.

Brian's broad shoulders practically filled the doorway. Suzanne could see the wild in his bright, bloodshot eyes. *Drugs? Coke? Drunk? Fuck. Fuck.* The flannel shirt he'd had on was gone. A ratty, stained "wifebeater" tank clung to his muscled torso. Faded greenish-black tattoos, words, and images that Suzanne could not make out popped all over his arms.

He placed both hands on the door's frame, closed his eyes, and bent his head down to inhale from his pits, sucking air into his nose deeply, methodically. With a satisfied smile, he raised his head, scanning across the room to Dannie first, then sliding his gaze down to Suzanne, his smile transforming into a sneer.

"Hello, bitches! Miss me? Don't you worry. Daddy's home. And Daddy's ready to get this fuckin' party started!"

He hooked his thumbs into the wide black belt wrapping around his waist. A knife sheath popped off his belt, just behind his right hand. *No. No. No cutting. Oh, Jesus. Please no cutting.* Her body tensed. She curled her hands into fists, instinctively trying to protect her extremities. Her left hand slid backward an inch.

Suzanne was startled to feel her left hand moving. She uncurled her fingers and felt the pressure of the strap across her wrist slacking. It was slight, but it was there. *Come on. Yes!* She flexed and pulled back slightly. A wave of euphoria lifted her for a split second. She flexed and pulled. *Fuck!* And pulled again.

Chapter 40

Look sharp

What's he doing? Suzanne's eyes shifted focus, catching movement beyond Brian's waist. The boy was fidgeting. In the soft, shadowy light, just beyond the battered, twisted body of the sheriff, she could see his arms working. *You're trying to get free.*

Panicking at the sudden thought she might be looking too long, Suzanne snapped her head up, as straight and defiant as she could manage, pressing the back of her skull into the cold wooden chair, simultaneously flexing her arms and balling her fists against the straps.

Hope made a quick visit into her mind as her left arm lifted slightly, pushing against the strap. She felt the fleeting sensation of air slipping under her forearm before she lowered it. She looked dead ahead, steeling herself for whatever brutality was coming next. Across from her, the dark, taped-over window beckoned. *Freedom.*

Visions of her wilder teenage self unrolled in her mind. She played back the hot summer nights she would sneak out of her parents' basement window with deft skill, popping the unsecured window out of its frame, shimmying her lithe body through the opening and onto the lawn outside. Ready for anything. Right now, she could almost taste the fresh air, feel the adrenaline.

Static of distorted electric guitar blasted across the concrete room, jarring Suzanne, making her tense, snapping her out of her fantasy. *What the . . .*

I like to dream, yes, yes
Right between the sound machine
On a cloud of sound I drift in the night
Any place it goes is right
Goes far, flies near
To the stars away from here
Well, you don't know what
We can find
Why don't you come with me little girl
On a magic carpet ride . . .

The throwback party song sent sharp waves of panic through Suzanne as it bounced around the room. The lyrics felt all wrong and warped, the words sending new meaning into her mind. Out of the corner of her eye, Suzanne saw Brian gyrating while he messed with something against the wall beside the door. *Probably that stupid old boom box.*

Dannie slinked by, working her movements to the beat, and pushing out a thick stream of smoke into Suzanne's face

281

as she crossed toward Brian. *Jesus. Fuck. They're priming up.* She jerked her left arm up and down in a frenzy.

Dannie got behind Brian, hands lifting through her hair, reaching up to the beams before grabbing his shoulders and grinding her pelvis into his backside. *Fuck. Fuck. Fuck.* Dannie's hands slid down Brian's back, working over his lats, then wrapping around his waist. Brian's head tilted back as he bucked into Dannie.

"Whooooo! You fuckin' feel that, babe? Fuckin' ready to go!" Brian spun around, still gyrating and bucking to the song. He grabbed Dannie's hair, yanking her head back as he buried his face in hers. His wild eyes looked up and over to Suzanne.

A surge of bile swelled into Suzanne's throat. *No. No. No. Stay with her.*

Brian jerked his head up, closed his eyes, and circled his tongue around the outside of his mouth. With one fast shove, he tossed Dannie to the side, sending her to the concrete floor. His eyes popped open and he looked directly at Suzanne.

"Bet you taste better than this old ashtray." He pointed at Dannie who was trying to right herself. "Just too bad Carole's not here yet to join in the fun. Looks like it'll be sloppy seconds for her."

Brian licked his lips, making slow, exaggerated motions with his tongue, then mouthed the words to the song.

Close your eyes now
Look inside now

282

Suzanne jerked her arm again, pulling up as hard as she could. *Just keep going. Come on!* She flexed and jerked again and again. Brian moved toward her, pacing each lurching step in time with the song.

Let the sound
Take you away

Brian paused as the song shifted gears down. He closed his eyes, swaying in place. Behind him, from her fallen position on the floor, Dannie whipped her head around, her disheveled hair flopping into her face. Her face was twisted in rage, staring after Brian, heaving breaths in and out. *Do it! Get up! Get him!*

He raised his arms. *Jesus. Fuck.* Once again, he bent his face down to his pits, inhaling from each one, his face taking on a slight smile. *Bet you fucking reek, you fuck!* The frenzied organ solo in the song was screaming in her ears. Suzanne stole a glance out the door. One of the boy's arms was reaching up over his body. *Oh my God. You're getting loose.*

Suzanne's glance out the door was interrupted by the swoosh of Brian's arms dropping. She turned her attention back to him. *Come on. Keep looking at me. Don't look out the door.* He opened his eyes, and indeed did look directly at her, his gaze drifting down from her eyes to the rest of her exposed body.

An icy wave of dread raced through her, making her shudder from head to toe. He stepped toward her, drawing closer with each rising beat of the song that seemed to be stretching on forever. His tangy foulness invaded her immediate space as the distance between them tightened.

A hot bubble of bile surged in her throat, but she caught it and forced it back down. *Don't you fucking lose it! Come on! Stronger than him.* Suzanne steeled herself, willing her face to stone. She focused her energy on her arm, silently telling it not to flex again. *Not yet. Too close. He'll see and just tighten it. You've got one—maybe two—more solid pulls. Make them count.*

Well, you don't know what
We can see
Why don't you tell your dreams to me
Fantasy will set you free

The song finally faded away as he reached the chair, positioning himself squarely between her stretched-open legs. His jeans brushed against the insides of her knees. Suzanne's breathing was coming quick now, catching in her throat, anticipating, dreading. *What? What? What, you fuck? Fuck me? Whip me? Cut me?*

He looked down at her, expressionless. His face was flush, mottled, beads of perspiration dotting his forehead. Black stubble spiked out from his cheeks and neck. He bent toward her, placing his powerful hands on her thighs, then squeezing them hard. He got close to her face and she was overwhelmed by his smell—the foul, sour stink of him, old sweat mixed with booze and fish. Her stomach churned and her heart pounded. She held her breath. *Jesus. Jesus. Get away from me!*

Then his tongue was on her, rough and wet, dragging and pressing across her raw cheek, crossing over her mouth, stopping at her right ear. An involuntary, desperate moan escaped from her throat.

His breath came at her hot and quick as he whispered into her ear. "I see you. I see you. Yes, I do. You scared? Scared of me?"

His wet tongue jammed into her ear. *Ohhh, Jesus!* Suzanne seized up, groaning in disgust and fear. Music blasted across the room again. Harder, rougher, electronic grunge.

Change my pitch up
Smack my bitch up
Change my pitch up
Smack my bitch up

In a wicked instant, his mouth shifted, biting down onto the top of her ear. Suzanne screamed out, guttural and raw, at the sudden, sharp pain of his teeth crunching down on her.

"Stop! Jesus! Please! Stop! Stop!"

Every muscle in her body tensed, fighting to get free. Everything in her fought to get away, but her head remained hopelessly trapped beneath the straps. Her left forearm shot up, lifting higher off the chair's arm. The force of his bite grew with every second.

"Please! Please! Stop!"

Change my pitch up
Smack my bitch up

Change my pitch up
Smack my bitch up

Brian released, pulling away from her. Cold, basement air hit her fresh wound, stinging it. Trickles of wetness slowly ran down the back of her ear, slipping to her neck. *Fuck. Spit? Blood?* Her mind flooded with fear, images, and horrifying scenarios all at once, panic overriding her plan.

Brian's lips were now splotched with fresh, crimson blood. He looked into her eyes as he circled his tongue around his puffy lips, slowly, deliberately.

"Mmm. Mmm. Tastes grade A to me. Rich bitch got herself all mixed up in all kinds of no good. Dannie there showed me your fuckin' notes." Suzanne stole a glance at Dannie, who looked to be sitting more upright now. "Thought you'd try to fuck me up, huh? Some kind of revenge for your little cunt of a girlfriend?" Brian punctuated "cunt," popping it at her.

He slid his hands up her legs, reaching the soft, tender skin of her inner thighs, just under her groin. Suzanne couldn't stop her mind from jumping ahead—anticipating his finger—*or fuck, fingers*—punching into her. She tightened her groin, tensing and pulling in with every muscle she could. She wasn't even close to ready for his next move.

He dug his thumbs into her abductor muscles. Suzanne screamed at a pain she'd never felt before, her body writhing in a futile attempt to get out of his grip. His thumbs felt like they were actually punching holes through her muscles.

Change my pitch up
Smack my bitch up

Change my pitch up
Smack my bitch up

　　Leaning in closer, Brian's mouth grazed her ear. His foul body odor struck her again, jolting her senses, waking the fight in her, and pushing her past the pain.
　　"You know . . ." His tongue darted into her ear. "I got a little secret for you." He licked behind her ear. "That little cunt weren't even mine." He laughed. "I might have been her daddy, but I weren't her *fuckin' daddy*." He laughed. "Bet you didn't know that, did you, smartass? Daddy. Fuck that. Nah, she was just a gorgeous little present from my girl, Carole. Just a sweet, tasty . . . little . . . fucking . . . present. I have no fucking idea—fuck, I don't even care—who Carole got her from. All I know is she was a good bitch and gave that sweet, young pussy to me when it was time—time to make me happy."
　　The words reverberated in Suzanne's head, filling her with rage and horror, making her want to vomit and rip his cock off all at the same time. *Twisted, fucked-up fucks!*
　　"She ever tell you I used to call her my little veal chop? No? No? Aww, she was tender and juicy in all the right places." He squeezed Suzanne's thighs, causing her to yelp, then sighed into her ear. "Fuck. Tore me up when that little cunt got it all in her to jump ship."

Change my pitch up
Smack my bitch up

　　Suzanne's heart started pumping fast, adrenaline coursing through her. *Do it. Get the knife.*

Change my pitch up
Smack my bitch up

Brian bit. Hard. Fast. The expected shock was unavoidable. Suzanne seized the rush of pain, let it fill her, power her. *Do it! Do it! Do it!*

Change my pitch up
Smack my bitch up

She yanked her arm back, pulling with every ounce of strength she had. Her hand exploded through the leather strap, its rough underside ripping at her skin. Her arm freed from the restraint, she seized Brian's waist, landing just before the knife sheath. *Fuck!* She fumbled, her arm and hand feeling wildly detached from her will.

She felt the flap, the cold metal snap on the leather. Yanked up, her fingers scrambling inside. *Fuck! Where is it?* She clawed Brian's neck.

"Get off me! Get off me!"

Brian released his locked teeth from her ear and removed his death grip on her legs.

Change my pitch up
Smack my bitch up

"You wild little fuck! What you trying to do?" He didn't look angry, just sort of bewildered and amused. Her glancing blows, landing on his chest and arm, did no damage. He let her hit him a few times.

Then, in one brutal, arcing move, he grabbed her wrist and slammed it down onto the arm of the chair, pressing his full weight onto it. She yanked and pulled, screaming against the defeating reality creeping in.

Change my pitch up
Smack my bitch up
Change my pitch up
Smack my bitch up

Both pissed and frightened more than she could have ever imagined herself being, she stopped trying to pull her arm away and stopped screaming. Her breath came hard and fast, spittle flying out of her mouth. Hurling sheer hatred up to his face, she glared past his cold eyes. Her breath choked in her throat.

Dannie stood behind Brian, a scowl crawling across her lips. She held a mean-looking hunting knife in her right hand. In her left, a syringe.

Change my pitch up
Smack my bitch up

Chapter 41

You can't stop the beat

Suzanne screamed, raw and primal, "Noo! Jesus, noo!" The blade came barreling toward her. She was unable to look away, unable to twist her body free, unable to stop the inevitable. "Noo!"

Dannie slammed into Brian, plunging the knife deep into the side of his thick neck. Blood sprayed across Suzanne's face. Her mouth snapped shut against the drops spattering across her lips. Brian let out a wet, garbled roar, stumbling sideways, smashing into Suzanne's bound leg, before crashing to his knees.

Drums and distorted guitar blasted from the boom box. His left hand gripped Suzanne's arm. With his right, he pulled haphazardly at the knife's handle. Suzanne's heart felt like it was going to explode. *Fuck! Just die! Die!* She couldn't look away from Brian's blood gushing out in rhythmic waves, like they were keeping time to the beat of the new song. Building then flowing from the blade's edge and soaking down into his dirty tank.

Whoa, Black Betty (Bam-ba-lam)
Whoa, Black Betty (Bam-ba-lam)
Black Betty had a child (Bam-ba-lam)
The damn thing gone wild (Bam-ba-lam)

"You... you fuck... aarrgh... you... bitch!" Brian croaked, spitting the words into Suzanne's face, but looking past her, his eyes wild and searching.

She said, "I'm worryin' outta mind" (Bam-ba-lam)
The damn thing gone blind (Bam-ba-lam)
I said oh, Black Betty (Bam-ba-lam)
Whoa, Black Betty (Bam-ba-lam)

"Fuck you!" With a violent yank, Brian jerked the knife out of his neck. The force sent his arm down, slicing into Suzanne's exposed left calf. She whelped in pain. The knife went skittering across the concrete floor.

The pain sucked away as quickly as it had come, like she had vacuumed it up into her, forcing it out of her nerves. *It's okay.* With fresh adrenaline, she flexed her right arm, working it up and down as fast as she could to loosen the strap.

She really gets me high (Bam-ba-lam)
You know that's no lie (Bam-ba-lam)

Warm rivers of blood flowed around her calf and down to her heel. *Is that mine? Jesus.* She could not see the cut, her strapped-down head turning her knees into fleshy mountains on a cruel horizon line, but she could feel the heat and sting rising from deep inside the gash in her calf. *No! No! Not going to die . . .*

She's so rock steady (Bam-ba-lam)
And she's always ready (Bam-ba-lam)

She fumbled at the strap holding her head. *. . . in – a – fucking chair.*

Whoa, Black Betty (Bam-ba-lam)
Whoa, Black Betty (Bam-ba-lam)

Brian gagged and gurgled, slumped just past her knees. Her eyes darted to the window. *Get out.* She began working at the strap around her head. Slick liquid met her fingers. *My ears. Fuck! Fuck!* A motion in her peripheral jolted her from her task.

Whoa, Black Betty (Bam-ba-lam)
Whoa, Black Betty (Bam-ba-lam)

Suzanne tore her eyes away from the window, her hand stopping. Dannie bent down and came up quickly, the bloody knife held tightly in her hand. *Don't! Jesus! Jesus!*

She's from Birmingham (Bam-ba-lam)

As Dannie rose, Suzanne could see she was panting, her body heaving. Head cocked, Dannie stared down at Brian. In her other hand, the syringe's needle jutted out. *Fuck. What's in there? Don't you stick that shit in me!*

Whoa, Black Betty (Bam-ba-lam)

Suzanne could feel Brian now, writhing, struggling. The sounds of his blood-choked coughing and gagging mixed with the song. Suzanne kept pumping her arm, eyes locked on Dannie, a million thoughts bombarding her mind as she raced against the next horror.

Whoa, Black Betty (Bam-ba-lam)

Brian's hand latched on to her wounded calf, his thumb jamming into the gash in her leg. *Fuck!* Suzanne's face contorted in pain, her eyes squeezing shut as she screamed.

Way down in Alabam' (Bam-ba-lam)
Well, she's shakin' that thing (Bam-ba-lam)
Boy, she makes me –

She popped open her eyes at the banging crunch of the boom box hitting the floor. The music cut off instantly and Dannie, now at the shelf, was looking at her, head still cocked. *Oh God*

"Two down," Dannie hissed. She held up the knife, backhand-flipping her hair away from her face. "Two to go." She sniffed in, sucking up mucous.

Two down. The sheriff. The math wasn't working fast enough in her head. *Two down. Brian? Carole? Two to go. Me. The kid? The kid. Say something!*

"Please, please. You—you don't have to do this," Suzanne pleaded. "He hurt you, too" *The kid. The kid.*

Dannie threw her head back, laughing. After a few seconds, she snapped her head back down to look squarely at Suzanne.

"Oh shit." She smiled, shaking her head and waving the knife back and forth. "I was wrong. Mm-mm-mm. Forgot all about Carole." Dannie's eyes lit up. "That's three! Three down. Fuck me! Four! That other fuckin' pig, too! That's four! Sweet fuckin' Jesus! And by my score, kind of looks like I'm winning all your asses."

Dannie broke into a hysterical laughing fit. *The kid.* Squinting past Dannie, Suzanne's breath caught, making her gasp. The lump was gone. The mattress lay flat. *He's gone. Jesus. Where? Run, kid. Run.* A strange wave of joy mixed with fear washed through her. She closed her eyes. *Go get help.*

Dannie stopped laughing.

Chapter 42

Into the light

In the darkest corner of the basement, crouching behind Angel's suitcase, Hagas watched with wild, terrified eyes. He stared into the other room, seeing only what the door frame would allow him to, thinking it was just like watching his movies, not being able to see what was off the sides of the glowing screen, but knowing something was always there, waiting in the dark, scheming. *The woman. The chair. I know what's next. But Brian. He's not moving. Not how it goes. Ma.*

With the music cut off, he could now hear. Ma's laughing had sounded more wicked than it ever had before. More than all those times when she'd stood by, watching Brian have his fun with him. Her laughter chilled him, rooting him to the concrete floor. *Stabbed him. Going to kill her. No. Kill me.*

Ma stood in the door frame, holding Brian's big knife and a needle. Gray plastic chunks and shiny bits of metal from the smashed boom box lay scattered on the floor around her. *Why? Why? What's she going to do?*

He squeezed the jackknife's weighty body in his hand; its rusty three-inch blade pointed out. His eyes darted from the door frame to the wall hiding the stairs leading up to the kitchen hall—and the screen door. *I can just run and run and run. But I won't make it. She'll see me running. She'll get me.*

His breathing was fast and his heart racing. He'd been so afraid she'd catch him—or Brian would come get him—before he could get the tape poked enough. But they didn't. For a moment he'd felt ready with the old jackknife in his hand.

But now, looking at the large, bloody blade Ma was holding, hearing the woman screaming, his fire faded. He was scared. A bead of cold sweat ran down his spine, collecting just above his waistband.

Angel, what do I do? What do I do? He caressed the dry, bulging leather of the suitcase like a fortune teller trying to conjure an image in a crystal ball. *Angel. Help me.* He pictured his hand touching her blonde hair, assuring her he'd protect her.

From the stairwell, he heard a low groaning creak. *Someone's coming!* Everything slipped into slow motion.

The stairs creaked again. Hagas looked back to the room. *Who is it? Where's Ma? Scream!* But he couldn't. Fear had grabbed hold of him too tight. Ma was gone, out of sight, somewhere beyond the illuminated frame of the doorway. The woman in the chair stopped thrashing and pulling at her straps, frozen in place.

296

The light in the room went out, plunging the basement into pure black. For a split second, Hagas's mind saw the dull afterglow outline of the woman in the chair, but the darkness stole it away in a heartbeat. *Oh no.*

A beam of light shot out from the stairwell. The circle of white light bounced across the basement walls, before landing on the policeman who'd almost gotten away.

"Sweet Jesus!" A woman's voice called from the stairwell. "Sheriff! Sheriff! Is that you? Oh, my God!" Dull bangs on the steps followed.

He waited, holding his breath that the woman was real, that she would come into view any second. She did not emerge; she had stopped short of the concrete floor. The beam of light trained on the policeman. "Sheriff? Answer me." The man did not move.

Hagas wanted to call out to the woman, but he couldn't get his brain and muscles to work together. His tongue was thick and sticking inside his dry mouth. Waiting. Watching. He became aware of his hands. His left knuckles were tense and hurting from his grip on the knife. The other hand felt loose and detached, still resting on a bulge just on the other side of the suitcase.

A few metallic clicks came from the stairwell. The woman yelled, her voice shaking, but loud. Loud enough to spark a little fire back into his frozen system. "Who's down here?" Silence answered her. "Show yourself! I got a gun, goddammit."

The woman in the chair screamed out, her panicked voice piercing the dead air. "Jesus! In here! They're crazy! Watch out! She's down here!"

297

The woman emerged from the staircase. She was dark and hard to see behind the glow of the flashlight she held out in front of her. Besides the flashlight, Hagas also saw the profile of a long gun. Just before she turned the beam away, pointing it into the room, he could see her finger on the trigger. Quick, sharp feelings of excitement and dread hit him hard, ripping through his mind. *She's gonna get Ma. Gonna shoot her!*

The flashlight shone upon the woman in the chair. She whipped her arm up to her face, using her hand to cover her eyes. In the light, all the dark, shiny splotches of blood around her face and neck stood out against her pale skin.

Dropping her arm, she revealed her full face. She looked scared, squinting her eyes and darting them side to side, but she looked a little hopeful too, with a skittery energy coming out of her—just like some of the people in his movies. *This is always the part. They never make it.*

"She's in here! Be careful! She's got a knife!" The woman in the chair yelled. "Where the fuck are you, you bitch?"

"Who? Who's in here? I've got a gun!" The woman with the flashlight yelled back. Her flashlight illuminated the woman in the chair. "Oh, Lord! Shit. It's you—from High Bridge!"

"Yes! Please hurry! She's down here. I lost her. Jesus, get me out of here!" The woman yelled, using her free hand to yank at the strap holding her other arm to the chair.

The light from the flashlight circled, sweeping the walls as the woman inched deeper into the room. *She's going in.* Sinking dread crept into his stomach. *Don't. This is always the part.*

"Stoppp." Hagas wheezed no more than a whisper. Fear would not allow his voice to come.

The beam of light landed on Brian's blood-soaked body, slumped against the legs of the woman in the chair. To Hagas's horror, Brian's eyes stared out, cutting across the dark, locking onto his own. *He sees me!* His muscles seemed to seize all at once, forcing him to crouch lower behind the suitcase. *No. He's dead.*

Hagas rose again, watching the jerking beam of light darting around the room. But he wasn't looking at the woman in the chair; he was looking for Ma—sensing, knowing, fearing. *Where'd you go? Angel, help me. Show me.*

The woman crept farther into Brian's room, zeroing the beam on the woman in the chair. The long, slender gun barrel glinted in the beam of light. *Yes! Get to her.*

Hagas was rooting for the two women as he inched himself up from behind the suitcase, the spark of fire in his belly growing.

"Come on. Come on," he whispered.

"Hurry, please." the woman in the chair gasped. "Come on. Get me untied."

Hagas saw a dark shape slide behind the silhouette of the woman with the flashlight, merging with it, blocking his view for a second. *Oh, no.*

Chapter 43

You go boom

For a fleeting moment, Suzanne's panic gave way to recognition as the woman behind the flashlight got closer. *It's the lady from check-in.n. You. Margie... Margaret.*

"Sh. Sh. Jesus. Oh my God." Margaret dropped the butt of her rifle down, gripping it between her legs. "Him," she said, darting her eyes down to Brian. "Saw him. Driving the sheriff's truck up the driveway. Knew. Knew something was . . . Jesus. Jesus. Jana and me were just . . ."

Margaret bent in, and Suzanne sensed panic behind her eyes.

"Honey, hold on. Hold on—sent Jana back. She's going to check in—to the check in cabin to radio—to get my radio. Going to get the cops—get them up here. Just – just gotta get you out of this goddam chair."

Margaret jammed the flashlight under her right armpit, grabbing the tether that secured Suzanne's right arm to the chair. Suzanne felt Margaret's cold, boney fingers grazing her skin.

"Dannie! Her name's Dannie. Hurry! She's – She's fucking crazy! Hurry. Jesus. Come on! Pull!"

Suzanne couldn't see. The flashlight's beam of light kept flashing into her eyes, filling her vision with fuzzy, greenish, glowing dots every time it swept away. Catching a whiff of outdoors from Margaret's coat—pine and dust, Suzanne tasted the freedom. *Come on! So close!*

The deafening blast of the gun came from somewhere behind Margaret. Hot, wet chunks landed on her chest, arms, and face. The blast ricocheted in her ears. The taste of the outdoors in her mouth ripped away, replaced by a strong metallic flavor.

In the next instant, Margaret crumpled, her forehead banking off Suzanne's arm, her dead weight sliding down Suzanne's thighs, joining Brian on the floor.

Pain hit Suzanne. Sharp. Hot. Pain. Near her right shoulder. Suzanne twisted her eyes down, seeing nothing beyond the bouncing spots. *Fuck! Oh, God. Shot me.* A scream welled inside her as the pain from the bullet hole spread through her.

"Noo!" Her scream was dull and distant, blocked out by the ringing in her ears. She hyperventilated, her breath hot and fast, spitting Margaret's blood from her mouth.

"Aaargh! You fucker! Fuccck!" Suzanne was boiling with rage, fear, and pain.

The overhead lights blazed on. All Suzanne could see was dark, inky blood oozing toward her breast. Chunks of flesh and bone peppered her blood-soaked torso. She heaved, catching a surge of bile in her throat. Clamping her eyes shut

301

against the pain and horror, she could feel hope draining from her, right along with the blood inching down her skin. *Oh, Jesus. This is it.*

"Fuck," Dannie said with a low rumble of wonder.

Dannie walked toward her from the doorway, a large gun hanging from her hand. Suzanne mustered a glare. *You cunt. Just do it!* The high-pitched ringing in her ears was dull and throbbing. She pulled and jerked on her right arm, feeling the strap loos*en*.

Giggling, Dannie shoved Margaret's body off Brian. Suzanne winced at the fresh zing of pain in her wounded leg. Margaret's shotgun and flashlight clattered on the cement as her body rolled onto the floor.

Suzanne looked down in horror at what used to be Margaret's face, now mostly just scraps of ripped flesh with a gaping hole where her right eye and cheek used to be. Her mouth hung down, torn. Blood pooled on the floor under Margaret's head. Suzanne averted her eyes, fighting back another wave of vomit.

"Shit. Now my count's all off." Dannie turned her eyes to Suzanne. "Where was I? Three down? No! Four! Four down. Two to go! But, shit. Looks like I got me a bonus!" She laugh-sighed, raising her hand, fingers outstretched in a high five—but no one to connect it with. "So, that's five. You know, I almost thought it was Carole when I heard that stair creak," Dannie said with an edge of excitement.

She rubbed her hand across Suzanne's face and lips, then, like a rattlesnake striking, delivered a quick, stinging slap. "But. But. I remembered. Yes, I did. You said she's dead, dead, dead." Suzanne squeezed her eyes shut as Dannie smeared Margaret's blood around her face.

"Then, though, I thought, fuck, this little bitch might be lying. Might just be trying to save her ass. Making some fucked-up plan with that tired, old bitch." Dannie dropped her hand.

Suzanne mumbled, "I didn't lie to you. She's dead. She's fucking dead."

Dannie jammed her finger into the bullet hole above Suzanne's collar bone—pulling it out and poking it back in between every word she spoke next. "Are–you—fuckin'—sure–you — ain't — lyin'—to—me?"

Suzanne screeched in agony at every poke. "Aaaiiieee! Fuck you! Fuck! Stop it! She's dead." Suzanne was sobbing now. "She's dead!"

"Okay! Okay! Christ all-fucking-mighty, you're a screamy bitch. Just settle the fuck down so I can think," Dannie said, yanking her finger out of the bloody hole, then pacing between the chair and the door. "Five down. Two to go. Five down. Two to go. Five down. Two to –" Dannie stopped moving, standing still in the doorway, her back to Suzanne.

"Jesus! Fuck! Just shoot me!" Suzanne thrashed. "What the fuck do you want?"

What Dannie wanted didn't matter to Suzanne. Nothing mattered now. She felt weak, drained, like she was detaching from her body. *I tried. Too much blood. I tried. Connie. I can't. Too many – fuck – too fucking many holes in me. Connie. Connie. I'm dying. I'm sorry.*

"Hold your goddamn horses. What's your rush?"

Suzanne flinched when Dannie dropped down, right at her legs, then popped up with the Margaret's flashlight in her hand. The flashlight's silver length had blood smeared all

303

over it. A wave of fresh panic flooded Suzanne. *Fuck. Oh God. What are you doing? Don't. Don't. Don't.*

Dannie held the gun up, shining the flashlight along the shotgun's dull, black barrel as a slight frown worked across her lips. Dannie lowered the flashlight, resting it on the chair then shoving it forward, between Suzanne's legs. The cold metal connected with Suzanne's inner thighs. She gasped, tensing her muscles. *Please. Jesus. Don't put that in me.*

Dannie leaned in, her smoky, foul breath washing across Suzanne's blood- and tear-streaked face. "Shhh. I've got a secret to tell you. Looks like my little fucktard decided to get himself out of bed. He's a bad, bad boy." Then she whistled. "Whip–poor–will. Whip–poor–will."

Dannie jerked the flashlight back and tiptoed toward the door. "Hagas. Hagas. Momma's here. It's all good. All good." Her voice was almost sing-songy as she made her way to the door.

"Ha–gas. Come out. Come out." Dannie swept the light side to side. "Come to Mama, boy." The boy did not appear. The light stretched into the room. The beam grew softer as it reached far into the dark. Suzanne struggled to see. Shadows played tricks on her eyes.

Throbbing pain swelled in her shoulder, her leg, her ears, spreading through her, almost taking over. In the dull, wide glow, an old suitcase came into view. *Did it just move?* Dannie raised the gun, bringing it up against the side of the trembling flashlight.

"There's my girl. My sweet, sweet Angel. Oh, baby girl. Baby girl," Dannie whispered, raising the gun higher.

"Nooo!" Suzanne screamed. "Run! Run!"

The crack of the gun firing reverberated through the basement. Dannie's arm bounced up, bringing the flashlight's beam with it, but not before Suzanne saw the hole tear open in the suitcase.

"And her! Goddamn! Fucking brother!" Dannie yelled into the darkness.

Dannie raised the gun again and pulled the trigger. But there was no blast and Dannie threw the gun to the floor. Her arm came up with Brian's knife glinting in the flashlight's beam. Suzanne's last ounces of hope slid into the darkness.

Chapter 44

Make or break

Hagas pressed his body as flat as he could, his back tight to the wall of the stairs, his breath sucked into his lungs as far down as he could get it. His ears were ringing from the blast, the high-pitched drone making him strain to hear what was happening in Brian's room.

He stared dead ahead, trying to focus on the dark suitcase sitting in the far corner, its shape just out of the reach of the light leaking from the room. Even in the dark, he could see something hanging out the front now. *Angel. She shot Angel.* He couldn't hear Angel any longer. Her voice had been blown away.

The burning flame of anger and adrenaline rekindled in his stomach. He squeezed the jackknife. Hagas was unsure he was concealed in his spot with the light pouring from Brian's room. He pressed himself harder against the wall, forcing himself to be still.

He checked his feet, making sure every part of him was in the dark, beyond the edge of light. The sharp pangs of needing a breath spiked in his chest. Slowly, shakily, he opened his mouth and expelled the air from deep in his lungs, then breathed in new air through his nose. *Quiet.*

It had taken more nerve than he thought he had to sprint over to the wall. He was so sure it would go wrong. It always did. Somewhere, deep inside, he was mad, enraged at himself for not being brave enough—then, now, everywhere in between.

Images of his past swirled in his head. But Angel had told him to go. To run. He had to. For her. He darted from behind the suitcase, across the floor, and directly to the wall. *Angel. Angel. But you're gone now. Really gone.* He couldn't hear her anymore. He didn't know what to do next. He couldn't let go of the wall. *She'll get me.*

"Ha-gas." Her voice sounded close. Too close. Hagas held his breath again. The flashlight illuminated a swath of the floor, going across the policeman, his mattress, and finally onto the suitcase. He heard a soft sobbing coming from Brian's room. *The woman in the chair. Alive.* "Whip-por-will. Whip-por-will. Five down. Two to kill."

Ma's call filled Hagas with instant fear. *Death is close.* Every muscle was frozen, sweat trickling down his back. It felt like the wall was pushing him forward, like it wanted him exposed. *She's coming.* The flashlight beam grew brighter on the suitcase. *Angel. Angel.* His stomach knotted. But his rage and fire grew. He felt it filling him.

"Whip . . . por . . . will. Two to kill." Ma's raspy, whistly voice was much closer. Too close.

He could see the light spilling around the corner of his wall like it was the sun peeking above the horizon in the morning. *Gonna see me. Oh God.* Ma's hand, wrapped tightly around the flashlight's handle, came into view. In her other hand was Brian's knife. Dirty. Bloody. *Hate you.* He squeezed his eyes shut, feeling the jackknife in his hand, working his mind up to what he knew he'd need to do—to try.

Grunting from the floor made him pop his eyes open. The flashlight's beam spotlighted the policeman. He still wasn't moving—but the sound—the sound came from him. *Angel. You saved him! Knew you wouldn't leave me.*

The flood of energy he'd felt running from the suitcase came rushing back. As fast as a lightning bolt, Hagas pushed off the wall, raising the jackknife and screaming out with rage. "I hate you!" His arm hurtled down just as Ma swung the light onto him. The blade sliced open her forearm. Ma screamed out, dropping the flashlight and Hagas lost his grip on the jackknife. Both items smacked to the floor. The flashlight sent beams of light bouncing across the floor.

Hagas did not try to get his knife. He pushed past her, shoving her sideways as she grabbed at her wounded arm. His legs churned, yet he felt like he wasn't going fast enough. His feet felt too heavy. *Too slow! Don't look back!*

Ma grabbed his shoulder, her strong fingers digging into him for a split second. But he had the momentum, he was moving fast enough, and her fingers lost their grip.

The stairs—freedom—right there. Hagas could see it all. The climb. The screen door. Running down the road. *I can make it!* He looked back at the woman in the chair. She turned her head towards him.

In a split second, Hagas ran instead to Brian's room, jerking to a stop, spinning, skidding, grabbing hold of the door, pulling it, then pushing it, heaving his weight against it.

"Close! Close! Close!"

Ma screamed after him. "Hagas!" Her arm shot through the closing gap, knife in her grip. She flailed it around, slicing and stabbing at the air. The blade caught his arm. He winced but kept pushing and pushing.

Ma was pushing back, yelling. "You fucker! Hagas! Gonna—kill—you!"

Hagas shoved with everything he had, but Ma was stronger. The fresh cut on her forearm appeared. He punched down on it. She screamed, dropping the knife. With a wicked clanging, the door ricocheted, bouncing off Ma's arm. Ma screamed out again and then her arm was gone from the gap.

Hagas grabbed the moment, desperately howling "Close!" again as he mustered one more, mighty shove. The door obeyed, latching into place. In a flash, he reached up, ignoring the pain in his arm, and twisted the deadbolt knob, feeling the thick metal shaft slide home. His breathing was fast and heavy. His heart was going so fast, that it felt like it was going to explode. *I did it. I did it. I did it.* On the other side of the door, Ma banged and screamed, cursing and calling his name.

"Hagas! You fucktard! Let me in, you little bastard!"

He jumped at the sound of her voice. *Right there still!* He pushed away from the door as it rocked and shook in its frame. He jumped at every bang, praying the door would hold, picturing Ma's twisted, enraged face just on the other side.

Brian's knife lay on the floor, blood on its blade. *Got you.* Lunging, he snatched it up, then bounced backward, away from the onslaught of banging and screaming. Frantic, unsure if she'd come through at any second.

"Help . . . help me . . ." the woman whispered from behind him. "Kid . . ."

Chapter 45

The ties that bind

Hagas stared at her, his eyes wide, fear and confusion etched on his face. The banging on the door intensified, and Dannie's screaming, now muffled, was still coming on strong. He flinched at every bang. *Fuck. Think, Suzanne, Think.* She sucked in a deep breath, picturing the oxygen filling her – giving her strength, then pushed her voice forth, forcing calm into her own fear.

"Please. My name is Suzanne, and I can help you, Hagas."

He cocked his head and took a hesitant step toward her, then another, still flinching at Dannie's banging and screaming. The door shook in its frame, banging against the deadbolt. *Keep coming. Come on kid. Come on. You can do it. Come on.* The boy

Hagas paused just a few feet from her. He looked down at the bodies on the floor. Then hugging himself tightly, he bent down just a little. "Are . . . are they . . . dead?"

"Yes. Yes, they are. I'm . . . sorry, Hagas."

"You sure?" He pointed, glancing down at Brian. "Sure he's dead. He . . . he was looking at me. Before. Before I got in here." His eyes drifted back to Brian's slumped body. "Sometimes they're not really dead. Just a trick sometimes. Then . . . then they come back."

The banging was slowing. So was Dannie's yelling, becoming just short bursts of 'Hagas!' *She's getting tired.*

"Hagas." She paused. No reaction. She tried again, using a hint more force. "Hagas." The boy snapped his gaze back to her. "He's gone. I promise. He can't hurt you. Untie me. We can get out of here."

Hagas moved, circling Margaret's body, arriving at the chair just to Suzanne's right.

"Okay. Good. Good boy." *So close. Keep going.* Suzanne looked at the door. *How long?* Her voice was calm but urgent, and she pressed Hagas. "Now, just untie the strap. It's loose already. You can get it. You can finish it, Hagas."

"Okay." Hagas bent in and moved his hands to the leather strap. "I'll try."

"You can do it. Just have to hurry." She felt the leather brushing against her, moving around her forearm. *Too delicate.* "Don't worry. You're not going to hurt me. Go 'head. Pull! Pull!" Suzanne fought the urge to yank her arm upward. *Just make it tighter. He's getting it.*

"Okay. Trying." He pulled harder, grunting under his breath. "Knot. Stupid knot. Just gotta . . . get it –"

312

The strap slackened. She felt it instantly, yanking her arm back and out to freedom, like a bear's paw being freed from a trap. The bullet hole under her collarbone came back alive with a vengeance.

"Aaargh! Fuck!" Her breath came heavy and fast. Hagas recoiled from the chair.

"I hurt you. I'm sorry. Sorry. Sorry. Sorry—"

Suzanne grimaced, fighting back tears. "No. No. You got it! You're a good boy. Good. Good. Okay." *Keep him going.* "Now, my head. Need you to undo my head. Can you get this one?" She raised her left arm to point him behind the chair.

"I—I think so. Think it's like this one." He pointed at the slacked leather on the arm of the chair.

"Okay. Go for it." She tried to smile, to reassure him. "Go ahead, I'm okay. Just got to keep moving as fast as you can." She stole a glance at the door still slamming in its frame. *Dammit. Fuck.* She prayed he didn't register her angst. *Focus, kid. Hurry up!*

Once again, her words worked. Hagas circled to the back of the chair. His tugging began quickly. Suzanne pressed her head back, trying to make some slack. She squeezed her eyes shut as the leather pressed into her forehead, coming in hard bursts as Hagas worked to undo the strap. With every burst of effort from his pulls, her head pressed harder into the wood of the chair. *Come on. Come on. Jesus. Just get it.*

The strap slipped down her forehead. *Thank God.* Hagas pulled on the leather and it slid across her forehead until it was fully away. *Thank God.*

Suzanne bent forward slightly, rolling her head, wincing again as her motion agitated the bullet hole. Hagas came

313

around, again standing by her right side. He looked better. Brighter. "Now what?" Legs? Yeah?" Hagas asked with urgency.

A giant boom filled the room, making them both jump and look to the door. Another boom Wood hitting wood. Heavy. Fierce. Dannie yelled out, "Fucker!" A few more seconds ticked by, then it was back to the banging on the door.

Suzanne refocused back to Hagas. "Yes. Yes. Get my right leg. I'll get my left. Need to move quickly. Okay?"

Suzanne glanced down at Margaret's lifeless shape, then back to Hagas who was looking a little shell-shocked. *Can't wait, kid.* She realized she had to push, to motivate him.

"Might have to move her. It's okay. She was trying to help me. It's okay. You can do it."

Hagas bent down but winced, hopping backward.

"It's okay. It's okay. Just—just don't look at her," Suzanne urged.

Hagas recovered. He took hold of Margaret's outstretched left arm, wrapping his hands just above her wrist. With a quick, steady pull, he dragged Margaret's body, her clothing making a soft whooshing sound as it moved across the concrete, a couple of feet away from the bottom of the chair.

Suzanne felt almost revitalized. *We're getting there! Making progress.* She looked down at Hagas. "Good. Good job. That should do it. Now, go ahead, get the strap undone."

Suzanne tried to work on the strap around her left leg. Her right shoulder sent a shockwave of pain through her and she felt fresh blood pumping from the wound.

"Fuck! Jesus!" She snapped back up, sucking in breaths, spittle flying with each exhale. "Mmm. Eee. Eee. Mmm."

"What? What'd I do? Sorry. Sorry. It's just really—" he said, backing away, looking up at her with furrowed brows.

"No. No. It was me. You're good." Suzanne continued sucking in her breaths, trying to make the pain subside. "Keep going. It's okay. Got to keep going."

Hagas bent down, and his tugging began again. Bracing herself for the unavoidable pain, Suzanne slid her hand down her leg. Brian's body, still warm and bloody pressed against her sliced-open calf.

She gasped. A vicious, curving gash ran down her calf, blood flowing from it. She was horrified by the amount of blood. *Jesus. Jesus. I'm bleeding out.*

The banging on the door suddenly stopped. Hagas' tugging stopped. Suzanne waited, her breathing shallow, a dew of sweat forming on her forehead. The door remained silent. She could see it was still locked, still holding. Yet, fresh panic rose in her. *Oh God. No. No. Shit. What's ae you doing? Where are you?*

Slinking under the door and across the dead air, came the soft creaking of stairs.

Chapter 46

Easy as one, two three

Tense moments ticked by. Suzanne's mouth went dry. Waiting. Wondering. Dreading what Dannie would be coming back with to get into the room. *Screwdriver? Hammer? Axe? Jesus. Chainsaw?* Footsteps on the floor above snapped Suzanne back to the moment.

"Got to keep moving," she said, her eyes still trained on the door.

Hagas did not respond. He stood stiff, looking up at the rafters.

"Hagas." He did not look at her. *Oh, come on. Come back to me.* She kicked her right leg, sending it nowhere. The leather was still wrapped around it, but she felt the slack from Hagas's work. *Fuck! Almost there. Almost there.*

"Hagas!"

He looked at her, his face void of expression.

"You have to keep going. Please. We—we don't have much—" *Don't. Get him back.* "You're almost there. Just need to get my legs."

He looked at her. *There we go. There we go.*

"I promise I won't let her get you. But you have to help me. Okay?" She kicked out with her leg again. "I need you to get my legs out."

"Okay." Hagas glanced at the door before he bent down by her leg again. "I'll try. I'll try." *Come on. Come on. Hurry.* She listened to the footsteps above. *What are you doing?* Her mind raced, trying to figure out their next move. *Block the door. Wait it out. Run? Hide?*

"Got it!" Hagas popped backwards, pulling the leather strap with him.

"Good! Good boy! Now, get the other one."

Suzanne moved her right leg away from the leg of the chair. Her inner thigh muscles were stiff from being spread, stuck in the same position for so long. But the relief was immediate. *So close. So close.*

"You sure he's dead?" Hagas pointed at Brian.

"Yes. He's gone." Suzanne looked down at Brian, feeling his weight pressing on her mangled leg. "He can't hurt you."

Dannie's footsteps pounded above. Suzanne positioned her foot against Brian's shoulder. Her breath came short and fast as she moved it. She figured she had one good shove in her, knowing it would send a wave of pain through her.

"Together, okay?"

Hagas touched Brian's left shoulder, and his hands recoiled. But he brought them back, placing them on Brian again.

317

"There. See. Nothing." Suzanne looked up to Hagas's scrunched-up face. "Now, on the count of three, we'll shove together, okay?"

"Okay." Hagas looked at Suzanne with determination. "Count of three."

"One . . . Two . . . Three!" Suzanne gritted her teeth and pushed with her right leg.

Pain shot from her shoulder and her sliced-open leg, but Brian's weight moved away. Hagas pushed just beside her. Brian's body reached the point of tipping forward, but Suzanne's foot slipped, and his weight shifted back, twisting toward the chair.

"Fuccck!" She jammed her foot back into position.

She gave everything she had, shoving again, ignoring the pain. Hagas kept pushing. Brian's body tipped and crashed forward. Warm streams of fresh blood trickled down her leg, running to her ankle and down around the bottom of her foot. *Fuck. Gotta move. Can't stop.*

"You did it!" She tried smiling at Hagas. "I know it's bloody. But you have to hurry."

Hagas dropped down, getting to work. "So much blood."

The strap finally dropped away. Her leg was free. She was free. *Oh my God.* She was feeling light and distant, her mind drifting to images of Connie. She let her head loll forward.

"Lady! Lady!" Hagas squeezed her forearm. Suzanne raised her head. "Your leg. What do we do?"

Suzanne forced her head back. Nausea swirled in the pit of her stomach. *Fuck! Focus.* "The strap. Tie it around my leg. Just under my knee. Can you do that?"

318

"Yeah. Okay. Seen it done. Turn off the blood, right?" He squatted down in front of her, then looked up quickly. "Here goes."

Hagas worked quickly, and the bursts of pain as he tightened were tolerable, coming in hot like an unexpected knife cut. On his final wrap, she sighed with relief. *Okay.* He buckled the leather strap, and it cinched tight. Guttural screams erupted from her.

"Aaaaargh! Fuck! Fuck!"

She kicked, sending Hagas skidding across the blood- and gore-covered floor. Suzanne heaved in air, trying to calm down. She watched Hagas prop himself up, noticing the blood trickling from his lip. "Shit. Sorry. You okay?"

Hagas looked a little dazed. "I'm. I'm okay," he said, wiping at his lip with his forearm, smearing blood across his chin.

"Okay. Let's move," Suzanne said. A flash of pain shot up her leg when she put weight on her leg. She grit her teeth, determined to keep going. "Help me stand."

Hagas reached under her arm and around her back. "Ready?"

"Count of three. Just like before." She tensed her muscles, steeling herself again for the inevitable pain to come. "One . . . Two . . . Three!"

She pushed off, trying to keep her weight on her right leg. Hagas pushed from behind. She rose from the chair. Pain tore through her, traveling down from her shoulder and up from her leg, connecting in her gut.

"Fuck! Oh Jesus! Mmmm. Mmmm. Mmmm."

"You did it! You did it!" Hagas exclaimed, "Now . . . now what? What do we do?"

"We move." Suzanne looked toward the door. "And we fight."

Suzanne bent, picking up Margaret's gun from beside the chair. She was surprised at the weight. Pointing the barrel down, she used it like a cane. Huffing and hobbling, the pair made their way to the door.

Suzanne grabbed hold of the big shelf to steady herself. She noticed Hagas was holding Brian's knife. It looked even bigger in his small hand.

"Hang onto that. I have a feeling we might need it."

"She's out there. I know it. She's, she's waiting. For me," he whispered.

Suzanne was thinking the same thing. Staring at the door. Knowing, dreading what was coming next.

"It's our only way Hagas. We're going to have to be brave." *Not going to make it. Not both of us. Maybe we'll get her too though. Maybe.*

"There's – maybe – there's another way." Hagas was looking behind them. He pointed across the room. "My window."

Suzanne looked back and saw it. *Oh, you brilliant little shit! Yes. Yes.* A surge of hope hit her. *Can I do it? Shit. Shit. Just some more pain. Screw it.* She leaned down to him, whispering at him.

"You've done it? Done it before? You've gotten out there?"

"Yes. It's, um—it's my secret." Hagas said, looking down at the floor.

"Not anymore. It's okay. It's okay. Your secret is going to save us." Suzanne looked at her hand on the shelf, forming

320

her plan on the fly. "We have to move this shelf. Block the door. Can you help me?" Hagas looked up and nodded. "Good. Good. You get on the other side and push. I'm going to pull."

Hagas put the knife on the floor, readying himself on the opposite side of the shelf. She gripped the shelving with her left arm.

"One more time. Count of three." She readied herself. "One . . . Two . . . Three!"

The shelf skittered, its steel frame jumping maybe an inch toward the door. It leaned precariously toward her.

"Stop! Stop." *Too heavy. Wasting time – strength.* "Okay. The window." She nodded her head forward. "You know the drill." She sucked in a deep breath. "On three."

Chapter 47

One small leap

As Suzanne said "three," Hagas braced for her weight. She was light enough, but he knew the walk across to the window would be awkward with her leaning on him. Mostly, he was afraid he'd hurt her. *Just gotta move easy.*

Stepping away from the door, Hagas felt her arm tensing across his shoulders. They moved forward, half-shuffling, half-walking, the gun barrel tapping on the cement. He kept his eyes locked on the window. For a short path he'd taken many times before, he couldn't remember when it felt so long. In his mind, he kept picturing Ma bursting into the room. *Just like the movies. Just when they think they're gonna make it.*

Halfway. Past the chair now. Suzanne was grunting and breathing heavily. *Dragging that leg. Shoot. She gonna be able to climb?* Suzanne's weight felt heavier with each lurch forward. Hagas kept pushing.

"Okay!" He released his hold on her. "Grab the shelf."

The window, dark and covered in old duct tape, his secret gateway, looked just a little farther away than normal. Suzanne stood, trembling, right at his spot. Right where he climbs up. He pictured the three quick moves, the moves he knew backward and forward, to get to the top. *Easy. Easy.*

"You have to go first," Suzanne said. "Got to show me the way."

Hagas spied a long, braided whip on the shelf. "I can pull you up," he said, pointing to the whip.

Suzanne nodded. "Okay."

Hagas looked over at the door. The image of the blasted, tattered suitcase popped into his head. He took a big breath, squeezing his eyes against the start of a tear. *Love you.* He blew out his air, and then looked back to Suzanne.

"I won't—I won't leave you. I promise." Hagas felt like he had to assure her. Familiar feelings of fear and excitement coursed through him, the rush of freedom so close. Balancing on her left leg, Suzanne held the whip up to him..

He tied it, shoelace-style, leaving one end hanging long. *Too short.* He scanned the shelves and found a second whip. He quickly double-knotted it to the first one, giving their makeshift towrope another few feet. Satisfied the extension would work, he turned his focus to the shelving. *Easy. Easy.*

Hagas swung the gun and knife onto the top shelf. He paused to look at Suzanne. "Just watch me. It's easy."

One more big breath and he launched, his feet and arms propelling him up, finishing at the top with quick roll onto the top shelf. Laying on his back, legs dangling over the top the shelf, he reached out to the window and pushed. It popped outward, just like it always did. A rush of fresh, damp air washed over him. *Almost there!*

"You got it! Oh, good boy! Go Hagas, go! Take this." She held out the end of the whip to him, hopping herself back into position, closer to the corner of the shelving. "Keep going. We can do this."

With the whip tight in his fist, Hagas shimmied into position. He spun his body to get onto his side. *Halfway. Halfway.* The air had that familiar smell, the best smell ever. Grass... dirt... trees.

Wriggling with new energy, he clutched at the grass and weeds outside the opening, clawing his hands forward. He felt the familiar rush of his whole body emerging from his prison, through the opening, and into his secret world. Legs sliding over the cement sill. Feet bumping over it. Shoving the duct-taped window out of his way. Then he was on the ground. Cold. Damp. Air. Stars. Freedom.

Whip still in his hand, he pushed up from the ground, getting to his knees. *Quiet. No Ma. Going to make it.* He looked down the length of the house. Light blazed from the windows, spilling onto the yard, mixing with shadows from the trees.

He didn't see any movement behind the windows. But he did see the back edge of Ma's car in the driveway. *Still here. Okay. Get her out. Hurry—*

A whip-poor-will called out. Dread flooded Hagas. *Gotta hurry.*

Dropping back down, he flattened himself to the ground and wriggled into the window opening. Suzanne looked up at him, her hand already grabbing onto the shelf, second from the top. *You can do this. You can. I just gotta pull hard.*

324

"You ready?" He looked into her eyes. She looked scared. Tired. *You got to.* Then—something else—a sudden shift. Her eyes widened and her mouth dropped open.

"What's–"

Chapter 48

Swing and a . . .

The shadow that moved across Hagas's shoulders was slight, but Suzanne knew instantly it was her. Dannie. She tried to scream out, to warn him, anything, but nothing came out.

For a second, she saw his face questioning her own. Confusion. Then a brief moment of realization.

Dannie's scream ripped through the window opening. "You fucktard!"

The head of an ax came down, landing high up on Hagas's back with a sickening thud. His face registered a flash of surprise and then quickly twisted into anguish.

He wailed, high-pitched and frantic. "Eeeaaahh!"

Suzanne clung to the shelving. She was horrified, frozen. *Oh, God! No!* For an agonizing second, Hagas's eyes were locked on hers. *Oh, God. Oh, God. Oh, God.* Then, she watched in horror as Hagas' body jerked through the opening. His chin hit the sill edge, bumping and skipping across. His hands were still reaching out to her.

"Heh . . . help . . . me," he half-whispered, pleading.

Suzanne lunged toward him. Her fingertips brushed against his, but they did not stick. *No!* Tears streamed down her face. Finally, His arms disappeared into the dark. Suzanne's muscles tensed, locking her to the shelving, keeping her from falling.

Another grunt from Dannie was followed by a wet, wrenching sound. Then, Dannie's skinny legs appeared just outside the opening. The dark silhouette of the ax lowered into view. Suzanne's breathing came fast, erratic. *Jesus! Jesus! Jesus!*

Dannie's face dropped into view. Suzanne saw her rage and hate zeroed in on her. Dannie wiped her drooling mouth with the back of her sleeve.

Chapter 49

Long way from the top

Dannie looked at Suzanne, "Oooh fuck! Look. At. You! Think I didn't know?" Suzanne shrank down, her hand slipping down the corner post.

Dannie grabbed hold of the whip and slammed the ax onto the sill, then maneuvered her head and shoulders through the opening.

"Think I didn't let you fuckers do this?"

Suzanne bent farther away. *Where you going, bitch? Gonna kill you.* Yanking on the whip, she pulled Suzanne tight into the shelving, eliciting a frightened squeak from her. She grabbed the axe from the sill, dragged it through the opening, and heaved it onto the top shelf. *Gonna chop you the fuck up.* Below, Suzanne tugged the whip tied around her.

"Knew my little fucktard would drag your ass over here. Fuckin' moron." She yanked on the whip again to disrupt any progress Suzanne was making. "Course I fuckin' knew! I'm his goddamn mother. And mothers . . ." She slid her body across the sill, almost to her waist, hovering herself above the room, bracing her weight with her hands. "Always . . ." She pulled her torso back. "Know!"

Her legs swung down from the opening, all dead weight, connecting with Suzanne's head and shoulders. The shelving heaved. Dannie latched her arms to the edge of the shelf and scrambled her dangling feet to find a purchase. She saw Suzanne drop away, crashing onto the floor and screaming out. The shelving rocked and swayed, twisting under Dannie.

"Goddamn it!" She screamed, flailing her feet for a few seconds before connecting her left to a low shelf. She looked down. Suzanne was on her ass, moving away, using her left arm to pull herself away, her legs trailing, the whip dragging along in her wake.

Dannie saw the ax and a gun. She reached for the gun. The shelving rocked. Metal and wood crashed to the floor. She landed hard on the cement. Objects dropped around her. She tried to move, but her leg was pinned. She jerked, trying to pull it free

"Fuck! Fuck! Fuck!" She screamed out, wildly twisting her body.

You fuck! No. No. No. Suzanne was halfway across the room, near the chair, still dragging herself away, and getting closer to the door.

In a frenzied, body-twisting scan of the surrounding floor, Dannie saw the gun. She grabbed it "Die, you fucking whore!" She squeezed the trigger, filling the room with a deafening boom. Suzanne dropped flat to the floor.

"Ha! Got you, you fuck! How's about one more for good fuckin' measure!"

Dannie leveled the gun a couple inches off the floor, pointing it straight between Suzanne's legs. She reveled in her viciousness. "Going to fuck you up good!" She squeezed. Click. "Fuck! Fuck! Fuck!" Dannie threw the gun aside.

Chapter 50

Stick the landing

Suzanne looked up at the door, her eyes fixated on the hole the bullet had ripped open. It had missed her, whizzing somewhere above her left shoulder. But somehow it also got her, fucking with her fight or flight instincts enough to land her here, on her back, stuck in a limbo state.

In the echo of the gun's blast, Dannie's muddled words, even the click of the empty chamber, the thought of staying right there, accepting her demise, swam into her head. Her entire body felt like it was on fire. *All done. Nowhere to go now. Fight's over.*

The image of the ax landing in Hagas's back flashed in her mind. His face. The pain. The confusion. The sadness. *So close. So close.*

Dannie's furious grunts pulled Suzanne back into the moment. She raised her head, looking down the length of her battered, bloody body. The whip was still wrapped around her, its length running out past her feet like a mouse's tail just begging to be snatched by a cat.

Her eyes landed on Dannie next, who was full-on battling the shelving on top of her leg. *Move your ass!* Suzanne pulled herself along the floor again. Pain filled her body. *Move!* She looked over her shoulder, wincing at the pain under her collarbone. The door was closer – or at least seemed it was – than a few minutes ago. She sucked in air and continued pulling. She looked back at Dannie, struggling and fighting to get free of the shelving. She glimpsed the gun, and not far past it, the ax. *No! Just move your ass. Go. Go!*

The sensation of feeling the wood, her way out, energized her. She braced for the pain, then, with a powerful thrust from her right leg, she pushed. Her abdomen muscles clenched as her back slid up. She slapped her left hand to the door, steadying her rough, awkward rise. Her left leg dragged up with her. She grit her teeth, stifling the scream. *Fuck!* Her back moved, higher, higher. She was up. Exhausted breaths spewed out of her. Then she saw that Dannie was almost free. *Oh, God. Shit.*

Dannie's leg popped out, sending her onto her back. The shelving crashed and clattered one last time. Suzanne spun. She grabbed the handle and pulled, hobbling backward to swing the door open. Dannie was crawling, then hobbling, now bending. She came up straight, ax in her hand. *Fuck! Oh, God! Move!*

Fear and adrenaline raced through Suzanne. With a screaming lunge, she staggered forward, pulling the door with her and slamming it behind her. Frantic, she gripped the doorknob with both hands, using every ounce of strength in her to keep it shut, to keep Dannie from opening it.

Their inevitable, final, bloody battle flashed into her head. Then, she saw a metal hinge with an open padlock hanging from it. She grabbed at the padlock.

"Coming for you!" Dannie screeched out from the other side of the door.

Jesus. She's right there. Suzanne fumbled with the lock. The door jostled. "Nooo!" Suzanne yelled. Even though the thick hinge bounced, it held and did not allow the door to open. *Fuck!* She crashed the padlock through the eye.

Just as she was about to jam it closed, Dannie yanked on the door again. Suzanne staggered backward, lost her balance and braced for the fall. Her back landed softly, surprising her. Underneath her, Chris let out a low moan. The unlocked padlock bounced wildly. But it held.

On the floor, she saw a glint of metal. A blade. She shoved off the sheriff's body, scrambling to get to it. Grabbing the jackknife, she dragged herself to the stairs.

A blistering, cracking sound made her turn. The ax head was sticking through the wood, right next to the padlock. *Jesus!* She pushed up, dragging her butt onto the first tread. She pushed up again, using her right leg now too. The sudden jerk to her body dropped her back to the first tread and popped the knife out of her hand. *What . . . ?*

In the light spilling around her, she saw the line of the whip. Realization hit her hard. She was held fast, unable to move any farther. "Noooo! Jesus!"

The knife! Suzanne grabbed it from the tread and sawed at the leather. Suzanne saw shards of wood splinter away in the growing hole as Dannie hacked at the door. The lock still held. She moved the knife as fast as she could.

Suzanne watched in horror as Dannie reached straight up, grabbed hold of the lock, and threw it. As Dannie flung the door open, Suzanne felt the violent tug of the whip hauling her forward for a brief second. Then slack. She thudded back onto the tread. *I'm loose! Jesus! She's right there!* In the dim light, Dannie's face contorted with rage as she stepped through the door frame.

"You stupid fuck. I'm gonna split you open from your pussy to your fucking mouth."

Suzanne spun, facing the stairs, pulling up, up, up, her elbows and knees smacking off the treads. Sheer terror flooded every fiber of her, canceling out the pain of her movements. The light of the upstairs was just ahead.

Crushing pain hit Suzanne as the axe buried into her calf. Before she could even make full sense of it, Dannie lunged up the stairs and latched onto her throat.

"I'm gonna fucking kill you!"

Suzanne's eyes bulged as she flailed under Dannie's fierce grip. She couldn't breathe. Couldn't scream. The light from the kitchen was getting dimmer. Dannie was squeezing harder. Suzanne felt her neck and throat tightening. Dannie's face blurred. Somewhere past them, somewhere in the light above, a door banged. Vicious barking echoed into the stairwell, loud and piercing. A yellowish-white blob appeared at the top of the stairs. The barking grew louder.

Derby thundered down the stairs, a wild blonde blur, hitting Dannie at full speed. He snarled and barked, latching onto Dannie. Suzanne gasped for air but got out three croaking words. "Kill, Derby! Kill!"

Derby's barking mixed with Dannie's screams and swearing. Dannie's head took form, coming into focus.

With the last of her strength, Suzanne swung the knife, stabbing Dannie in the neck.

Dannie screamed, trying to pull out the knife. Derby stayed latched onto her right arm. Suzanne kicked out with her right leg, connecting with Dannie's midsection. "Die! Die! Die!"

Dannie flew backward, Derby still attached to her, hitting the concrete with a sickening, cracking thud. Derby yelped. Then, silence.

Suzanne pushed herself upright, heaving in air, staring down at the Dannie. Dannie's eyes stared straight up to the ceiling, the knife sticking out of her neck. Suzanne waited, sure Dannie would pop up. Blood pooled around Dannie's head, spilling out across the concrete. *She's gone. She's gone.* Suzanne crumpled onto the stairs.

In her twilight state, Suzanne's mind drifted. She thought she heard the door above slamming. *Didn't that happen already?* Then pounding footsteps. *Who's here now?* Below her, Derby whimpered, and in her mind, she smiled. *Made it, boy. Good boy. Good boy . . .* Someone was yelling down to her, the voice all echoey and muted. *I know that voice. That girl. That park girl.*

Blackness came, slipping across her from the outside in, erasing the pain of her cuts, burns, and broken parts as it wrapped her in its warm cocoon.

Epilogue

Well, they say it's kinda frightenin'
How this younger generation swings
You know it's more than just some new sensation
Well, the kid is into losin' sleep
And he don't come home for half the week

Chris turned onto the KI road. It had been a year since everything happened and he still felt the lingering effects of his harrowing night. Not so much pain anymore, but twinges of discomfort if he moved the wrong way. Even after all the therapy, the reporters, the re-election cementing his future here, the biggest twinge, the one he couldn't shake, was that gut-flipping feeling he got every time he turned onto this road.

To fight through it, his immediate response was to crank up the radio and let the music take over him. And so, as he'd done for the past eight months, he did exactly that, blasting Van Halen into the cab of his new Bronco, slapping his thumbs on the steering wheel to the beat.

You know it's more than just an aggravation

And the cradle will rock
Yes the cradle, cradle will rock

The road never changed – just the same rumbling dusty vein bringing people, good and bad, in and out of the heart of the North Maine Woods. He scanned the road and surrounding woods, looking for what, he wasn't sure. It was mainly his trained habit of keeping his eyes and mind open, to look for anything . . . off. *Hell, everything's off up here.*

Nearing the house where it all happened, he thought about all the houses like it, scattered across his county, blending into the woods and fields. A lot of people didn't spend much time thinking about what was going on behind the walls of those kinds of houses. *Or, choosing to ignore because their realities, their secrets, were too damn scary.* He slowed to a stop at the base of the driveway. Looking up to the now boarded-up structure, his mind raced back.

The horse tranquilizer had damn near killed him. He couldn't remember much past his beat-down from Brian. Everything was dark and fuzzy, and once in a while flashes of images and snippets of sounds would come through. He just couldn't quite piece them together into a coherent recollection.

The one thing he remembered, that he could feel, that he was sure about, was the cold of the cement floor. The thought of it sent a wave of shivers through him.

And when some local kid gets down
They try an' drum him outta town
They say "Ya coulda least faked it,
Boy", fake it, boy (Ooh, stranger, boy)

He gripped the steering wheel, forcing himself to steady, and looked down the length of the house. His eyes landed on the plywood covering the basement window. In his mind, he replayed the movie of what he'd been told happened. *An ax. The decomposed body of the little girl, the kid's sister, in the blasted suitcase. The kid. That poor friggin' kid. Never knew why he was taping up those animals. They must have really fucked him up. No way to end.*

A low rumble brought his attention back to the road. In the distance, a logging truck raced toward him, its massive tires churning up a growing plume of dust in its wake. As the truck drew closer the dust cloud blocked out the bushes and trees on the sides of the road.

Chris stared into the hazy tan cloud, his mind wandering to the nagging questions keeping him up at night *How many other fucked-up stories are going on right now?*

At an early age he hits the street
And winds up tired with who he meets
An' he's unemployed
(Unemployed) Oww
And the cradle will rock, ow!
And the cradle, the cradle –

Chris snapped the radio off and glanced at the new picture of his boys. *Jesus. Poor kid. Didn't deserve any of that.* As the truck roared by, its driver sounded out a couple of loud honks. *Never had a chance though. If a tree falls in the woods and no one is there, does it . . .*

He dragged his hand across his eyes. *No one even knew he was here.* He threw the Bronco into drive and rolled away in silence.

The dust from the logging truck lingered in the air for most of the remaining stretch to the check-in cabin. He parked and got out. For a moment he just stood, breathing in the crisp spring air, looking around at the tall pines, listening to the stream's chortle. *So much beauty. So many secrets.* He took in one more deep breath, then began gimping over to the porch.

Jana looked up from her logbook as he swung open the screen door and stepped inside. She smiled at him.

"Well, hello, hello, Sheriff," Jana said, her voice bright and chirpy.

Chris smiled back, glancing at the vase of fresh flowers beside the framed picture of Margaret. He missed the surly attitude of her greeting.

"What time's she coming?" Chris asked. "Should be here soon. Called this morning when she was leaving Boston." Jana glanced down at her logbook and tucked her hair behind her ears before looking back up at him. "She booked all of them, High Bridge one, two, and three. Normally wouldn't allow it. Margaret never would have, but I figure she needs it. And she doesn't need any gawkers. She, um . . . she sounded good. Almost happy, or at least normal."

Chris furrowed his brows. "Any press or anyone?"

"Nope. Thinking this all might finally be old news." She tilted her head back and raised her hand, wagging her forefinger. "Actually, some guy—a writer, he said—did call a few weeks ago. Shoot. I can't remember his name." She chuckled. "Feel like I have the curse of Margaret or

339

something. Anyway, he wanted to book High Bridge two, for research, he said. But I told him it was already taken."

Chris smiled. He was glad she had decided to stay up here, taking on Margaret's role. It was partly her strength and fearlessness that had convinced him to run for sheriff again. She didn't turn her back on this place. And he would be forever grateful she was there that night. Things could have wound up very different for him and Suzanne.

The distinct sound of tires crunching along the gravel made its way into the check-in cabin. Chris and Jana went out to the porch to see the black Range Rover pull into a parking spot across from the cabin. There was a moment of silence when the engine shut down.

For a few seconds, Chris wondered if she might be changing her mind. *She might just start it back up and turn right around. Wouldn't blame her. Hard for me to come down here.*

The slight popping sound of the liftgate broke the silence. A second later, blonde paws appeared. And there he was. *Derby. Just as feisty.* He leaped out of the back, dropping his haunches down to release a forceful stream into the dirt. Then he was up, yapping and barking as he raced around the lot. His tail was in full wag as he greeted Chris and Jana with excited barks, wiggling and bumping around their legs before his nose hit the ground for some exploring. Jana jumped off the porch, following him as he began zig-zagging his way behind the cabin.

"Let's get you some water," Jana said, clapping her hands to get Derby's attention.

Chris turned back to the Rover. *And there she is.* Suzanne stood still, just beside the driver's door, arms crossed, her back to him. Looking down, he felt a pang of guilt, seeing her left calf with a plastic and metal brace secured around it, long scars visible through its gaps. Chris waited, wondering what was going through her mind, giving her space to soak it all in.

He didn't have to wait long. Suzanne turned, opened the rear passenger door, and pulled out a techy-looking hiking pole. She shut the door, sending out a solid whoomph. Chris couldn't help but smile at her as she limped across the lot. Suzanne stopped just shy of the porch and locked eyes with Chris.

"Hi, Sheriff. What's new? Anything, uh . . . exciting?" Suzanne asked, a hint of a smile curving her lips.

"Not a thing, Suzanne." He chuckled. "Not a thing."

They stood looking at each other, searching each other's faces in silence. Jana and Derby broke the moment, tearing around the corner of the building. Derby went directly to Suzanne's side.

"My God! He's so fast!" Jana said. "Suzanne! Hi!" She wrapped her arms around her. "So good to see you. You look great!"

"Well, hi back, Jana. It's good to see friendly faces."

"Let's get you checked in," Jana said, hopping back onto the porch and through the screen door.

Suzanne looked at Chris. "So, Jana told me I can get the resident rate. Hope that's not a big legal issue with you."

"No issue with me. It's a state thing. I'm just county. But you'll be first to know if any legal issues come up. I'll drive right up to High Bridge and tell you in person."

Suzanne laughed. "With all due respect, Sheriff—and I know we go way back now—but I really hope I do not see you driving up to my site at all."

Chris chuckled. "Understood." He paused. "You should know, Dannie's still in a coma. Checked myself. But something tells me you checked, too. Even if she ever wakes up, she's never going to see the light of day—at least not without bars blocking her view. The laundry list of charges just keeps coming. Maine. New Hampshire. Who knows what else we'll find the more we dig into the warped world she made for herself?" He stopped. *Too much. Bring it back.* "You, uh . . . it's just really something seeing you again."

Jana yelled out from inside. "Day's a wasting!"

Suzanne made her way onto the porch, pausing and turning to look at Chris, before going inside. "Thank you." She cleared her throat. "Oh, and, yes, I checked on Dannie. And I'm digging, too," she said, the corner of her lip curling up before she and Derby went inside.

Chris descended from the porch and started gimping over to his Bronco. He opened his door, but before getting in, he took another long look at the endless expanse of trees stretching past the giant furnace. *So beautiful. So off. What other secrets are you hiding out there?* He heaved himself onto his seat and just as he was shutting his door, he heard a familiar call coming from the trees on the edge of the lawn.

Whip-poor-will.
Whip-poor-will.
Whip-poor-will.